The lights of her intra-tat bounced around in erratic pulses in a frightening way that wasn't alluring like when he first touched her hand. Tonight they were a physical sign of whatever horror she was experiencing.

He brushed her damp hair back with his fingers and whispered words of reassurance, knowing this could be the biggest mistake of his life. She had been sent here to flush out a fragger operative, that much he knew. Right now she and the Embassy thought David was their man—he didn't know whether to laugh at the absurdity or be insulted. If that's what her Embassy intel was saying, then it might be easier to bring down this government than he thought.

"Sean." She reached out to the empty space beside her.

He put his hand over hers. "I'm here."

When she whimpered and shook, he lay down next to her because he knew what it was like to go through this alone. He knew what it was like to go through everything alone. He folded Sara in his arms and pulled her tight against his chest. Her body relaxed against him. He kissed the top of her head.

If she betrayed him later, he'd deal with that when it happened. It's not like he hadn't thought of offing himself, and not the pleasant way with passing drugs and a bedside full of family crying for him. Maybe she'd be doing him a favor. Sean's older brother had killed himself. He told Sean before he did it that Sean wouldn't understand because he had never known their father, so couldn't really miss him. But, Sean did miss having a father…and an older brother.

Sara's breathing deepened with exhaustion. So did Sean's. He rested his cheek against the top of her head and fell asleep.

dr steve
— thank you for being part of the ambasadora-verse in so many ways!

AMBASADORA

heidi ruby miller

Heidi Ruby Miller

Copyright © 2011 Heidi Ruby Miller
Union City Publishing
Cover Image © 2007 Byron Winton
All rights reserved.
ISBN: 0615481124
ISBN-13: 9780615481128

For Jason—Even after all these years I still have an emotional fallacy for you.

ACKNOWLEDGMENTS

Because *Ambasadora* was my thesis for Seton Hill University's Writing Popular Fiction Graduate Program, I have more people to thank for the completion of this novel than I have room for, but here are some of the highlights:

Thank you first to my critique partners, Mary SanGiovanni and Christopher Paul Carey. Mary, you lived in the world of my novel with me, getting to know my characters until they became real. You are my Jersey sister and a best friend. CPC, our common background in anthropology allowed me to create a culture with real world rules and all the drama and fascination they entail. You understood my vision better than anyone else.

Thank you to Michael A. Arnzen. You are a dear friend and confidant.

Thank you to my mentors and final readers, Thomas F. Monteleone, Tobias Buckell, and Lawrence C. Connolly, who each brought their individual expertise to my manuscript while helping me to maintain my vision.

Thank you to Mike Resnick, Patrick Picciarelli, and Timons Esaias for taking time to be unofficial mentors.

Thank you to Becca Baker, Kristina Buchanan, Hanna Gribble, KJ Howe, Russ Howe, Jared Maraio, Mike Mehalek, Rachael Pruitt, Bruce Siskawicz, Maria V. Snyder, Steven LaTullipe, and K. Ceres Wright for read-throughs of drafts that should have never been read.

Thank you to all the Seton Hill Writers who workshopped parts of this book over two years. We had fun coming up with names and techiness. I know this isn't all of you, but here are some whose comments helped to transform this story: Mike Brendan, Penny Dawn, Ron Edison, Elaine Ervin, Lee Allen Howard, Adrienne Kapp, Chun Lee, W. D. Prescott, and Shara Saunsaucie White.

Thank you to Liz Coley. You were there with me to the very end of this one!

Thank you to my brother Tom Ruby, my brother-in-law Mike Miller, and my cousin Michael Ruby, who will forever have their old gamer tags immortalized in the V-side.

Thank you to my parents Albert and Sharon Ruby and my grandparents John and Wanda Hawk for supporting me in writing and all of my life's adventures and for passing down the creativity gene accompanied by an insane work ethic. I couldn't have done this without both. And, special thoughts for my Grandparents Ruby, Albert and Anna, who never got to see this project come to completion.

Finally, thank you to my husband Jason Jack Miller. J, you read, you listened, you encouraged, and most of all you loved. How did I get so lucky? Oh, wait, that's right, I picked you. You didn't really have a say in it all.

·

ONE

"They're watching us again," Sara whispered against the smoothness of Chen's cheek. His soft bergamot scent mixed with her vodka-tinged breath.

A voyeur hovered six meters above them, narrowly missing the snaking track of blue lights suspended from the hippodrome's ceiling. A man from the balcony overhead reached out in a drunken swat for the voyeur, but came nowhere near the mass of cameras and directional microphones. His mates pulled him back with loud guffaws when he almost toppled over the railing.

Sara laughed, too, basking in the celebratory atmosphere. Hot pink swirls of light traveled along the floor and walls in complex patterns, painting the opulent furnishings and beautiful guests with dizzying, ephemeral artwork. The hypnotic beats pulsing through the speakers worked in time with the lighting, enhancing the dream-like quality of the evening. She found it hard to believe this cavernous playground, this entire stunning complex, was once part of an ancient worldship.

The voyeur descended closer, several of its cameras telescoped through the darkness to capture the couple from varied angles. Chen pushed Sara up against the bar and nuzzled her neck, hiding his face and hers for the third time since they'd arrived tonight. His actions annoyed her. The whole point of coming here, at least in her opinion and every other Socialite worth her birth right, was to be seen, and not just by the party guests.

She wanted the whole system to see her at a function for the Sovereign's nephew, even if it was an honorable passing celebration. Normally she declined invites to suicide parties because she felt a morose mixture of jealousy and pity for the guests of honor. Jealousy because of the lavish attention bestowed upon the celebrants; pity because the next morning the honorees would take the passing drugs, choosing to die honorably than to live sterile lives and bring shame to their family circles.

She much preferred the charm of formal dinners and the exhilaration of techno-dances, and even the one sex party she had attended a few months ago for her eighteenth birthday, but Chen was insistent, finally winning her over by mentioning that her cousins and half-sister would never turn down this opportunity.

Plus, she was going with a contractor—though still part of the Upper Caste Socialites, contractors may as well have been their own sub-group with very strict marriage and family traditions. Her mother, who didn't approve of Chen, perpetuated the gossip that contractor children underwent secret reconstructive surgeries to look so perfect, and to hide the inevitable consequences of a shallow gene pool.

Apparently her mother chose to ignore the little tweaks the doctors did during Sara's matriculation through the nursery, and the bigger tweaks to her half-sister when they hit puberty. Laws regarding reconstruction were often overlooked in this society, unless you were a Lower, then the Embassy assumed you were trying to hide your birth caste. That warranted a Writ of Execution. Sara pushed those thoughts from her mind. If she left them wander around inside her head too long, she started to question the traditions, the History. That could only lead to trouble.

"You'd think the voyeurs would be more interested in the guy who's about to kill himself and head to the Otherside," Chen said.

"I guess the Media will take news and gossip wherever they can get it." Sara ran a hand through her short chestnut hair, showing off the new obsidian cuff on her forearm, just in case one of the cameras was still interested.

With his usual warped sense of timing, Chen decided this occasion was the perfect way to celebrate his gift to her. The coveted offering of black jewelry meant Chen was ready to marry her, take her on as his third amour, and have a child with her. So, tonight they would celebrate the linking of their genetic lines while the party's honoree pretended not to mourn the end of his. Another tenet of their society she barely understood, that the continuing of your lineage was one of the most important measures of worth, second only to the person you chose to procreate with. But, it was from the History, handed down by the archivists of millennia past, so who was she to question if a man wanted to kill himself rather than live with the shame of being a non-breeder.

She had more pressing concerns, she thought, mesmerized by her new bracelet shimmering in the hazy blue and pink light. Chen was finally living up to the title of prime amour, her first conceiving partner. He already took two women before her, and no doubt she, too, would have many amours one day, *but only one prime*. That's why his aloofness this past month bothered her, left her suspicious that he was already getting bored with her. Even after he gave her the cuff, she still felt a tinge of that suspicion return tonight.

Sara scanned the sea of gowns and formal suits, looking for familiar faces, either friends or rivals. A woman with long blonde hair and a short green dress reminded her of a classmate from graduation last year, but Sara couldn't concentrate enough to be sure. She was distracted because Chen was distracted, and had been from the moment the transport dropped them off here in Palomin.

He hadn't said much tonight, not even at the gravity lift security point when a contractor still employed by the Embassy chided Chen about his rogue status, the type of subject which normally led to heated arguments or physical confrontations. Contractors went rogue all the time, especially those in their twenties, but many of the older generation stuck to the idea that contractors had traditionally been the Embassy police force and that's the way it should always be, punctuating the sentiment by marrying only other contractors, homogenizing their family circles with dark hair, blue eyes, and olive skin in varying shades.

Chen shared those same physical features, but differed in his allegiance to the government, especially when independent contracting promised higher monetary compensation and faster occupational mobility than the Embassy could offer. It wasn't illegal to leave the Embassy, but most rogues broke as many rules as they enforced and ended up on the wrong side of the law eventually. Sara had never witnessed Chen doing any rule-breaking, but admitted it was the air of danger he projected that originally attracted her. On occasion he expressed regret at leaving the Embassy, but said returning was next to impossible; rogues had shown they couldn't be loyal, and the Embassy demanded the utmost loyalty.

"See anyone we know?" Sara noticed Chen scrutinizing the dark hippodrome with purpose and calculation. She followed his gaze to the illuminated exits at the far end. "What's wrong?"

Chen looked at her as though snapping out of a daydream. "Nothing, Luv. Old habits."

Now that they were enamoured to one another, she no longer liked his *old habits*. In fact, if he kept them up, she might threaten to find another prime. She'd had plenty of offers, boring as they were. Only, that kind of ultimatum could provide him a way out. Her mother's warning came back to her about never trusting a contractor.

He gave her a quick kiss to the forehead, a benign gesture that any man here could have bestowed upon her in formal greeting—not the type of kiss she expected from her prime. Of course, he wasn't her prime yet, not until the amour ceremony bound them legally. She almost asked him if he was having second thoughts about their relationship, then chided her paranoia. Chen was stubborn and wouldn't do anything out of a sense of duty. If he wanted her, he wanted her. The marriage token confirmed it.

Shouts at the other end of the long granite bar sent the voyeur floating toward three arguing men. This drama, feigned or genuine, would ensure the trio some precious broadcast minutes on the Media channels, helping to build their minor celebrity status and making them more desirable mates.

Chen relaxed a bit now that the cameras had found new subjects. Before the interloper could return, he said, "I'll be back in a bit. Enjoy yourself. Have another drink." His gaze lingered on her bracelet for a moment before he left.

Sara noticed the purple glow highlighting each individual filament deep inside the cuff. Maybe the phosphorous lights in the hippodrome caused the effect, the same way they made the pink calcite fluoresce in the arabesque designs on the floor and walls. When she visited her family tomorrow, the lighting would have to be similar so they could appreciate the glowing filaments. Sara hadn't seen her family in months. Adventure had called her from a young age, so she followed it as soon as she could. It left her sisters and cousins with the perfect mix of awe and jealousy. Now, she'd also have the distinction of being the first to marry out of her generation.

A quickening tempo from the percussionists brought guests into the dance area to her right. The guest of honor, a man in his twenties, moved among the dancers, gyrating and laughing. Though all of his amours were in attendance, none of them shared in the antics. The rumor was that his third had gone public with his sterility in an attempt to save face for their childless relationship. Sara wondered if he would eventually be reunited with these same amours on the Otherside.

The honoree seemed not to notice his inattentive amours, knowing he could count on one or more of the anonymous young women surrounding him to make his last night memorable, if only to give them a chance to tell the story at parties. To be someone's last, now that was special.

Since tonight's invitation came to Chen, Sara didn't even know the man's name, only that he was part of Sovereign Prollixer's distant family circle. She felt guilty that she really didn't care who the celebrant was and uneasy because of Chen's behavior. She finished her vodka, enjoying the vanilla-tinged fire as it slid down her throat.

She watched Chen's suited figure cross the expansive dance floor to the dining area. He stopped at a table near the balcony exit, leaned toward its sole occupant, a female with short, sleek hair, and helped her up. Her leg peeked from a waist-high slit in the silver gown she wore. Chen placed his hand on her lower back, and they left.

Looking for a new amour already?

The thought of him with another woman so soon pinched, but it was better than the alternative, business—probably the rule-breaking kind. For once she worried. A rumor that the Sovereign himself would be attending tonight made security at the party tighter than at any other social event she'd ever attended. Embassy contractors, clad in their traditional black clothing, floated on the edges of the party, watching as closely as any voyeur.

She moved to follow Chen, but a man stepped into her path. "Enjoying the celebration?"

Though he wore a formal charcoal suit, the man's black hair and deep blue eyes marked him as a contractor. He reminded her of Chen, though a dozen years older, with his short jaw and the perfect angle between his nose and upper lip. Without a doubt, the two men came from the same distant lineage. In other circumstances she might be interested, but her anxiety multiplied the longer Chen was out of her sight.

"It's a beautiful party. Unfortunately you caught me on my way out."

The contractor slipped a hand around her wrist and brought her arm up to admire the cuff. She caught a whiff of musky sandalwood on his skin.

"Is this for your first child?" he asked.

"It will be." She tried to pull away, but his grip tightened.

"So you just recently received this?"

"I'm sorry. I didn't catch your name."

"Rainer Varden, Head Contractor for the Embassy."

Her mouth went dry.

"I didn't catch your name either," he said.

"Sara Mendoza." She ignored the shiver moving down her spine and tried to play confident. "You obviously come from an impressive line, but I won't be in the market for a new amour until after my child is born."

He chuckled, his look making it clear that he would never be in the market for her.

She blushed, but ignored the insult.

"Have you already conceived?" he asked.

"No." She hated admitting that she was still on mandatory birth control.

He didn't look surprised, and that turned her annoyance into anxiety.

"Maybe we can talk later," she said with a shaky smile. "Right now I have to meet someone."

"I'd like to meet him, too." Rainer pushed aside his long formal jacket to reveal a gun strapped to his thigh. All Embassy contractors carried the same static charge weapon—an incendiary pistol commonly called a cender. Chen carried one, too, but not when he could be searched, like tonight.

Rainer kept a firm grip on her elbow as they moved through the mass of bodies. To anyone watching, they would look like two newly met individuals stealing away to get more intimately acquainted.

Her heart raced. She looked around for Chen and tried to offer pleading looks to the people they passed on their way out. Most of the returning glances showed drunken indifference, some expressed a hint of envy, none recognized her fear.

Rainer gracefully maneuvered her through the exit. The door shut out the energy of party guests and fast music. Outside, the sudden stillness rang in her ears. She fidgeted from foot to foot as they entered the grav lift and waited for it to activate. From the curving outside balcony of the hippodrome, she stared into Palomin Canyon Reserve. The moon illuminated the orange and pink undulations of the sandstone walls surrounding them. A fleeting scent of sun-baked rocks trickled into her lungs, and she shivered in the cooling evening.

Two other white rotundas, like the one she just left, sprouted from the purpled stone of the ancient river valley like bloated mushrooms. Even from six hundred meters up Sara could make out the ambient light circles below each building. An amalgam of salvaged worldship sections, these edifices provided a home to all the archives of the Embassy's six-moon system, its short, but all-powerful History. She hadn't thought about any of this in years. Her anxious mind grabbed onto these solid, school-taught facts as a distraction, so she wouldn't have to think what might happen next.

She tucked wisps of her hair behind her ear and considered asking questions as they waited for the lift. Rainer's grip on her other elbow kept her tongue still.

The trip to the canyon was her first, and a certain feeling of *arriving* had accompanied it. Not just arriving at a party hosted by the Sovereign, but her debut within high society, a world her modestly-ranking family circle had yet to penetrate. She might be a Socialite, but even among the Upper Caste there was a hierarchy.

The energy walls of the grav lift enveloped them and hazed her view. She thought of her ride on the lift earlier tonight, how Chen kept promising it would be a night to change their lives. How quickly perspectives changed.

The lift activated. Surprisingly, the sensation of being *pulled up* was somehow more comforting than *falling down*, though the one meter per second speed was actually the same both ways. When ascending, it simply was easier *not* to look down and see there was only a hazy nothingness between her and the dizzying drop into the mottled canyon.

At the canyon's rim, the lift slowed to a stop. Her heels tapped a nervous cadence across the portable metal gangway then fell silent when she stepped onto the sandy ochre earth. Six other contractors waited for them. Sara stumbled as her knees buckled. Rainer held tight to her elbow.

Where was Chen? She willed herself not to stare at the weapons strapped to the contractors' thighs. One on each leg. Seven contractors, including the one holding onto her. Fourteen cenders, each capable of hurling a sizzling shot right through her.

Rainer tugged on Sara's arm, pulling her closer to the group. Her legs froze.

"What's happening? I don't understand." Her voice sounded small; she barely recognized it.

"We're going to ask you a few questions."

"About what?" She forced a little strength into her voice.

"About this." He thumbed the cuff just below her elbow.

Her breath caught. The once purple filaments now burned white inside their black casing. What had Chen given her? A listening device? An explosive?

She tried to jerk away, but Rainer held her fast. Racing through escape scenarios in her mind, she saw none that wouldn't get her shot or killed.

Her peripheral vision suddenly caught movement on her right. Chen? Hoping for an intervention she almost cried in relief. Chen could handle this. She was in over her head.

The figure zipped past, not Chen, but a man surfing the air on a swivel board, rocking on his heels to turn the board where he wanted to go. Another followed. Then another. They were dressed in a motley assortment of workers' pants, t-shirts, and leather. Their eye sockets reflected with silver lenses.

Fraggers.

Her muscles tightened in agitation. She wondered if the rumors were true about the anti-government techno-militants, that the v-mitter lenses they wore could allow them to see the real world like a virtual arena, giving the wearers sharper reflexes and more efficient kills.

Fraggers were killers.

Around her, the contractors drew their cenders, blasting at the incoming attackers. Rainer was already on his communicator. "All units to the rim."

He let go of her and directed her to a nearby boulder before adding his guns to the fight. She never hesitated. Thanks to Chen she would add *running for her life* to the list of things she'd never experienced before tonight.

TWO

"Stay alive. Stay alive." Sara chanted the mantra during her dash across the scrubby ground. She needed to be able to think, to act fast, to find a way out of this. If she let one tear fall, it would unleash a mind-numbing torrent of sobbing; she'd save that luxury for when she and Chen were traveling back home.

The boulder rose up to greet her. She ran faster, her ankles twisting in the strappy heels. Adrenaline shook through her limbs and she dove for cover. Sand clung to the perspiration on her cheek and arm where she'd landed. Scrambling on bare hands and exposed knees, Sara crawled further behind the boulder. Her back scraped against the sandy surface. She pressed her palms to her eyes. "Stay alive."

Even in her hiding place she couldn't feel safe. Her mind flashed through a hundred stories she had heard about fragger brutality.

She chanced a look around the boulder's side.

A handful of boarders flew out from the canyon's depths. The snap of cender fire echoed off the rocks and far canyon walls. Hoping not to be noticed, she staggered for a tall stack of rocks further away. The sandstone grabbed at her silky dress, ripping patches away and shredding her skin. She fumbled with the straps on her shoes, then kicked them off.

The fraggers unhitched from their boards and dropped onto a dozen more contractors unloading from an open-air desert transport that had arrived from the direction of the setting sun.

The contractors charged on the outnumbered fraggers, their cenders releasing enough supercharged energy to power her ancestral home for a month. Each invisible round left a wake of static-charged air sparkling in the darkening evening. The heavy smell of ozone made her cough and wheeze. Flying sand, gritty and thick, coated her tongue. Her hair follicles expanded with the change in temperature and static heat in the air.

Activity on the far side of the battle scene near the rim drew her attention. It was Chen, scaling the canyon wall with grapplers. He slipped up and over the rim nearby, unnoticed; the woman he'd left the event with was nowhere to be seen. Looking at readings on his palm screen brought his gaze up to the rocky outcrop where Sara huddled.

Part of her wondered if he had known where she was because the bracelet had a tracker. Mostly she just felt relieved. She pushed away from the rock, but he quickly gestured for her to stay put.

An intense light emanated from the battle arena, blocking her view of Chen. On the fringe of the light, she could discern three fraggers backed into a circle, directly in the center of the cender onslaught. The contractor weapons seemed to have no effect on them. The fraggers stood calmly with their hands thrust out in front of them, palms glowing. It looked to her like the fraggers were absorbing the energy from the cender bursts, turning it into orbs of intense light that they could manipulate and hold in their palms.

She almost couldn't look at their brilliance any more. Then, the fraggers threw the glowing orbs back at their attackers.

Sara didn't hear any screams.

No explosions.

Silence grew as the orbs expanded and engulfed the contractors. When the flash died down, six victims lay in a charred heap in front of the fraggers. The scent of burning hair and flesh fouled the air.

Lights flooded the plateau. A small ship's engines screamed to life from behind a high escarpment. Chen signaled Sara toward it. A boarder spotted the movement and pulled a vertical three-sixty to dive on him. Chen fired double cenders. When the fragger orbed the energy back at him, Chen slipped behind a sandstone arch extending from the escarpment.

Sara ran to help, but came face to face with a pair of silver v-mitter lenses.

A deboarded fragger thrust his triton knife at her throat, its three silvery blades already tinged with blood. Her left arm blocked it, but the knife glanced off the cuff on her forearm and sliced through the skin. The cuff flew to the stony ground several meters away.

The fragger grabbed her by her neck and threw her to the ground. He dropped a knee into her stomach, forcing the air out of her body. Pain shot through her abdomen and erupted in her head. She felt like she would vomit. The man punched her, shattering her nose and spilling blood down her throat.

The transport's lights reflected in the fragger's v-mitters. In desperation, Sara ripped the right one from his eye. He shrieked and rolled off her.

She crawled away.

Chen ran toward her. Another boarder closed in on him. With a well-timed shot to the board's center, Chen forced the rider to dismount. Sara tried to scream for his attention, but choked on blood.

Just before he reached her, Chen stopped to pick up the bracelet.

Someone tackled Sara by the legs and threw her onto her back. She met the dead stare of the fragger. His functioning v-mitter taunted her, but the frenzied look in the bloody, exposed eye was terrifying. He straddled her, pinning her arms to the ground with his legs, then wrapped his hands around her throat. She thrashed, but he cut off her air, slowly, as if savoring her panic.

She silently begged Chen to hurry.

Blackness spotted her vision. The fight died inside of her.

Suddenly the pressure released. Her assailant's head snapped back, then the fragger pitched over onto her.

She gasped and choked, struggling to push the heavy body aside. With the small amount of strength remaining inside of her, Sara rolled the dead weight off her. Lying on her side, sand sticking to the blood and tears streaking her face, she stared into the harsh landing lights ahead. She saw Chen pocket the bracelet and board the ship.

He never looked back.

The door closed. The lights dimmed, and the ship's green hull shimmered in the ascent, before disappearing into the cloudless night.

He left her.

A shadowy outline eclipsed her starry view. She grabbed the fragger's triton knife, but the dark figure leveled a cender. She knew it was the same cender which had forced her away from the party and up the grav lift, the same cender which had brought down the fragger trying to kill her.

She grasped the fragger's knife in desperation, but the hair on her arms was already rising with the static discharge of Rainer's weapon.

THREE

"You'll be fine."

The words penetrated Sara's semi-conscious state. Her vision remained dark, but she smelled sandalwood.

"I dialed down my cender after killing the fragger." The man's husky timbre sounded familiar. Chen?

No. Chen had abandoned her.

The man speaking to her was the contractor from Palomin. Rainer.

Black turned to shades of grey, sharpening into an outline of a person stooping over her. The desert sky peeked from behind the escarpment here on the rim. She almost expected to see the ghostly trail of afterburners from Chen's ship.

Rainer's hands roved over her waist and belly, then moved to her breasts.

"Stop it." She grabbed his wrist weakly, but he shook it off.

"What happened to your part of the data?" He slid his hands down to her thighs. "Your bracelet?"

Sara's vision focused on Rainer's thick black brows and blue eyes.

He slipped his hand between her legs.

"I don't understand." Sara swatted at his hand. Her face felt crusty and her tongue lay thick in her mouth, the metallic bite of blood swam in the back of her nose and throat.

"That's what you said before. You want me to believe it's just a coincidence that you're attending a function this close to the Palomin Data Reserve wearing a bit siphoner disguised as a piece of jewelry?"

Bit siphoner?

Disbelief washed over her. Chen's *gift* was intended to siphon data, not represent their bonding.

Lights approached from the escarpment, their beams narrowing to reveal a blue ovoid ship. Upon landing, three contractors stepped out, sweeping the area with their weapons. Following them, Sovereign Simon Prollixer.

Awareness clamped down on Sara as she struggled for full consciousness. She squeezed her fists and curled her toes. What had Chen done?

"Have you recovered my property?" The Sovereign's gaze passed over the fragger's body then Sara's.

"The fraggers weren't here for extraction," Rainer said, his voice growing huskier in the settling smoke and dust.

"How do you know? You a mind reader now, Rainer?" A female with pink and black hair spoke up.

"Because the scans record the siphoning coming from multiple contacts *inside*...a full nine minutes before the attack," Rainer said.

"What about the woman?" the Sovereign asked.

"She doesn't have it. Neither did the woman in the silver dress we found dead on the valley floor. The runner took what he needed before leaving them both."

"Do you know who the man was?" The Sovereign's small mouth barely moved.

"Not yet." Rainer looked down at Sara. "Probably a rogue. Only way he could know how to get by security in the first place."

"Was he working with the fraggers?"

Rainer snapped his head up. "No contractor, not even a rogue, would do *anything* with that kind of halfcaste techno-militant trash."

"I don't need the cultural lesson, nor your contemptible tone. What I need is my data." The warning in Sovereign Prollixer's gaze belied the stoicism in his voice. "Get her to a behavior modification cell. My life won't be the only one forfeit if that data is not returned."

Sara fought to stay awake, to find a way to plead her case.

"I don't believe she's strong enough to undergo interrogation. If she dies, you've lost the best lead we have and the runner won't come back for a dead partner." Rainer's words brought her little hope.

Chen wasn't coming back. She saw it in his eyes when he picked up the bracelet.

FOUR

"You don't have to do this." Sara pleaded through her tears.

Rainer held her arm once again, and she believed that as long as she could touch him, she could persuade him not to hurt her. Maybe it was only her mind's way of keeping her sanity, but she felt protected by him. She didn't dare look at the others following behind them or at the Sovereign walking out in front as the group returned to the hippodrome's balcony. Relief set in when she saw the door to the passing celebration. Maybe it would be all right after all. Then they walked past the entrance and headed into a service stairway.

"Please don't." Sara put her hand over Rainer's and squeezed.

"We're just going to sit down and talk a bit," Rainer said without looking at her.

The small party reached a freight elevator halfway down the grey hallway. Rainer motioned Sara inside and followed her in.

The Sovereign spoke up. "Contractor Varden, if you wouldn't mind returning to my nephew's celebration."

"Don't I have more immediate concerns?"

"No. Contractor Renault will be handling this matter."

The pink-haired female slid past Rainer into the elevator and tipped the corner of her mouth in a gloating smile. She slid her hand around Sara's arm, emphasizing her new found ownership.

"Faya's interrogation record is less than stellar."

In response, Contractor Renault—Faya—dug her fingers in between the muscles of Sara's bicep, pinching nerves and practically bringing Sara to her knees in pain. She cried out in shock, but kept her gaze pinned on Rainer.

"Please help me."

He stared at her, then at Faya, his expression turning from sympathy to alarm.

"On your way, Contractor Varden."

The Sovereign stepped inside the lift and closed the door. Faya held Sara tight, but Sara barely felt the woman's fingers digging into her any more. The numbness of her unabated vulnerability replaced the panic. She floated outside of her body now, as if somehow watching through her own eyes from above the group.

She clawed to stay inside the elevator once it stopped, but Faya's strength and years of combatant training easily overpowered her. Faya grabbed a fistful of Sara's hair and dragged her down the hallway to the room Sovereign Prollixer had referred to as a behavior modification cell. Two of the other contractors bound her hands to a chain hanging from the ceiling. Her screams allowed her to hear only parts of what Faya said to her: "You'll really get into the drugs. Well, not at first." The woman laughed, then attached a doser patch to Sara's neck. A tiny pinprick followed. "Before you know it, you'll be begging me for more."

A hot sensation split through the muscles of her neck.

Faya held up manacles lined with hundreds of contouring blades. "Ever seen blade cuffs? They're low tech, I know, but I'm more hands-on." She winked and ripped the gown the rest of the way from Sara's body.

Sara cried out in fear and shame, but the screams only echoed in her own head as the fog of Faya's drugs burned through her system. She was dimly aware of her feet being chained to the floor.

Faya approached, the blade cuffs dangling from her fingers. She smelled like strawberries. "The spring action keeps them snug as they slide along your skin. They can travel unencumbered all the way from thigh to ankle."

"I'll tell you everything about Chen."

"Yeah, you will. But let's have some fun first." Faya clamped a manacle to the top of Sara's thigh.

FIVE

SIX WEEKS LATER

"It's not real. None of it's real."

Sara dragged herself across the entryway by her elbows. Blood oozed from hundreds of cuts on her legs, a miasma of red streaks on the geometric design of the olive tiles. She would rest here at the Sovereign's apartment within the reserve until he decided it was time to return her to Faya's dank cell.

This guest suite was like a gilded cage. Only here the torture wasn't needles or shockers, but knowing that even if she escaped the windowless room, she'd never make it out of Palomin Canyon alive. Not that she had the strength to even try it. Maybe when the Sovereign first imprisoned her here—twenty, forty days ago? She had lost track.

Was this how the citizens on the worldships felt for all those millennia? Trapped and hopeless? Sick and dying? She'd thought about them during these hateful days spent in the remnants of their old ship. She never cared about those ancient days, never understood, but her present circumstances mirrored those of the Lowers back then. The Lower Caste had been shut away from the rest of society for being unclean, damaged.

Thinking that even those people managed through their horrors sometimes gave Sara resolve. Sometimes.

The cold tiles stuck to her skin as she crawled the short distance to the bathroom. Her teary vision morphed the intricate white archway at its entrance into a hazy apparition. The normally straight and regal columns bent at irregular angles as though melting.

She stopped to wipe her nose on her arm. A pair of disembodied silver eyes appeared in the archway.

It's just the dosing. Another hallucination.

The eyes flew at her. She ducked her head and screamed. They hovered there, within touching distance. Just like the fragger v-mitters, but they had wide black pupils in their centers. She buried her face to hide her tears from them.

"Get away from me."

She should have expected to see some residual images. Faya had finished her latest modification session only an hour ago. And this time she had stepped up the hallucinogenic dosers.

The eyes aren't real. There aren't any fraggers here.

Sara never told Faya about her fear of the techno-militants or what really happened at Palomin. She never would, no matter how many torture sessions she had to endure. But Faya didn't need to know what inspired Sara's terror, only which drugs would make it manifest.

Her hatred of Faya gave Sara a moment's courage. She clawed at the fresh cuts on her legs, begging that the horrendous sensation of splitting skin destroy the horrid images. Pain had become her only tether to reality these past weeks. Another secret she had kept from Faya. The more intense the pain, the less the dosers worked.

Sara looked up to stare at one silver v-mitter, now featureless and dead, its mate, the bloodied eye of the fragger she had fought outside these walls.

"You're not real." Sara slammed a fist against the tiles. Why wasn't the pain working this time? Had Faya finally dosed her so much that the visions would never go away?

Angry and frightened, Sara continued her crawl toward the bathroom. The raw eye stayed just ahead of her, rolling around as though still in a socket. Sara ignored it and counted tiles, anything to force her focus elsewhere.

Inside the bathroom, the eyeball plopped onto the back of her hand and stared at her. Screaming, she flung it off.

The stench of charred flesh wafted from where the eye had rested. There were no signs of burns, but the acrid smell overwhelmed her. She heaved and pulled herself up to the toilet. Bluish mucus and bile burned her esophagus and mouth as it came back up from her stomach. The taste reminded her of cleaning chemicals. The throat-searing pain overloaded her senses. The eyeball rolled around on the tiles a few times, then vanished.

Now that her mind cleared, the pain in her legs grew in proportion. She smiled weakly at the trade-off.

With mustered strength, she propped herself up and grabbed a thick towel from the washstand. The towel caught on the rim of an empty water glass and sent it tumbling to the floor, shattering it into tiny pieces. Dark red streaks soaked through the towel's pale green fabric as she pressed it against her legs. The contact of even the softest fibers sent needles of reassuring pain through her.

Blade cuffs. What sick mind came up with that idea?

Faya favored the devices over the shockers, which had stopped Sara's heart once, and dental torture, though there weren't many molars on her right side left to pull. Faya was at least kind enough to rub anti-microbial salts into the cuts and empty sockets and rinse them with chlorate, to keep down the infection.

Can't have you dying on me yet, Faya had whispered against her cheek.

Sara could still smell the pungent chlorate here in the sterile bathroom, mixed with Faya's strawberry scent.

But, the worst part was the nightmares; they stayed after the split skin and contusions healed.

Sara thought of the one thing that would stop her slide into insanity. She thought of *him*. He would come to her soon. He always did.

Trying not to move her lacerated legs, she grasped the side of the huge bathing tub and dragged herself into a sitting position. Her naked back absorbed the coolness of the tub's side. She closed her eyes and panted.

"I see Faya went for the blade cuffs again."

Her eyes flew open and her heart jumped. He was here. Rainer was finally here.

Glass crunched under his boots as he approached. "At least she stayed away from your face this time." He nudged her head up to look at her scars.

His skin had tanned since a few days ago, or was it yesterday? Or last week? The bronzing complemented his sculpted face and dark hair. She was deathly pale and her face now bore no resemblance to the woman she used to be. Faya had succeeded in her humiliation.

Rainer reached past Sara and turned on the water for the tub. Its rushing noise brought comfort, static to fill her mind. When he bent down beside her, she smelled the subtle woodiness of his scentbots. Breathing deeply, she allowed his scent to calm her.

"I'm giving you the stims first because it's going to be painful when you hit that water." Rainer pressed a doser patch into Sara's neck before she could protest.

She barely noticed the pinch of the tiny needle or the endorphin stimulants pumping into her bloodstream.

"Let me see what damage she did." He lifted the towel and set it aside. A brief sadness crossed his face. After a careful inspection of her cuts, he grabbed a crystal atomizer from the wash stand and sprayed her legs with an analgesic.

"You'll still feel some pain, but that should help until the stims flood your system."

Rainer was always gentle when ministering to her wounds, but very clinical. When his actions became too tender, his touch too caressing, he detached himself from the work and became methodical. Nevertheless, she craved his touch, any touch besides that of her tormentor.

"Thanks," she whispered.

"Hold onto my neck." He lowered her into the tub.

As the warm water inundated the shallow cuts, bright red clouded the bath. The shock sent her head spinning. Her fingers dug into Rainer's neck, and he waited for her to relax before pulling away.

"I take it you haven't told Faya what she wants to know yet." Rainer moved toward the tall cabinet to the right of the tub.

Suspicion crept into Sara's ailing mind. Was this part of Prollixer's ploy? Faya roughed her up, then Rainer would come in as trusted healer.

"I've told her everything I know about Chen. And I don't know anything about *Simon's* curse." Her voice broke when saying the Sovereign's given name, but the endostims kicked in enough to make the insult sound strong. "I just hope he dies from it."

"He might." Rainer left the room.

Maybe Simon figured the male contractor could seduce information from her that Faya couldn't procure through behavior modification. Only, Rainer had never tried to seduce Sara. In fact, he always turned down *her* physical advances.

How could she blame him? She'd bashed every mirror in this suite just so she wouldn't catch a glimpse of herself. With a sick little look, she spotted a brand new shiny mirror above the sink. Simon always made sure to replace them just before she returned from another torture session.

Rainer stood over the tub with a crystal shaker and poured a silvery powder into the water. Sara held her breath in anticipation of the burn from the metallic antiseptic, but its pinch was subtle compared to the chlorate. When Rainer turned off the water, the silence was stark and unnerving.

"I believe you don't know anything more," he said.

His words almost stopped her heart.

"Otherwise, why put yourself through all this? To cover for a man who left you to die? A man who led you to believe he'd have a child with you." Rainer swirled the powdery solution around her legs.

The burn in Sara's heart matched the sensation on her sliced skin. She couldn't even think of Chen without wanting to wrap her hands around his throat and crush the life from him. The sudden surge of emotion brought with it a panic, and panic often brought on—

She looked to Rainer, then past him into the bedroom. *It was there.*

Her body shook as she stared at a hovering orb of light, no larger than a pebble. The expanding sphere drifted toward them. Rainer scanned the room, even drawing one of his cenders.

He couldn't see it.

On some level she understood it was just another deranged image in her mind, but that didn't make her reaction any less real.

The fragger energy orb augmented, its speed increasing, until it hurled its room-sized mass directly at her. She threw her hands in front of her face, afraid its energy would char her body as it had those contractors on Palomin's rim.

"Sara." Rainer's voice sounded distant, like he still fought to be heard over running water. "Sara, there's nothing there."

He pulled her dripping arms from her face and tilted her head up. "Look at me. Sara, look at me."

Ashamed of her scarred visage, she twisted out of his grasp. Scraping at her legs drew fresh blood and calming pain.

Rainer grabbed her hand to stop her. "What did you see?"

She shook her head and closed her eyes.

"Tell me what you saw."

"A fragger orb." The absurdity of it disgusted her.

"Do you still see it?"

"No," she said, then defiantly, "Do you?"

Rainer ignored the question and took a fresh towel from the cabinet. With careful hands, he helped her out of the tub. Her legs still screamed with pain, but she could at least stand if she leaned up against him. That physical contact felt better than the stims, than the pain. He wrapped her legs in silky gauze then guided her around the broken glass and into the bedroom. She rested her head on his shoulder.

He held her with one arm while he turned down the bed with the other. When he laid her down, she held onto his forearm and rubbed her thumb over the fine dark hairs.

"Can't you stay with me a little longer? Just hold my hand, until I fall asleep?" She craved affection, gentleness, someone to hold her and say it would be okay.

Rainer stared at her, his expression unreadable. "This is business, Sara. The healthier you are, the stronger you'll be to defy Faya."

"I'm not defying her." The thought was more absurd than a fragger orb detonating inside the room. "I don't know anything, including why Faya's failure is so important to you."

"That's business, too. Mine."

"Would it be different if I didn't look like this?" She placed a shaking hand on his, trying to hold onto its warmth. "I just need someone to be near me." She wanted her mother, her father, one of her cousins, even her sister to hold onto right now. Most of all, she wanted Rainer because he was here and he was always the one to take her pain away, to listen to her ravings.

A commotion in the hallway put them both on alert.

Rainer tugged his hand away and looked at her. Not quite a look of pity, but it still stung. "I've been here too long already," he said. "If the Sovereign knew about this, we'd both be dead. You won't need me soon. He has other plans for you, ones that don't involve torture...or at least not like this."

Watching him leave, Sara couldn't even muster the strength to care what the Sovereign would do to her next.

SIX

A faint blue ellipse decorated a large circle of pavement outside the Embassy's expansive halfmoon-shaped complex. Rainer caught glimpses of the faded symbol within a mix of drably dressed Embassy staff, flamboyant Socialites, and black-clad contractors. Bodies crisscrossed in kaleidoscopic regularity to and from the ferries and ship berths at Shiraz Dock here within the Hub.

Tampa Quad's largest urban center used to be a different kind of hub. Rainer formed a vague image from stories his family told of archivist ships constantly arriving and departing from the system's six moons, before Sovereign Archivist Simon Prollixer dropped the archivist part of his title and managed to gain control from a council too willing to give up its power. Now there was only the Sovereign.

Like Sara, Rainer didn't believe Prollixer deserved his manufactured title.

Thinking of her brought mixed feelings, ones he pushed aside as he passed the defunct landing pads and avoided the commonways used by most pedestrian traffic to the Hub. He never entered via the grand main entrance with its sparkling chalcedony wall, preferring to maneuver through the Hub's underground tunnels. Head Contractor had its privileges, including access to places most citizens couldn't imagine.

Though Prollixer originally commissioned the tunnels' construction for quick getaways at the onset of his take-over, he now preferred to be as high profile as possible in order to bask in the appreciation of his citizens. Maybe he forgot that not everyone celebrated the regime change like he did.

Contractors and fraggers protested the loudest; Prollixer made sure to turn one against the other very early. Those contractors who found working for the Embassy too restrictive left the guild to become rogues for hire. At first, Prollixer denied marriage rights to the rogues, but quickly changed policy after the guilders threatened to mutiny as well. Once any group of Uppers was denied rights, others could easily follow.

The Sovereign might pay Embassy contractors to be loyal, but no price was worth losing their family privileges. It was too much like what had happened on the worldships when the diseases ran unchecked and the quarantines were first enforced. A negative growth in population left the citizenry in serious jeopardy of extinction.

Without the archivists' History lessons, the Sovereign might have thrown the population into decline, or worse, allowed the purer lines to become tainted. Reinforcing the need to marry within one's caste and with multiple partners ensured a thriving populace among the six moon-planets. Of course interpretation of *caste* varied. Most took it to mean any from the Upper Caste, but family circles consisting mostly of Embassy contractors took the mandate to a new level, nearly becoming a sub-class themselves. Most of them formed their family circles with other contractors exclusively. Rainer's family subscribed to this tradition, as was evidenced by the lineages of his amours.

Three figures rounded the corner ahead. Few traveled the featureless white corridors with their overly bright ceiling lights, so Rainer often used his transit time down here to disconnect from everything, allow his mind to rest and wander. It annoyed him to have this meditation interrupted, especially today.

The approaching forms became recognizable as Archivist Phoebe Lewellyn and her contractor bodyguards. The woman's blue-streaked blonde hair almost glowed in the harsh lighting.

"Hello, Contractor Varden." Phoebe motioned her escort ahead. "May we speak?"

The mayfly holo-broach securing her pink wrap fluttered its wings.

"I have a few moments before the Sovereign expects me." Rainer kept the movement of Phoebe's bodyguards in sight at all times.

"The Sovereign hasn't been himself recently. He dismissed the quorum today without even making an appearance. I hope he's not still ill." The gaze of her dark green eyes watched Rainer closely, but he was too disciplined to display any tells.

"He was fine when I saw him yesterday. He's a busy man."

"Too busy to meet with his own advisors?"

"Maybe he no longer needed your advice." Rainer and Phoebe both knew the Quorum of Archivists served only as figureheads to make Prollixer's rule fall more into line with the History teachings. There had always been archivists, would always be. Even the Sovereign couldn't change History, but he could decide how History was interpreted, like giving the other archivists no real political responsibilities.

"Anything else?" Rainer asked.

"No, just my concern for our dear Sovereign. Good day."

Rainer had regarded the woman with suspicion for some time. Normally his instincts were dead on. He imagined it wouldn't be long before Archivist Lewellyn met with misfortune.

Within the medical suite, Rainer followed a white beam of horizontal light as it passed over Sara's naked form and projected its readings into the air above her. A doctor studied the scan silently.

Sara's will to survive continued to impress Rainer. An urge surfaced to touch her hand, but he quelled it immediately. Each time he had left her at Prollixer's mercy he took with him the memory of her touch; the pressure, the swish of her thumb, the signaling of need. The power he held to elevate her mood, take away her pain, and give her hope fed his emotions almost as much as his ego.

A hint of roses enveloped her, thanks to new scentbots. Breathing a little deeper, he couldn't remember how she smelled before. It didn't matter; this smell was as fresh and new as her body. He stared at every detail of her.

The changes to her appearance played with him. Her lips were fuller, her nose a little wider. And the scars were all gone.

Sara's reconstruction didn't technically constitute a breach in law. Allowances were made for little fixes all the time, but her alterations took away any natural attributes she had once had, at least so far as Rainer was concerned. Mores and tradition still held more sway with him than laws.

Seeing her lying there both excited and disturbed him.

"How is my newest ambasadora?" the Sovereign asked from the doorway.

The doctor stood straighter.

Rainer stepped back from the post-op table and avoided Prollixer's stare.

"I didn't expect you to personally check on…I mean, you didn't visit any of the other ambasadoras," the doctor said.

The Sovereign made no response.

The doctor cleared his throat and continued. "She'll be coming out of the anesthesia soon."

"The implantation was successful?" Prollixer walked over to the bed where Sara lay, exposed and vulnerable in her drug-induced sleep.

The doctor peeled back the single bandage covering her right arm. "Yes, all the cells grafted well. And, as you can see, the intra-tattoo's design is flawless."

"How can you tell with all the bruising?"

Hundreds of puncture wounds in varying shades of purple and black covered her entire arm from the back of her hand to her shoulder. The site of more marks marring Sara's new skin angered Rainer.

"It looked much better when the light matrix covered her skin during insertion. But, not to worry, the contusions should heal quickly."

"Fine. Now, if you wouldn't mind leaving us."

"Yes, Sovereign."

Prollixer waited until the doctor left the room. "Contractor Varden, what do you think of my modifications?"

Rainer stared at Sara's hand to avoid looking at the rest of her. He had more discipline than to let his physical desire show, but involuntary responses like pupil dilation were more difficult to control. Few citizens ever overcame that genetically hardwired reaction to sexual stimuli.

Except for the Sovereign.

Had he lived so long that coupling was no longer important to him? Perhaps that would explain why he hadn't produced any offspring for nearly sixty years. Speculation about a true genetic link to his previous children still surfaced occasionally, mostly due to their early deaths, but most citizens shied away from gossiping about the Sovereign for fear of repercussions. Of course, most wouldn't have guessed that his longevity bots were more than a myth, that his scientists had found a way to lengthen his life, and that this technology wouldn't be shared with anyone who couldn't pay the exorbitant price.

Rainer wondered if, now that Prollixer's supposed immortality was threatened, the panic of being heirless gnawed at his guts.

The Sovereign dissolved a sedative strip on his tongue as if in answer.

Rainer's gaze drifted to Sara's breasts, which were larger now, but he quickly pulled it back to her face. Considering the circumstances, any type of arousal displayed by Rainer would be expected, but he feared Prollixer knew of the unauthorized visits to Sara during her modification.

"I don't see much difference except for the longer hair. Good color choice, by the way. I'm kind of partial to dark-haired women." But, changing her hair color still wouldn't make her a contractor, and that disappointed Rainer more than he cared to admit.

"I'm glad it pleases you. I chose a similar hue for her eyes."

"Quite a change from the honey color they were," Rainer said.

"You remember the color of her eyes? Surprising. I believe it was quite dark and dusty the only time you saw them."

Rainer gave Simon a guarded look, but his response was even. "Eyes are just my thing. Some guys focus on a woman's mouth or her ass. I always go for the eyes."

"Precisely why I didn't hire you for the modification."

Rainer's mouth folded at the corners. "You didn't even know about the eye thing until just now."

"I knew there was something you liked about her. You took great care of her..."

Rainer didn't blink.

"...before Contractor Renault took over that night."

"I took care that she didn't die before we got any information from her. Then you cut me out of the modification process. I would have charged less than Faya."

"Really? Contractor Renault wouldn't accept any payment to break the woman."

Rainer's breathing paused for just a moment, but the Sovereign had caught it. His smile said so. "Not to worry. I have more important jobs for you."

He looked back at Sara. "And you, Ambasadora Mendoza, have the most important job of all. You get to lift my curse."

"Why her?"

"Bait. The rogue who left her at Palomin will be very interested to know she is still alive, and now serving as one of my ambasadoras. He will either come back to save her or to kill her. But, either way, he will come back."

Prollixer's rising tone hinted at desperation, a trait emerging more frequently in the ailing Sovereign. Rainer supposed curses would do that to a man.

SEVEN

The deafening hum of the engine room aboard the *Bard* drowned out the sound of Sean Cryer's fist slamming repeatedly against the bulkhead. It wasn't a technical problem like he often faced here on the luxury cruiser turned science vessel that vexed him, but rather one of a more personal and illegal nature.

"How could my prints not smear?" He threw an electric wrench into the shining metal framework just to the right of the open console. If someone monitoring his last exit from the V-side traced his digital prints back to this ship, they could also find out which virtual worlds he'd visited. He'd be swept away by a contractor patrol and imprisoned as an Embassy agitator. Until they found out he was a node in the fragger organization, then he'd just be tortured and executed and forgotten.

Sean had suspected someone shadowing him during his last couple of ventures into the V-side, the virtual world. Possibility leaned toward probability now that he found the door to the comm chamber slightly ajar.

Inside, snuggled into a protected wall, lay the secret port he had installed six years ago after initially purchasing a suite aboard the *Bard* and becoming the ship's engineer, or mech tech as the others referred to him. This port allowed him access to the V-side without detection, without shadows tracking him, without suspicious Embassy officials lifting his digital prints from this source. Or at least he thought. He probed the port and watched the readings scroll over his palm from a wrist reporter implanted under his skin. Everything checked out. Maybe there hadn't been a shadow, just his paranoia.

David would enjoy hearing that.

The new nav leader on board already hinted at Sean's stim abuse and his consequent bouts of paranoia. But what did he know? David Anlow was little more than a hired pilot who flew a bunch of independent scientists to appointments throughout the system. Problem was that David, being a former Armadan captain, fancied himself still in charge of a ship.

Sean had caught him looking around the engine room on one other occasion. The ensuing argument had turned physical on Sean's part. Risky since Armadans were bred to be warriors, how their caste came to be named after the military in which most of them served. As a result, their bone and muscle structure was stronger than that of Socialites, the other Upper Caste. Of course Sean's real father passed along some of that Armadan strength to him, even if no one but his immediate family circle knew Sean's true genetic history. That wasn't the biggest secret, though. Sean's mother had been from the Lower Caste. His father took care of them anyway, even helped to buy them into Socialite society before he died. But Sean and his brother always knew they were different, not as deserving as other members of their father's family circle, including their siblings by other mothers.

Heading to the *Bard*'s bridge, Sean reminded himself to be calm when confronting David, to keep his head. He didn't want to tip his hand if David didn't already know what was happening.

As soon as Sean burst through the open bridge door, he flew into David. "What were you doing in the engine room again? Thought I told you to stay away from there."

David swiveled his nav chair around inside the orb of holo-controls.

"How you doing, Sean? Coming down from a binge?"

Sean resisted the impulse to leap across the shining black floor of the bridge and grab the bigger man by his throat. Truth was Sean had just taken several restors to bring him back to equilibrium.

"Just asking if you visited the engine room recently."

"It sounded to me like you were accusing me of something." David manipulated an airscreen in one side of the orb.

His nonchalance and cheery disposition grated on Sean's nerves. "Just tell me if you were there." Sean scratched at his chin and neck; an itching sensation rose with his blood pressure, a restor side effect. He forced himself to stop before David noticed.

"Like you said, I'm not welcome in there. Besides, it's too bright. All those glowing white walls give me a headache."

David's lack of eye contact proved he told the truth. After six months, Sean could read the man well. Most Armadans were open and happy, the latter most likely a result of certain aggressor genes being turned off at birth. Sean envied that. He secretly suspected some of his problems fitting into society stemmed from being an intercaste hybrid, a halfcaste. His mother had him classified as a Socialite so he wouldn't have to spend his life in the military, but as a result, he never underwent the *appropriate procedures* that would have helped him to adjust, that would have *calmed* him.

He certainly wasn't calm now. Maybe he was overreacting. He could have left the door ajar during his last visit to the chamber. That seemed unlikely; he was seldom careless. He was about to hurl another accusation at David when a whir in the back of his brain clipped off his response. The fragger bosses had just summoned him to another meeting in a specified world in the V-side. Second one today. Something big was breaking out.

"Just...stay out of there," he managed, making a less than graceful exit.

The only time Sean lay on his bed was to enter the V-side. It was more comfortable to sprawl out on the puffy mattress than to fold himself up on the couch in the sitting room where he normally slept. Plus he could get the bedroom dark enough that his pupils opened to their fullest. The bigger his pupils, the faster the neural stimulator would kick in.

With the tips of his fingers, he slipped the silver v-mitters onto his corneas. The tinny smell of the conductor fluids was unpleasant, but would allow his brain waves to hitch a ride on an electro-magnetic stream emanating from the engine room's secret port.

Ninety-nine percent of those citizens who entered the V-side were gamers looking to escape from a bad day into a fantastical landscape or flex their muscles through neural stimulation. Some users sought out stimulation of another type, which was why sex worlds proved so lucrative.

To fraggers, it was a medium for discreet training and communication without need of a physical headquarters. Compliments of the Embassy, the virtual submersion worlds and plethora of drugs associated with them were meant to serve as an outlet for aggression amongst the more unruly Uppers and mindless entertainment for the Lowers.

The original V-side source was the now defunct comm system from one of Palomin's worldships. But once new, unregulated technologies sprouted up all over the V-side, the Embassy attempted to shut down the virtual arena in order to control the latest advances. The Sovereign withheld the tech from the normal population until such a time as he and his corrupt council could profit from it.

A group of tech savvy individuals staged a protest by taking over the Media for exactly nineteen minutes and thirty-three seconds to broadcast anti-Embassy sentiments and to expose Simon Prollixer's illegal takeover of the Embassy. The first fraggers were born, and abruptly died by the hands of the Sovereign's contractors.

Fortunately, others listened and managed to create a secret array with the remaining comm systems scattered around the six moons. No matter what the Embassy did, they couldn't bring down the V-side. For years no protests arose, but all that time the fraggers were regrouping, Uppers and Lowers, Armadans and Socialites, even a scarce few rogue contractors, coming together for the same purpose—policing the Embassy and its oppressive policies.

Sean relaxed as the sensation of a cool liquid flowed behind his eyes, preceding the insertion of his avatar, Zak, into the virtual lobby.

Okay, Zak, time to go to work.

It was like a very lucid dream. Sean was completely immersed as though he were physically there, not just lying motionless on his bed aboard the *Bard*.

His ears buzzed and popped. The space around him transformed from dark nothingness into a purple sea and silver-grey sky.

Inside the V-side lobby Zak stood on a floating platform that was barely a meter square. Sean's stomach on the *Bard* detected the rise and fall of the softly undulating virtual sea as Zak kept his balance on the slate-colored raft. The popping in his ears gave way to a gentle lapping. His brain reacted with the phantom smell of the Archenzon Shore on Tampa One, but the salty scent faded immediately. In the V-side, nothing had a scent. This little detail kept the immersive world from ever becoming truly real.

Six fist-sized globules rose out of the sea in greeting and encircled him. Each was a different shade of blue, indicating the type of invitation being extended. The darkest came from a group of regular gamers Zak and Topper had befriended during a slasher session. Zak had joined them once, but he didn't get into gaming like many fraggers did, just the training.

With a wave of his hand, Zak sent the globules into a slow orbit around him until the palest one whirled front and center. It was almost transparent and took on the purple sheen of the surrounding sea on bottom and the silver of the sky on top. He reached his hand out and made contact with the slippery surface.

A quick pulse began in his fingertips and rushed through his body, probing for his identi-markers. His av was recognized immediately through the idents. The globule opened at the top and fanned out, enlarging enough to allow Zak to step through to a training world.

On the other side, grassy plains welcomed him. Half a dozen dragons with purple heads and green and silver iridescent bodies eclipsed the dwindling light of a late day sky. Zak observed three of his virtual companions figure the trajectories and energy expenditures needed to bring down one of the iridescent beasts. Six others practiced hand to hand techniques in a field nearby.

Topper, sporting his reptilian av, stepped aside as Ariel took aim with a rocket launcher and fired a round into the lead dragon. Silvery scales disintegrated. The animal flapped its great wings once before falling to its death behind a distant white mountain. The other timid dragons hesitated, but when Ariel fired a second rocket their way, another beast took point and led their flight formation away, into the darkening horizon of this virtual world.

"Zak, did you hear me?" Topper sent a hot plasma blast into Zak's shoulder from a crafter, a modified cender. The nickname came about because the originator said it was craftier than anything the obtuse contractors could come up with.

Zak's vision blurred as the shot triggered a neural stimulation of his pain center. His virtual arm dangled uselessly at his side. Blood splattered his grey armored vest and soaked the sleeve of his blue shirt.

"Can't hear anything above Ariel's rockets." Zak called up the healing program in his mind. Catching Zak off-guard was one of Topper's favorite games.

"So, what's your take on the ambasadora thing?" Topper's voice took on a reptilian hiss to match his present lizard form.

"Just one of Prollixer's pet projects. Most likely to draw attention away from current Embassy mis-dealings."

"But how's this new element going to affect our plans?" Topper asked.

"Won't. Ambasadoras are just another Embassy show, as impotent as Armadans." Zak thought of his earlier run in with David back on the *Bard*. Thinking of David as impotent made him feel better.

The system might have a highly trained military, but the Armada was all show. With no intra-system conflicts brewing, they never used their skills, weren't even allowed to carry arms outside of their Armada ships. The Embassy wanted it that way. Yet the Sovereign's pet contractors were given free reign of the system after they put down those first fragger protesters.

"The ambasadoras are just another Embassy spectacle of shallow grandiosity." The pain subsided as Zak's arm healed. He looked down to confirm the blood was fading, then checked to see the sleeve had been properly repaired.

"The Media have been calling them the *Faces of the Embassy*. Rumor has it they're all women." Bullseye's marmoset-like mouth morphed into a lascivious grin as his furry, prehensile tail flicked back and forth.

"*Of course* they're all women." Ariel's brown braids swished against her almost bare backside as she sidled up to the meter-high Bullseye. When she scratched under his furry chin, he snaked his tail up her booted leg.

Just as he was about to reach the skin at the top of her thigh, she clasped a hand around his throat and threw him to the ground. "Women make better distractions than men." She gave him a kick to his mid-section.

Everyone laughed, except Zak. He hated to waste time socializing with a bunch of dosed-up fraggers, especially in the V-side. The anonymity it afforded allowed egos to run high with avatude and behavior to go unchecked. Of course the entire fragger organization was set up that way, and with good reason. Even if the Embassy found out the identities of a few fragger operatives, the loss would be minimal. Only select bosses knew all their members.

Zak looked around at the dozen members of his contingency and wondered if, as a fragger node, he should secretly learn a little more about the people he led. He trusted them because they hated the Embassy. Aside from opposing the Embassy's suppression of technology, his fraggers also rebelled against the society's millennia-old caste system. All this reflected Sean's own ideology. Putting their lives at stake to make a difference made them honorable.

There were still flaws in the system, though, like when someone's ideology changed.

Zak looked from av to av. It was more to show authority than to get a read on any of their faces. The expressions weren't real anyway, just the result of each fragger's preferred programming. Nothing in this world was real. Of course, most of society was fake, too—the Uppers cosseted existence, Sovereign Prollixer with his claque of Socialites, the Lowers wasting away in menial jobs, unseen and unheard.

"The bosses confirmed a leak." Zak kept his tone even.

"They sending us in to take care of it?" Ariel loomed a head taller than any of them.

Take care of it, as big a euphemism as the word *fragger*, both just a nicer way to say *kill*.

"Yep. That's why the invites went out for today."

Even the fraggers who weren't already plugged into a gaming world were summoned.

"Is it because of the Palomin siphon?" Bullseye used his tail to swing up onto Ariel's shoulder. "That was a month ago."

"I thought one of the other contingencies took responsibility for that." Ariel shoved the marmoset back to the ground.

"They were there, but not responsible for the extraction," Zak said. "A group of rogue contractors pulled the siphon from inside."

"Rumor has it we lost three fraggers during that siphon. That true, Zak?" Ariel trailed a finger down his gun arm. He felt the sensation through his neural transmitter, and though it registered in his pleasure center, he casually twisted his arm out of her reach.

"That's true. The rogues caused complications, but the virus we gave Prollixer is back to doing its job. Sources say once the quarantine was siphoned, his cell sweepers ceased functioning. He's now aging normally. Calls it his 'curse.'" Zak dropped a hand to his side and secretly unlocked the safety on his weapon.

"Can't think of someone who deserves to be cursed more," Topper said. "Guess he can't have the rest of us knowing about his longevity bots. Might have a societal mutiny on his hands."

"He already does," Zak said.

"Those rogues did us a favor then," Bullseye said.

"Except…." Zak wrapped both hands around his weapon, ready to level it. "Someone slipped in a data miner to a fragger hub world."

"If that's true, then a streamer either breached some pretty elaborate security or—"

"Streamers are average citizens coming to V-side worlds to get laid or watch the sun set somewhere they'll never get to see in person. They barely have the knowledge it takes for insertion," Zak interrupted.

Someone accidentally stumbling into the wrong part of the V-side was almost impossible. The random combination of idents implanted during fragger initiation were not only scanned upon entering the hidden V-side fragger worlds, but also monitored during any session, preventing a mainstream user, dubbed streamers, from entering fragger territory by accident or otherwise. Zak often wondered where all of his idents were; in his arm, his thigh bone, his tongue? Only the doctor who performed the operation knew.

"What we have is another informer problem," he said. *Someone who found a new ideology.*

"Do the bosses know who?" Ariel gripped her rocket launcher in both hands.

"Yep." Zak leveled his weapon at Bullseye. "Confirmed just before I called you in."

The marmoset's large eyes bulged. "Not me." He morphed into a human av, green spikes of hair rocketing upward from a youthful visage. He had called up his own crafter with the morph and wielded it in trembling hands.

"Come on. You know me better than that."

Zak was the first to fire, a point-blank shot to the forehead. In the real world Bullseye would have been obliterated, but in this virtual existence, it just blew off the top of his head without killing him.

He managed to choke out a plea. "Zak, please. Don't do this. I wouldn't betray the fraggers."

The little guy stalled, trying to call up better weapons, activate his healing programs, or just unplug from his V-side host. But Zak had lockout codes for every fragger in his contingency. Bullseye no longer had control of his fate.

"Please." Bullseye screamed when he realized he'd never be able to unplug. "No. Help me." He crawled toward Zak's feet.

Zak fired into Bullseye's newly healed face. The others fired their weapons until Bullseye could no longer call up his healing programs. Then Ariel aimed her rocket launcher at his spasming chest and finished the job.

Whoever Bullseye was in the real world was now experiencing a neural overload. The result would be either a cerebral hemorrhage or a heart attack. Then the idents would break down with the cessation of cell activity. All traces of fragger involvement would be erased, making it look like another gamer who dialed up his neural stimulator too far or a streamer who couldn't handle insertion. That was if anyone even found the body. Most fraggers were anti-social and chose a life of solitude, except in the V-side.

Probably did him a favor, ending his lonely existence.

Zak looked at his contingency and knew one day that favor would probably be returned.

EIGHT

FOUR WEEKS LATER

"I really hate your sister." Sara uppercut Dahlia's jaw. Her head snapped back, her ponytail slapping her face. Dahlia lacked Faya's spirit. That must have come from Faya's father's side since she and Dahlia shared the same mother. Dahlia had quite the horrible shadow to live in, but that wouldn't win her any sympathy from Sara. As soon as she found out that Faya Renault's little sister was training here as well, Sara focused all of her energy for this one fight. Masked as a simple scrimmage, she meant to exact revenge on Faya today, through her sister.

A small group of Simon's private contractors cheered from the edges of the grass sparring ring. The bare-footed females traded blows on the aqua-colored sod of the training garden, which was fenced in on three sides by tall hedges.

A mid-morning grey sky hung close above the clouds in the Prollixer Territory, a thousand miles from the Palomin Reserve and Sara's hateful modification cell. Her silver top and form-fitting black shorts, which exposed her navel and the bottoms of her cheeks, remained cool and comfortable in the temperate climate, even though she worked up a sweat. Much better than the desert heat.

Sara leaned backward at the waist, denying Dahlia any contact from a side kick. In one motion, she twisted upright and pushed her open palm into the other woman's chest. The force landed the contractor on the ground. Only a month ago Sara was recovering from major reconstructive surgery, and weeks before that from Faya's torment. Sara kneeled on Dahlia's chest, a small part of her pretending it was Faya, and pressed her knee into the woman's throat. She grabbed a handful of pink hair and ripped it from her head. Out of desperation, Dahlia punched at Sara. Only one of the three jabs found a mark, on the side of her jaw, but Sara didn't flinch.

The crowd whipped into a frenzy as Dahlia struggled beneath Sara. The contractor's fist unballed and her arm fell to the grass. Her magenta streaked hair splayed in the grass around her.

Strong hands lifted Sara up and dragged her aside. She struggled against them until she saw it was Rainer holding her back. "Make sure she's still breathing." A couple of the contractors surrounding the ring jumped to help Dahlia. Some meandered away now that the show was over, but a few just stood and watched Rainer. Being Simon's Head Contractor, Rainer probably battled those killer looks constantly, and most likely the actual attempts that sometimes accompanied them.

Dahlia sputtered to life. Rainer used his reporter to call for a medical team and ushered Sara to the cool-down area outside of the hedge ring.

"Hello, Rainer." Sara smiled at him, a little knowing smile that spoke of the secret they shared. She overheard one of the remaining male contractors tell his companion, "Should have figured she'd be with *him*." Because Sara was an ambasadora, training in contractor techniques, she was a novelty here, which afforded her a fair share of nightly proposals, none of which she ever accepted.

Seeing Rainer again after so many weeks reminded her why. She stole a glance at him while they walked together and was surprised to find his gaze on her, as well. "Nice to see you have your strength back. I'm not sure Dahlia deserved that, though."

Those were his first words to her? Nothing had changed. Disappointment flooded through her, then a slow simmering rage. Sara had more than her old strength back—she was stronger than ever, both physically and emotionally. Months of torture were bound to kill her or force her to adapt. She was thankful it was the latter.

"Dahlia was an unfortunate victim of her lineage," Sara said. "She's no more her sister than you are yours."

Sara stiffened at the mention of her family. Until a week ago, she had had no contact with them since Palomin. Then, just before the announcement that Sara would become one of the honored ambasadoras, Simon allowed her to speak with her mother. He stood beside her during the video call, seeming like the proud leader, when really he wanted to monitor what she said. The threats he had made against her family should she reveal her true circumstances kept her tone light and a smile on her face for those few moments. Her mother expressed her pride, but Sara could see confusion and worry behind her expression, especially as she took in Sara's enhanced appearance. Thankfully, Simon hadn't noticed.

Rainer lifted a towel from the table and handed it to her. The shade was the same light green found in Simon's apartment back at Palomin. Rather than pulling away from the memories of torture it evoked, Sara accepted it graciously. The swirl of her purple intra-tat glowed a bit brighter on her right hand.

Rainer watched the glowing speckles beneath her skin, too. "Do you ever find it unsettling that your new body art owes its beauty to a tree crustacean?"

"Actually, I didn't know where all these lights came from." She'd simply been told the bio-lights were an exclusive mark of the ambasadoras and that they would be a part of her for the rest of her life.

"I asked the doctor in your recovery room," Rainer said. "They're protein cells from proto-shrimp living in canopy pools in the Archenzon Cloud Forest on Tampa One."

"That's unnerving. To think I have another species living comfortably inside my body." She patted her forehead dry then ran the towel over her neck.

"Harvesting them must have been no simple task. Those forests were the first in the system to be terraformed. The trees are enormous because they were never touched once Tampa Deux opened for settlement."

"I've never been there." Traveling to the system's farthest moon had never appealed to her, but she would hop on a freight ship headed to the mines of Deleine this second if she could get away from Simon.

"Most people haven't since the Embassy imposed the trade embargo on Tampa One. That means your little friends are probably worth more than this entire territory."

"Expensive livestock brand," she muttered.

"You haven't embraced your new role as a Face of the Embassy, I take it?"

She hoped Rainer didn't suspect she just played Simon's game until she had an advantage of her own. "It's better than the alternative." She squeezed his forearm in an attempt to change his focus.

She was a little surprised to see it had worked when he traced his finger along her jaw to her neck and down to her cleavage.

"You missed a spot." He rubbed the moisture from her body between his thumb and forefinger.

A mix of desire and anger welled within her. She slid her hand up his arm. "You like the new me, don't you?" she asked.

"It's different," he said.

"Better? More like a contractor?" Sara caressed his neck with the back of her hand.

"Better, but you'll never be a contractor, even with the hair and the training. It's not in your genes."

"That's right," she said as though just recollecting some odd fact. "Unlike normal Socialites and Armadans, contractors only mix with other contractors. You even take your profession based on your heritage, or is it the other way around?" She leaned a little closer. "But, doesn't that lead to a lot of inbreeding?" Sara thrust her fingers into Rainer's neck, pinching the nerves. Before he could react, she kicked his feet out from under him and held him at bay with one of his own cenders.

"But you'd be willing to overlook that for a tumble," she said. "It's still me. Just with a prettier shell. Apparently the shell is all that matters to you." She looked up at a newly gathering crowd. "To anyone."

Rainer made it to one knee before Sara pressed the cender into his temple.

"Don't worry. I'll dial down the energy before I shoot you, like you did for me."

A few chuckles and a smattering of applause drifted her way from the crowd.

Rainer grabbed Sara's wrist. With his thumb jammed in between her tendons, she lost her grip on his cender.

She punched him in the jaw with her other hand.

"Enough." Simon's tinny voice stopped the escalating fray. "Your training is paying off, Ambasadora Mendoza. Now I suggest we try it out on someone other than Contractor Varden."

Rainer's look was as hard as Simon's.

Sara picked up the cender and offered the silver grip to Rainer. He grabbed her hand with it, crushing her fingers into the metal. The action matched the threat in his eyes. They both knew he wouldn't do anything in front of Simon, but he had just warned her about any future encounters.

She'd be waiting.

"Leave us," Simon said to the crowd of contractors.

"I found you a ship, ambasadora. The *Bard*. It's registered as a science vessel, but was originally a pleasure cruiser, so the accommodations should be reasonable. You will need a suitable transport to shuttle you from engagement to engagement."

"Found me a ship? Like you found me a new body and a new title? Don't expect me to be honored by any of it."

Simon whirled on her. "Never speak to me like that again or I'll send you back to Contractor Renault, and this time I won't hold her back."

Sara's face flushed and she avoided Rainer's gaze. "I apologize. Maybe it was the shock that you're sending me out on social engagements."

"I am sending you to get information on a suspected fragger operative who lives aboard the *Bard*. To keep up appearances, you will be expected to attend certain social functions of my choosing."

Sara forced her mouth to stay closed.

"Don't forget this new title and new body are gifts. I have personally chosen each ambasadora based on exceptional breeding lineage, beauty, and social skills. I chose *you* because you have a connection to my curse. The training I've given you should have been reserved for a contractor. And, my doctors had no choice but to improve your assets. How else could you charm the fragger operative and bring him into your confidence?"

Sara's fists balled up when Simon mentioned her improved assets. Before Faya sliced Sara's face to bits, she had been pretty, if not striking or beautiful. More importantly, Sara's face had been *hers*. As the tears threatened, she warned herself to quit mourning who she used to be and embrace this chance at a more powerful life. Beat Simon with his own tools.

"How do you know it's a *him*?" Sara asked.

"Because my sources suspect someone in particular."

"Who?" Rainer spoke up.

Sara wondered why Rainer wasn't privy to this information ahead of time. Perhaps the Sovereign and his Head Contractor weren't as close these days. The implications of how that could benefit her raced through her mind.

"The *Bard*'s Armadan pilot," Simon said.

Rainer sniffed. "That doesn't surprise me. Armadans are only three steps away from being Lowers, and since fraggers are anti-caste, well...." He shrugged.

"How old is this guy?" Sara asked. "I thought Armadans stayed with the military until their century mark, then lived their last sixty or so years in retirement on Yurai."

"Are you afraid you won't like the shell?" Rainer asked.

Sara ignored the jibe.

"This particular Armadan captain left service of his own volition halfway through his commission. His record at the time was superb. He was even due for a promotion, one of the reasons my sources suspect him. Why abandon your professional life in its prime?" Simon looked at Sara. "He's still in his prime sexually, as well, so I don't think you'll find what I'm asking to be too unpleasant."

Simon didn't know what unpleasant meant. But he would.

NINE

She should be close.
David watched Mari's golden-tipped hair bounce over her eyes as he pressed her back against the grey wall of his suite. With her legs wrapped around him, she slid up and down the smooth wall quite easily. It was the only wall that would work since it was the one without wooden screens attached to it.

With a forty year age difference, Boston Maribu and David Anlow had nothing in common. *Well, almost nothing.*

Mari's jaw slackened. Her breathing came in shallow gasps. When she seized his shoulders in a death grip and clamped her mouth over his, he knew he had her. And none too soon—he'd been close for a while and his legs were ready to give out.

Their bodies both tensed. David kept Mari pressed to the wall as he pumped inside her one last time. And, he kept his mouth on hers in a tight kiss because she had a tendency to be loud when she climaxed. It was hard to be discreet on a ship with thin inner walls, especially with Mari's vigor for sex. David found it more and more difficult to keep their couplings secret, and he knew Mari liked the thrill of clandestine meetings in the beginning, but was ready to announce to everyone that she and David were officially together. He wasn't. Not only did he fear it would cause problems with the others, but he also worried that the magic of their relationship would somehow end if it were exposed to the world.

He tossed her playfully onto the thin mattress on the floor. As soon as he collapsed beside her, Mari wrapped herself up in half of the royal blue duvet and snuggled against him. The citrus notes of her scentbots played in his nose once again.

"How could you possibly be cold after all of that?" He curled an arm around her under the blanket.

"Because you keep this place like a cave." She shivered. "It's not very homey. You barely have any furniture. And what you do have is ugly."

David scanned his bedroom. Three of the walls had large black screens adhered to their surfaces. These were inset with an occasional white square over the grey backing that covered the other walls and the ceiling. On the wall opposite the entrance was a large framed line drawing of the Koley Mountains on Yurai, David's home planet. Besides the low bed and the freestanding lamps, the only other piece of furniture was a light blue wooden chair that was more comfortable than it looked...and apparently ugly.

The spartan interior housed everything he needed, but more importantly, it looked like his quarters on the *Argo Protector* just before he left his commission there.

"It's better than the neon world where you live." He smiled and closed his eyes, knowing the tease would get her riled up.

"What's wrong with a little color?" she asked.

"A *little* color? It looks like the bottom part of the light spectrum exploded all over your suite in green and blue globules." He peeked out of one eye to see her reaction.

"Well, when you become my prime, maybe I'll let you have a say in the redecorating. Unless we stayed in your suite, then I'd have a say in the redecorating. Whose suite is bigger? I think mine is, but yours is closer to the bridge, so that's something to consider."

Mari prattled on. David stared at the ceiling. Sometimes she talked so fast and about so many different topics all at once that David had a hard time following the conversation. Not that it ever really was much of a conversation because Mari didn't often give him a chance to get a word in, except when she was mad at him and during sex. The latter had to become a rule, though, after the first couple of times that he and Mari were in the throes of coupling and she talked through half of it. He managed to smother her mouth with kisses during the other half, but as soon as he would come up for air, she'd find something new to tell him. So they had agreed that unless it was dirty, encouraging, or telling him that he was doing something wrong, it could wait until afterward.

The room was suddenly silent, and since they had just finished docking, it meant Mari was irritated.

"Nothing to say?" she asked.

"I was just enjoying the moment." David tried to play innocent. He knew she was referring to the marriage subject again, but he hoped to avoid a fight.

"David."

"I thought we agreed not to talk about this for a while."

"It's been almost a month since I mentioned it." She propped herself up by an elbow.

"That's only a month, not a while." He knew that wouldn't pacify her. They would end up in the same argument they always did.

"You think you can do better than me, don't you?" she asked.

How could he do better? Mari's insecurities about her coral-colored eyes were unfounded in David's opinion. She couldn't help that she had a reaction to a vaccine while living on Deleine. Besides, it gave her individuality in a society of tired copies. David's real concern was Mari's age and inexperience. Not only was he her first real relationship, but the first and only man she had ever been intimate with. That worried him. She was too young to be thinking about marriage and children. There was too much life for her yet to live. Armadan males often started families much later, after their service to the fleet came to an end, but Socialites always jumped right in, practically after puberty. Just the cultural variations, he supposed. Still, a guilty little part of him felt as though he were taking advantage of her. He needed to be sure of his feelings and hers before they took another step.

He realized she was still talking when she asked, "Or are you just holding out for a battle maiden?"

"I've had lots and lots of battle maidens," he said. He meant it as a joke, but she didn't need to know it was true.

She flicked him in between the eyes, the purse of her lips daring him to continue.

"All I meant was if I had wanted a military woman as my prime, then I had lots—*a couple of*—opportunities to do so." He stroked her cheek, enjoying the feel of her soft skin. "We'll talk about this another time, I promise." He leaned over and kissed her until he could think of something else to talk about, wondering at the morality of using his kiss as a distractor.

"Are you coming with me to the Hub to pick up our ambasadora today?" he asked. Mari was always ready to venture off the ship.

When her mouth became very small, he knew this morning would end in a fight no matter what. "*Our* ambasadora?" she asked. "So, that's it, isn't it? You're waiting for a chance to snag a Face of the Embassy. Go ahead and deny it." She sat up and folded her arms over her bare breasts.

David caressed her thigh under the duvet, hoping to soothe her a bit. "Mari, you're making me crazy with your jealousy."

"So, you aren't going to deny it?"

She hadn't heard a thing he said. He rested his head against her leg in defeat. "Deny what, Mari? Deny what!" This just reinforced his earlier opinion that she was too young for him. Dealing with a nineteen year old's insecurities frustrated him, but it also made him feel alive in a way even combat hadn't. Each day he stayed with Mari, he came closer to reconciling those opposites. Even with today's fight, he favored feeling alive.

"I need to go," she said. "I promised Geir I'd help him with the mid-day meal." She rolled out of the duvet and away from

David, a little pout on her thin lips. It was petulant, but arousing.

"Mari."

She walked over to the chair where her clothes lay. David forgot their fight as he watched her slip on her little mauve top and shorts while she hummed some song he had never heard before.

"Mari."

When she pulled on matching thigh-high boots, he considered taking her back to bed, boots and all. She might be a little short, but her legs were long, and those boots made them even longer.

"Mari."

She studied the line drawing on the wall, trying to ignore him as he pulled on pants and a shirt, but he caught her peeking at his body anyway. It was one of things she liked best about him. He walked over to her and hugged her from behind. She liked when he chased her after a fight, and he was usually happy to oblige her. He figured if they parted on bad terms they might never find their way back to one another.

"So, we'll talk about this again in a while?" she asked.

"I promised we would, and I will always keep my promises to you," he said against the softness of her hair. It smelled like a combination of her citrusy scentbots and the gentle floral shampoo she favored.

She spun around in his arms, stood on her tiptoes, and gave him a little peck on the lips. "You better," she said, and with that announcement, she was out the door.

David spoke into the empty room. "I'd marry you tomorrow and start making babies if I thought it was the best thing for you." He was already sure it was the best thing for him.

This was why civilians irritated David Anlow, especially scientists. You couldn't just order them around—they had *opinions* and wanted to debate every decision.

"So, it's true. The Embassy is forcing this woman on us even after our petitions to them state we don't have room for her?" Sean Cryer spoke from across the jadeite dining table. He and David were the only ones standing, as if squaring off against one another. Though larger than average, Sean's frame couldn't match David's, but the light from the curving sculpture lamp behind Sean made him look bigger. And, the younger man had the presence and aggressive confidence of an Armadan, which served to reaffirm a certain suspicion David had about Sean Cryer's ancestry. Of course, it was hard to tell how much of the attitude and bravado came naturally and how much he garnered from the mind and mood-altering poisons he swallowed, injected, or sniffed. Plus, Armadans could control their confrontational impulses; Sean could not.

Everyone else watched intently while enjoying their meal.

"I'm sure those petitions you sent out were read by a sub-official, then filed away forever," David said. "Let's try and make the most of this."

"If the *Bard* keeps gaining passengers, you might have enough for a squadron soon," Geir Shang said in jest. "Then it would be like you were navigating one of those big Armada cruisers again, instead of piloting around a handful of scientists, though I imagine we're better looking and more fun."

Odd that Geir would make a military joke when he was an Armadan who had chosen a life of science over joining the fleet. David had mixed feelings about Armadans like Geir mainly because one of his brothers and a sister had taken the civilian route upon graduation. Though not unique among Armadans, his siblings were the first in the Anlow family circle to break tradition, and David, even though he left service early, seemed to be the only one who had difficulty accepting their choices.

Still, Geir had become a good friend. The dark man would see things David's way; he always did. David shoved Geir's booted foot out of his chair. It landed with a thud on the lilac and blue swirl of the floor. "I'm not exactly thrilled with the idea of a new body myself," he admitted. "I'm still trying to get used to some of you after three months." He looked pointedly at Sean whose expression dared him to say more.

If Sean hadn't performed technological miracles several times on this antiquated pleasure craft, David would have petitioned to have him jettisoned into the deep dark weeks ago.

"Look," David reasoned. "We all knew this was coming. We've been preparing for it for almost a month. There's nothing we can do about it now."

"Scientists need room for their research," Mari said. "We're already sharing the public space among the six of us. *Her* room was going to be a laboratory for Kenon and Geir."

David wanted to punch Sean in the mouth for getting Mari worked up about this issue again. "Then why haven't they gotten around to using it all of these years? Or even within the three months since I got here?"

Sean jumped in again. "What about all the rerouting? We're expected to change all of our schedules to accommodate her shopping trips and parties."

"That's not true."

"So, we're not rerouting?" Sean asked.

Sean was shrewd. He knew the answer already because he had confronted David about that very issue yesterday. Now, he wanted the rest of the passengers to hear it.

"We're tweaking the schedule like we would for any of the rest of you, and not for shopping trips. She's new. We can be a little accommodating."

Sean was relentless. "And what about the next passenger they saddle us with? Because you know this is just the beginning unless we show the Embassy we can't *accommodate* any more bodies on board. And, why would Prollixer want the *Bard* to carry a diplomat anyway? Doesn't make sense." Sean's features softened when Solimar Robbins came through the door next to him and placed her palm against his chest in greeting.

The mocha-skinned woman looked every centimeter an Upper female in her navy, shape-hugging dress. She paused in front of Sean, while he returned her greeting with a kiss to her forehead. For someone who was supposedly so anti-establishment, the mech tech still followed the dictates of polite society, even in the heat of an argument.

An argument that was a waste of time. David ran his hand over his face.

Sean, paranoid doser that he was, acted as though the ambasadora's presence was a personal affront to him, so had asked these questions on a daily basis since word came down from the Embassy last month. Now he wanted one more open forum.

To keep that from happening, David said the same thing he had before. "It doesn't matter *why*. The Embassy owns the *Bard*. They say so, we do so."

"Then Sean's right?" Geir asked, before taking a forkful of the casserole he and Mari had whipped up for lunch.

"About what?" David asked.

"That the Embassy can force anyone or anything on us at any time and we have no say about it," Sean said. "How can that be okay with you?"

David looked around for support. Nothing. Just a bunch of metal utensils dinging against finely crafted dinnerware.

"It's a simple concept," he said to no one in particular. "Yet, I'm the only one getting it."

Apparently not caring about *why* was blasphemy to a group of scientists. He would be glad to get off this frigid ship and visit the Hub today.

"I'd like to think of this as an opportunity." Kenon Brudger spoke up.

David was pleasantly surprised; the foppish geological observer disagreed with David almost as often as Sean did.

"Finally a man of reason," David said.

Mari sniffed.

"Opportunity for you to snag a new amour, you mean," Sean said.

"If she finds me appealing, I would welcome her," Kenon said.

"Right into your bed." Geir slapped Kenon on the back, nearly sending the slight-framed man sliding out of his chair.

As Kenon complained of a bruised shoulder and indigestion, Sean slammed his palms on the table. Dishes jumped up and landed with a crash.

David's hands balled into fists.

"Easy, Sean. I feel like you do," Mari said. She reached a hand out and touched his arm. David didn't like it, but he kept his calm.

"Can't the rest of you see it's just a way for the Embassy to control our independent operations here?" Sean asked.

Geir laughed and wrapped a dark arm around Sean's shoulders. "That's our Sean. Always thinking too much."

"Always paranoid," David said.

"Some of you aren't thinking enough." Sean pushed off the dining table. "Kenon, transport leaves in three minutes, with or without you."

Part of David wanted to follow Sean out of the room and settle this once and for all, but mostly he was just glad to be rid of him for a while.

"We should call him Sunshine. What do you think?" Geir laughed.

"That's nicer than what I call him," David said.

"And nicer than what he calls you." Kenon stood up from the jadeite table.

"Really? What's he call me?"

The others looked at each other and laughed, even Mari.

A beep sounded from David's reporter. "Now I'm late."

"You better go." Mari cleared the dishes without looking up at him. "Wouldn't want to make our guest wait. She's too important." She walked over to give a departing kiss on the cheek to Geir.

If that's how Mari wanted to play it, David could certainly hold out longer. "You're right. She is pretty important." Mari's head whipped around, but David wasn't letting her off the hook for siding with Sean.

"Ready, Soli?" David made for their own planet side transport. He waited until he and Soli were out of earshot of the others, then leaned over and asked, "So, what's Sean call me?"

TEN

Sean heard Giselle moaning as soon as he and Kenon entered the rounded foyer.

Kenon slipped off his shoes and moved quietly over the smoky-colored tiles toward the sitting room. "So that's why we had to let ourselves in. Obviously, Giselle didn't want any intrusions today, including from her own servants."

Sean contemplated undoing the series of snaps and fasteners holding his boots in place and decided the servants would be back after Giselle's tryst to clean up anyway. Still, he walked stealthily after Kenon, who had paused in the foyer's gallery to smile at the latest vid of his daughter, Hailey. The six year-old spun around in a circle, her long blonde curls bouncing on the sleeves of her baby blue dress. He held out a hand as if to touch her face.

"This sweet child carries my genes, my heart," Kenon whispered.

"Yet, like every other Upper Caste parent I know, you send your children off to nurseries, only to see them a few times a year."

Kenon didn't seem to hear. "Watch." The little girl twirled in her holoscape again. She looked just like Giselle with her heart-shaped face and upturned nose. Only her blue eyes were unmistakably Kenon's.

"*You* could have probably done with a more proper education." Kenon sniffed.

If only Kenon knew. Sean's childhood had all the proper education and etiquette, even having a Lower Caste mother, but he saw no reason to practice good behavior when few Uppers around him ever did. The system's motto seemed to be that so long as the whole system was aware that one *knew better*, one never really had to *do better*. He hated the hypocrisy. That's why he left school at thirteen to learn as much as he could about the V-side and join the fragger organization. He wasn't sure what would appall Kenon more, the fact that Sean was a halfcaste or a fragger.

They followed the curve of the white-walled gallery into Giselle's sitting room. Tall-backed couches in lush mauve patterns and dark wooden tables of assorted sizes separated them from the large windows covering the far wall.

In the center of the tiled floor lay a silver rug. On top of it Giselle straddled a man. She wore nothing but the onyx necklace Kenon had given her for Hailey's conception. He told Sean he'd take him to the same jeweler for a good deal when the need to finally marry stirred within him.

So far it hadn't, and Sean didn't anticipate it stirring any time soon.

The heavy, black pendant seemed large for Giselle's delicate frame. It smacked roughly between her small breasts as she moved up and down on the male under her.

"That's Mikail," Kenon said. "The amour she took after me."

Sean probably met the auburn-headed man at Hailey's naming ceremony, and then again when Soli had talked Sean into attending Hailey's induction into the Tampian nursery a few years back. The induction was Sean's last formal function. He even adopted a scruffy appearance to detract anyone from inviting him anywhere again.

Giselle and Mikail were so involved with their coupling that Kenon and Sean went unnoticed. Sean said he'd wait in the other room, but Kenon placed delicate fingers on his forearm. He mouthed, "He has bad form. Schooled in Witho."

The schools from Mikail's home territory on Tampa Deux were known more for their attention to the Media than their attention to sex education. Mikail wasn't helping their cause. His rhythm was already slowing just as Giselle picked up her pace. Sean had his doubts Mikail would be able to match her as she moved faster and pushed down harder. It wouldn't be long now, judging by Giselle's heavy breathing.

Kenon smiled and elbowed Sean when Mikail finally lost the rhythm completely, then let his hips rest and waited for Giselle to finish them both.

"At least she got something out of it," Kenon whispered, then loudly, "Hello, Giselle. Mikail."

Giselle's big, grey eyes looked up at them from under mussy locks of blonde hair. She flashed a sly smile to say she knew they were there all along.

Mikail obviously did not, as his annoyed tone implied. "Do you mind, Kenon? We're in the middle of something."

"It would seem you're at the end of something, Mikail."

Sean coughed to cover a laugh. Posturing among Socialites always amused him.

They all knew Kenon had privilege as Giselle's prime. Mikail would have to defer if asked.

"We'll come by later, Giselle," Kenon said.

Tricky bastard. Kenon knew they'd find Giselle and Mikail here alone. That's why he suddenly needed Sean to reprogram his wrist reporter for access to the systems in Giselle's manor.

"Wait, Kenon. He was just leaving."

Ouch. A dismissal. Not Mikail's day.

Sean half-expected a fight to ensue. Domestic incidents between competing amours were few, or at least few were reported. Kenon probably respected Giselle too much to push the issue, and more importantly was fearful of bodily injury from the larger Mikail. Another reason Kenon had brought Sean along.

"Fine. We'll be in the viewing room. Sean needs to make some adjustments to my reporter anyway. Nice to see you again, Mikail," he said over his shoulder.

No response issued forth.

"He's always hated me." Kenon led Sean through a back hallway to the more comfortable viewing room with its casual furnishings and fully stocked bar.

"Imagine that. Jealousy among amours."

"Jealousy?" Kenon said the word as though it were the most ridiculous he'd ever heard. "Giselle is just one of three. I enjoy them all the same. And they enjoy each of their other amours in turn. Just one perk of a large family circle. You should try it."

"Keep telling yourself that." Sean decided long ago that many Lowers had the right idea—one partner, less headaches. Of course, the Embassy restricted their marriage rights, so they didn't really have a choice, but few complained of a monogamous life.

Kenon switched on the Media with his *faulty* reporter. A large viewscreen materialized in the air opposite the bar and dominated the room. Two round sienna faces with short platinum hair flashed to life in mid-commentary.

"...Socialite Mariam Datwal chose the Passing Ritual this morning after a medical exam concluded her ova were not viable. Her lineage remains intact due to her sacrifice. She died honorably and comfortably after requesting her doctor to administer...."

Kenon muted the sound.

"Thought your reporter was non-responsive to these systems," Sean said.

"Hmmm? Oh, it seems to be working fine right now. Yurian scotch?" He held up a blue tumbler.

"I can't believe you, Kenon. What a waste of my time. Just an excuse to spy on Giselle."

"I think she's planning to take a third amour." Kenon became serious and downed his glass.

"Thought you wanted to expand your circle."

Kenon's voice remained pleasant. "Of course. I figured she would want another child soon. She and Mikail had Sasha three years ago. Hailey is now six. I just thought we'd be planning for another of our own by now."

Sean almost felt sorry for Kenon. Trapped in the tenets of a society and trying to make the best of it because it was *the right thing to do*. He couldn't blame him for that. Misery was always the side-effect of any ideology. Sean sniffed at the scotch and gave it a swirl.

On the screen, the image of gossip-mongering hosts gave way to the sharp features and pale skin of the most recognizable man in the system, Sovereign Simon Prollixer.

Sean's mood darkened further. He put the glass to his lips, but thought better of it. Mixing alcohol with double dosers could produce debilitating side effects. Too bad he'd taken that last batch of stims before they left.

Bubbles with video clips from the day's headliners bounced along the screen's edge, expanding and contracting. A clip of a particularly beautiful, redheaded woman bounced by, the word *AMBASADORAS* rotating within it. Sean used his implanted reporter to expand the window. It manipulated all of the systems in Giselle's residence just like Kenon's did, though the couple didn't know this.

When the redhead began to speak, Sean turned up the volume. She proved more interesting than Mikail's whining from the other room.

"...can't tell you what an honor it is to be a Face of the Embassy. I'm sure you'll be hearing good things about the ambasadoras. The Sovereign was wonderful to give us this opportunity. I think all the women will agree he has been like a father to us. He is a very generous man with a wonderful heart."

Sean wanted to hurl his untouched drink through the screen. Naïve bitch. All the ambasadoras were being used to redirect attention away from the true intentions of the Embassy.

The woman's light green eyes were almost as shiny as her glossed lips. She played up to her audience by angling her head and smiling, techniques that wooed only the weakest of men.

"Isn't she incredible?" Kenon stared transfixed at the screen as the ambasadora sang another round of praises for the Sovereign. "So much beauty, so much poise."

The camera pulled back to a half-body shot to show a glimpse of violet lights pulsing up one of her shapely biceps, then the angle returned to her laughing face.

"This whole ambasadora business is nothing more than a publicity stunt by the Embassy," Giselle said from behind them. She slid past Sean in an orchid-colored silk robe. "I don't know how the Sovereign found sixty Socialite women willing to demean themselves that way."

Giselle attempted to hide the jealousy in her voice with a nonchalant posture. Sean knew better. Anything that placed one Upper above another in societal standing was always a cause for envy.

"I agree," Sean said under his breath, but Giselle had picked up on it.

"Hello, Scientist Cryer." Giselle winked.

Kenon pretended not to notice her flirting and poured another scotch.

"You can skip the title. It means nothing." Sean finally swallowed the smooth liquid, no longer caring about the consequences.

"Then how about mech tech? Isn't that what you all call him aboard ship, Kenon?" The term was meant as an insult, but Sean had found many more mech techs he liked than Socialites.

"Just Sean. If you have to talk to me at all."

She had already lost interest in him anyway, nuzzling up to Kenon and telling him she had something to discuss.

Sean made to leave, but Sovereign Prollixer's reappearance on the Media pulled his attention back.

"The ambasadoras will fill the roles of our once cherished archivists, sharing information about our projects and bringing back wonderful news of success within the system."

All of which could be accomplished faster and with less expense via the Media or virtually. That tingling feeling inside Sean that said he was right made him angry because the situation was actually worse than he thought. Rather than acting as passive distractions, the ambasadoras would be actively spying for the Sovereign and few would question it in order to be a part of the fanfare. Now one of those women would be living with him on the *Bard*, watching him, maybe reporting on his activities.

"I'm heading back, Kenon. Have fun."

Sean needed to make another stop in the V-side to find out more about Ambasadora Sara Mendoza's history before she insinuated herself into his life. What he found out just might determine the length of hers.

Shots ricocheted off metal. A huge hand grabbed the top of Zak's armor, pulling him to the floor. Three projectile rounds sparked in the darkness against a metal railing just centimeters from where he had stood. The soft echoing of the shots told him he was inside a cavernous room. The swaying floor and the aerated metal slicing into his cheek where he fell hinted at a catwalk of some sort.

"Haven't seen you around in a while," Topper said, the scarred face of his human av scarier than his normal reptilian form.

"I've been keeping a low profile, but thanks for the welcome back." He wiped the blood on the back of his hand. No healing programs in a true combat world.

It had been almost three weeks since his last session—when he had pulled Bullseye's plug.

"I think he's got a new woman." Cuzco chuckled from somewhere behind them. Zak's sight adjusted to see the big man crouched at the end of the catwalk taking aim at a rival contingency among the industrial machinery down below. Cuzco had been away on some special op for months. He had even missed Bullseye's elimination.

"Been finding better ways to work out, haven't you?" Cuzco asked.

"Hmmm. I always thought Zak *was* a woman." Ariel opened up on an enemy trying to sneak up a nearby ladder. Her crafters weren't as powerful as the rocket launcher she used on the dragons, but in this training scenario rockets weren't allowed.

Ariel probably wasn't joking about him being female. It was common for fraggers and gamers to switch genders in a virtual world. Sometimes it was an extra concealment technique. Sometimes it was just for the arousal. Considering Zak had always shrugged off Ariel's invitations for v-sex, she must have figured he was either into same gender or a woman.

But, Sean had never had v-sex with anyone. It creeped him out to think who might be on the other end of all that stimulation.

"Who's down below?" Zak asked.

"Eclipse's contingency. She's been waiting for you to show. Wanted to convey her condolences about Bullseye." Cuzco handed off a new clip to Vishnue as he belly-crawled past the smaller man.

"It took everyone by surprise, I'm sure. Bullseye had a lot of friends in the organization." Zak half-stood to let Vishnue squirm by and almost took a round to the head.

"Yeah, the whole incident caused quite an uproar. At least thirty fraggers have come forward with overthrow strategies," Cuzco said.

"Overthrow strategies?"

"This is the third case of faulty intel resulting in wrongful elimination. Next time it could be one of us." The coldness in Ariel's voice didn't match the chill running down Zak's spine.

Faulty intel. Wrongful elimination.

"What are you talking about?" Zak grabbed Ariel's bare arm and yanked her down beside of him.

"Easy, Zak, if you want a little, all you have to do is ask. I'm always willing." She grabbed his crotch.

He knocked her hand away. "No, I mean it, what's this about faulty intel?" Why hadn't the bosses contacted him? Hearing it from his whole contingency after the fact made him look like a fool. But maybe that was the point someone higher up was trying to make.

"You have been out of the loop, haven't you? Bullseye had nothing to do with the data dump. It came from an orbital source." Ariel shrugged. "Sorry. I thought you knew."

Zak slumped against the perforated railing.

"The head idiots had us take out one of our own guys based on bad info," Vishnue said beside him. He stood up and screamed, unleashing a torrent of strafing fire upon the contingency on the floor. His upper body jerked as he took several rounds in the chest. He fell against the handrail. The entire catwalk shook violently and threw Ariel backward over the railing. Zak stood up to grab her arm. An explosive round impacted on his back before he could catch her. He steadied himself against the handrail only to take another hit to his shoulder. It was enough to throw him off balance and pitch him forward, over the railing.

Sean's heart thudded and his stomach tightened as Zak's body went into freefall. There were no healing programs to bring him back; those were the rules of training engagement. Adrenaline pumped through his veins as he heard the crunch of Ariel's body hit the concrete. Zak's body hit seconds later.

Sean's connection was automatically severed with Zak's demise, but his physical body back on the *Bard* responded to the impact. He fought to catch his breath as he frantically pulled the lenses from his eyes.

Quivering from the pain of a hundred virtual broken bones, Sean screamed in the darkness of his own bedroom. He rolled off the bed and fell to his knees, then he balled his hands into fists and smashed them into the floor until the pain he felt turned into a numb afterthought. He concentrated on his breathing, the scent of conductor fluid, blood, and sweat pushing into his nose.

Today marked the first time in a decade he had been *killed* in virtual combat, but that wasn't what hurt most. His mind crept back to one thought: wrongful elimination.

His breathing became more labored. Resting his forehead on the cold floor, Sean rocked back and forth in an attempt to push out the grief…and with it, the guilt.

ELEVEN

I wish I had brought some shades.

By the time David and Soli stepped off of the magno-ramp inside the Embassy, they had to squint against the sunlight filtering through the six-story chalcedony atrium. A translucent wall of pale blue light buffeted the huge reception area.

David looked around the spacious lobby for somewhere to sit. Several intimate groupings of cushy white couches and chairs clustered around immense green pillars that spiraled toward the thirty meter high ceiling. He found an empty couch and motioned for Soli to join him.

He sat down heavily in a chair and put a fist to his chest. After stifling a painful belch, he said, "Solimar, don't ever let me eat maznee again. I don't care if I'm starving."

"Serves you right for going to that filthy diner. If you were too late for the Embassy dinner, why didn't you just go to Oso Negro's or Yama's? They're both right across the street." She looked at him with her coffee-colored eyes from under a baby blue braid. Her blue hair contrasted with her tawny skin in a very fetching manner.

"They're out of my pay range," David said, sorry now that he had settled for the special at-what *was* the name of that place? He couldn't even remember, though he did remember the special. It ended up being a fermented bowl of maznee-spiced chowder he had forced down in three swallows.

"Do you see a medmarket anywhere?" He pounded on his chest.

Soli laughed.

"Are you enjoying my misery?"

"No, it's just typical you," she said. "You get an Embassy stipend for piloting one of their science cruisers, and you're afraid to spend even that."

"I'm not afraid of anything. Armadan, remember?" He gave her a wink.

"Who left the military for life as a civilian pilot."

"Don't remind me," David muttered. "By the way, there's nothing wrong with being frugal."

"We only get one hundred sixty cycles if we're lucky, so I say there's no need to be frugal." She playfully squeezed his forearm.

He wasn't going to argue with her. Soli was used to being pampered and taken care of, like most of the other Socialites on the *Bard*. Warriors, or even ex-warriors, were self-sufficient as a point of pride. It separated them from other Upper Caste citizens. And, no doubt, put them a step closer to acting like Lowers through a Socialite's coddled eyes.

"So, you never mentioned how you felt about our new passenger," he said.

Soli had always been affable, but David only recently developed a good rapport with the woman. Her job as a social archivist made her one of the biggest busybodies in the system and that made David uncomfortable. Soli's constant recording of daily activities aboard ship was disconcerting and still took some getting used to. Was this why the original archivists were revered, because they knew everything about everyone?

"I'm anxious to meet her. The Media has shown interviews with some of the ambasadoras, and they are quite beautiful, even by Socialite standards."

"Hey, you and your prime are ready to have your first child." *Or her brother's child, to be exact.* Same gender, or SG, amours relied on siblings as donors and carriers. "You're not allowed to look at another woman for a while," David said.

"No one really follows those mores anymore, David."

"Kenon does."

She pondered the statement, watching a young mother parade her toddler proudly around the atrium. "I suppose you're right. It's endearing how he's so ingrained in tradition. Shows his upbringing. Good circles."

"Like Trala?" David asked, liking the way Soli's eyes lit up with the mention of her prime's name.

"Exactly like Trala. She's very refined and more gracious than I deserve, perhaps. I would never stray from her during the carrying. Besides, I don't believe any of the ambasadoras are into SG. This one is all yours."

"No thanks," David said.

"You don't think you'll find her attractive?" Soli asked. "Or have you been seeing someone else?" Her tone sounded playful and insinuating.

"It doesn't matter," David said too quickly. "You know my philosophy about tumbles between crew members."

"I never mentioned crew, and technically, David, we're not crew, only passengers."

"It's all the same."

"Do you really think your philosophy would stop, oh, say Mari and Kenon from having a tryst? Or, more likely Mari and Sean?"

David's eyes narrowed at the mention of an assumed attraction between Mari and anyone. "What do you mean? Have you heard something?"

Soli laughed. "It was a hypothetical thought, though a conceivable one. I could even imagine Mari with *you*."

David wasn't taking the bait, though he shifted a little uncomfortably in his seat. "Shipboard romances make things awkward. If something goes awry, you have to see the person every day. That's why Kenon lives in space, far away from all of his trysts, and especially his amours. Did you ever wonder if he even likes the women he has children with? Wouldn't he want to be by their sides as much as possible?" David paused. "Why do *you* live in space?"

Her full lips shrunk up a bit before she said, "You're interesting, David Anlow. I don't know if your views are a product of your Armadan upbringing or just a way to hear yourself talk."

"It'll take you another three months to figure that out."

A sudden rise in the conversations around them drew David's attention to the shimmering magnos on the next tier. Their elegantly curving surfaces transported society's political elite to and from the Embassy offices. Standing at the top was the head man himself, Sovereign Simon Prollixer, flanked by a pair of Embassy contractors and a woman.

David had only known the Sovereign from clips on the Media so was surprised to see that, in the flesh, the man looked to be only ten years older than he. *Probably had seen the reconstructive surgeon a few times to achieve that.*

Sovereign Prollixer's real age seemed to be the biggest mystery in this arm of the galaxy. David guessed about one ninety, but some sources postulated it was twice that.

He felt underdressed even in his brown uniform pants and light blue button up shirt. The Sovereign stood rigid in a formal suit. David knew just how uncomfortable the starched fabric could be, having sported the side-zipped tunic and front-zipped pants on more than one occasion. The tunic proved too hard to get on, the pants too hard to get off. The Socialite ladies went crazy for the look, though, which led him back to the part about the pants being too hard to get off…which led him to the woman who stood next to Sovereign Prollixer.

She wore a black full-length gown suspended from her neck by one thick strap. He followed a V of sheer black netting past a swell of breasts. Slits ran down both sides of the gown, beginning at her thighs and reaching the floor. The focus, though, was a six-inch wide purple corset cinched at her waist.

Her hair sat atop her head in a crown of black and purple ringlets. The only adornment David could see was the most obvious and the most captivating, a swirling pattern of purple lights pulsing slowly under the skin of her bare right arm.

The bioluminescence mesmerized him. Though the Media were all abuzz about these ambasadora-exclusive intra-tats, this was the first time he had seen one in person.

"She *is* beautiful," Soli said in David's ear.

He nodded, thinking of a particular chestnut-haired, coral-eyed nineteen year old back on the *Bard* who was not going to like this one bit.

They waited at the bottom of the magno to receive their newest passenger. The ambasadora leaned forward, as if to whisper in the closest contractor's ear. Instead, she chopped him in the back of the neck, then pushed the other into the Sovereign. The men tumbled partway down the ramp.

She kicked off her shoes and slid over the handrail to an ascending magno, disappearing onto the office level.

David looked at Soli. "I didn't see that coming."

TWELVE

"Move!"

Sara flew past a startled Embassy staffer, her bare feet slapping the onyx floor. As she raced through flanking planters of giant wax ferns, their iridescent leaves strobed green then lavender. When she broke into the office hub proper, she slowed her pace and stayed close to the obsidian fountain wall on her left. It would be best to avoid the outer offices which lay to the far right, inset behind the grey corbelled arches.

She needed to be on the other side of the fountain anyway. That's where the elevators were. Upon approaching the end of the fountain barrier, which separated the descending and ascending walkways to the magnos, Sara noticed a pair of contractors heading toward her from under an arch. One had his long, black hair pulled back into a knot at the nape of his neck, the other had his short hair combed into the more common center ridge style. Just like another Rainer.

Sara watched the contractors walk in opposite directions. Their casual black pants and jackets made them dark spots among a spectrum of green-suited staffers. Even if the men hadn't been donning the unofficial uniform, the twin side arms strapped to their upper thighs still advertised their profession.

No one besides Embassy contractors could carry a weapon here.

When both men were out of sight, Sara headed for one of the large cylindrical communications ports. There were three of the silver kiosks on this side of the hub. Each one could provide cover to the emergency elevator at the far end of the lobby.

She circled the first cylinder and saw most of the doors scrolled a pink holographic message: *OCCUPIED-OCCUPIED*.

Without stopping, she moved onto the next kiosk and then pretended to wait for it to open as several people walked past and chatted about the upcoming Tertian Verdant Gala. She was about to head to the third kiosk when she saw the ponytailed contractor reappear beside it.

He stayed between her and the lift, but luckily hadn't seen her. Circling the cylinder, she kept her right arm close to the port doors in an attempt to hide her bio-lights. Too many passers-by liked to gawk at the purple pulses that were now glowing wildly with her increased heart rate. It was hard not to be noticed with those dots advertising her location like a skyway v-board.

She peeked around to see the ponytail still hovering in between the kiosks. Had the contractors guessed her plan to reach the emergency lift, or were they just covering all possible exits? She could have thought this out a bit better, but there hadn't been time. The impulse to escape had only come to her as she was *escorted* through here on her way to the magnos. She should have waited until she was on her way to her new ship. Impatience had gotten the best of her. Ironic, considering she had bided her time for two months while Simon kept her under lock and key. She couldn't have waited a few more minutes?

The ponytail circled the far kiosk. Sara ducked around the side of the communications port. She looked around and saw the other contractor turning the corner at the fountain wall. Her only recourse would be to hide out for a while. Of the six ports on this side, all scrolled pink.

One of them had to empty soon.

One did…all the way down at the far end. She headed straight toward the man vacating it and smiled. He nodded, then looked down at her arm. Before he could comment about the lights flashing under her skin, she touched the controls to open the door and ducked inside.

A viewer attached to the narrow wedge wall directly in front of her glowed bright azure and the white overhead lights began to dim as the door slid shut. It had almost closed completely when the overhead lights came back on. She turned to see if the long gown had impeded the door, but something from behind pushed her roughly and threw her face first against the communications viewer.

Quick reflexes allowed her to jab an elbow backward into some kind of soft flesh. Strong hands wrapped around her wrists and pushed her back into the viewer, its blue glow washing into her vision as the door finally closed all the way.

She attempted to struggle, but the small space, meant for only one occupant at a time, left her no room to move, not that she could have anyway as the intruder pressed his body against hers from the back. When she smelled a familiar woody scent, she relaxed.

"Rainer?"

"What are you doing, Sara?" he asked near her left ear.

"Trying to take back my life. You could help me, you know." She pushed her backside against his crotch.

He loosened his grip on her wrists. "I've already helped you too much. And, you don't seem to appreciate all the gestures."

She threw her head back and made contact with his temple. He slammed her back into the viewer.

"You know, Simon's going to be pretty upset if you muss up one of his pets. And, by the way, you were helping yourself when you slipped me those stims. You always came conveniently *after* my modification sessions with Faya."

"I did what I could for you, yet you assume the worst of me."

"Rainer, I don't believe that you, or any other contractor, has ever done a good deed without getting something in return.

You wanted Faya to breech her contract. What better way to prove to Simon that he'd hired the wrong *woman* for the job. You're petty and pathetic." She didn't believe those words entirely, but she couldn't trust anyone after the nightmare of these past months. She wanted to trust Rainer, and that was reason to push him as far away as possible. She would never be caught with her guard down again.

"Such a mighty little darling you've become. Not at all like the bloody, weeping mess I used to find curled up on the floor of the Sovereign's guest quarters. What was it Faya used to rub into those shallow little cuts? Chlorate?"

Sara stiffened. She wouldn't let him into her head with memories of torture. "Bet you wouldn't have thought of that. Guess she was the better choice."

"The stims helped, didn't they? That's why you offered yourself to me all those times, out of gratitude." He leaned closer until she could feel his breath on her ear, his whole body pressed against hers. "But, whatever made you think I'd want to touch you? Let's face it, you weren't exactly at your best."

If she could have turned around, she would have spit in Rainer's face. Her stomach churned with the memories of her obsession with him. It had nothing to do with him; it was all about relieving her misery, if only for a short while. She was right not to trust him.

"Don't flatter yourself, Rainer. I was so desperate for the comfort of a warm body even a fragger would've done."

"You're a liar."

"Piss off."

The overhead light blinked on.

"Contractor Varden, do you need any help?"

Rainer pulled Sara out and flung her into the awaiting guards.

"No, I think our ambasadora is willing to go quietly. You still have a little dignity left, don't you, Sara?"

"Have a seat, Ambasadora Mendoza." Simon's back was to her as the guards pulled her into his office. He watched a large viewer that covered almost half of the dark green wall. It showed a man and a woman sitting in the waiting area just outside. That's why they brought Sara in through the back, so she wouldn't be seen.

She slid into a metal-framed blue chair. The dimly lit office unnerved her. Maybe he just didn't want her to see his many shelved trinkets. He branded her a thief, after all. That was the reason he kept her alive, to catch another thief, a fragger who had stolen Simon's most prized possession, his longevity. He also probably hoped to flush out Chen in the process.

During those first few weeks of the hallucinogens and Faya's cuts, Sara believed Chen would come back. Now she knew better. She was on her own.

"Do you see the man and woman waiting out there?" Simon stepped aside to offer her a better view of the airscreen. "Their names are David Anlow and Solimar Robbins, respectively. *He* would have been your pilot. *She*, a fellow passenger, perhaps even a friend."

"And that means what to me?" Anger welled in her.

"It means they are no longer unknown to you. You've seen their faces. You know their names." Finally he looked at her. "When they die because of your actions, you'll remember them."

"Why would knowing their names make me care if you hurt them, Simon? A lot of people knew my name when Faya was hurting me." She glared at Rainer. To her surprise he looked away.

"I wouldn't just hurt them. I would kill them." The blunt statement was more for clarity than dramatics.

If he had wanted them dead, he would have ordered it done, especially after they witnessed her escape attempt. She wanted to call his bluff. "I don't care, Simon."

"You should at least care about Navigational Leader Anlow." He walked closer and leaned in discreetly.

She avoided looking into Simon's eerie grey eyes, but couldn't avoid his scent. It was woody like Rainer's, but with a hint of spice. Though not unpleasant, it made her want to gag because the scent was specific to him...and she hated him, more than anyone she'd ever known, except maybe Faya. She should have taken the time to snap his neck on the magno.

He whispered to her then. "He's the fragger operative."

"Then why not have Rainer just cut the information out of him?" she asked.

"Because fraggers have an exceptionally high tolerance to pain. It's all that dosing and training, you see, mixed with some absurd code of loyalty. We're finding that our modification sessions with many of their operatives produce no useful information. But one thing fraggers can't ignore is their biology. They are still ruled by their physical desires. It's interesting to see what even the most disciplined will do if the attraction is great enough."

Sara didn't miss Simon's glance in Rainer's direction. Rainer stared at the viewer.

"This society's need to preserve its genes has been its greatest weakness. You might say it's like a *curse*. Not so different from my infected cell sweepers." He stood straight again, but Sara didn't miss the worried shadow that crossed his eyes.

"I think it's time you understood what it's like to have your future threatened."

"What more could you possibly do to me?"

"I had hoped it wouldn't come to this, but your antics on the magno-ramp today show me your disobedience is inevitable, so I'm taking *your* immortality by hijacking your lineage."

"How? Would you really stoop to raping me?" An iciness crept down her spine.

"Don't be crass. While you were still unconscious from the grafting, I had the doctor implant dormant irradicae cells on your ovaries."

The revelation was a cender blast to her psyche. Irradicae had been used to fight the most virulent diseases back on the worldships. It was used on citizens today only in extreme circumstances and after they had conceived at least one child because the supercharge to one's immune system had many side effects, the most devastating of which was sterility.

The scent of spiced wood drifted on Simon's breath. "You lift my curse, ambasadora, I lift yours."

Sara's cheeks felt cold as the blood drained from her face. Anxiety flooded her system. Then near panic. Then....

No hallucinations. Not now.

She kept the semblance of calm, not even blinking as she jammed her thumbnail under the seat's metal lip. The sudden rise in respiration and her accelerated heartbeat provided quite a show as her bio-lights pulsed and twinkled.

She pushed her thumbnail against the metal edge until it started to pull away from the skin. The sharp pain stayed with her.

On the viewer Solimar Robbins paced and rubbed her mocha-colored arms as though she were cold. Sara would gladly exchange places with her. David, the fragger in hiding, said something to Solimar that prompted her to sit once again, then he put an arm around her as if to ward off her chill, or her fear.

The endearment, the protective gesture made Sara's throat dry and her eyes threaten to well up. In a society where affection was openly shared, she had no one. For months, all she wanted was the caring touch of another person, a reassurance that she hadn't been forgotten. She ventured a glance at Rainer's unreadable visage. Maybe if she had looked like Solimar Robbins, or like Dahlia, he would have protected her, consoled her.

She sat up straighter and lifted her head a little higher. The hardened experiences of her modification made it quite clear that the only person who could save Sara Mendoza was Sara Mendoza. She *was* truly alone. And, she needed to take back some control.

"You were right," she said with a calm she didn't feel. "Charming *him* definitely won't be unpleasant. Nice body, thick hair, great profile." She received the surprised look from Rainer that she had hoped for.

"Glad to see you've changed your mind," Simon said. "Isn't that a good thing, Contractor Varden?"

Rainer took a moment before answering. "Just so she doesn't get too distracted from her task."

What a terrible task it was. Sara contemplated David Anlow's image on the viewer. Could she manipulate someone, kill someone, to save her lineage? If he were guilty, yes. And if he were innocent? She feared it might still be the same answer. If David were a fragger, he was just as bad as Simon in her eyes.

THIRTEEN

"How far is it, Navigational Leader Anlow?" Sara couldn't take the lonely whir of the roadway transport any longer.

"That's a long title. Let's stick to David." His pleasant demeanor helped her to relax, but made her job here more difficult. "The *Bard*'s berth is only a kilometer out. We should be there soon."

Given an opening, David prattled on conversationally, as though he didn't get to talk much, but Sara barely listened. She followed the lead of Solimar Robbins, who sat in silence and stared out of the rain-streaked window.

Shiraz Dock's nightscape slid by. A fog rolling in from Carrey Bay muted the signature glow of Shiraz's myriad blue and green lights. The nightly water show would be in full swing by now, but they'd not get a glimpse of the synth spiders weaving their webs of colorful light with long mechanical arms in time to the music they generated. As a child she had spent many evenings entranced by the floating musical artists. Maybe she'd hear some of the spiders' music once they made it to the berth.

Sara shifted uncomfortably, crossing and uncrossing her legs too many times as she willed the transport to move faster. Solimar kept an arm curled around David's, but the lines on her face said he was of little comfort right now. Being taken into Embassy care had shaken her.

Things like this don't happen to Socialites, she had complained tearfully to Rainer and the other contractors upon release.

Sara thought her a tad melodramatic, but then Solimar hadn't spent a month under Faya's modification at Palomin so had no idea what true discomfort was.

"You hate space travel, huh?" David asked.

"Excuse me?" Sara couldn't tell if David were being serious or trying to feel her out. His cheery Armadan tone surprised her. She'd not met many Armadans during her childhood. They were as foreign to her as contractors had been, probably why Chen's promise of rogue adventure pulled her into his criminal world.

Life with Chen seemed so long ago, another lifetime, when Sara was still Sara, not Ambasadora Mendoza.

"I mean, there had to be some reason you shoved those contractors down the magno, then took off running."

David's implication startled Sara, about as much as Solimar's eager attention to hear the response. Was the archivist recording this interaction? Sara would have to get used to having a snoop around.

"By the way." He cocked his head to look down at the skirt hem covering her feet. "Did you get your shoes back okay?"

Sara wiggled her toes in the black pumps. "Yes. Thanks for picking them up for me."

"No problem. I had to do something while waiting to be detained by Embassy officials," David said.

Solimar nudged him in the ribs with her elbow, but kept her wide-eyed focus on Sara.

The transport stopped. Solimar waited for David to help her out. When he turned back to do the same for Sara, she touched his hand long enough to be polite, but pushed out of the transport all on her own.

Before her rested the sexiest craft she'd ever seen. The silvery ship reminded her of a woman lying on her side, all pregnant curves, dips and mounds of opalescent metal. Purples, greens, and blues shimmered from the hull in the berthing lights of Shiraz Dock. The sheen of her new home certainly fit the ideal of a pleasure cruiser, even one acting as its own kind of prison.

"Good night, David." Solimar leaned up to kiss his cheek and whisper, "Thanks for coddling me today."

"My pleasure."

"Forgive me, ambasadora." She took Sara's hands in her own. The gesture of friendship, though expected in polite society, still softened Sara's mood a bit. "It's just been…an unusual day."

"I understand, and please call me Sara."

Solimar smiled, then headed for the *Bard*'s covered gangway.

"I don't make a very good first impression, do I?" Sara watched the archivist disappear under the soft chartreuse light of the gangway. "Not like the *Bard*."

"You were just nervous about the flight. Who could blame you?"

Sara found a real smile creeping onto her face for the first time since that night at Palomin when Chen had given her the ill-fated black cuff. She wondered who was charming who. Surely David realized something was off about her behavior, yet he didn't push the issue. Was he being polite or biding his time?

"She's a pretty shell, isn't she? The *Bard*, I mean."

Sara's smile evaporated. *Pretty shells,* that's all they wanted.

"I promise to be more considerate of the other passengers," she said.

"Don't bother. Some of them aren't too considerate themselves."

He offered his elbow. With the tips of her fingers lightly on his oversized bicep, she allowed him to lead her into the glow of the gangway.

"I doubt you'll even see the others much, except at dinner. They're independent scientists, so they stick to their labs or their suites and do what they want. Not a very social group while on the ship."

David stopped at the entryway. "Unless there's something astir, then apparently they're more than happy to make an appearance."

Sara counted three faces, besides that of the supposedly exhausted archivist, waiting for them inside. No doubt Solimar apprised the other passengers of the magno incident before she even left the Hub. The sweeping glances at Sara's concealing hemline confirmed the call ahead. The breech of privacy unnerved Sara, but she knew it was just the woman's social nature. She was an archivist; it was her job to record and inform.

Maybe it was Simon's inference that Solimar could have been a friend, or maybe it was the fake sentiment in the greeting gesture which made Solimar's actions disappointing. More likely, it was Sara's own need to reach out to someone. When would she learn?

David put his hand on the small of Sara's back in presentation. The action drew a sharp glare from a young woman about Sara's age with golden streaks in her hair and amazing irises the color of the sunrise. She offered nothing but clinically dissecting looks in greeting.

The two men were all smiles. The larger, darker skinned man's was good-natured, but the smaller man seemed calculating. His appearance screamed Socialite, from his delicate stature to his high cheek bones and full lips. He was the first to come forward.

"Ambasadora Mendoza, I am privileged to make your acquaintance." The man's shoulder-length black hair was tipped in deep blue and brushed her arm as he pulled the inner part of her wrist to his lips for a kiss.

To her dismay the lavender dots involuntarily stirred. She gave no other indication of interest, however.

"This is Scientist Kenon Brudger," David said.

"Hello Scientist Brudger. What type of science do you study?" Not that she really cared.

"I'm a geological observer. I make sure these terraformed worlds don't break apart at the core."

"Huh. I didn't realize your job was that important," David said, drawing an irritated look from the other man.

"And *Kenon* will do. I always thought making *scientist* a title was a little pretentious anyway. Everyone on board goes by their first name. May we include you in this little custom, Sara?" Then as smooth as Deleinean silk, he stroked his thumb over the back of her hand.

This time the bio-lights barely flickered.

"Of course. It's odd how all Socialites claim titles are so gauche, yet we continue to invent new ones. I think we should just drop them entirely."

She gently pulled her hand away.

"You can call me Geir." The jovial man surprised Sara with a big hug. Judging by his mass, she guessed he had Armadan genes as well.

"That's some pretty intense body art. It complements your hair," he said with a wink.

Sara smiled at the genuine affinity she already felt for Geir. Her bio-lights seconded the feeling.

A draft blew in then and introduced herself as Boston Maribu, Mari to her friends. Sara was sure she hadn't made it into that circle just yet. A broad smile showed on Mari's lips, but it didn't extend to those unusual eyes, proving that golden orange wasn't necessarily a *warm* color.

Mari's delicate features, round eyes, and thin nose mirrored Sara's own, until Faya had butchered her. Now she resembled a contractor more than a Socialite, not that she cared. In the past month she had learned how little one's appearance truly meant.

Kenon moved in on Sara again, this time feigning interest in her purpose aboard their ship.

Her gaze drifted past him to the interior of the ship's rotunda lobby as she recited practiced responses; "…using the *Bard* as a transport and temporary home…honor of being a Face of the Embassy…spreading cheer…liaisons…."

It was Solimar who saved her. "Would you like to see our crystal trees?" Without waiting for a reply, she took Sara by the arm and led her away from the others.

"Thank you," Sara whispered.

A light melody played upon their approach to the rotunda. Meandering past the rounded grey chaises which circled the intimate three-story space, Sara stopped just before reaching the rotunda's center. Here the circle of clear Celestite floor reflected powder blue puddles from the overhead chandeliers. The fixtures' stained-glass surfaces bore butterflies, dragonflies, and blooming flowers, all in varying shades of blue.

The three crystal trees branched up from the floor, not quite reaching the swirled, white ceiling, but passing over the third-floor balcony. A thin line of cerulean glowed within each trunk and naked branch, giving them the appearance of iced-over electrical arcs. They even gave off a distinctive scent that reminded her of the half-frozen lake which flowed through her family's estate on Tampa Deux.

She missed her family, but the burden of lying to her mother and pretending how happy she was with her new honor had Sara finding excuses not to contact her home. Plus, Simon's warnings remained fresh in her mind.

Sara breathed deeply. Everything would be okay now. She was away from Simon and she had time to plan. Without his grating voice in her ear, she would find a way out of this mess. She clung to that thought in reassurance.

"Pardon me, Sara." David stood beside her. "There's an important call waiting for you in your suite."

FOURTEEN

"Is everything in here white?" Sara looked around her new sitting room. The marbled floors, the fabric-coated walls, the bulging lines of the furnishings were all bright and shining and completely devoid of color. What wasn't white, like the table lamps and a row of empty vases lining three tiers of shelves on one wall, was made of crystal or clear glass. She had been given a lifetime's worth of white from her incarceration at Palomin.

She stared at the controls which would activate the viewer. So long as she didn't answer the call she could pretend it was her envious cousins or her mother sending her congratulations on becoming a Face of the Embassy.

Mother. A title she might never attain. The constricting feel of her corset amplified her anger and shock.

Sara worked another fastener free as she sought out the bedrooms. Bearing left and rounding the short curving hallway brought her to another door, also white. Her irritation grew and she fumbled with another hook.

Upon releasing the last of them, she ripped the piece off and exhaled. She willed herself not to take another breath, just let it all slip away with the tears rolling down her face. But she wasn't ready to go out gently just yet, so she took a deep breath and tapped the door controls.

The bedroom lights illuminated to reveal an alabaster twin of her sitting room. Only an addition of a large canopied bed covered in shiny white linens set this room apart from the other. She dropped onto the bed and closed her eyes.

Her mind fired with shifting thoughts and images. Thankfully there were no hallucinations in the mix at the moment. With a clear head, Sara focused on strategy. She had been working out several plans, some to carry out Simon's orders, some to muck them up. She devoted great care deciding which of the paths to follow.

A tone sounded from the sitting room's viewer. She tried ignoring it. She already knew who it was, but walked out to answer it anyway. A tap to the manual control prompted the screen to illuminate.

She needed one of those wrist reporters. David had mentioned she should see the ship's mech tech for one. Maybe she could even gather some information about the irradicae if she was discreet about it.

Simon's visage peered at her from the viewer's airscreen.

"How are things progressing with the pilot?" he asked.

"What, no 'how are you settling in?' or 'do the other passengers like you?'"

"Your social standing on board the Bard *is irrelevant. Retrieving my data from the fragger should be your only focus. Your escape attempt may have worked in our favor. He will trust you if he sees you also loathe the Embassy."*

"I just got here. I need some time to finesse the information from him."

"I warn you not to take too much time. I've sent your itinerary ahead and will be monitoring it closely, just in case you had plans of escaping again. One unscheduled stop, and everyone on that ship will pay for your betrayal."

Sara remained silent.

"If you can't get results, I will be forced to intervene. I'm giving you the opportunity to repay your life debt, Ambasadora Mendoza. Isn't that what you want? To please me?"

She'd like to cut off Simon's testicles and make him choke on them. That would please her. Instead she said, "Of course that's what I want. You'll have your information."

"And once you obtain what I need, be sure to kill the fragger. It will be one less to worry about."

Simon's image and the screen blinked out.

For once, she and the Sovereign agreed. After what happened at Palomin, she would have no problem killing every fragger who crossed her path.

FIFTEEN

The head-splitting sound of fast drums and shouted lyrics filled Sean's suite.

He unfastened his pants. Brushing his fingers along his left hip bone, he felt for the doser patch. It took a few passes to distinguish between his real skin and the piece of synth-flesh. He removed the fingernail-sized doser and its tri-needle backing. The prick of each millimeter-long tip comforted him with its time-released concentration of stims.

Sean threw the old one into the toilet and picked up the one he had just prepared, ready to apply it on his right side this time. He alternated just to keep track of how many times a week he was dosing. Usually he limited it to three, but this was already number six in half as many days.

Bullseye's death weighed on him. It was more than guilt over killing an anonymous operative—the bosses had passed him bad intel. Now distrust ran rampant among the organization, and the fraggers were splintering. That could be catastrophic.

The surprise in all this tossing of blame was that the only one who blamed Sean was Sean. The rest of the fraggers, including those within his own contingency, knew he was just carrying out orders. *Blindly carrying out orders, putting his faith in unseen entities.*

The music muted, a wispy tone sounding in its place. Someone was at his door. The music blared on again. Whenever his door chimed, which wasn't often, he made a note to change it or deactivate it completely. Just another left-over from the *Bard*'s time as a pleasure cruiser, as was his suite's décor. The others had theirs customized, but Sean was too apathetic to change anything. Heavy swags and worn drapery still covered some of the walls, while decorative cornices sprouted from each corner of the dulled white ceiling.

He applied the doser and zipped up his pants before answering the repeated tone with a shout of impatience. "Yeah. I'm coming."

It was probably David with a tech problem or Soli to tell him all he missed with the arrival of the ambasadora.

Sean called up the music control, the blue prompt glowing across his palm. With a tap from his middle finger, he turned down the cacophony and followed with the entry code for his lock.

He came out of the bathroom and stopped.

The first thing he noticed about the woman who stood inside his messy sitting area was her face. Pouty lips. High cheekbones. Big, sad eyes. Or maybe he mistook weariness for sadness. Either way, she carried a burden that her rigid posture and elegant clothes couldn't quite hide. Sean knew about burdens. He also knew about weariness and sadness.

The next thing he noticed about her was an armful of swirling purple lights. They may have been one of the most beautiful things he had seen in this world, or a virtual one. But maybe not as beautiful as her face.

"Scientist Cryer?"

He snapped his focus away from the little dots. "Sorry. They're distracting."

She looked down at the tops of her breasts which were piled high behind some black netting.

"Your tat," he said, though now that his attention had been drawn to the rest of her body, he liked what he saw there as well.

"The bio-lights certainly get me noticed." That's not what *he* noticed first, but admitted her intra-tat was more mesmerizing in person than the ones he'd seen on the Media. "I'm Sean, by the way. No need for a title." His responses sounded clipped and rude, even to him.

"I've been hearing that a lot. Nice to meet you, Sean. I'd like to be one of your clients." Her gaze moved subtly from his eyes to the rest of him as she spoke.

He resisted the urge to scratch at the dark blonde stubble on his neck and pat down his dishelveled hair or smooth the wrinkled shirt he wore, maybe even rub the dark circles from under his eyes. Unlike the rest of his colleagues, he hadn't cared about his appearance for a long time. It bothered him that she made him care now.

"Why would you need to hire me?" He made his tone less severe, but still businesslike.

"David said you could reprogram my scentbots."

"You don't like roses?" He enjoyed her soft scent, or maybe the pheromones attached to it.

"Not so much," she said.

When her gaze lingered on his face, Sean felt a twinge in his chest. *Just the new doser kicking in.*

"Oh, and a reporter," she added with a small smile.

He relaxed a little. "Have a seat."

"Thank you." She dropped down on his couch near a pile of shirts that had recently come back from the cleaners. Like everything else, he had just never bothered to put them away.

Sean scanned the rest of the room. Empty alcohol and drop bottles rested on the glass and stainless tables. Clothes hung from every available piece of furniture. A blanket and pillows splayed from the other couch onto the floor. A little embarrassed, he walked into the extra bedroom, the one he had converted into a tech lab. He grabbed a reporter and tried not to worry about her impression of him. *She came uninvited. What did she expect?*

Sean never brought clients here, no women at all for that matter. Aside from Soli and Mari, who were strictly colleagues. There were plenty of clubs and hotels when he got the urge for a tumble. His body tingled like he was getting that urge now, either from the stims running through his veins or because he was experiencing an emotional fallacy. Instant attractions often resulted in false feelings for another. That's why when he felt this way, he usually ran in the other direction. It was the best way to avoid using bad judgment.

When he returned to the sitting room, he watched with a mix of interest and annoyance as she unfolded a couple of his shirts from the pile.

"Are all your shirts grey?" She studied the designs on each one before casually refolding them.

"Mostly. Might find a couple of blue ones in the closet."

"No black?" She looked up.

"I wouldn't want to be mistaken for a contractor," he said, only half-joking.

She stiffened at the comment. His gaze took in her black hair, making him wonder.

"You don't like contractors?"

"Don't know any personally," he lied.

"Neither do I."

The graphic on the shirt she held showed a blindfolded woman diving naked into a volcano, a logo for the group whose song played through his suite.

"Are you a fan?" he asked.

"Not really. The artwork just spoke to me."

Watching her carefully handle his shirts, he felt calm return, almost a warm feeling in his fingers. Usually he only found this peace by taking restor drops. Though, recently even their narcotic bliss proved evasive. It was why he had withdrawn from the others completely. Not that they would have noticed; he wasn't exactly social to begin with. The remoteness of his personality sometimes made it tough to live in a society built upon social connections. His height of socialness was drinking enough to start a fight or two at whatever bar he found himself in.

Sean's head felt a little fuzzy, and he fell into a trance watching the slow pulse of the intra-tat on her arm. He followed the lights from the spiral on the back of her hand, onto her wrist, where it disappeared briefly as it encircled her arm in an upward vortex, then fell over her shoulder in a swirl. His gaze continued up her slender neck and past her strong jawline to return to her lips. Maybe he crossed the line from respectful admiration to blatant ogling, but he didn't believe in boundaries.

She, on the other hand, was a slave to boundaries because she worked for the Sovereign.

The thought reeled him in and reminded him why he didn't want her on board to begin with. She was part of the Embassy, an enemy. The ambasadora project put friendly faces to the government's hidden politics while it manipulated its citizens. This woman represented everything he despised about the system.

Maybe she knew how much he hated the Embassy, knew of his attachment to the fragger organization. That could be why she conveniently needed her bots reprogrammed as soon as she arrived. Was there a Writ of Execution out on him, and she was thinking of cashing in?

"Do you mind?" He snatched the shirt from her hands. His tone was harsh, but didn't contain the acid he felt in his stomach.

"I'm sorry." She lowered her gaze, and he thought he detected a slight flush on her olive cheeks.

That threw him...unless she had receptors implanted just under her skin to call the blush reflex at will. It could be very endearing, very arousing to the right man. Well, she could forget it; he wasn't the right man.

A pinch at his hip reminded him the doser was doing its job. Was it also making him paranoid? David accused him of stim-induced paranoia all the time, though Sean had never admitted his dosing to anyone. He may have done too many stims this week, but the feeling he had about her motives was more than the drugs.

"I also had another question. After watching something earlier on the Media," she said. "A woman had her lineage hijacked."

"Hijacked? Was she raped?"

Rapes were few in the system because of the societal stigma attached to having to force your advances onto another, but laws were ignored on occasion, even when the penalty was death.

"Not from the report. It sounded more like she had an adverse reaction to…irradicae that were injected to rid her body of an unwanted cyst, but they attached themselves to her ovaries as well." She fingered his shirts again.

"Why would that bother *you*?" he asked.

She paused. "Just imagining how she must feel, facing something like that. They said she never even found out until months later when she was going through a security scanner at the Hub." She was almost whispering now.

Something was off and it had nothing to do with the drugs in his system. "That story's a fake."

She nearly jumped out of her seat. "What?"

"Treatment with irradicae is illegal, plus you would need specialized equipment for implantation, or even detection. Only Embassy med facilities have that kind of tech. The Media airs fake stories all the time, just to get a reaction like yours, get people talking and scared."

"You're probably right," she said, though her expression said otherwise.

She seemed genuinely afraid. That sent him into a protective mode. After Bullseye, Sean became drawn to human suffering in a way only the penitent man ever can be. It messed with him, made him want to curl into himself and pretend the rest of the world didn't exist. Hard to do when it came knocking at his door.

"You have good taste in shirts." She spoke loudly, bringing them both out of their thoughts.

Did the silence bother her? Sean hated it, too. Maybe if he had a quiet mind...but his thoughts were just too loud.

He took a deep breath. "Here's your reporter. Already programmed for the ship. Won't take me long to program your suite codes." He pushed aside the shirts and sat down next to her. She smelled liked the garden at his childhood home.

"Are you sure you want to change your scentbots?" Gently taking her hand, he slipped the reporter on her wrist. She could have done it herself, but in spite of all his concerns, Sean wanted an excuse to touch her. He didn't want David to be right, about the paranoia, about brooding alone, about a lot of things. That would mean Sean had lost his perspective, and he couldn't afford that.

"Actually, I was hoping you could get rid of them altogether," she said. "I never had any before...I became an ambasadora."

She caught him looking at her, and he caught her involuntary pupil response. It made him lean in a little closer.

That could be faked too.

It shouldn't matter if it were real. Sean refused to be ruled by those DNA sharing impulses. Yet, here he was holding her hand and close enough to kiss her, all because she seemed a little upset and looked at him a certain way.

He cleared his throat. "Ever use one of these before?"

"No."

"Easy to master." He turned her hand over palm-side up and rested the bracelet's silver node just at her pulse point. Her heart rate was a little elevated. He pressed the node to activate her reporter, but kept hold of her hand. A blue light zipped across the olive skin of her hand, a menu scrolling along it.

"Touch a finger to your palm to activate the menu." He dragged his middle finger down her palm and noticed the flurry of violet erupting on her other arm.

Damn. That was a lot better than a blush. And he was only touching her hand.

Sean's stomach tightened as he imagined what would happen if he kissed her neck or ran his hands down her back or over her breasts. And what would it be like if he were docking her? Actually, he'd been wondering about that since he first saw her.

"What's this mean?" she asked, her voice a little breathy.

Sean realized she had leaned a little closer, too, so their heads were almost touching. He forced his gaze to a message blinking on her palm, but was acutely aware that she still looked at his face.

"There's a message waiting for you, welcoming you to the system. From someone named Rainer Varden."

"Oh." That one little word broke the spell. She pulled her hand away. "Embassy business. I should probably get back to my room and respond. Maybe we can take care of my scentbots another time?"

"Sure." He walked her to the door, telling himself it was because he wanted a final read on her.

After she left, the scent of roses remained, as did his heightened emotions.

SIXTEEN

"Rainer?" Sara suddenly regretted responding to his earlier transmission, but she would need her nerve to coerce him.

"That was faster than expected. Actually, I'm surprised you responded at all." His expression said he was pleased. That was fortuitous, but somehow uncomfortable.

"I was going to contact you anyway. I need...your help." Just asking humbled her.

"With what? You need some tips on charming the Armadan?"

She ignored his taunt. Now that the time had arrived to present her plan, she felt sick in her stomach. If Rainer refused and went to Simon with her betrayal, she was finished. Sterilized and as good as dead.

"Is it with the irradicae?"

Tears filled her eyes and she hoped he couldn't see them through the transmission. "Yes."

"I didn't know he would break our mores for his own gain. Behavior modification was one thing, even if he would have killed you outright, but hijacking your lineage went too far, even for the Sovereign."

Rainer shocked her; he was openly criticizing the most powerful man in the system. Still, her words came out tinged in anger. "You have an odd value system. No problem with murder and torture, but let someone mess with this society's breeding traditions and you're suddenly a crusader."

That rant may have cost her his help. She waited for the retort.

"It's not the people in the society that matter as much as their traditions. History tells us how to live, what works and what doesn't."

"Now you sound like an archivist." She evened her tone.

"Sometimes even archivists don't follow the History."

He was obviously referring to Simon's former title.

"Does that mean you'll help me?"

"Tell me what you need first."

Sara passed through the crystal trees on her way to the gangway. Thankfully, the passengers of the *Bard* didn't seem bothered to be staying at Shiraz for an extra half-day, and only David questioned why. Sara's vague response about an Embassy meeting hadn't quite placated him, but he didn't force the issue. He was obviously just as suspicious of her as she was of him.

"Heading out?"

Sean's voice. Sara would recognize that low pitch and soft timbre anywhere.

"Embassy meeting," she said, remembering the instant attraction she had for him earlier. Seeing him again reinforced her first impression. There was absolutely no polish to him, but that meant he had nothing to hide. She found that to be a very attractive quality. It helped that she found the rest of him attractive as well.

"Share a transport? I have a client to see near the Hub."

Sean's offer threw her because she had hoped to sneak away. He motioned her down the glowing gangway. Excuses ran through her brain, then she spotted the voyeur waiting for her outside. Of course the Media would want any chance to report on the ambasadoras, especially the one they knew little about. She was sure Simon was watching her, too.

Being with Sean Cryer might provide a distraction until she could slip the cameras and get to the tunnels for her meeting with Rainer. If asked, she'd convince Simon that this was part of her plan. She had yet to decide what to do about David. If this trip went as anticipated, she wouldn't have to worry about it.

Upon exiting the gangway canopy, a pair of voyeurs flew into orbit around them, casting short shadows in the midday sun.

"Parasites," Sean said.

Several airscreens along the platform echoed, *"Parasites,"* and showed Sean's face on a split screen next to Sara's. Then the image cut to them standing beside each other, only the forced angle implied more of an intimacy.

Sean's irritation made her self-conscious, like her life was spilling over and affecting others.

"Still want to ride with me?" she asked.

"Gotta get there somehow."

Media commentary followed their walk to the transport station. Sara caught snatches of it among the dock's perpetual airship and boat traffic, live musical groups, and chattering citizens either passing through or spending the day among Shiraz's amusements:

"...Scientist Sean Cryer, a fellow passenger aboard her ship."

And,

"It didn't take this most secretive of ambasadoras long to find a potential amour, though we expected her sights to be set a little higher, like maybe her Armadan pilot. He's a retired fleet captain...."

If Sean were insulted by the Media banter, he didn't show it. In fact, he placed his hand at the small of her back to guide her through several passersby that gathered near them. Three young girls hurried up to Sara just as the transport pulled in.

"Excuse me, ambasadora, can we get your print?" The bravest one asked, while the other two watched the pulsing of Sara's bio-lights.

Sean pushed his palm against the transport door to keep it open. A man looked out of the front train car, but didn't say anything, most likely because of Sean's challenging stare.

Sara pressed her index finger against the girls' digital bracelets, allowing them to capture the time, place, and a holo of their encounter. Her digi print would verify it all for bragging rights later.

The girls moved along, and the transport finally went on its way.

"That ever bother you?" Sean asked.

In the enclosed space she could smell the more earthy notes of his scentbots, mixed in with a little melon, maybe. It was very pleasing.

"Actually, that was the first time it ever happened. I guess the ambasadoras are becoming popular." She didn't smile when she said that last bit.

And, he didn't smile when he said, "I don't doubt it."

"So, what's your client need?" She hoped to change the subject.

"Huh?"

"Your client? The one you're going to meet now?"

"Reporter implantation."

Sara didn't miss the jerky eye movements just before his answer.

As if sensing her suspicion, he said, "That's something you should think about." He held up his naked wrist. Blue pictures and words swirled across his palm. "You could get an implant like this. It's almost universal because the reprogramming is fast and easy."

"I don't like the thought of any more foreign objects being implanted into my body."

"Yeah, I bet those were difficult to get used to."

Heat ran up her neck. Did he know?

She fumbled for a response, but saw him looking at the purple lights deepening on her arm. Of course. How could he know about the irradicae?

"Yes, they were...*are*." She needed to get away from him. Her emotions could only be kept at bay so long and this idle chit chat was starting to feel invasive. Reaching a hand to the console by her side, she pressed the destination button, alerting the automated train to drop her at the next stop.

"Not going all the way to the Embassy?" Sean asked.

"It's better for me to use a back entrance. Less attention, you know."

"I can see that being a problem."

The train stopped.

"Thanks for the company. See you back aboard." Her heart sank a little realizing that if she could be free of Simon, she'd have to run pretty far, and probably wouldn't ever see Sean again. She squeezed his hand on the way out. He held onto hers a little longer, then pulled away as if taken with shyness.

She hoped to recall the genuineness of his reaction someday, preferably on a secluded beach away from Simon and his threats. That comforting feeling waned as she boarded the next transport and continued on to her meeting with Rainer.

SEVENTEEN

"You look well, considering," Rainer said.
"Is that a compliment?" Her anxiety heightened in the glaring tunnel lights.
"It is."
Silence followed until Sara's thoughts got the best of her. "You're taking a lot of risks to do this."
"You want to know why, is that it?" He touched her shoulder to guide her through a doorway on the left. The sensation brought back memories of Palomin, aftermath of torture, his care, his rejection.
"No, you made your feelings about what Simon did to me very clear. I guess I was trying to say thank you." Her heels echoed off the concrete stairs.
"There's nothing to thank me for. I'm not even sure what will come of this visit."
"Still..." she said.
Rainer motioned for Sara to wait while he opened the door at the top of the landing.
"Is it secure?" he asked someone she couldn't see.
"Yes," a nervous voice answered.

"Ambasadora Mendoza?" Rainer tended to use her title when others were around. He gestured her inside the med facility.

Shining silver and white surfaces greeted her, putting her on edge.

The doctor who had attended to her bio-light implantation stepped forward. "Ambasadora Mendoza, it's wonderful to see you again. You look beautiful. The black dress complements your intra-tattoo."

Sara glanced down at the short sari she wore and realized she had been wearing black almost every day since becoming an ambasadora. Was it her subconscious fascination with contractors or an attempt to battle the constant white surrounding her?

"Thank you. Did Contractor Varden explain why we came here?"

The doctor licked his lips. "Yes, and I have to be up front. I'm not comfortable with all of the secrecy."

"Trust me," she said. "It's better for all of us that way."

"You haven't mentioned this to anyone, have you?" Rainer had been walking around the bright, sterile room, noting the colored glass bottles lining the shelves, inspecting the medical equipment attached to the walls, and feeling under the exam table with the tips of his fingers. Now, he stood toe to toe with the doctor.

The other man pulled his shoulders in and tried to shrink away without actually taking a step backward. "I told no one, as you instructed."

"Then let's get this over with," Sara said.

"The scanner is back this way."

Sara slipped off her sari, catching Rainer's scrutiny of her naked body. She stepped into the scanning cylinder. There was a possibility that Simon had bluffed, that even he couldn't resort to such measures.

A few minutes later, the man's voice carried through a speaker inside the cylinder. "You can step out now while I read the scan."

So fast? As much as she wanted this all to be over quickly, the rapidity heightened her anxiety.

She emerged from the cylinder to see Rainer and the doctor watching readings and impressions of her body scroll over an airscreen. Sara dressed with automatic movements, her mind occupied by what the scan would reveal.

The doctor said something low to Rainer.

"Speak to *me*. This is about *me*." She yelled because she sensed the truth.

"I'm sorry, ambasadora. I've confirmed that the irradicae are attached to your ovaries. It had to have happened after the insertion of the intra-tattoo because my scans would have picked them up before your surgery."

"I guess Simon's desperation outweighed his sense of society." Bitterness laced Sara's words. "Get rid of them. I don't care how much it costs."

The doctor looked from Sara to Rainer, then quickly back again. "I can't."

Acid burned in Sara's stomach. "Can't or *won't?*"

"They're set to trigger should anyone try to tamper with them. Most likely there's also a remote trigger, could be through a sort of wave, probably transmitted via a large network like the Media."

"Those signals are everywhere. They blanket the entire system," Rainer said.

There it was, the truth. Numbness crept into her limbs. Her vision funneled into a narrow dot of brightness as she stared into the empty scanning cylinder. She wasn't getting out of this. For the first time since Palomin she felt like ending it all. Maybe she should just let the doctor give her the suicide drugs now, bypass the humiliation, stave off any more pain. Just end it.

Rainer folded her in his arms, and she wept.

EIGHTEEN

The doleful electronic screeching of the street player echoed Sean's mood. It reeked of uneasiness and deceit. Waiting in the shade of a metal awning, he kept out of the scurrying Hub activity. As the Embassy staff finished their day, they loaded into transports or sat and chatted in one of the many perimeter cafés.

The whole corporate scene bugged the shit out of him.

The tracing program he put on Sara's reporter just before he gave it to her showed she was still inside the Embassy. Maybe she really did have a meeting. He imagined her sitting around sipping neons or another fruity drink with her sister ambasadoras, discussing what they should all wear at their next appearance.

He hoped that were the case, but something about the way she acted at their first meeting said otherwise, said she was into something more sinister.

A buzzing in his palm alerted him to her movement. She was coming this way, out a side entrance. He ducked in among a crowd of female staffers.

"Hi," a brunette in a dark suit said. "Come to join us?"

He looked around at the handful of women and knew by their expressions it was an invitation for more than casual conversation and a drink.

"Just passing through." He maneuvered to a spot concealed by a giant planter overflowing with clematis stakes. From this vantage he could see and hear Sara without being noticed. A contractor escorted her.

They emerged from around the corner of the marble building. Sara had a scarf covering her shoulders, perhaps to keep her bio-lights hidden and keep the voyeurs at bay.

The contractor led her by the elbow. Sara stared at her feet as she walked. They remained silent until moving several meters past Sean's position.

"Will you be all right returning to your ship?" the contractor asked.

Sara never looked at him. "Yes. The sooner, the better."

From different vantage points, Sean and the contractor watched Sara board a transport heading back to Shiraz. Her entire being showed her emotional state at the moment. The contractor, on the other hand, was a blank slate.

Those times when Sean became a blank slate to the outside world were when he had the most to hide. So, even though his first impulse was to follow Sara, he chose to shadow the contractor.

Waltzing into the Embassy wasn't the best idea Sean had, but no one knew him from any other citizen. No one would guess he was a fragger node, in charge of a few dozen commandos who would rather blow this building up than take a stroll inside it. Moving among the lobby crowd, he kept an adequate distance behind the contractor. Sean thought about the lost details of this place when it was mapped and placed into a training world. The programmers had forgotten the green floor lamps and didn't have the lighting quite right on the chalcedony wall. The planters were a few meters too short, as well. Not even V-side architects paid attention to details any more, and that was always a good way to mess up as far as Sean was concerned.

They'd gotten the magnos perfect, though. Probably a different team working on that lay-out than the lobby planners. Consistency was sometimes difficult to manage with so many anonymous contributors.

The contractor moved steadily toward the corbelled arches of the office area and medical facilities. He stopped to speak to a female contractor who approached him from an office. They both glanced in Sean's direction. Though his pulse pounded, he maintained his pace, but altered his path slightly so it would seem he was heading toward the elevator bank. He kept them in his periphery, however, ready to bolt if they looked his way again.

But they weren't interested in Sean any more—they looked to be arguing. Sean was almost to the elevator when the woman stormed off, her pink and black ponytail flipping after her. The male contractor continued through the medical arch.

Sean changed course again, but slowed his gait. He hesitated to keep on the contractor, wondering if perhaps he'd misread the man, if he really had nothing to hide. Moving further into enemy territory chilled Sean, yet he couldn't ignore his instinct.

They meandered through mostly deserted dark green hallways, Sean hanging a hundred paces back. The contractor rounded another corner. Sean could see the man's reflection in the smoky colored glass of a nearby office door where he stood waiting. Sean tensed. If the man attacked, Sean had the advantage of being able to see the contractor coming, but he couldn't outrun cender fire. The only weapons he had on him were a half dozen razor discs plated with a special nickel alloy undetectable to Embassy scanners. When used properly, the bottle cap-sized discs could be lethal, but he wouldn't get more than one or two off before the contractor fried him.

When the contractor looked back toward the corner he'd just rounded, Sean backed up a couple of steps and grabbed a disc from a sheath sewn into his belt. The contractor keyed in an entry code on the door in front of him, then entered. Sean siphoned the code with his reporter.

When he reached the door, he keyed in the code, but didn't open the door. The contractor could be standing just on the other side, or a whole room full of people who would know he didn't belong there. Judging by other rooms he'd passed on this floor and whose doors were opened wide, there should be a foyer and a hallway leading to either side.

He was this far—he had to take that last step.

With quick movements, which he hoped mimicked someone who was accustomed to entering this area, Sean pushed into the room. A darkened foyer with small lights along the floor met him. No sign of anyone.

He stealthed to the inner hallway and listened for signs of the contractor. Footsteps on a tile floor reached him from the left.

"Contractor Varden?" A doctor stood at a metal terminal inside the marginally lit office.

Varden. The name on the message waiting for Sara earlier was Rainer Varden. It made sense.

"I noticed you recorded the results of Ambasadora Mendoza's scan today."

Not a meeting. A doctor's appointment.

"That's just an automatic—"

"Is it also automatic to send those results elsewhere without the patient being told?"

Surprise registered on the doctor's pale face. "I would never...."

"That's what you're doing right now. I put in a security measure to alert me if you accessed this system within thirty-six hours of the ambasadora's scan. If it's not her results you're sending out, then there's nothing to worry about."

"I'm sending them to the Sovereign."

"Why would you do that?" Rainer moved closer to the doctor.

"So he knows I had nothing to do with this." The doctor sounded nervous. "I'm sorry if the ambasadora is your amour—"

"She is not."

"Then *would* have been your amour had you not discovered the truth of her condition."

Rainer shouldered next to the doctor and grabbed his wrist. A finger-sized portable transmitter slipped from his grasp and fell to the floor with a clang of metal on tile.

"How are you going to explain this?" the doctor asked.

"One of my duties as Head Contractor is to apprehend those who might want to blackmail the Sovereign and further their own interests."

Shock washed over Sean. He'd been tailing Prollixer's Head Contractor. Suspicion trickeled through his mind as he wondered just how involved Sara was with this man. He should have expected a woman like her would have a powerful man somewhere in her background.

"Blackmail?" The doctor looked confused, then paled.

Before Sean could blink, Rainer fired his cender into the doctor's head. The body slumped to the ground. Rainer stooped down to grab the transmitter.

Sean had just enough time to set up a siphon. As the data was erased, he collected it. Rainer called for a clean-up team from his reporter. Soon the place would be swarming with contractors. Sean headed out the way he came and made for the nearest descending magno. He never looked back until he boarded a transport for the *Bard*.

In transit, he scrolled through the siphoned data. His heart almost stopped when he read the contents streaming across his palm.

Prollixer had given Sara a slow death sentence.

It was a tragedy in Upper Caste society to be naturally sterile. Like Lowers, fraggers didn't share this attitude. Sean never cared about his own breeding capabilities precisely because his society thought he should. And maybe because he had the option to father a child any time he chose. What if that option were taken away, like it was with Sara? Anger boiled inside him. If the Sovereign would do this to one of his ambasadoras, who else could be or had been a victim? Just another reason to hate and fear the Embassy. And another reason to bring them down.

NINETEEN

"Not now," Sara muttered.

Solimar practically pounced when Sara emerged from her room. Back only a few hours and already someone wanted a piece of her. Without stopping, Sara moved down the hallway toward the grand staircase.

"Have a nice meeting?" the archivist asked. Her short tunic revealed the bottoms of her mocha cheeks and opened to more than a little cleavage.

"Nothing special," Sara scurried down the stairs, her shorter heels giving her more leverage than Solimar's platformed monstrosities. At the bottom of the grand atrium, she hesitated, not wanting to head into the dining room, but needing to escape Solimar. Too late. The woman was quite adept in her crazy footwear. Sara moved to get past, but Solimar clasped her hands and stopped her.

"I saw that you and Sean were getting on well."

"Sean? When?"

"On the Docks."

That's right. As an archivist, Solimar Robbins probably watched the Media non-stop, had several feeds transmitted directly into her brain, if they could really do that.

"How can you know what you saw is what's real?" Sara pulled her hands away.

"I'm sorry, ambasadora. Did I do something to offend you?" Solimar's voice held true dismay.

Sean walked in just then. Sara felt foolish thinking she'd never see him again after her appointment at the doctor's. But, she was truly a fool to believe Simon upheld the society's mores and to think Rainer could help her this time. As far as she was concerned, Rainer had never *really* helped her, even on Palomin. Her survival was her own. It still would be. Somehow.

Solimar greeted Sean, and Sara took the opportunity to meander further into the circle of glass trees. Without their thin arc of blue electricity spreading through their branches, the trees would be empty shells, beautiful, but without function and purpose. She understood that sentiment.

Sean's smell drifted through the airy foyer. It was clean and masculine and probably loaded with pheromones, judging by how she always felt that little flutter around him. "Solimar assumes everyone enjoys time on the Media, even if the stories about them are false," he said.

"I know she didn't mean anything. I'll apologize later." Sara followed one azure branch, stopping when she reached the spot where it split into two because she couldn't decide which to choose. So many choices had been made for her since Palomin that she no longer trusted herself to decide anything.

"You hurting?" Sean asked.

She looked at him and noticed his gaze rested on her belly. She had unconsciously placed her hands over her womb. She immediately dropped them.

"Something I ate."

"I had food poisoning once when I was six." He sat down on one of the white benches and patted the empty space beside him.

She stayed where she was.

He continued anyway. "My family took us on a holiday to a beach on Archenzon, way before the embargo. I remember seeing lights like yours in the trees at night."

She wandered over next to him and sat down, but pointed her knees away from him and didn't make direct eye contact. "I decided I should try some of the local seafood, straight from the surf. Puked for the rest of the trip. Ended up in a med facility while my brother played around in the sand. Worst holiday I can remember."

She faced him. "Sorry. I just can't imagine why you thought that story would make me feel better right now."

"I don't know either." He smiled, and it was just like she thought it would be, shy and true.

A shrill alarm startled her out of the moment.

Sean consulted the messages scrolling across his palm.

"Some spacer's going to ram us. I have to get to the engine room. You should go to the bridge, just in case."

"Ram us?"

He pulled her to her feet. "That way."

Sara ran down the commonway and burst onto the bridge. It was empty.

David squeezed past behind her. He was bare-chested and muttering over the alarm, "...could have interfaced immediately on the *Protector*. Told Sean I needed an updated cerebro implant."

He called up a nav chair from the middle of the black floor. An orb of holo-controls immediately sphered around his large frame.

"You'll want to strap in. Mari should be here soon if you need help."

Sara looked behind her to find a crash couch. The harnesses were the same type as on Chen's ship. And in their line of work, she'd had plenty of practice using them.

"Sean was heading to the engine room," Sara said.

"Did someone just get out of the shower?" Mari's tone implied she knew the answer firsthand. She swept in and called up a nav chair of her own.

David killed the alarm without acknowledging Mari's comment, then opened a visual feed to the engine room. Sean and Geir stood before several airscreens, manipulating data on the holographic panel with their fingertips, much in the same way David and Mari controlled the manual flight of the ship. Only, Sean's and Geir's screens were stationary while the nav chairs and orbed controls of the bridge were gyroscopic.

"Sean, who's in our lane?"

"Some ship called Aracenzo.*"*

"Opening com on all lines," David said. "Attention *Aracenzo.* Change your heading. Repeat, change your heading. We have right of way in this docking lane."

David stared at the readings on his screen. The alarm blared anew.

"*Aracenzo*, change your heading!"

"They won't move off," Geir said.

"I'm going to pull us out and punch through the atmosphere."

"Not enough juice for that kind of maneuvering," Sean said.

"There'll be enough. Add another fuel cylinder to the engine."

Sara didn't know anything about the *Bard*'s propulsion system, but suspected adding a cylinder wasn't normally recommended, nor was zipping into the air on a vertical trajectory. A rash of curses from Sean confirmed her thoughts.

"Loading sixth cylinder now. And strapping in," he said.

No protests. Were they that desperate?

Sara was accustomed to jostling and pulling soft gees in the many small craft necessary for Chen's work, but hadn't felt a truly strong g-force during space travel since a trip years ago when the private transport she and some girlfriends were on lost partial power to its gravity suppressors. The current force pushing her chest through her back and into the soft couch behind her was infinitely worse.

Seconds passed slowly. Ringing in her ears overcame the alarm's shriek. She could no longer suck in air. Her heart pounded and her vision tunneled. Small purple explosions dotted her right arm. She wanted to tear at her restraints, but her hands remained pinned to the armrests.

The alarm's pitch reached a crescendo, accompanied by the squeal of the metal hull.

The pressure released.

Silence.

Sara gasped for breath and closed her eyes to the dizziness.

"Clear of the atmosphere," David said. "How are things in the engine room?"

Belicose laughter erupted from Geir, who seemed to be having the time of his life.

Sean was less celebratory. *"Blew a couple of cylinders. Easy to fix, but time consuming."*

"Well, you have about three minutes until we land at Nanga Ki, so I guess you better get started." David flicked off the feed from the engine room, but not before Sean got out a few choice words.

David pivoted in his eggshell of holo-controls to face Sara. "You okay?"

"Never better," she said. Her arms twitched a little, and she had to focus on not bouncing her knees, but otherwise she was intact. "You're a good pilot, but I suppose that goes without saying considering you were a captain in the fleet."

"The best," Mari said. The way she looked at David spoke volumes. Sara thought she saw that same look returned. If these two were in a relationship, that could complicate Sara's plans. It shouldn't. She should just use her *improved assets* and make David forget about his co-pilot/biological observer, at least until Sara could get some information from him. The thought sickened her. She judged Mari's age to be around her own, but Mari had a wonderful trusting innocence that Sara would never get back. Mari saw only the best of her life ahead of her—Sara saw nothing. Could she really take that from another person?

"So, how are you liking the *Bard*?" Mari's question startled Sara out of her thoughts. It was the most the other woman had spoken to her since she boarded. Then she noticed David giving her an encouraging look, as though he had prompted her to talk to Sara. Still, the effort was sweet on both their parts.

"It's been fun so far," Sara said.

Before she knew it, Mari launched into a one-way conversation about a concert she wanted to see next month on Tampa Deux and segued into a gossip session about three different Socialites that Sara didn't even know. David seemed pleased as he flew the ship, ocassionally glancing at Mari to nod at something she said which he probably didn't even hear. Not exactly the kind of behavior she expected from a fragger.

"Incoming transmission from Nanga Ki," Mari said in between dualing lectures on the variety of begonias on Tampa One and the quality of silk from her home world of Deleine. Sara was sorry for their *discussion* to end. She knew Mari was just feeling her out, but enjoyed having the distraction of system gossip and another woman to talk to, one who wasn't training to be a killer. That's why Sara had stayed on the bridge after their scare. In another life she and Mari would have been best friends.

"Already?" David asked. "They must be excited about your visit. Let's hear it."

"Welcome Navigational Leader Anlow and Ambasadora Mendoza. Supervisor Bakkin Venture would like to welcome you to Nanga Ki and extend your and the ambasadora's dinner invitations to all of the passengers this evening. An escort will meet your transport at the hangar."

The com clicked off.

"Hmm, free dinner," David said.

Sara couldn't muster his enthusiasm. Was this what she could expect as a Face of the Embassy? Many inconveniently cordial get-togethers where she could chat about nothing and pretend to be fascinated by everything. Refusal came to mind, but Simon needed to believe she was more biddable than ever; otherwise, her next escape attempt would end like the first. Or much worse. No matter how desperate Simon might be to lift his curse, he wouldn't give her another chance. So, instead of steaming in a bath and going to bed early, she would have dinner with a local nobody. Before she changed her mind, she asked, "So, who's up for some Nanga Ki fare?"

"I can always eat," David said. "And, it sounded like they expected me. I guess civvy pilots do get a little respect sometimes."

"Mari? You coming with us?" Sara asked.

"I can't. Thanks." Mari stood to leave.

Sara felt a little dismayed that perhaps Mari's earlier niceties were false, or maybe Sara was nervous that she would finally be alone with David and have to put into action what Simon had asked.

"You're always wanting to get off the ship," he said.

"I have extra work to do since my schedule was set back a few weeks due to so many unexpected stops. I'll just see you later." She leaned toward David as though she were going to kiss him, but thought better of it. David looked like he wanted to ask her to change her mind—both about joining them and the kiss.

"What about everyone else?" Sara wondered specifically about Sean.

"Kenon never misses a chance to scout out new territory." David's tone told her what he meant. "But, Soli's probably lying down, trying to recover from all the latest excitement."

"Geir?" She didn't want to be too obvious and ask about Sean specifically.

"He might join us after he helps Sean with that cylinder. It's not like Sean would go anyway."

A surprising disappointment trickled through her, but she pushed it aside. She didn't need the distraction. This would be the perfect opportunity.

"I'll prep the transport for three then," he said.

"David?" Sara walked past him.

"Yeah?"

"I think they're going to expect you to wear a shirt."

He looked down at his bare chest and looked offended. "So, it's *that* kind of place."

TWENTY

"Why is Nanga Ki on the highest, steepest mountain range on Tampa Quad?" Sara asked from the back seat of the small transport, Nanga Ki's hangar being too small for even a mid-range ship like the *Bard*. The whole mountain came into view, snow streaming from its tri peaks like steam.

"I don't know," David said. "But, that's why it's easier to come in from such a high altitude than trying to climb all the way up here."

"Nanga Ki's location was chosen by Tertians," Kenon said, referring to the citizens of Tampa Three, the most inhospitable of the four Tampa moons and Tampa Quad's closest neighbor in the system. He leaned in close enough for Sara to smell his amber scent and feel his breath on her cheek. "They aren't exactly known for their logistics, considering their ancestors originally chose *that* rock for their settlements. Some of them wanted to incorporate part of Tampa Quad, too, but this was the only piece of land left." He squeezed her hand. His proximity and tone left no doubt of his invitation.

After spending so much time around contractors, Sara had forgotten how forward Socialite males could be. For them, it was easier to be forthcoming than to waste their efforts on an unrequited attraction. But, the fawning and innuendo irritated, rather than flattered, her. Maybe she had just gotten used to Rainer's reserved demeanor. Or, maybe she preferred the shy respect Sean had given her.

"Nanga Ki, this is Navigational Leader David Anlow of the *Bard*'s transport. Are we a go for landing?"

The hangar replied with an all-go signal.

"Understood. All-go."

A blinding wall of white cut in front of them as the descending sun reflected harshly off snow and metal. Sara discerned green landing lights flashing around three metal doors.

"Nanga Ki, this is the *Bard* transport. Why are the hangar doors not open?"

Without their own ear buds, Sara and Kenon couldn't hear Nanga Ki's response.

"Should we abort?" Kenon asked, his focus now more on the sealed hangar doors filling their view than on Sara's attentions.

"Nope. Everything's fine," David said, slightly amused.

The seconds ticked by without a hint of movement near the huge metal doors encased within solid rock.

"David!" Kenon's face drained of color. "What are you doing?"

"Ever buzz a scarecrow?" David asked.

The doors rushed at them. Kenon threw his arms up to protect his face. Sara remained frozen in her seat. No crash, no impact, just a pass through a holo-screen that looked for all the planet like solid metal hangar doors.

David decelerated and came to a complete stop at the end of the landing tunnel. No one spoke. Kenon laughed nervously, then smoothed his hair, the navy blue tips shining in the transport's soft light.

"You could have told the rest of us it was just a holo-screen," Sara said.

"I figured you knew what a scarecrow was." David's nonchalance annoyed her.

Sara liked to know what to expect from the people around her, and David had just proven he could be unpredictable. Simon's fragger theory gained ground.

"I should have worn a coat." The freezing air assaulted Sara as soon as she entered the hangar's atmosphere. Her bio-lights danced up and down the goose flesh on her arm, and she shivered in the brilliant light as it reflected off of the glossy white walls.

A group of six approached the trio from the *Bard*. All but one woman were clad in black coats with cenders strapped to their thighs. Every one of them stared at Sara's intra-tattoo like streamers at a v-game screen. Those dots would forever define her as an Embassy project. The other ambasadoras relished such favor. Sara viewed it as a permanent reminder of her slavery.

She felt gentle hands wrap a jacket around her shoulders. Her appreciative gaze met Kenon's smiling face. *Ever the society gentleman.*

Once the purple lights disappeared, the spell was broken, and the weaponless female stepped forward in a form-fitting silver coat that practically dragged the floor. Its color contrasted beautifully with her mocha skin.

"Ambasadora Mendoza, I am Liloch Ramon, deputy supervisor of Nanga Ki." She bowed deeply.

The action made Sara uncomfortable, as did seeing each contractor with their hands at the ready over the silver handles of their weapons. She instantly ran through defensive scenarios in her mind and within seconds had one that would allow her to take out the three closest contractors in about that many moves. Rainer would be proud.

"It is a pleasure to meet you, Deputy Supervisor Ramon. May I introduce the handsome and charming men of the *Bard*, Navigational Leader David Anlow and Terra Observer Kenon Brudger."

Liloch nodded her pony-tailed head at both men, though her coffee-colored eyes lingered on Kenon's soft features much longer. She was rewarded with a propositioning smile.

Worried more about their armed escort than amused by the woman's obvious infatuation, Sara prodded, "May we proceed inside?"

"Forgive me. This way."

"Good to know you still got the touch." David chided Kenon as they followed Liloch and her security entourage through a pair of double doors and into an antechamber.

"Once the doors behind us close, we'll be able to proceed into the main hall," she said. *Good way to keep out the cold and unwanted guests.*

The party of nine squeezed into the small antechamber. Given the choice of pressing against a male contractor or David, Sara chose David. She caught a whiff of that green tea smell she had come to associate with Armadans, well at least David and Geir, the only two she really knew. Rather than coming from bots, the scent seemed to be natural to their caste.

A whisper of conversation from the female contractors drifted her way. Her heart skipped a beat when she realized they were talking about Rainer. Without looking directly at them, Sara tried to concentrate on their words. All she heard was "reassigned" before the male standing beside them spoke loudly to his companion.

"Don't often see a birth Armadan pulling civvy duty. Unless his own kind doesn't even want him."

"What makes you think I'm an Armadan?" David lowered his head past the contractor's bright green and black ridge of hair in order to look into the man's eyes.

Sara chuckled, drawing an angry stare from Green Hair.

David's expression was an amused calm. Still, she imagined him with v-mitters. Her first impulse was to pull away, but that would have been too obvious. Better to let him play at protector and not bruise his ego.

The *swooshing* seal of the front door brought their chatter to an end. Even the slight change in temperature made her cheeks and lips loosen their grip on her capillaries. She gave into a small shiver and hugged Kenon's jacket closer, loving its warmth and subtle smell.

The white inner doors of the antechamber opened within seconds onto a bustling atrium of dark stone and fuchsia light. It was a pleasant surprise after the spartan hangar.

David elbowed out first, guiding Sara by the shoulders. Green Hair exited close behind them.

"This is the Great Hall," Liloch announced. "As you can see, we took our inspiration for the interior from digitals of several ancient Yuraian cultures found among the first worldships."

"I thought this looked a little familiar," David said.

"So, you *are* an Armadan," Green Hair said.

"Not all of Yurai's citizens are Armadans. Only the best ones."

Trying to diffuse the situation, Kenon asked Liloch about the wall coverings.

Sixteen tapestries cascaded down from the ceiling along the dark stone walls. Fuchsia birds of prey, perhaps indigenous to Yurai, raced down the black, silky wall coverings, wings folded behind them, claws at the ready. Thirty of the beasts flew, self-contained in a world of perpetual flight. The brilliant pink tone of the holo-birds mirrored the flame erupting from flanking wall sconces. Each tapestry canopied its own seating nook. The cozy alcove benches were carved into the chamber itself.

The Great Hall's centerpiece, however, was the floor to ceiling fireplace. It stretched nine meters above them and was half as wide, a natural pillar of the mountain. Kenon moved toward the fiery tower and its small platform of dark steps which encircled the fireplace on all sides. Circumnavigating the stone benches of staring occupants, he climbed the stone staircase.

Sara almost wanted to join him as he neared the mesmerizing pink fire. An inferno of fuchsia burned within large openings at its bottom. Smaller holes pocked its remaining length to expose the traveling pink glow.

The firelight lit upon Kenon's face as he climbed closer and tilted his head back to view the ceiling.

"I'm surprised Kenon's playing the role of a terra observer so well. I assumed he just wanted a scientific title to feel more important than other Socialites. You know, without actually doing any real work for it," David said.

"Like Mari?" Sara was surprised to see him frown.

"Mari devotes a lot of time to her work, and though I don't quite understand what it is she does, I know it's important, at least to her."

"I was joking, but best not to tell her I said that."

"I won't. Not that we talk that much anyway. I mean, we don't see each other that often. Or at all." He mumbled something else, then changed the subject quickly. "By the way, I should have gone over emergency procedures with you as soon as you boarded. I always did for new crew on the *Protector*. I guess I'm slipping too far into civvy life already."

Green Hair sauntered past, his knuckles white from a tight grip on his cenders. He watched Kenon, but Sara knew his attention was really on David and her. Was the contractor edgy because he had been told of her escape attempt?

Kenon rejoined them. "It's basalt."

Sara looked at David in faux amazement.

"Nanga Ki is volcanic," Kenon said to none of them in particular.

"Extinct, I assure you," Liloch said.

"Maybe." Kenon stopped beside her.

"Truly, Scientist Brudger—"

"Please." He took her hand, and said, "Call me Kenon," before going into the same speech about the pretension of titles he gave upon meeting Sara.

"Kenon," Liloch said. "I was just about to explain to the ambasadora that our beautiful and functional fireplace is what remains of an original lava tube. Five million years ago, this chamber would have been flooded with magma. Now it's our Great Hall. And, I'm sure you already know why there is heat produced, but no smoke."

"I wondered about that," Sara said.

Liloch waited for Kenon to respond.

"It's because of what feeds your fire, here in the chimney and the flames in the wall sconces. Vulcan gas in the vernacular, but I prefer the poetic term Hephestos' breath, though I'm not certain where the term originated."

"Exactly." Liloch pushed closer to Kenon.

Sara and David exchanged bemused glances. She avoided looking too deeply into his eyes. David's smoky irises were earnest and pleasing, and nothing at all like a fragger's heartless orbs. On second consideration, the scarecrow prank earlier wasn't enough to convince her that David was an anti-government operative. She had first-hand experience with fraggers. David wasn't acting like one of them.

She heard Liloch laugh and looked at the darker woman's response to Kenon. It was as though they were the only people in the room. Sara couldn't imagine being that carefree again. She was acutely aware of everyone surrounding her at all times, and had even learned from Rainer how to assess the level of each individual's threat to her. If this was what her life would be from now on—assessing threats and planning escapes, she would gladly go back to being a bored Socialite and watching the Media with her cousins. Now, they were snuggled in at home watching her on the Media. Sara should be proud, flattered, but it was all a lie, and she hated liars.

"The major supervisor is waiting for us in the dining hall. If you'll follow me." Liloch took Kenon's offered arm.

When they walked past Green Hair and his companions, David gave them a taunting wave good-bye.

Sara smiled a little, then thought, *I hope I'm right about you, David Anlow. Otherwise I'll have to kill you to save myself.*

TWENTY-ONE

Heavy drums and whining guitars pounded through the V-side, energizing the combatants. Zak kicked Cuzco's legs out from under him and sent the bigger guy tumbling down an ascending magno. When Vishnue rammed his head into Zak's stomach, Sean gasped for breath back in his dark suite in the real world. Pain registered in his head, his left shoulder, and finally his knees as Zak and Vishnue rolled after Cuzco.

At the bottom of the ramp, Zak jumped up and right into Cuzco's fist. The jab to his mouth drove his teeth into his upper lip and left him reeling backward. Before Cuzco could get a second jab in, Zak ducked around behind him and chopped the back of the man's neck with the edge of his hand. Then he shifted his weight onto his front foot and kicked sideways at a newly charging Vishnue.

Cuzco spun around. Zak circled the big guy and spit a mouthful of blood onto the onyx floor. He hoped to turn Cuzco full into the sunlight that filtered through the chalcedony atrium. The only difference between this virtual world and the real Embassy was the lack of people rushing through.

And no green floor lamps and a dozen other details no one cared about but him. In a training ground, every detail had significance because strategies could be infinitely altered by one green lamp.

He'd mentioned the slip to the bosses again. No one was concerned.

Out of the corner of his eye, Zak saw Vishnue coming up on his right. Cuzco would wait until the two of them could attack Zak from both fronts. Zak knew what to expect because their partner strategies were always the same. It was time for some new moves.

Waiting until the last possible moment, Zak spun away from Cuzco and took Vishnue head on with a combination of punches to the jaw. He threw the dazed man into Cuzco so hard they both tumbled to the ground. The pair rolled back to their feet, ready to lunge at Zak.

A portal opened in front of them.

Ariel stepped through and looked at them. "Why didn't anyone invite me? I would have dropped this background search and come running, ready to rumble…or tumble."

She wiped some blood from Zak's lip, then sucked it off her finger.

"What did you find out?" Zak wiped the rest of the blood onto his sleeve.

"That Ambasadora Sara Mendoza didn't exist for the past two months. I mean she doesn't show up anywhere in the system again until very recently."

"Where was she prior to working for Prollixer?" he asked.

"Officially, she was a Socialite living on Tampa Quad with her family," Ariel said.

"Unofficially?"

"Enamoured to a rogue contractor. Guy named Chen Starrie."

"Sounds like an Embassy snitch to me," Vishnue said.

"Do you know where she is now, Zak?" Ariel asked.

"No," he lied. "But I'll find out and take care of it. Such a high profile position will need to be dealt with delicately."

Without waiting for any objections, Sean pulled Zak out of the V-side.

He wiped the lenses from his eyes and stared into the darkness of his bedroom. He hated to be right about Sara. It left him empty.

The fraggers would expect him to eliminate her before she did any damage. But he would make that decision for himself. Fragger intel had failed him once already. Never again would he act on another's word. Waiting could be risky, but the rational part of him wasn't convinced of her guilt yet. His first instincts were usually right on. That's why their initial encounter had meant so much; it told him there was something more to her. He was determined to find out how much more.

He kicked his legs off the bed and tapped his palm to activate his bedroom lights. If he started now, he could search her suite long before she returned from the social on Nanga Ki. Deciding not to bother with shirt or shoes, he strode through his sitting area and tapped open his door.

He jerked his head back when he met Soli's smiling face in the commonway.

"Isn't this a nice look for you. Are you going out?" She placed her hand on his bare chest and gently backed him up into the room. "I was just coming to visit."

"Now's not a good time, Soli. I kind of have something I need to do."

Her eyebrows raised in interest. "Oh, you have somewhere to be? Someone to see?" She moved past him without waiting for his answer and walked to one of the couches and stood.

Resigned, he followed her. With one swipe of his arm, he cleared a space for her to sit on the couch's blue fabric surface. The shirt Sara had fondled earlier lay on top of the pile, its blindfolded occupant still paused in mid-dive. He picked up the shirt and held it, as though it would bring back the memory of that day. Then he tugged it on, catching just a slight whiff of roses, or so his mind imagined.

"Don't get dressed on my account," Soli said. She tucked the graceful lines of her tailed tunic under her before gliding onto the couch. The low-cut white front drew Sean's eyes to the matching curves of her amber breasts.

"You like this?" she asked. A sly smile peeked from the corner of her cornflower blue lips.

"If only you were interested in men, Soli."

"Then you'd want nothing to do with me." Her smile faded, and a stray braid fell over her forehead.

"What do you mean?" he asked.

"Because you would think I was only after your DNA. You assume that's what all women want from you."

"I'd be right. It's a tenet of our society. Don't you remember your studies? 'Sex is life. Value your drive. Choose your couplings well.'"

"Is that why you haven't taken a prime yet…at your age?"

"My age?" He knit his brows. "I'm thirty. I have a good 140 years left in my projected lifecycle." When she didn't look convinced he added, "David's almost twice as old as me and still hasn't taken a prime."

"David's an Armadan. They normally don't have children until their late sixties. You're a Socialite."

Not even by half, Sean thought.

"Kenon's the Socialite. He started at sixteen and has had three children over the past six years. And, he's looking for a new amour already."

"Yes, I know," Soli said with an innocent smile. "He has his sights set on our ambasadora."

"Sara? I should have guessed." Irritation worked into Sean's jaw. Though Kenon was probably more her type and certainly closer in age if Sean had guessed right.

Soli perked up. "On a first name basis already? You didn't even come to greet her."

"She came to me for a reporter and asked if I could reprogram her scentbots."

"Did you?"

"I gave her a reporter," Sean said. *And a very thorough lesson on how to use it.*

"But no new scentbots?"

"Not yet."

"So you'd have an excuse to see her again." Soli didn't mean this as a question.

"What? No. She had a message waiting for her." Sean crossed his arms.

"Maybe she wanted an excuse to see *you* again."

She probably did want to see him again, but not in the way Soli suggested. If anything, Sara Mendoza might be plotting to capture or kill him at their next meeting.

"Quit trying to matchmake, Soli." He kept his tone light, though he was annoyed because she hit a little too close to the truth. It amazed him how she seemed to know what they all were thinking on board.

"You know, an amour would do you a world of good. Make you more social, less brooding."

"I may spend a lot of time in my head, but I don't brood."

"You're one of the loneliest people I know, Sean. Perhaps you really prefer it that way. Or are you just afraid of intimacy?"

"I get all the intimacy I need, thanks." Though there hadn't been any of that recently, either.

"There's a difference between sex and intimacy, otherwise no one would bother to take on an amour."

"For me there's no distinction. You'd be surprised how many Uppers think that way. They just won't admit it. I don't need someone permanent in my life."

And no one needed him. The truth caused an ache that traveled from his throat to his stomach, but he never let the reaction show on his face. He knew it was time for Soli to leave, before he said anything he'd regret.

She must have sensed his irritation because she stood and walked the few paces to him.

"You're one of my favorite people. That's why I care about you." She brushed the back of her hand along his jaw and gave him a sad, little smile.

He took her hand and looked down at it. "Thanks, Soli. Nice to know."

"Now, I'm off to cheer up Mari."

"More David troubles?" Sean asked.

"What else?"

Sean worried about Mari's very obvious emotional fallacy for David. He had known her during the year she had been on board. When she first arrived, he'd been interested, then she immediately opened her mouth and he couldn't take the constant chatter, even for a man who hated the silence. Still, he liked Mari because she was genuine and kind. He hoped David had only the best intentions toward her. So far, that seemed to be the case. He put up with her immaturity and basically taught her about intimacy in a safe and gentle way, at least according to all the graphic details she had shared with Sean and Geir when they were trying to work on the engine core one morning. David would blow a circuit if he knew Mari talked about their relationship and their sexual habits so openly.

"Does he still think he's keeping their tryst a secret?" Sean walked Soli to the door.

"Of course he does, dear. He's an Armadan." Soli headed out with a wave.

Sean waited until he saw her round the bend for the stairs before heading out himself. Sara's suite was only three doors down from his on this side, but he didn't want to take any chances being seen. If he did have to eliminate her, he didn't want anyone drawing a connection between the two of them.

TWENTY-TWO

"I hope that's not dinner." Sara put her hand to her nose and kept it there, for once relishing in her scentbots' rosy bouquet. Kenon coughed several times. An odd smell of burnt hair and flowers detracted from the room's elegance.

Several nicely dressed guests were already enjoying their meals at a long stone banquet table. In a strip down the middle glowed a fuchsia fire, its flames not reaching higher than a few centimeters. More sconces lined the walls, though without the tapestries that had accompanied them in the main chamber.

"The major supervisor likes to do his own introductions." Liloch motioned toward the head of the polished basalt table. "So, if you'll excuse me...."

"You're not joining us?" Sara held out hope for an alternate dining facility.

Liloch threw a quick glance at Kenon. "I usually dine in my quarters."

As the pony-tailed blonde turned to go, Kenon strode up to David and said, "See you in the morning. Enjoy your social."

A whirring drew their attention to the shadows at the far end of the table, where the major supervisor floated toward them on a hover chair. He had a girth not unlike a small moon, and apparently no table manners to speak of. His light grey tunic displayed a preview of each course that had been prepared for the evening. When he licked his food-encrusted lips and adjusted himself, Sara wrinkled her nose.

"Is that a floating throne?" David asked.

"Maybe that's what smells," Sara whispered back.

The stench worsened when the major supervisor stopped in front of them. He looked her over, his gaze never quite made it to her face. Speaking to her cleavage, he said, "Ambasadora Sara Mendoza, you are everything I had imagined."

The man's soprano voice made her think there wasn't much there to adjust after all.

"I am Major Supervisor Bakkin Venture." He took her hand, his greasy fingers massaging her palm.

She pulled her hand back and easily slid free of his grasp. "It's nice to make your acquaintance. May I introduce Navigational Leader David Anlow."

"Hello," Venture muttered.

She noticed that neither man was punctilious enough to offer his hand.

"You don't know how happy I was to hear that an ambasadora would be staying with me."

"We'll actually be returning to our ship after dinner," Sara said.

"*Immediately* after dinner," David added, then muttered something about this being worse than some dive at the Hub.

Venture's look said he liked David better when he was silent. "You must be hungry. I do hope you don't mind, but when we were informed of your tardiness this evening, we started without you. But, I have seats reserved for you at my side."

"I thought we were right on schedule," David said. "I'm usually on time."

"I don't think it really matters at this point," Sara said, but David remained irritated by their supposed tardiness. No doubt he was regimented about such things from his time in the fleet.

None of the diners offered more than a nod of acknowledgment, and most of them were almost finished eating. She and David had been given the honorable seats to either side of Venture. Attendants loaded both of their plates and filled their glasses with a clovered alcohol. She wondered how the six people seated at the other end of the table could be eating with such gusto when the odor in here had killed her appetite completely. Already tired of playing at the good Embassy diplomat, she would've happily returned to her horrible white room on the *Bard*.

After several minutes of pushing food around on her plate without taking a single bite, she realized David had simply shoved his meal away without touching it. He had downed several glasses of the honeyed mead, however, including Sara's when she offered it to him.

Venture tried to peek under Kenon's jacket at her bio-lights. She snagged his thumb and bent it in on itself, not enough to break, just enough to make a point.

He retracted his hand and glared at her. "Best be careful, ambasadora, or you'll ruin the Sovereign's little set-up."

The whispered words struck her in the stomach. "I guess I was moving too slow for him?" She kept her voice low, trying to coax out what he knew.

"The Sovereign is not a man to be kept waiting. But, he is gracious, so he arranged tonight for you."

"What happens tonight?" Her voice sounded tight, and not just because she was whispering.

"Ambasadora, if you need a demonstration, I'll be happy to oblige." He grinned, a huge piece of blackened meat caught between two of his upper teeth.

"This was not part of the plan. The timing isn't right. By rushing this, Simon is only hurting himself."

"On a first name basis with the Sovereign? You must be something special," Venture chided.

"I'm not playing this game. I do this on my terms or not at all." She threw her napkin down and pushed away from the table. Speaking loudly, she turned to David. "Ready to go?"

"Yep."

"How regrettable. I was informed shortly before you joined me of an impending storm moving toward Nanga Ki." Venture spoke up.

"I've flown in severe weather before." David started to walk away.

"You don't seem to understand. We operate on a mandated lock-down during storms. Barring an emergency or Embassy directive, those doors open for no one. Not even the *Sovereign*, if he were here."

Sara stiffened.

Before David could mouth another protest, Venture continued, "Not to worry. I've secured one of our best guestrooms for you. Though, I regret that it is the *only* one available. Lucky your terra observer already found a bunk mate...."

"What about the crew on the *Bard*?"

With another burst of irritation, Venture raised his voice in finality. "Your passengers have already been notified that any traffic into or out of the hangar is strictly prohibited for now. The message was received by your archivist."

The doors to the dining hall opened, allowing Green Hair and his friends access. The other diners fell silent.

"I could offer you a holding cell for the evening if you'd prefer."

Squeezing David's arm, Sara said, "No, that won't be necessary. The guest room sounds very cozy." If Simon were part of this ruse, it was best to be careful until they knew more about the real situation.

"I figured as much. If you've finished, I'll have you escorted there now."

Green Hair motioned them out the doors and through a stone passageway. David encircled Sara with his arm and pulled her close. It would appear as an intimate gesture to unknowing eyes, instead he used it as a way to communicate through a whisper. "This whole thing doesn't make sense. Do you think keeping us here is some type of political move? Maybe Venture is buying time to work our *rescue* to his advantage."

"I'm not sure he's smart enough to have plotted something so fast." But Simon certainly had plans for them.

"I can take the two guys on the right, and that would give you a chance to make a break for it, like on the magnos that day."

Sara felt confident she could take the guys on the right and the woman directly in front of her before David made a move, but now was not the time to stir up a group of edgy contractors. "Neither of us would get very far. I think we should play it cautious."

They rounded the corner.

"Maybe you're right. There's no way any of these idiots would touch an ambasadora."

"Of course not." She hoped she kept the sarcasm out of her tone.

"Here's your room." Green Hair stopped in front of the first door in this annex. He flung open the thick Oak door and waited for David and Sara to step inside. As she passed, the contractor leaned in to say, "Have fun."

"You can't break down the door no matter how hard you pound," Sara said.

David smashed his fist against the solid wood again. "Someone is bound to hear us. I've been pounding on it for twenty minutes. I can't understand why they locked us in."

She was sure someone *did* hear them. Without being obvious, she had scanned the room for cameras or listening devices. They could be anywhere—camouflaged in the stone walls, built into the canopy bed, sewn into the pillows, or molded into the tray of cooling drinks and pastries that waited for them on the table.

Simon hadn't missed a detail. The cozy quarters were meant to be an interrogation room of sorts, to aid Sara in retrieving information by a particular means. The thought tore at her. Flirting with a potential partner and consensual couplings were one thing, using her sexuality to extract information was quite another. It reminded her too much of contractor behavior, selfish, deceptive. She thought about the stakes, the permanent loss of her breeding right, maybe even death. Then she thought about the fraggers who had attacked at Palomin and their brutality. She thought especially about the fragger who sat on top of her and would have squeezed the life from her if not for Rainer.

Rainer.

Where there were memories of him, memories of Faya and her torture followed. Better this than a modification cell. David should consider himself so lucky.

"They have to let us go eventually. I'm an ambasadora, remember? The Media follows my every move. Didn't you see the voyeurs in the dining hall? The whole system knows we're here."

In truth, she hadn't seen a voyeur in the entire place, an oddity which had needled her. There was no public arena void of Media spies, not even somewhere as remote as Nanga Ki. It all made an eerie sense now and put her on edge—Simon didn't want any more witnesses than necessary. She realized how much comfort she had taken in their transparent society, a false safety that someone was always *watching out* for you, not just *watching* you.

"Then how is Venture going to explain holding us here?" David asked.

"He'll say you were a security risk." She sat down on the bed, as there was no place else to sit. "That you refused to obey the storm lock-down, putting the entire complex in jeopardy. That he had no other choice. Or something along those lines." She patted the bed beside of her and tried not to think of the way David had looked at Mari earlier. Sara felt guilty enough.

David sat on the edge of the bed beside her. "I'm not sure I believe that."

"Venture won't do anything to upset Sim—the Sovereign. His post and title would be forfeit." This same threat may have been how Simon managed to secure Venture's cooperation in the first place, or maybe it was a promise of a better position.

Too bad for Venture, Simon wasn't the type to keep his promises.

David grabbed a dainty pastry from the tray and popped the whole thing in his mouth, then offered her one. "They're good."

"Yes, they are." Her appetite was back. "What do we have to drink?"

David took a sip. "Chai, with a little something extra. Bourbon, maybe. My father added Bourbon to everything he drank. Come to think of it, so did my mother." David took a larger swallow.

Sara followed suit. The spice of the chai definitely hid the underlying notes of some type of alcohol. Some of the anxiety eased. She had a little time to think now. So far, she had been a half step ahead of Simon. There was no reason to believe she couldn't keep that lead. She pulled her feet under her and leaned against one of the large tassled pillows, some of her inhibitions fading as she let her knees rest against David's hip.

He noticed and looked decidedly uncomfortable. When he handed her another pastry, she made sure their fingers touched in the pass, her own comfort level rising as the alcohol dulled the edges of her conscience.

"So, how did you become an ambasadora anyway?" David's hand rested on her knee.

"I have Sovereign Prollixer to thank for it." She sipped at the chai and lay back on the pillows.

David's hand had started a slow move up her leg, pushing the bottom of her dress with it. "Were you chosen because of your lineage or did you apply to the position?" His speech sounded a little off. He had a slight accent anyway, tending to draw out certain vowels. It suited him, just another of his attractive qualities.

"It's a long story," she said.

"According to Bakkin Venture, we've got all night." His hand was almost to her thigh.

Something about the way David said *Bakkin* made Sara laugh. She knew exactly what Mari saw in the older man. He was big and safe and the type to handle any situation that came his way, probably how he had worked through the fleet ranks to become a captain. A man like David Anlow would have gotten her out of Palomin. Sara wondered how those thoughts floated into her head. Like on a cloud. She felt cloudy, as though *she* were floating a little and couldn't see through her blurry peripheral vision. Taking another swallow of chai, she wondered if that was what caused the dreamy feeling. It certainly warmed her throat and belly and several other parts of her that were responding to David's hand on her leg.

He chugged down his drink. In this light his facial features vaguely resembled Sean Cryer's. Maybe they shared some type of common ancestry. She took another sip, wishing the scruffy blonde were sitting next to her. Stretching her legs out, she allowed that white cloud to build around her.

David leaned over her, his face just centimeters from hers. She smoothed one of his eyebrows with her thumb.

"Are you tired, Mari?" he asked.

"Not really," Sara said, though her lids felt heavy. Wait. Did he just call her Mari? Sara thought he had. She tried to shake the cloudy feeling, but her inner voice was garbled like static.

"Me neither." David, *or was it Sean*, traced the swirls of purple on her hand, stirring them into a quickening pulse. Then he slid his hands up her arms, all the way to her shoulders, sending the satiny blue straps of her dress falling away. She giggled and wondered where the sound had come from.

He whispered something in her ear. It was a far-away whisper, though, and the words were incomprehensible, as though he spoke another language. She wanted to respond, but couldn't form her own words. The white clouds threatened from all around her now. Understanding poured through her. She was sliding. The chai fell from her hands. This time David laughed, a deep throaty rumble that reverberated through her body.

"Drugged," was all she managed to whisper. Her hand reached for him, but he now had three faces. She couldn't find the real one, though she swore she had tried to touch each of them at least once. When he brushed his lips against hers, she knew she'd found the right one, but the clouds interfered with her movements. Confused, she kissed him back. He tasted like chai. She parted the clouds for just a moment and tried to warn him again.

"Drugged," she said against his mouth. He kissed her harder.

Didn't he realize something was wrong? She said in a lazy voice, "I'm not Mari."

He pulled away from her and sat up. She heard him say something in that other language, but couldn't respond. She froze when she saw Rainer in David's place. Her conscious mind battled her sliding subconscious. Rainer wasn't here. Just her and David. Right?

The feeling of helplessness and disorientation bloomed into panic. Her skin felt too hot and her breath wouldn't come easily. Dizziness struck. She crawled past David and grabbed at the canopy's silky curtains, but they tore under her weight and sent her spilling onto the cold stone floor.

David stumbled to help her. Was his balance affected by the drugs or was it her perception? The thud of his body hitting the floor at the other end of the bed brought her answer.

"David," she choked out.

There was a distant groaning, which slowly formed into whispered words, just not David's. *"Can't have you dying on me yet."*

Faya.

Sara looked around the room. No Faya, only a pinpoint of light caught in her peripheral vision. She looked at the area straight on, the light jumped to the other corner. It bounced around, appearing to her left then her right. Now it swam directly in front of her, reminding her of the way light reflected off a razor disc when it was thrown just right. She was sure she'd seen one of its silvery blades.

Faya's voice morphed into Simon's. *"You've seen their faces, you know their names. So, when they die because of your actions, you'll remember them."*

The disc spun directly above her. As its rotation slowed she could discern individual specks instead one large mass. They weren't blades; they looked like her bio-lights. She glanced at her arm. One by one the lavender dots popped out of her skin and rose into the air, swarming together. She stifled a scream and crawled to a wall. Using its nooks and crevices like handholds, she climbed to her feet.

Rainer's voice was at her ear. *"You're a liar."*

"Stop!" She punched at the stone wall. The pain of smashed knuckles brought momentary clarity.

The door opened. Green Hair and a female contractor pushed inside.

Sara rushed the woman, knocking her to the ground. She struggled against her opponent and the half-dream state ascending on her again. She allowed a punch to connect with her side. The pain did as she'd hoped and parted the clouds long enough for her to shove the contractor's head against the stone. The woman went limp.

Sara snapped her attention to Green Hair. But, David was up from the floor and charging the male contractor. She'd heard that Armadans could produce excess adrenaline at will, but didn't think it was true, until David picked Green Hair up by his shirt and flung him three meters into two more contractors guarding the doorway.

"Head for the hangar," David said.

Sara skirted the contractors sprawled in the doorway, but one grabbed her ankle. She yanked it from his grasp and kicked him in the face, then took off. Scuffling sounded behind her. She considered going back to help David, but lost her balance as the floor shimmered in front of her. She barely felt the turn of her ankle or the rock slamming into her knee. She crawled to the wall, but it kept bending away from her at irregular angles. Pulling herself to her unsteady feet, Sara closed her eyes in an attempt to thwart the dizziness. Heavy footfalls raced up behind her.

"Come on." David grabbed her arm, dragging her along beside him. She tried to look back to see if the contractors followed but saw no one. If a retired captain could dispatch a handful of combatants by himself, contractors would be in trouble if they ever had to face Armadans in a real fight.

When she and David rounded the corner back toward the Great Hall, he gave into his disorientation, tripping and slamming his shoulder into the stone wall, dislodging one of the giant tapestries. The birds continued to fly as the black sheet of fabric folded to the ground with a snap.

"Can you make it to the hangar? I have talk to someone about opening those doors," David said. His voice seemed normal now. She could barely get out a "Yes." She wondered if he could fly them *out* of the hangar.

Sara continued navigating the hallway, trailing a hand against the stone wall to steady her wobbling form. The fuchsia light from the Great Hall sconces warped into long flames then retracted to compact orbs. When she passed the massive stone fireplace, several people still milled around, but as she had suspected earlier, no voyeurs. No real witnesses. A woman up ahead caught Sara's attention. Magenta-streaked dark hair. Faya. So she was here.

Sara staggered up to her, rage pulsing through her thoughts. She spun the woman around and grabbed her by the throat. A startled whimper escaped too small of lips, and green-flecked eyes stared back at her, not Faya's grey irises. Sara released her.

David stood yelling at a guard to open the airlock doors. A voyeur floated just above him. Relief surged through Sara; the live feed to the Media would ensure their safe passage out of Nanga Ki. Venture wouldn't dare allow her to be hurt in front of the Media, and neither would Simon. As if on cue, the inner chamber doors opened. David stood in the doorway and ushered her inside. He no longer seemed to be under the influence of the drugs. Had they already worn off for him, his size able to handle more than her small frame, or did he take something to counteract them?

She needed something, something to stop her slide, and she knew exactly where she would get it.

TWENTY-THREE

"Open the door, Sean." Sara slapped at the door's sensor. Its half-moon of bluegreen light made her uneasy. She watched it collapse into a small orb and jerked her hand away before the energy could burn the flesh from her bones.

"Stop!" Her voice echoed in the empty commonway.

She slid further into a hallucinogenic reality. She might be able to minimize the effects, at least keep part of herself ground in the real. She beat the sensor with her skinned knuckles.

No respite came this time. She barely even felt the pain.

Please answer the door.

It was obvious after meeting Sean, and seeing the mess of bottles and paraphernalia in his suite, that he was a doser. She'd pay triple for whatever he had on hand or just break down the damn door and take it. She needed a distractor to keep Faya's horrors at bay.

The metallic smell of chlorate burned through her nasal passages. She bit her lip against the onslaught of a thousand pins pricking the lining of her sinuses, and pushed her palms against her closed eyes. Holding her breath helped.

Sweat dampened her hands and crept down her wrists. Only it felt gummy and too sticky. She wrenched her hands away from her face and stared at the blue mucus that covered her palms. Her breathing came in shallow bursts. In a panic she wiped the mucus onto her gown. The fluorescent ooze ate through the shiny fabric and dripped onto her legs like acid. She grabbed handfuls of the gown to keep it off her skin.

It's not real.

She didn't care. Most of her believed it was real. Carbonizing flesh overpowered the ammonia-stench as her fingernails blackened. She watched each finger curl up and burn like leaves.

"Sara, what are you doing?"

She spun at the voice. Her gaze settled on a pair of silver v-mitters. She screamed and backhanded the fragger before falling against the closed door. With one shoulder pressed into the wall for support, she stumbled forward. Hands grabbed her shoulders. She whipped forward and smashed her forehead into the fragger's chin.

She heard a grunt in response, but the hands only tightened.

"What is your problem?"

The voice sounded familiar. Rainer? The hope gave her pause.

"Sara, what's wrong with you?" She saw a square jawline and a thin upper lip. Her gaze moved past the trail of blood coming from the man's mouth up to his eyes—Sean Cryer's brown eyes, not colorless v-mitters.

She fell against his chest in relief, then remembered her burnt fingers. "My hands." She inspected them to find healthy olive skin, except the bloody, swollen knuckles on her right hand.

Sean loosened his grasp on her wrists and turned her hands over in his, inspecting them. "What did you hit? Besides me?"

She looked at him, but saw Simon's face. Her hands balled into fists. "Let go of me."

"You're sliding, aren't you?" It was Sean's face again.

"Yes."

"Judging by your pupils and breathing, you're headed into a full slide. I didn't take you for a doser."

"I need something. Please."

Sean helped her into his suite. She saw him take a step into Faya's modification cell and pulled away from him. "I won't let her touch me again. I'll kill her and you and Simon. He put you up to this, didn't he? How could you?"

She grabbed an empty bottle from the table in front of her and hurled it at Sean's head before running down a corridor. She had imagined escaping down this corridor before every session with Faya, but never had the chance to until now. She ran into a sitting room and stopped. This wasn't part of the modification area, not part of Simon's complex. It lacked his cold luxury. This place was familiar. She lost her panic to confusion. A quick survey took in all the bottles and pillows scattered about and the piles of clothes covering the couches. She bypassed all of these and stumbled over to a chair and picked up a crumpled grey shirt.

She held it to her chest. Instead of the comforting woody scent she expected, she thought she smelled clay mixed with freshly raked leaves. Her mind flashed to fingertips brushing across her open palm and a face full of dark blonde stubble.

"Sean?"

"Yeah." His voice carried from across the room.

She glanced in his direction, then quickly away. "Do you work for Simon?"

"Prollixer? No."

Her peripheral vision caught his slow movement toward her. She'd forgotten what she'd asked. This was how her games with Faya always began, volleying questions at one another until Faya became bored and either started to break Sara's toes or hooked her up to the blade cuffs.

Sara squeezed the shirt like it was a lifeline to sanity. "Sean?"

"I'm here."

She couldn't find him.

"Why don't you tell Faya what she wants to know?"

Not Sean's voice. Rainer's. She shook her head.

"David Anlow isn't a fragger," she said.

"I could have told you that." Sean's voice, right next to her. He slipped an arm around her and pressed something into her neck. Images of blade cuffs slicing her face and neck played through her mind as she twisted and fought against Sean's grasp. He held her tight to his chest. Her breath came in shallow spurts, and her mouth moved in unvoiced words.

"It's okay. Calm down." His voice was soothing as he rubbed her back. "This'll stop the slide and take care of all that stuff in your head. You'll work it out of your subconscious through a few bad dreams."

The dreams were worse than the reality. Sara was already drifting into unconsciousness. Her knees buckled. Sean lifted her and carried her to his room. She didn't want to be alone to battle her way back to the real through endless nightmares. Her mind separated from her physical form, but she thought she clung to him, burying her face in his neck. If Sean left her alone, she'd never know. It would be okay. They always left.

And she still survived.

Several bottles clinked to the floor as Sean hurried to grab one of his clean shirts from the stack on the couch. He doused a corner of the soft cotton shirt with cold water from the bathroom faucet. Cries from the connecting bedroom sent him straight back to Sara. She thrashed against the mattress as though fighting an invisible opponent. His throbbing lip reminded him to approach her cautiously. She'd also caught him above his right eye during her last episode.

"Sara, it's Sean. I'm the only one here. You're safe." He placed a tentative hand on her shoulder.

She stilled. Only her chest moved, rising and falling with ragged breaths. Her eyes never opened. He didn't know if she could actually understand him or if she was just responding to the tone of his voice. He sat beside her. Sweat beaded on her forehead and the scent of roses suffocated the room as it dripped out of her pores. He was beginning to hate the heady smell as much as she did because he associated it with her torment.

He pressed the cool cotton of the shirt against her forehead. He could feel the heat radiating from her skin, and that worried him. Having survived a couple of full slides in his teens, he always relied on restors to put him out so he could sleep it off. He'd given Sara a double dose already, yet that hadn't calmed her much. He was afraid she'd overdose if he gave her any more. She either had a tolerance that surpassed his own or someone had used some powerful shit to mess with her mind.

At least she slept, though it was more like a nightmarish trance. She murmured constantly, sometimes shouted. He could make out a small amount, pleas for help mostly, which made his chest tight. And names. Some he recognized like Rainer, Chen, and Simon. He was pretty sure that last one was in reference to Simon Prollixer. Though there weren't many familiar enough with the Sovereign to throw his first name around, except in secret and adding a punchline to follow it up.

One name that he didn't recognize always brought about the most violent episodes. If this Faya had been around tonight, he believed Sara would have torn her apart with her bare hands. At this point, Sean could have done that himself.

The lights of her intra-tat bounced around in erratic pulses in a frightening way that wasn't alluring like when he first touched her hand. Tonight they were a physical sign of whatever horror she was experiencing.

He brushed her damp hair back with his fingers and whispered words of reassurance, knowing this could be the biggest mistake of his life. She had been sent here to flush out a fragger operative, that much he knew. Right now she and the Embassy thought David was their man—he didn't know whether to laugh at the absurdity or be insulted. If that's what her Embassy intel was saying, then it might be easier to bring down this government than he thought.

"Sean." She reached out to the empty space beside her. He put his hand over hers. "I'm here."

When she whimpered and shook, he lay down next to her because he knew what it was like to go through this alone. He knew what it was like to go through everything alone. He folded Sara in his arms and pulled her tight against his chest. Her body relaxed against him. He kissed the top of her head. If she betrayed him later, he'd deal with that when it happened. It's not like he hadn't thought of offing himself, and not the pleasant way with passing drugs and a bedside full of family crying for him. Maybe she'd be doing him a favor. Sean's older brother had killed himself. He told Sean before he did it that Sean wouldn't understand because he had never known their father, so couldn't really miss him. But, Sean did miss having a father...and an older brother.

Sara's breathing deepened with exhaustion. So did Sean's. He rested his cheek against the top of her head and fell asleep.

TWENTY-FOUR

Rainer looked out the curved window of the Embassy council's chamber. The noon sun glinted off the water at Shiraz Dock far below, and small shadows followed the bustling pedestrians scurrying along the elliptoid pattern of the Hub's blue pavement.

The interior here was cold and gloomy today, and not just from the dark filters on the massive skylights or the room's climate controls. Lately, it was always dismal whenever the Sovereign met with his council.

"Does this have anything to do with the recent fragger uprisings?" Archivist Harlo Andravo asked.

This was the argument Rainer had been waiting for after ten minutes of strained pleasantries and mundane business discussions. He shifted his attention to Prollixer's diminutive frame draped gracefully over a leather armchair at the head of the long snaking table.

"Yes, I have evidence to prove that fragger operatives plotted the attempt on Ambasadora Mendoza's life."

The lie never showed on the Sovereign's gaunt face.

"Why would fraggers go after an ambasadora?" Phoebe Llewellyn's tone was more critical than questioning.

Rainer hadn't seen Phoebe since that day in the underground corridors, on his way to see Sara's new body. The archivist avoided his gaze now.

"They did it as an affront to the Embassy," the Sovereign said.

"There are more worthy adversaries in this system than a newly entitled Socialite and her pilot," Llewellyn said.

Rainer silently agreed. The three other council members also remained quiet.

"Do you suppose they did it to humiliate *me*, then?" Prollixer asked.

"It would seem from their previous protests that humiliating you would only be a bonus to fulfilling some higher ideology." Llewellyn's pitch raised enough on that last word to strengthen Rainer's suspicion that she was sympathetic to the fraggers. Yet, the Sovereign had never seen the signs. Rainer attributed the man's distraction to his failing health. Or perhaps he just hadn't shared his thoughts with Rainer. He'd kept quite a bit from him ever since Sara's time at Palomin, not that he was ever really open with Rainer or anyone else. As the years went by, there was coincidentally less and less history available concerning the Sovereign.

"Let's ask Contractor Varden."

Prollixer had never asked for Rainer's opinion before during a council meeting.

"Do you believe the attack on Ambasadora Mendoza is the result of fragger dissidence?"

"I don't think we have enough intel to say for certain."

The warning in Prollixer's stare reminded Rainer of the power the man still wielded, making him rethink his assumption of the man's frailty. Rather than subduing Prollixer, desperation energized his deviousness. Rainer would need to take more care in the future if he was to outlive his Sovereign.

"The most intelligent comment I've heard thus far," Andravo said.

Before either Prollixer or Llewellyn could respond, a contractor with lime and black hair ridging down the middle of his head strolled into the chamber. A synth-flesh bandage covered his forehead above his right eye.

"I'm afraid the meeting is adjourned," the Sovereign said.

Phoebe balked. "But, we've not—"

"Contractor Varden, perhaps you should escort the council out as they seem to have forgotten where the door is."

Retaining all the dignity they could, the archivists filed out of the chamber in silence…and without escort. They all understood that Sovereign Prollixer kept the council alive as a faux check to his unmitigated governing; only, he'd never made the point so blatantly until now.

Simon waved a hand and the windows tinted further, throwing the room into complete darkness. Airscreens popped on in front of each of the empty council chairs.

"Since you don't believe we have enough intel on the matter, I would like your perspective on this." The Sovereign motioned to his own viewer. "This is a feed from several cameras secreted in one of the Nanga Ki guest suites."

Magenta flame sconces accented grey stone walls. In the middle stood an elevated square bed with an open canopy, curtained at the posts in gauzy silver sheets.

The pilot from Sara's ship pounded on the suite's door. Rainer's chest tightened each time David Anlow's fist made contact with the metal. He was certain the door would eventually give under the Armadan's blows.

"Just think if we hadn't switched off their aggressor genes," the Sovereign said. "We'd likely be governed by our own military."

Since when did Simon Prollixer worry about losing power? His unnatural longevity and lack of interest in breeding separated him from the other citizens. Now he was cursed with mortality. That brought him just a little closer to his own kind and made him a little more dangerous; he finally had something to lose.

The shot switched to Sara. Rainer forced his fists not to ball as Sara touched the Armadan. He held his composure, knowing the Sovereign's gaze was as much on him as the people on the screen. It was an exercise in self-control for Rainer as Sara smoothed one of David's eyebrows while they chatted. He rested his hand on her knee, then moved it the entire way up her body. When they kissed, Rainer wanted to smash the viewing console.

His six amours engaged in this type of intimacy with other men on a regular basis, but Sara wasn't his amour and could never be if he wanted to maintain a pure line. She was never to be had by him. Yet he couldn't stop others from being with her. He had no control over her, nor his emotions concerning her, and that enraged him.

The screen showed Sara pull away from the kiss and look around wildly. Her behavior changed to that of a crazed person, stumbling to the floor, crawling around. The Armadan struggled as well.

"You drugged them," Rainer said.

Sara punched at the stone wall, and Rainer flinched, feeling her pain.

"She obviously had a bad reaction. The drug affects every person differently." Prollixer's matter-of-fact tone almost pushed Rainer too far. He gripped a handle on his cender, then forced his fingers away from the pistol.

On the screen, David Anlow sprung at the green-haired contractor standing in the room with them now. The Armadan lifted him off his feet, then hurled him at two other contractors. Rainer was unnerved by the larger man's strength, but not as much as seeing Sara fight off her attacker.

Prollixer had hoped to get his information, then dispose of them both. Drugged out of their minds, they would make easy prey, only the Sovereign hadn't counted on Sara's resistance to the dosing. Rainer knew how Faya had used more drugs than she had license to and what that did to Sara. He tried to forget he never stepped in to stop it.

The image switched to a voyeur view of a large hall decorated in the same grey stone and hot pink flames. Sara grabbed a woman who resembled Faya, but even at this distance, Rainer could tell it wasn't her.

From another angle, David argued with a guard until he opened the airlock doors, allowing Sara and him to escape. The viewer went blank and a dim light returned to the chamber.

"Why not finish it, even with a voyeur present?" Rainer asked. "You've already suppressed this from the Media with your delay protocol." No one else in the entire system could stop a live feed to the Media. And, no one knew the Sovereign could either.

"Because the ambasadoras represent the smiling, gentle aspect of the Embassy. I gave them to the masses so they could ignore the ugly resentments the fraggers have stirred up about my government. I can't take that away right now." He coughed, a rattling from down deep in his chest.

Recovering, he continued, "I need to release edited bits of this recording when it is most advantageous. It'll accompany an official response saying that fraggers attempted an assault while the ambasadora was coupling with her new pilot. David Anlow's fragger colleagues will see him compromised by an agent of the Embassy, putting his own carnal entertainment above the security of his organization. His loyalty will be questioned. Some of his constituents may even turn on him. That will make him reactive, prone to mistakes."

Even with the intel suggesting that an Armadan aboard the *Bard* was the fragger operative, Rainer could see that David Anlow was not the man Prollixer wanted. Nothing about his personality, his actions, his background pointed to involvement. Rainer knew it because he didn't have a hunch about the Armadan like he did about Phoebe Llewellyn.

"Don't you think it will make good viewing for the citizenry? This drama will get massive air time; such predictable Upper Caste behavior. Physical cues are so deeply ingrained in this society that actions and reactions are automatic, like androids programmed for coupling."

Rainer disagreed. Prollixer was the one becoming an automaton, single-minded in his obsession for a longer life.

"It's all those classes to make them aware of every signal, every gesture, both conscious and subconscious. But isn't that what everyone wanted, better gene stock?"

He noted how the Sovereign spoke of *them*, separating himself from society and its tenets. Maybe he needed to brush up on his History, remember what happened on the worldships and why all citizens, both Uppers and Lowers upheld the tradition of selective marriage. Or, maybe once the fragger threat was quelled, the Sovereign just needed to be dethroned.

TWENTY-FIVE

The small stream of water *whooshing* from the faucet thundered into the drain like a flash flood through Palomin Canyon. Somehow in last night's confusion, Sean had left the bathroom faucet on. He hadn't noticed it until about an hour ago when his full bladder forced him in and out of sleep.

He should have just gotten up, but Sara was lying on his arm.

Her shallow breath brushed against his hand. He barely felt it as his arm's circulation dwindled, but he couldn't bear to disturb her. Most of the night she'd slid in and out of the real, until he lay down with her. She whimpered a few times after that, but settled back down with a few coaxing words. For Sean, it was the best sleep he had had in years. He hated for it to end.

Sara shifted. He tried to slide his arm out, dreading the inevitable discomfort of blood flowing back into his limb. The action woke her. She rolled over and looked at him, her sleepy gaze not quite focusing as she touched hesitant fingers to his cheek.

He eased his arm from under her, feeling a bit awkward. She looked confused, as though searching her memory to find out how she ended up here. He held up a finger for her to wait a minute and sprinted to the bathroom. Once again he scanned her vitals with his reporter as he had done several times last night. Her heart rate and respiration were normal, but large amounts of chemical dosers still lingered in her system. He wanted to study the compounds to see if it was an Embassy brew or something designer.

Catching a glimpse of himself in the mirror above the sink made him self-conscious. Dark blonde tufts of his short hair stuck out at odd angles, and he hadn't shaved in weeks. A bruise hid near his lip, but the one blossoming above his right eye had nowhere to hide. He splashed water over his face and hair, but it did little good. He told himself it didn't matter anyway, that he'd let an emotional fallacy get the best of him last night. It was time he really woke up. She was here to spy on him, maybe kill him, whether she knew it yet or not.

He returned, a healthy chip on his shoulder.

Sara sat on the edge of the bed and smoothed her wrinkled dress and fingered the strap that had broken during one of her fits. She looked at him, her pupils still a little too large. Sean kept a safe distance. So she couldn't launch another attack, he told himself.

She ran her fingers through her hair. He could still feel the softness of it on his own fingertips. He shook off the memory. "How are you feeling?" he asked.

She didn't respond, just stared. It was taking her a while to come out of this.

"Sara?"

"I don't know," she finally said.

"Fair enough." What did he expect her to say?

"I'm going to make some tea. It will help." The stronger, the better. "The bathroom's right there if you need it." He looked around for a minute, wondering if there was anything else he should say, decided there wasn't and left.

As he rounded the hallway toward the kitchen, a fragger transmission whirred into his mind—mandatory briefing in three minutes. Standard invite was at least thirty. Something was up.

He grabbed a glass container of tea and added boiling water from the spigot. He'd have to get rid of Sara if he were going to respond to the invite. She would probably need a little time to recover this morning, though, so he shouldn't push her out if she wasn't ready to leave yet. He'd just say he wasn't near an insertion point. This was dangerous thinking. It wasn't so much that he was skipping out on the fragger invite, it was that he'd never done it before.

Sara walked into the kitchen, her hair falling over her shoulder in a long ponytail and her arms wrapped around her. She looked lucid, but her skin tone was a little paler, closer to Sean's.

He poured the tea into his last two clean mugs and handed her one.

She took a sip without looking at him. "Thank you for helping me last night…though I'm not sure I wanted anyone to see me like that."

"It was no problem. No one else needs to know." He took a drink and hit the mug against his busted lip. He pulled his head back in reflex.

Sara caught the movement. She studied his face for the first time. Self-conscious, he stepped away, but her hand on his forearm stopped him. "Did I do that to you?"

"Don't worry about it. I've had worse, though you are surprisingly strong." He attempted a smile, but it became a wince as his lip split open a little further.

She brushed her thumb over it as though she could heal it with her touch, and Sean almost swore she could. Her hand caressed his cheek, moving to his brow line. He closed his eyes as she traced the bruise there and trailed her light touch to the little cut near his hairline. He would have let her beat him senseless last night just to have her touch him like this a little longer.

"I'm so sorry." Her voice broke. "After everything you did for me."

Another whirring reminder entered Sean's mind. He ignored it.

"It's nothing. Really. An hour or two wearing mender patches and it'll be fine." Sean had never used menders because he couldn't see the need. Stuff healed eventually. Until then, it kept everyone wondering. But if seeing him like this reminded her of last night, he'd consider plastering a couple on.

"What else did I do?"

She didn't need him to replay the terrible night for her, especially if she was lucky enough to have forgotten most of it.

"You had some bad dreams."

"I have those even when I'm awake."

He had suspected as much, considering the intensity of her hallucinations when she showed up at his door. "We could try to overwrite those visions." He had debated mentioning this to her.

"I didn't know that was possible." She held the mug between both hands and drank the tea.

"It can be done. It's risky. Takes some serious dosing. Nothing I have on hand." He should just let her go. It was her problem, not his. "I could take you to a place if you want. I'd make sure you were safe." What the hell was he doing?

A spark of hope lit her eyes. "I'll go."

He hadn't expected her eagerness. It made him feel good that he could help her. "I'll set it up and let you know." Then, "Do you want something to eat? I don't really have anything here, but there's probably something left in the main kitchen."

"I think tea's all I'll have for a while. Can I take the mug with me?"

"Sure. It came with the suite."

Sara put the tea down and wrapped her arms around him in a weary hug and kissed his cheek. "Thank you, Sean," she whispered against his shirt. "Thank you for not leaving me."

He squeezed her a little tighter. She didn't know how easy it had been for him to stay.

Sean's ears popped as he slipped into the V-side. While Zak stood upon the metallic raft, three deep blue, watery spheres rose to greet him. All were of fragger source and all were pulsing with immediacy. He checked the hosts for each. An all-call and one from Ariel—why wasn't she at the all-call? And a closed invite from Ephemerata, one of the bosses.

He reached for that one.

The portal delivered him to an oceanside cliff. He looked over the edge into the rolling surf hundreds of meters below.

"Don't stare too long. You really will jump."

He turned around to see Ephemerata floating above him. Her violet wings changed from opaque to translucent with each contraction. The black skin of her bare body had a blinding sheen and contrasted with the silver strands of hair that fell over her shoulders. Not a bad av for a boss.

"Zak, you know about the intel dump." Her voice sounded like the higher octaves of a synth spider.

"Yes."

"Do you know that the source of the dump has been located?"

"No." Maybe that was the reason for the urgent all-call.

"It was brought in on a carrier wave from a ship. The *Bard*."

Zak showed no expression and remained silent as he called up the disconnect. He could make it look like a lost signal or a bad lag.

"You're locked in, Sean Cryer."

Acid churned in Zak's virtual stomach, but Sean felt its effects back in his suite.

She knew his real name.

Thoughts of Bullseye writhing in his lonely death panicked him.

"You can eliminate me, but that won't help you with the dump. I didn't put it there." He needed to stall until he could access a safety disconnect he had programmed for himself after Bullseye's wrongful elimination.

"I know. That's why I called you here privately. Don't go to the all-call. It's your trial and execution. Even with your blind safeguards, you'll never be able to pull out in time."

He was in it worse than he thought.

"Do the other bosses know who I really am?"

"You know the answer to that, Sean. We may be a loose confederacy of anarchists, but leadership still has its privileges. How else do you think I could bring you here without the others knowing?"

Sean stared at the roundness of her dark breasts without really seeing them. "I'll be marked now, have to go through an ident-change, reconstruction, the works. Not sure it's worth it."

Jumping into that turbulent, white sea was more appealing than ever. On his terms. That's how he'd go out.

"No. I can help—" Ephemerata's body jerked and her wings beat out of sync. "I'm needed at the all-call. I will give you what you need tomorrow on Tampa Three. Your ambasadora is scheduled to attend the Tertian Verdant Gala at the Tredificio. Everyone on your ship will be invited. Accept that invitation."

In plain sight. He didn't know how much he liked that. This could still be some kind of a set up.

"Be safe, Sean Cryer. Right now you are my biggest asset."

With a flutter of wings, she zipped into the air and was gone.

TWENTY-SIX

I hate these things.

David tried not to squirm in the bone mender encircling his ankle. He hadn't even realized his ankle had snapped during the scuffle with the contractors until the stims wore off. Sean would go into a tirade about David's hypocrisy if he ever found out David resorted to a dosing patch. It was an old habit from his military days—carrying an emergency patch, not dosing, though many troopers fell prey to the latter. The tickle/burn of the mender was irritating, but he lived with it often during his military training and once during a combat mission. By tomorrow he should be rid of the contraption.

He wondered if Sara had sustained any injuries. And what she remembered about their time in that room together. He needed her to understand it was the drugs and not him, that half of the time he thought she was Mari. It was the other half of the time when he knew exactly whose leg he was touching that made him feel like shit. But, no one, specifically Mari, would have to know otherwise.

He'd tried Sara's door several times that night and got no reply. Soli said he should check Sean's room, but David wasn't in the mood for jokes. Sara was definitely more than she seemed, and he was getting tired of being polite just because she was an Embassy diplomat. He suspected some of his anger came from his own behavior, but not all of it.

    The comm chimed. "There's a response coming in from your rant," Geir told David. He was trying to learn as many of the ship's systems as he could, whether out of true interest or sheer boredom, David didn't know, but he appreciated him taking the initiative.

    "It's from the Sovereign's office." Geir called up the transmission to display on the bridge's large air screen.

    Finally. All night David sent messages to Nanga Ki. When Venture pawned off the *complication* on the Embassy, claiming no jurisdiction over ambasadora affairs, David sent an alert directly to the Sovereign's office. He'd received the bureaucratic piss-off several times, but persistence had resulted in the current response. And it had only taken six hours.

    The lights automatically dimmed when the air screen animated. A woman with chestnut hair and wearing a grey suit appeared. *"Please hold for the Sovereign."*

    Geir looked at David. "Did she just say the Sovereign?"

    David stared at the screen, trying to recall the exact words in his messages. He regretted a few of his more creative threats.

    The screen blinked, revealing Sovereign Prollixer. At this resolution, David took back his earlier opinion that the man looked only ten years older than he. It was more like twenty or thirty. Forgetting his injury, David attempted to stand at attention. A shrill alarm sounded from the bone mender until he shifted the weight to his other leg.

    "Sovereign, I didn't expect a personal reply."

    "This is a sensitive matter, Navigational Leader Anlow. Your behavior at Nanga Ki was appalling, becoming intoxicated, brawling with contractors, seducing a woman I entrusted to your care. To commit such disgraceful acts, I wonder if you have a personal vendetta against the Embassy? Or is it against me?"

    David felt like he had stepped into an interrogation. Shock made him stumble over his words. "That's…not what happened. We were drugged and held against our will by Bakkin Venture. That's why I contacted the authorities."

"Those are some serious accusations, completely counter to the ones Major Supervisor Venture leveled against you. Perhaps I should speak with Ambasadora Mendoza to find the truth. She is safe, isn't she? I've attempted communication with her several times since the incident, but have received no responses."

"I imagine she's a little shaken up—"

"You don't know?"

David's jaw set. "She was fine when we boarded so I felt it my first priority to notify the authorities about the attempt on our lives."

"So the accusations are getting worse? Filing false testimony against another Upper Caste citizen is a punishable offense. It could shorten your life span significantly."

The acid in the Sovereign's last words loosened David's tongue. "Tell that to Venture. As a former Armadan captain, I stand by my word. I believe Venture planned the entire incident on Nanga Ki to gain favor, trying to put us in jeopardy so he could take credit for our *rescue*. But the voyeurs tell a different story. If you want to see the truth, it should be splashed all over the Media." Though David had yet to see a snippet of it this morning.

The Sovereign's tone hardened. *"Unfortunately, I've had to blacklist the event. It will never be reported in order to spare Ambasadora Mendoza the shame."*

David fell silent. He'd always heard even the Embassy couldn't inhibit the free flow of the Media. It was illegal. Obviously Sovereign Prollixer ruled above legality.

"Perhaps there was a misunderstanding on both sides." The Sovereign eased into a diplomatic tone. "I believe it best that we all just put the incident behind us. You and those aboard your ship should go about your normal affairs and speak to no one about Nanga Ki. We don't want any unfortunate consequences as a result of gossip, wouldn't you agree?"

The threat landed hard. "Yes, sir. I would agree."

The Sovereign's expression was unreadable while he considered the sincerity of David's response. *"Very well. As a gesture of good will and to allay any rumors that may have crept out about last night, you will all be expected to attend tomorrow's Tertian Verdant Gala at the Tredificio. You understand this is not a request."*

"Understood."

"Please give Ambasadora Mendoza my regards and ask her to contact me as soon as she's feeling better."

The airscreen went dormant.

"What was all of that about?" Geir asked.

"I'm not even sure, but it definitely has something to do with Sara."

"I guess that makes Sean right."

"I guess so," David said. He hated to admit it, but Sean had been the smart one by staying away from Sara.

TWENTY-SEVEN

"You're an idiot." Sara said the words once the airscreen blinked off and she was sure Simon couldn't hear her.

Nanga Ki had been a debacle. Sara knew for certain now that David Anlow wasn't the man Simon was looking for, but he was too blind to see it. She considered offering the possibility that Geir might be a fragger, but only because he was the only other Armadan aboard. That would be a waste of time, too. She couldn't imagine the gentle scientist as an anti-government agitator, capable of killing. Simon was running out of options. *She* was running out of options. If she didn't produce results soon, Simon would make good on his threats.

The door's chime broke into Sara's lamenting thoughts. She checked the time. Soli was early. She promised to help Sara with the eyehooks on her bodice. Tapping her door lock on her palm, Sara moved through the living room to meet Soli in the foyer.

"Come in." She tripped over the short emerald green train on the back of her gown and heard a little tear. "Figures. I am not in the mood for this." She pulled the train around front as best she could and searched for the rip with one hand while she held the unfastened bustier against her breasts with the other. "Soli, I think I'm going to change."

"I think that would be a mistake because you look really good."

Sara's head snapped up. Sean stood in the room wearing a formal blue shirt with its first two buttons open and dark charcoal pants. The clothes weren't the biggest surprise. She couldn't help staring at his face. Clean-shaven, his defined jaw no longer hid behind stubble. The bruises from last night had disappeared. His short hair was even combed and parted to the side so a couple of dark blonde locks settled onto his forehead. And those eyes—she thought about looking into those eyes more often than she should.

Having him stare back at her now brought a flush to her skin, partially because of her half-dressed state, but more because of how he had seen her last night. "You look good, too," she said, straightening up and pressing the gown's sparkly top tighter to her chest. "I guess you take your verdant galas pretty seriously."

"I'm not even sure what one is. Has something to do with botanical gardens and plants, doesn't it?"

"Something like that. Is everyone waiting for me? I'm ready. Just waiting for Soli to help button me up."

"There's time. I came by early to take care of those scentbots before we go, but I think I can handle a few fasteners." She studied his frame in the formal clothing, enjoying how the shirt hugged his shoulders and chest just the right amount and how the pants laid flat against his narrow hips.

He caught her stare, but didn't show a response. She hesitated before turning her bared back to him. "Thanks. I got as many as I could reach."

His fingers brushed her skin as he gathered her hair to the side. Her breathing quickened. She liked his large hands and had since their first meeting when he slipped that reporter on her wrist and ran his finger over her palm. Just like then, she was now hyper-aware of each time his fingers made contact with her skin. He fastened the small hooks one by one with a nimbleness probably honed from working with small pieces of tech and engine parts. No doubt his work left some of those scrapes and scratches on his knuckles. As he worked his way up her back, the bodice tightened against her breasts. She fantasized about him unfastening each one of the hooks he had just fastened, but a little more slowly, then peeling the gown away from her body.

"I think I got them all." His voice broke into her daydream. When he spoke, she felt the lightness of his breath on the back of her neck. She shivered, tattling on herself. His fingers lingered on her shoulders, like he wasn't ready to step away from her yet. He moved around to face her, standing so close, his jaw nearly brushed her forehead. He ran his middle finger over the skin just below her right ear. Her breathing nearly stopped.

"Is your port on this side?" he asked. The low timbre of his voice in her ear sent more chills down her spine.

"Yes." She tried to sound casual, but her bio-lights said otherwise, and he noticed. She caught him watching their quickening pulse.

"Nervous?" he asked.

"Yes. I don't like public appearances." What she did like was when the fabric of his shirt pressed against her dress.

"I avoid them myself." He removed the small patch with a metal pin. "But isn't that all part of being an ambasadora?"

"I suppose so." She breathed in his clean, earthy scent and had to stop herself from reaching out to touch him.

He stepped back to pull a small case from his pocket and showed her three small patches inside. "I wasn't sure what you wanted."

"Do you have a favorite?" she asked.

"There's one I thought you might like." He pulled the middle patch out and snapped the case shut, then put it back in his pocket. She looked at the small patch resting on his fingertip. "It's not flower-based," he said. "Comes from the Lalido tree."

"What made you choose this one?" She was flattered he had put some thought into a scent for her.

"My brother and I climbed the Lalido trees in front of our house when I was a kid. He showed me once how its clear sap turns deep violet when the tree is agitated. It reminded me of someone." He smiled like he wasn't used to the gesture coming so spontaneously.

"I guess you probably had quite a light show last night." She couldn't avoid talking about what happened.

"At times." He nudged her head to the side. "How are you feeling now?"

"Tired, but slides will do that, I guess."

He murmured in agreement as he inserted the new patch. "If you ever want to talk about anything, including your torture—"

She almost twisted away, but he held a finger to her neck. "Not done yet."

"Why would you mention torture?" She worked hard to sound like the idea was absurd.

"Because it's what happened to you." His words sounded pained.

Sara stared at the mosaic of white tiles on the floor and fought the urge to just collapse. Who knew what she had said last night in her delirium? After all of Sean's kindness, she may have put him in jeopardy. And this was different than charming David for information. David was a trained warrior who more than handled himself when she led him straight into danger. But, Sean...he was an innocent, a Socialite mech tech whose biggest fault was dosing.

A sweet, heady smell drifted in on the silence.

"There," he said. "What do you think?"

She couldn't look at him. "It's a good choice."

"Maybe I shouldn't have brought up all of that. What happened to you is your business." He touched her arm as he spoke. "I just want you to know I'll help you if I can."

She forced herself to face him. He deserved that much. The sincerity of his expression broke her. She leaned into him and brushed her lips against his. Just a hesitant little kiss, in the hopes that he wouldn't pull away. He wrapped his arms around her waist and returned the kiss just as gently. She swept her fingers up the back of his neck into his hair line. He hugged her closer and his mouth responded with more pressure. When she felt the tip of his tongue trace her bottom lip, she opened her mouth a little wider. He took the invitation. For once, she forgot her rage, forgot her fear. There was nothing in this system but their kiss.

She heard tapping on the open doorframe, and her illusion evaporated. Sara was the one to pull away.

"My apologies." Soli stood in the commonway, a silver and turquoise sarong hugging her curves. "I would have waited, but you didn't look like you were coming out of that kiss any time soon."

Sean ran a hand over the back of his neck where her fingers had been and cleared his throat.

"I take it you don't need my help now," Soli said.

"No. Sean took care of it," Sara said.

"I noticed." Soli was enjoying their discomfort. "You both look wonderful." She gave Sean an extra long appraisal. "The transport's waiting."

Sean ushered Sara through the door after Soli, then slid his hand into hers until they reached the top of the stairs. This innocent gesture felt more intimate than their kiss. After all, what they shared last night meant more to Sara than any tumble ever could…or did.

When the three of them entered the grey interior of the transport, all conversation stopped and everyone's gaze was riveted on Sean.

"Who's this guy?" Geir asked.

"Funny." Sean didn't look amused.

"I always said he would clean up well," Soli said. "He just needed the proper motivation." She looked at Sara.

"Still a little more cleaning to do, if you ask me, and you're missing half your suit," Kenon said.

"I think Kenon's jealous that he might not be the prettiest guy on board anymore," Mari said.

David's head snapped around from the pilot's seat. Mari put her hand on his knee and gave him a knowing smile. The others pretended not to notice.

"Those jackets look stupid," Sean said.

"You just have to know how to wear them," Kenon said.

Geir laughed. "I may take mine off before we reach the monorail station. But, seriously, Sean, in the three years I've known you, I've never seen you so shiny and polished. It's because of a woman, isn't it?"

Sean ignored them all and took a seat between Sara and Soli.

"Someone you're meeting tonight, I'm betting," Geir persisted.

Sara's stomach twisted. She hadn't considered Sean might be involved with someone. Their kiss suddenly made her feel foolish. She should be beyond these kinds of emotional fallacies. They had her imagining a future with a man she barely knew. Worse, they had her imagining a future at all. As the group continued teasing Sean and making predictions about the woman who waited for him at the Tredificio, Sara regained sight of why she was there in the first place and what she needed to do in order to save herself.

She couldn't be upset with Sean. He was just a kind person who helped her when she needed it. Shame on her for reading too much into his gesture.

TWENTY-EIGHT

The tinkling melody filtering through the monorail made Sean want to scream. It had taken forever to transfer from the *Bard*'s transport to the monorail station and even longer to wait for an available train. He should have brought an extra doser with him. Maybe it would have helped to stave off his sudden irritability.

When Kenon started to hum to the saccharine tune, Sean couldn't take it. "Why do they even make music like this? Nobody listens to it except when they're trapped in one of these things."

"I think it's pretty catchy." Kenon hummed louder, now that he knew it bothered Sean.

Sara's kiss was to blame for Sean's current mood, or rather, how that small gesture had made him feel.

He had to remind himself that *she* felt nothing for *him*, despite the kiss, which he kept replaying in his head until he thought he would go crazy. When he wasn't thinking about the kiss, he thought about her breasts nearly spilling out of the dress when he walked in and the control he exerted fastening each one of those little hooks. Thoughts of where that kiss could have led bombarded him until he could think of nothing else. That's why he chose a seat as far from her as possible during this ride, not that she had spoken to him while in the transport. In fact, she hadn't looked at him, even with their shoulders and thighs brushing against each other during the trip. Had he done something to upset her? It shouldn't matter. He never thought this much about a woman. It worried him.

Paranoia was setting in, but Sean welcomed it this time; it helped him to remember his earlier meeting with Ephemerata in the V-side and focus on who or what might be waiting for him at the Tredificio.

"That is beautiful." Mari drew Sean's attention to the opposite side of the transport. The polarized window showed the pink setting sun falling behind three glass pyramids suspended above a waterfall.

"The Tredificio is the only reason to come to Tampa Three," Kenon said. "They should just move it to Tampa Quad."

"Tampa Quad isn't so great," Mari said.

"You tell yourself that because you didn't grow up there."

"At least I *grew up*."

Sean tuned out the snarky comments they volleyed back and forth and watched the three buildings draw closer. He wondered why no one had ever thought to map this place and go virtual. The waterfall would cause some challenges, but techs liked challenges. Maybe some architect had already done a mock up, and Sean just hadn't run into it yet.

The three ziggurat-type buildings which made up the Tredificio cascaded down nine levels that were connected by covered walkways. With the sun dipping behind the horizon, the illuminated walkways glowed brightly. Magenta and purple hues at the top descended the spectrum into blues and greens at the base.

"Now those are viewers! They must have a different Media channel showing on every cantilever," Geir said.

All Sean could see were blurry images flickering on the cantilever faces. Less than perfect eyesight was a deficit inherited from his Lower Caste mother, but in the V-side he could compensate.

"What is that?" Mari asked, as they neared the transport monorail station. "David?"

Sean could see it now. Splashed nineteen meters high across the third cantilever face was a vid of David and Sara in a lavish bedroom. They all watched as David slid her dress up her thigh. It cut to a different angle, showing him pulling her straps off her shoulders, then nuzzling her neck.

Sean's irritability reached the teeth-crunching point. He stole a glance at Sara, but she stared at the viewer. Shock registered on her face first, then anger.

"That never happened," David protested.

"So you were never in that room together?" Mari looked like she might cry.

Sean never wanted to hit David more than he did right now.

"That's the room they kept us in, but there wasn't time for any of...*that* before they drugged us," David said.

"You were taking drugs, too?" Kenon asked.

"We *were* drugged. By someone else. And attacked by contractors," David said.

This bit of information gave Sean pause. Sara never mentioned it to him. Of course she was sliding out of her mind the whole night, so why would she? Especially if this was part of a set up by the Embassy. It was still hard for Sean to watch, though not as hard as it was for Mari.

"David's telling the truth, Mari." Sara's voice was calm, almost detached, even under Mari's accusing stare.

The transport zipped by, but the passengers picked up the Media action on the next building, sixth level up this time. David's shirt was gone, so was Sara's dress. Her bare back faced the camera as David lowered her to the bed.

"Is this where the contractors come in?" Kenon asked.

David stared him down, but spoke to Mari. "None of this happened."

Another image showed a tight shot of Sara's head on a pillow, then David leaning in and kissing her.

"Well, most of it didn't happen," David muttered.

Sean didn't like the sound of that. His imagination got the best of him, especially as the scene continued with flashes of skin. Mari looked away. Sean couldn't, so he was thankful that the monorail passed under the viewer as the vid started to get more graphic.

"It figures," Kenon said. "Right as we were getting to the good part." He scanned the next grouping of cantilevers. "Maybe it's on one of these."

"The whole thing is a lie," Sara said.

"Pretty hard to fool a voyeur," Soli said.

Sean tried to keep quiet, but never did have much control over his mouth. "She's right."

"Soli?" Geir asked.

"Sara's right." He glanced at her. "Those shots have been mixed and painted, probably reshot in sections with stand-ins or a compilation of digital images."

"How do you know?" Mari asked, a little hope entering her voice.

The real answer was because after spending the night taking care of Sara, watching her, and holding her in his arms, he knew her body. Instead, he gave them the technical version.

"For one thing, her dress is wrong. Sara's had deeper cleavage." Or, maybe it was Sara who had the deeper cleavage.

"They botched the bio-lights on her right shoulder blade—the pattern's not even close." He had stared at that particular swirl of lights so much he could map every little purple dot by memory.

"Her hair is shinier and softer." How he could know about the softness of her hair from just a vid? He hurried on.

"And, the arch of her body is all wrong." He remembered the feel of her curled up next to him, every slope and angle. "Sara's curves outward slightly from her waist to her hips, and her waist is a lot smaller than that. Plus, she has matching dimples just above her...." He should probably stop there. "On her lower back."

The train car was silent, except for the cheery music. The surprised stares said that he had revealed too much, implying more of an intimacy than he intended.

"You have to be kidding me." Kenon nearly sputtered in outrage. "Of all the people...."

Geir slapped a stunned David in the chest and said, "I guess he won't be filing anymore petitions with the Embassy."

Sean had definitely said too much and was worried he had betrayed Sara's confidence or painted a picture as false as the vid playing over the Media. He chanced a look at her, expecting to see disappointment or anger. He noticed his words brought a blush to her cheeks where even the vid hadn't.

Kenon was beside himself. He asked, "Why, Sara? Why him?"

The others waited for her to respond. Sean tried to think of a way to explain how he knew such personal details without compromising more of Sara's trust. He could say he had been watching her without her knowing it. He'd look like a pervert, but at least they wouldn't think Sara docked him right after meeting him. He could bare their judgement to protect her image. It's not like he cared much about his reputation anyway. He was about to bite the bullet when Sara simply shrugged and said, "He's sexy."

If Sean had a blush reflex, it would have burned through his skin. As it was, he couldn't hide the smile tugging at the corner of his mouth. Maybe that kiss did mean something to her, too.

As the train decelerated into the station, Geir said, "I told you he cleaned himself up for a woman."

Festive trills announced the group's arrival among a mob of extravagantly dressed Uppers, all clamoring to talk with Sara up ahead. Sean moved against the throng with David and Mari, who were in a full blown argument.

"Mari, that wasn't real. You know that, right? Sean proved it."

"Maybe it just proves Sara's working her way through every man on the ship," Mari said.

"She's not like that," Sean snapped out. He wanted to explain how innocent her time with him had been, but Mari pressed on.

"You're delusional, Sean. If a voyeur records it, the Media will air it. That's why they're so effective. They capture it all. Just look around."

He had counted six voyeurs since they disembarked and was trying to avoid direct eye contact with all the flying spies. It was the Embassy's way of saying once you entered public domain, you forfeited your privacy. He also suspected they could manipulate and suppress the *live* feeds for their own purposes—the incident with Sara and David proved it.

Kenon and Geir eddied out of the crowd in front of them.

"How do they expect us to be seen in a crowd this large?" Kenon asked.

Though Sean didn't like being smashed against so many people, he did welcome its temporary anonymity.

"There's a Media kiosk. I'm going to talk to somebody about that broadcast." David hesitated and looked at Mari, then pushed toward the kiosk a few meters away.

Geir put an arm around Mari and gave her a quick kiss to the side of her head. "Don't worry. David's crazy about you. We all see it."

Kenon leaned in. "Though everyone likes to sample something new now and then."

"Leave it alone, Kenon," Sean said. "You're just pissed because Giselle's taking an Armadan amour."

"An Armadan in *your* family circle?" Geir started into one of his loud, bellowing laughs.

Kenon balked. "Nothing's official yet."

Geir took Mari's arm and guided her toward the welcoming center. "You got nothing to worry about with David. Trust me."

Trust. One virtue Sean had a hard time finding in this system.

Several attendants from the welcoming center rushed at the new arrivals to upload v-maps of the Tredificio into the guests' wrist reporters. Sean could barely hear the brunette woman spieling to him about the Tredificio's amenities as she competed with a barrage of synth spiders playing around them. He walked away from the attendant mid-sentence, scanning the mass of people for Sara.

She was surrounded by clinging Socialites, and Soli was right in the middle of it all, acting as Sara's personal liaison and smiling pretty for the voyeurs hovering overhead. She looked more comfortable with the attention than Sara did.

A woman strolled up beside him and took his arm. "It's been a long time."

Sean looked the woman over, seeking recognition. Deep blue bangs framed her jawline but the rest of her shoulder-length hair was blonde. Her face was a homogenized combination of the usual Socialite features. He breathed in her citrusy scent, but still no memories came.

"Don't tell me you forgot about me already. Our friend, Zak, would be so disappointed."

It was then he noticed the mayfly hologram pin at the bottom of her cleavage. The wings fluttered.

"Our last meeting was kind of ephemeral," he said, testing his theory.

She put her hand over his ear and kissed him on the cheek. A puff of air blasted into his ear. He flinched.

"We have a subvocal connection now through this cocom." He heard her voice inside his head, but her lips never moved. The cocom devices were gaining popularity among the fraggers, but Sean thought using one was a good way to mark yourself as a criminal. Guess he no longer had a choice.

"Call me Phoebe and act like you're happy to be catching up on old times." What she vocalized for everyone else was, "I bet I could find a way to help you remember."

"I don't think we've met." Sara stood at Sean's elbow with Soli.

He looked only at Sara as he introduced the women. It felt awkward using her full title. Distancing. He didn't like it.

"Nice to meet you." Sara gave Phoebe's hand a pulse, then slipped her hand into Sean's. The subtle show of possessiveness sent little electric sparks through his fingertips.

"You're quite friendly with the ambasadora."

"She's just a passenger on my ship." The subvocal conversing was giving him a headache, or maybe it was just the new implant.

"Your body language tells me otherwise. You're worried about how she's responding to our implied intimacy."

Sean didn't say anything.

"Sara, there's someone you have to meet." Soli called to a friend.

Sara looked from Sean to Phoebe once more. "I'll see you at dinner, Sean?" She kissed his cheek.

"Sure." He squeezed her hand before letting go.

Phoebe said her farewell pleasantries to Sara as she reproached Sean. *"She's dangerous. I received the same background check on her that you did. She was trained as a contractor and most likely sent to eliminate you."*

"I considered that. I have it under control."

Sean watched Sara walk away.

"I'd say she has you under control."

"I said I—"

Phoebe cut him off. "Do you have a dance for an old tumble?" She took Sean by the arm and led him through an entryway to a large elevated platform.

Numerous couples held each other close and softly swayed around a darkened dance floor. Sean hesitated when he spotted the turquoise beams of mind minstrels scanning the dancers. It was bad enough citizens fell over themselves to have a voyeur record their actions and opinions for Media broadcast, but now the Embassy had taken transparency a step further by stealing a fragger interrogation technology and repurposing it to read a person's thoughts and emotions.

Not *actual* thoughts, not even the tech geniuses among the fragger organization could do that…yet. Rather, these thin floating parallelograms scanned a target to read their brain waves. Depending on what center of the brain was most active, they could interpret emotion, mood, and bits of memory, occasionally a word or two if the person saw words spelled out in his head. The odd result had been a tonal feedback that resulted in almost musical patterns. As a joke, someone worked up a randomizing program which assigned notes to certain data as it came in, then played the results back as musical entertainment, sometimes with lyrics snatched from bits of dialog.

One of the small devices hovered above a kissing couple to their right. Its beat became sultry and loud as the couple groped one another. The mind minstrel drew on their energy. Its rhythm followed the sway of their hips and the pounding of their hearts. A low female voice sang out of the energy amps, *"I'm waiting for you…to touch me."* A voyeur broadcast the dance and music across the Media, much to the couple's delight.

Sean steered clear of the area. He didn't need his thoughts and conversation put to music. His emotions were charged and a minstrel would detect the agitation through his respiration and heart rate. It was similar to the tech he had used to monitor Sara last night, only without the musical accompaniment, though part of him admitted he would like to have a read on her emotions.

Phoebe put her arms around his neck, and they fell into a rhythm with the music. *"If docking her is your idea of controlling her then you're not as smart as I thought."*

Sean narrowed his eyes and said out loud, "Don't assume anything."

"And, don't speak out loud!" Her grip on his shoulder tightened, and he felt the bite of her nails through his shirt.

"I'm not docking her."

"That's even worse. I could accept your sexual attraction to her, but from the way you're acting, I believe you're heading into an emotional fallacy. This behavior isn't like you. I've studied all of your training, your

anti-social and anti-Embassy attitudes, and I vouched for you personally. You had no interest in the Socialite scene, but now you'd let some Embassy bitch play you for a fool because she makes your pants a little tighter? Eliminate her. Make it look like an accident."

Sean crushed Phoebe's hand and grabbed the back of her neck to force her ear to his mouth. "You may have watched some vids and read some reports about me, but you have no idea who I am. And, I don't know you. There are very few people in this system I trust. You're not one of them."

She put her head on his shoulder to force an illusion of intimacy. *"You don't have a choice, Sean. The fragger bosses have splintered and that will soon trickle down the ranks. I have a way to hold the organization together."*

"How do I know any of this is true?"

"I know what the intel dump is and where it's hidden."

Sean stood still. "You know?"

She shot him a warning look about speaking out loud.

"You're involved?" Rage welled inside of him. *"I killed one of my own men because the bosses told me he was responsible. That's what trust got me."*

"It wasn't me who gave those orders. There are some of us who still want to bring down the Sovereign, end his illegal take-over. I believe your ideology matches ours, otherwise I wouldn't waste my time."

"Then tell me what's in the dump."

"The cure for Prollixer's curse. Patch codes for his cell sweepers."

Sean's mind raced with the implications. The idea of a doubled or tripled life span or the myth of eternal life sounded like society's ultimate dream, but the insanity that accompanied those with such an unnatural longevity would become a nightmare of world proportions. *"Who figured out the patches?"*

"An Embassy tech team, one of whom was a fragger operative. They needed test subjects, so injected cell sweepers into volunteer Armadan troopers."

"Not contractors?"

"Contractors aren't as loyal as they pretend to be. Armadans are bound by a higher sense of duty to the Embassy, no matter who's in charge."

"What happened to them?"

"Our man smuggled the patches into the V-side and destroyed the originals before they could be treated. The risks of repairing their bots were too high. The Embassy could use their DNA to reconstruct the patch codes."

So the Armadan volunteers were dying like Prollixer, and experiencing the same type of dementia.

"Where is the dump?" Sean asked.

"Later. We've been together too long and starting to draw attention. Meet back here tonight after dinner." Phoebe pulled away from him as a turquoise beam of light approached.

TWENTY-NINE

"I hope no one gets motion sick." Sara looked at the floating tables. The slightly scooped hot pink and green platforms were reminiscent of giant water lilies, the pedestal table standing at the center like an azure stamen. Hundreds of real lily pads floated around them in the huge inset pool, their blooms matching those of the dining platforms. The air was awash in flowery notes.

"Welcome to the Aqua Biome, Ambasadora Mendoza," said their male host. He wore white flowing pants cinched with the gala's official dark green sash, but no shirt over his shapely torso. He led them to a gangplank. After a few tentative steps Sara realized there was no sway.

"Stabilizers. They'll keep your table steady as well," explained the host.

The ethereal silver glow radiating from deep in the dark pool rivaled the twilight of the blue domed ceiling.

"We have already reserved a seat for each of you at the Sovereign's request." He gestured to the leaf-shaped place settings. At the center burned three flame flowers. The flowers' pale green glow didn't travel far from the botanical source before fading into the blue twilight.

Sara's name was engraved on a large, waxy leaf resting just above the metal plate. Immediately to her right was David. "Looks like we're dining partners again," she said.

"I knew you'd be pleased." The host beamed.

"I'm sure she is." Mari took her place on David's other side, even though Soli's name was written on the placeholder. The couple seemed to have worked out their issues after the vid fiasco, no doubt thanks to Sean's intervention.

Sara recalled the way he had described her body, not just the words he used but the almost dreamy way he recollected every detail. She knew he hadn't meant to imply they'd been intimate, but what he had done for her that night was as intimate as it got. Secretly, she didn't mind the others thinking their time together had a more carnal bent, and she'd meant it when she said he was sexy. He was by far the sexiest man she had ever met, mainly because he didn't try to be.

"What's for dinner?" Geir asked.

"Probably plants," Kenon said. "This *is* a gala celebrating foliage."

"Just so it's not Maznee," David said.

"Maznee's a spice made from ground up insects, not plants," Mari said.

"I had no idea." Soli pulled a face.

Geir played on her repulsion. "Now, are they still alive when they get squished?"

"Are what alive?" Sean asked. He spoke to Geir, but looked only at Sara.

"About time you showed up," Geir said. "Some of us were worried. We're talking about the process of making Maznee."

"Exciting." Sean took his seat across the table from Sara. Though he gave her a quick smile, he looked unsettled from his reunion with the blue-haired blonde.

"You should have asked your attractive friend to join us," Kenon said. "Or do you like to keep your tumbles separate?"

Uncomfortable looks darted around the table. Sean knocked Kenon's water glass over into his lap. Kenon stammered in indignation while Geir laughed. Their host appeared with extra cloth napkins, defusing the situation. A couple of scantily-clad females maneuvered hovering trays of food and beverages. Their labor roles said all three were Lowers whose looks put them on the fringe of Upper Caste society. Some Lowers were lucky enough to become absorbed into Socialite or Armadan family circles. Ironically, it wasn't until becoming an ambasadora, a top position among Uppers, that Sara felt more of a kinship to the Lower Caste. It was the feeling of not quite understanding your place in the world, or maybe not accepting that place.

"Once your food is served," the male said, "we'll set you adrift. Should you need anything or just wish to return to the staging area, press this sensor pad." He placed a green, fist-sized object near Geir.

"Is this because I'm closest or because I look like I'll need the refresher first?" he asked.

The table floated free. Sara held her breath, but the stabilizers compensated for even the slightest tilt.

"This smells wonderful." Soli uncovered her main course. "Curried cod with a yogurt drizzle and long-grained rice."

"I hate fish," Mari said.

It became darker the closer they floated to the center of the pool. Mind minstrels and voyeurs zipped around like dragonflies above the water, waiting to prey on unsuspecting diners. Several of them immediately zipped into orbit a few meters above their party's table. From that height it would be easy to zoom in on images and amplify even subtle sounds. It left Sara feeling exposed. Sean mirrored her unease.

"The Sovereign was quite kind to set us up in *this* biome, rather than the desert or tundra." Soli nudged Kenon into agreement.

Kind? That wasn't a word Sara associated with Simon.

She and Sean shared a knowing look and she was suddenly unnerved that she had revealed so much to him during her slide. His behavior tonight with the other woman caused prickles of suspicion to worry at the back of her mind. It reminded her too much of Chen and his old business habits.

The others continued to eat while Soli went on to describe each biome in detail. Mid-way through forkfuls of cod and sips of neons, a mind minstrel descended upon the table. Sara held her breath, willing the minstrel to move on. She noticed Sean's posture tense, as well. The turquoise beam settled over Mari. A slow rhythm undulated from the light green parallelogram overhead. David smiled at Mari and the beat stuttered into triplets.

Geir bobbed his head in approval and said, "Not bad."

A burst of *"not bad"* sang out in a throaty male voice in time to the beat's bounce and was repeated over and over, drawing appraising glances from other tables. Then, the voice faded out for a few bars while a synthesized guitar played a series of high, fast chords accompanied by a low-pitched female singing ominously, *"Waiting."*

Mari blushed. Only Sara could see David slip his arm around Mari as he made a small distracting joke about the food. Sara felt for Mari. She was obviously smitten with David and couldn't see how much he cared about her.

The fem voice sang out again, this time in a haunting whisper, *"Waiting."*

The lights went out.

The crowd hushed until Geir asked, "Is *this* what she was waiting for?"

Something crashed onto the table and several more somethings splashed into the pool around them. More crashes, splashes, and screams came from the other floating dinner tables.

Emergency lights blinked on and dusted the aqua biome in an eerie grey light. A quick look around showed the source of the chaos, every voyeur and mind minstrel had fallen out of the air and landed in the water, or on top of dining tables, or even on the head of one unlucky guest.

As the stars would have it, David had taken a mind minstrel in the main course, as evidenced by the corner of rectangle peeking out from curried fish and yogurt dressing, the same yogurt dressing that dripped from most everyone at the table.

"We're going to smell like fish all night." Mari pulled the gelatinous concoction from her golden-tipped hair. "You've got a little something right there." She made a circular motion to encompass David's whole face.

"Yeah, thanks." He grabbed the napkin from her lap.

"What happened?" Soli's voice trembled.

Surprise and irritation registered on the faces of nearby diners. The rest of the biome remained muted in darkness.

Metal dishes fluttered on the table and clanged against each other. Their table pitched slightly and water lapped against the padded benches.

While the others conjectured over the situation and Soli held onto Kenon for dear life, Sara saw Sean stare into the far darkness. He glanced absently around as though listening for something. His hand shot to his ear, but he pulled it away when he caught her look.

Her stomach tightened, and it wasn't from the gentle rocking of the table. She had the same bad feeling about him that she did about Chen all those months ago at Palomin. Those suspicions at the back of her mind moved front and center.

"We need to get back to the *Bard* as soon as possible." Kenon's visage was stone. "Do you remember my concern about Nanga Ki being volcanic?"

"A dormant volcano. Liloch reassured us it was dormant." David sounded accusatory. "And, what does that have to do with our present situation?"

"Who's Liloch?" Mari asked.

A distant rumble filled the air around them.

Sara knew what Kenon was going to say even before he said it: "Because the Tredificio is built upon another *dormant* volcano."

The rumble roared over them, rattling the dome above and rippling through the pool below.

The guests' screams overpowered the rumbling quakes, localizing the chaos for the first time. Sean held onto the table's round edges with both hands.

"It's tipping," Mari yelled. "The table is tipping!"

Neons spilled. Pointy leaf plates slid. Yogurt-covered scraps of fish tumbled. The lilypad table capsized.

The cool water sucked Sean down. He kicked for the surface and emerged into a world of panicked screams from the other sixty tables. Most floated on their sides, the long stabilizers protruding from the pool in all directions like huge green knives. Geir and Mari hung onto the table and helped Kenon get a handhold. David popped up beside Sean with a struggling Soli under his arm.

"Where's Sara?" Sean asked, ignoring the oily spills of yogurt and curry sauce sliding across the surface near his face.

"I don't know. She has to be in the water still. Soli, calm down. I'll be back to help you look." David swam toward the pool's side.

"Forget about her, Sean. That e-pulse has knocked out the pruithium cell pressure regulators on the Tredificio," Ephemerata said in his ear.

Sean couldn't believe the Tertians' stupidity, using regulators to keep their volcano dormant when any tech with half a brain could rig an e-pulse strong enough to shake the whole planet. The hard part was finding an orbital craft with enough energy to prime the pulse and not leave an energy footprint.

Chaos reigned in the aqua biome. He scanned the diners splashing around in the food-filled water.

"Was it fragger origin?"

"Yes. And it was from your contingency. You'll be blamed so you have to get that data out of the V-side fa—"

"Ephemerata?" Maybe the water in his ear had short-circuited the cocom. He took the chance to call for her out loud. "Ephemerata? Phoebe?"

"They found me."

"Who? What's happening?"

"The dump is in this part of the V-side." She sent a data burst through his cocom. Sean grabbed his ear against the shrill pitch, hoping his recorder was getting it all.

"The dump has to be moved as soon as possible." Then she screamed into his mind. A terrible scream, full of fear and helplessness. He felt her ebb away, and his sense of her fell cold.

"Phoebe?" Sean yelled above the panicked din.

He spun around to a hand on his shoulder. Sara stared back at him, her dark hair plastered to her cheeks. "Everyone else make it?"

No.

Another tremor hit, longer and stronger than the others. Amidst the usual mayhem came a distinctive popping. One or two random pops at first, followed by a deafening crack. All other sounds faded, and the motion of the quake seemed to still as every eye in the aqua biome watched the great twilight dome and the splintering crack that streaked along its glassy surface.

Sean and Sara were in the middle of the pool when a quarter of the dome plowed into the water just a few meters from them. The impact sundered the dome piece, and a large portion heaved to, breaching the pool's side.

Water tugged at Sean's feet and pulled at his calves.

"It's draining," Sara said. "The bottom of the pool must have ruptured."

They fought to stay on the surface, but the whirlpool's force strengthened. Sean locked a forearm with Sara before the water sucked them down. The darkness deepened. His only light now was the faint glow of her bio-lights, and they were just dizzying specks in the swirling water. The bottom of Sara's dress wrapped around his legs in a clockwise motion.

She kicked him. He tried to see her face, but the purple sheen showed her kicking at a stabilizer just below them that was plugging half of the breach. He kicked at the support, but it was futile. The water's resistance ate at his strength. He hoped the pool emptied into the next terrace rather than the waterfall a thousand meters below. But the suction was strong, and they didn't have much air left.

Part of the support caught at the breach's edge and broke open even further. An incredible volume of water whirled to evacuate the pool, pulling the tables with it. Sean lost his hold of Sara. He clawed at the rushing water to find her, but had to close his eyes against the water's force and the swirling debris.

Several objects sliced at his skin and pummeled his legs before he was flushed through the opening and fell.

THIRTY

Hopefully the Armadan rescue protocol is still in effect.
David no sooner reached the side of the pool when debris from the fallen dome showered those already out of the water. He watched a fist-sized chunk of the thick glass strike Soli's shoulder. She tumbled over the edge and back into the chaos of the pool.

He dove down after her. With a tight arm around her waist, he made for the surface. She didn't struggle this time, which made him nervous. They surfaced at the pool's side. Mari and Geir grabbed Soli from him. Blood seeped from a gash on her shoulder.

"It's okay, Soli," Mari whispered to her inert form.

David rubbed Mari's back. "Are you okay? Nothing hit you?"

She hugged him and said, "No, I'm fine. That was very brave going back for Soli."

He wanted to remember her looking at him like that forever.

"That's a lot of blood," Kenon whispered. "Is she going to be all right?" He barely got the words out before he stumbled to the side and brought up his dinner.

David ignored him and watched Mari assess Soli's condition with her wrist reporter. Part of Mari's biological studies had been medicinal, though she seldom had to use her training aboard the *Bard*. When Mari ripped off a piece of her own dress to wrap around Soli's wound, David's heart swelled a little.

"She needs a med facility."

A bare-chested host ran by, his sash hanging loose and dragging on the puddled floor. David grabbed his arm. "Show us the quickest way to the monorail station."

"Are you crazy? Half the people in here are bleeding or dead. Find your own way out."

David tightened his grip. "*You're* leaving, aren't you? We'll just follow you out." He let go and grabbed one end of a stretcher Geir had fashioned from some table linens and a piece of a pedestal.

"Are you planning to push us all the way back to the ship?" Kenon asked.

"What?" David snapped.

"The monorail will be out, too. No power, no trip back to the berths."

"I have the situation under control, Kenon. I don't need any insubordination."

"Insubordination?" Kenon clucked. "I don't see either of us wearing a military uniform."

"I'm trying to get us out of here."

Geir spoke up. "Kenon, do me a favor and shift Soli's leg back onto the board here. Don't want that pretty skin of hers to get scratched."

Kenon moved to Soli's side, keeping his eyes averted from the bloodied tourniquet around her shoulder. "What about Sean and Sara?" He looked back at the water.

David didn't look. He wouldn't see them anyway. Sara was quite capable of taking care of herself. And, Sean was a survivor.

"They'll meet us back at the *Bard*'s transport," David said, a quiver in his stomach making him doubt the statement. Maybe he should send Soli with Kenon and Geir while he searched for the others. Looking at Mari made him abandon the thought. His responsibilities lay here...with her.

A rumble shook the Tredificio and threw David into a wall. He managed to take the brunt with his shoulder and save Soli any unnecessary jostling.

Kenon helped Mari up from the floor. The gala host pushed himself to his feet. "You'll never get out of here in time carrying her." He took off down the commonway ahead of them.

"Wait!" Mari called.

"Forget him," David said. "We'll take the magno to the station."

"It won't have power either," Kenon said.

"That won't be a problem."

"It'll be tricky in the dark." Mari looked at Soli's small, unconscious form. "I guess we don't have much choice."

The group made a careful descent down the inert magno. Mari moved ahead while David and Geir carried Soli. Kenon clung close behind them.

"I've made it to the next level," Mari yelled from the descending curve of darkness. "And we're in luck because it's the Temperate Biome."

David looked to Geir and Kenon before asking, "Does that sound lucky to you?"

A cerulean glow appeared from below and illuminated Mari as she ascended the curve. In her hands she held six objects that looked like balloons.

"It's lucky," she said, "because these grow in the biome. Luminosa ampules. Now we can see." Mari handed over three ampules to Kenon, but his shaking hands dropped one.

David watched it blink out and fall dark to the magno's smooth surface.

"Sorry," Kenon said.

"It's not broken." Mari stooped for the ampule. When she grabbed its stem, the globule began to glow again. "Static electricity excites the gas inside."

"Good thinking. It should be easier going with some light," David said. He admired Mari's poise. Many women would have been paralyzed with fear, but she kept calm, used her brain.

They wound their way down the magno. Geir slipped but managed to keep Soli's stretcher in the air.

Kenon called from ahead, "We have an uprooted tree blocking the way. We'll never make it over this with the stretcher."

"We'll have to clear it. Geir, let's set her down."

They all pushed repeatedly, but only managed to break off a few of the weaker branches.

"This could take some time," Geir said.

"Maybe we can go over the side." Mari held an ampule out over the magno's railing. "The station is just one tier down. It looks pretty deserted."

"Because it's worthless without power," Kenon said. "This is ridiculous! We're going to die down here."

"Calm down, Kenon." David glared at him until he turned away. "Geir, we'll need to tear apart this stretcher to make a rope."

The building shook again. A loud rumble thundered through the monorail tube below. Metal screeched and concrete groaned. David, Mari, and Geir worked through it all to tie the cloth into a viable rope.

When the tremor subsided, David asked Geir to give the rope a test.

"Kenon. You're next."

With a less than graceful attempt, Kenon slid over the side. David waited until Geir had hands on Kenon, then pulled Mari into a deep kiss. "You're everything to me, Mari. Don't ever doubt it."

"Ready up there?" Geir called.

"On my way," Mari said. She squeezed David's hand before scampering down to Geir. David lifted Soli onto his shoulder and hoped the expensive cloth would hold both of their weights.

"Easy does it." Geir took Soli from David when he neared the station landing. David dropped the last meter.

The area was still. Damaged pillars surrounded them. Rows of track showed signs of buckling and warping. A faint smell of fire filtered through the station.

"Now what?" Kenon asked.

"They'll be here soon." David scanned the station. The light from the emergency ceiling units didn't quite reach the monorail tracks a meter below him.

"Who? Everyone else from the gala?" Kenon asked. "Do they know to bring their own table cloths or did everyone but us remember to pack climbing equipment for this evening?"

Sick of Kenon's mouth, David rounded on him, but let it go when he saw the smaller man could barely hide his fear.

A low hum floated through the concrete and vibrated in David's chest. The sensation entered his blood and flowed to the tips of his fingers, into his groin, and out the bottoms of his feet. The sound lowered an octave as it rolled through the station and shook the floor.

"Another tremor?" Geir asked.

David stared down the monorail launch tube at the backside of Tampa One in the northern sky. Ash fell from the sky like dark snowflakes against the starry night. A huge shadow snuffed out each sparkling dot one by one, then completely eclipsed the moon. The intense vibrations consumed his body.

"It's the *Argo Protector*." David wanted to cry at the sight of his old ship. It was like meeting an amour after a long separation.

THIRTY-ONE

"Ouch."

Sara landed on her wrist, but at least this new surface was spongy, not the bone-crunching concrete she expected. Her hands sank into wet springy foliage as she pushed herself upright. She could see by the scant emergency lighting how the plant material darkened wherever her skin made contact. There was only one plant which turned from snow white to space black at a touch, *corpselia*. The pungent smell of sulfur should have given it away.

A few meters from her on top of the immense corpse hedge Sean lay face down and motionless.

"Sean?" She gave his shoulder a quick shake, the wet fabric of his shirt clinging to her fingers.

No response. She shook him harder. "Sean!"

His reactive groan put her mind at ease. "What the…?" He struggled to push himself up from the softly latticed leaves.

"You okay?" she asked, noting several bloody scratches on his neck and face.

"Yeah. What did we land on?"

"I think it's the top of a corpselia maze."

"Lucky landing," he said.

She followed his gaze to the pool above. "Most of the debris...and people plugged up the breach. We happened to get sucked through first."

Sara shivered at the sight of bodies smashed among lily pad tables and stabilizers. A few faces were pressed against the pool's glass bottom and stared wide-mouthed with vacant eyes, their expensive clothing swirling about them.

"I've never been lucky before," Sean said. "Maybe it's you."

"I'm not sure I believe in luck."

Something zipped between them and stuck into the spongy surface. Sean plucked the small metal cylinder from the corpselia, then dropped it like it was poison. He grabbed Sara and rolled them off the top of the hedge. Her left hip hit hard, but she knew Sean had taken most of the impact.

"What was that?" she whispered.

"A dart. They carry a quick-acting poison that's difficult to trace. Used to be a contractor weapon."

Sara scanned the muted darkness above.

A tremor rumbled through. Her grip tightened on Sean as they lay together next to the spongy corpselia wall. It lasted longer than the previous quaking.

"We should be able to follow this thing to an exit," Sean said.

"Some of these mazes cover an area the size of a sports fie—." She heard a squish from above and held her breath. Someone was walking along the top of the maze. She looked down at her glowing arm. Tracking them would be pretty easy.

"Come on." Sean helped her up, and they took off into the darkness.

Sara slid her fingertips along the corpselia wall to her right in order to navigate the maze and to hide her intra-tat as best she could. The massive three meter tall hedge towered over them. Moving quickly, they curved around corner after corner. They should be nearing an exit soon. A hedge wall blocked their path.

Sean swore. "Was there another turn off on that last left hand curve?"

"I don't remember. Maybe."

She hated to backtrack. The assassin following them could be anywhere. With every step back the way they came, Sara prepared to take a dart to the neck or an eye.

Sean put a hand on her arm to stop her, then pulled her to the left. She curved into another extension of the maze. Her bio-lights provided just enough light to discern an intersection. She prodded Sean to go left.

Something slammed into the sopping hair piled on the back of her head.

"Hold still." Sean untangled another projectile from her hair and threw it to the floor. They ran through the darkened corpse maze, bouncing off the spongy walls until finally reaching another confluence. Sara grabbed Sean's shirt and pulled him left again.

Once they rounded the bend, he pressed her against the hedge wall and covered her glowing arm with his. Then he covered her ear and whispered, "Gotta get back on top. I saw a damaged section back on the right."

The already scant emergency lighting dimmed further. Someone blocked the light coming from the confluence.

An explosion shook the building, more violent than the preceding tremors. A deafening blast shattered the windows on every cantilever around them. Sara looked at Sean, and he nodded in understanding.

They waited for the figure to pass through the confluence and disappear around a curve to the right. Sean slid out of the passageway and went left. Sara moved on his heels, willing herself not to look back. As she followed him around the curving maze, she lost her sense of direction. Sean grabbed her hand and pulled her around a sharp right turn. The damaged section waited in front of them.

After a quick glance behind him, Sean steadied Sara as she climbed. The extra weight of her wet gown strained her muscles. Sean pulled himself up next to her. Their feet padded along the spongy surface awkwardly. Sean was having a worse time of it because he still wore his waterlogged shoes; Sara had left hers in the whirlpool. Though they could see the way out from this vantage, getting there would prove time consuming.

"There." Sean gestured ahead where the corpse maze came within a meter of a blown out window and a skywalk connecting this pyramid to another. She thought it was raining until she realized ash fell from the night sky. Screwing up her courage, Sara hopped across the expanse to the walkway. When she hit the synthstone flooring, it shifted under her weight, spilling her forward.

She got up to warn Sean of the damaged bridge, but he had already landed next to her.

A series of booms staccatoed around them from the walkway's buckling supports. It dropped down three meters, cutting off their way back into the aqua biome. They had no choice now but to continue to the other pyramid.

They started across before several more pops sounded. Scrambling along the collapsing walkway, they made it little more than halfway when the railing on the left gave out and threw the whole skyway off-balance. As she pitched over the side, Sara grabbed for the dislodged railing. A section of it pulled away from the bridge with the addition of her sudden weight. Sean dove for her, landing on the dangling railing just below her. Hundreds of meters below them, the waterfall rushed in the darkness.

Their wet clothes made the ashy build up on the metal slippery. Sean stopped Sara's sliding foot with his shoulder. She intertwined her arms within the railing as though it were rungs on a ladder. Sean kept a tight grasp on her ankle.

"You okay to climb?" he asked.

"Yes."

He released her leg.

Sara ignored the railing's groaning protest and climbed. It took effort to drag her body back onto the twisted walkway. Once she made it, she crawled to a section where the supports still anchored it to the other pyramid. Sean moved more slowly. The creaks from his heavier frame made him more cautious about his foot and hand holds. She helped pull him up to the stable part of the walkway with her. They still had a few meters to go. Moving as quickly as they dared, they finally made it to the other end.

The glass door remained intact on this side. Sean tried to pull it open. "It's sealed."

Sara shivered from the chilly night air and the adrenaline pumping through her veins. She studied Sean's face for signs of hope, seeing only smudges of ash mixed with dried blood. "What do we do now?"

"I can get us inside. I think." He pulled a razor disc from the inner lining of his belt.

She should be surprised a simple mech tech would carry such a lethal weapon. She wasn't. There was no more doubt in her mind who or what Sean Cryer really was.

A loud hum filled the air. Sara looked to the sky and saw a huge ship in the upper atmosphere. The glass rattled in the windows beside of them. "Get down. They're gonna blow out like the others." Sean threw her to the walkway and covered her body with his.

THIRTY-TWO

"The Armadans sent a rescue ship?" Kenon's face relaxed. "I'm surprised they even made it into the atmosphere."

"Their entry was one of the big booms we heard earlier, not that we would have noticed with all the tremors. Alerting the fleet is standard protocol for an accident on the Tredificio. And this monorail station is their drop off spot."

"It's good to have insider knowledge. Knew you'd come in handy for something," Geir said.

David's gaze remained fixed on the blue lights pulsing around the ship's immense door frame. Even from thousands of meters away, he would know that pulse anywhere.

"They can't land that big of a ship here," Kenon said.

"They won't need to land."

The electronic crackle of an energy well danced in his ears. *Deployment.*

He beamed at the massive field of circular green energy. At that moment, more than anything he wanted to be slowly falling through that well. The suppressors made even the heft of an Armadan's body light and graceful as a bird.

But, when the first round of troopers dropped, so did David's elation…and his stomach. They were armored. There was nothing standard about that.

Flashes of indigo breast plates and helmets disrupted the lime-colored walls inside the energy well as Armadan troopers dropped to the monorail platform as gently as if settling on the ocean floor. But once clear of the well, the pounding foot falls of armored boots roared through the station. Mari and Kenon covered their ears. The cadence of a thousand troopers rushing toward them was deafening. The others must be terrified. David's heart was pumping, too.

"What in the world?" Kenon's breath came in gasps as he moved to run.

"Stand still," David snapped. He motioned to Geir, who grabbed Kenon firmly by the arm to keep the younger man from bolting.

Only one thing brought out an armored force. Threat containment.

So much for a rescue.

The lead personnel were on them in seconds, energy rifles raised. David stared at the figures, standing a few centimeters taller than he in their heavy boots.

The grey organic-alloy blend of their armor shifted subtly from indigo to green without aid of outside light. It was almost form-fitting and extremely heavy, but Armadan bone structure was twice as dense as that of other citizens. The look of a fully armored Armadan was intimidating, even to an ex-captain.

A group of six troopers diverged from the group and headed for David and the others. Geir and Kenon moved back to where Mari kneeled over Soli. David didn't flinch.

"Retired Captain David Anlow." The voice coming through the helmet was clear and distinctly feminine.

David turned up the corner of his mouth in a little smile. *Lovely Lyra.* That should make things easier. Just not with Mari.

"Captain Simpra, it's good to see you." David pictured Lyra Simpra's blonde hair curling just above her shoulders behind the opaque face shield and boxy helmet. It was the only soft part about her.

"I expected to find you, but not so soon." Lyra's tone remained void of emotion or any further recognition.

That stoicism was why he'd given up on battle maidens and why Mari's tempestuous moods delighted him more than annoyed him. She knew how to feel, and her responses were honest, not filtered with practiced restraint. When Mari was happy, she was giddy. When she was pissed, she was adorable.

"How did you know I was here?" David asked.

"Word came down from the Embassy that your ambasadora would be attending this event. We have your new ship docked within the *Protector*."

"That's service," Geir said with a little laugh and edged closer to David. He seemed to be curious about a lifestyle he could have had.

"Where is Ambasadora Mendoza?" Lyra asked.

So much for reminiscing.

"The ambasadora became separated from our party."

Lyra cocked her head to the side. David knew she was giving subvocal orders to her deployment. He'd tried many times to break her of the tell.

"Sara will be fine with Sean." Mari's voice quavered. "Soli could be dying. She needs attention right now."

"My troopers will take care of her."

While three of the Armadans prepared an expandable stretcher for Soli under Mari's watchful eye, Lyra leaned toward David. "Just so you know, the contractor waiting on board your ship is not going to be happy about the loss of the ambasadora. You better have a good reason why you're coming back without her."

"The military is answering to contractors now?" David asked.

"We answer to the Embassy, nav leader." Lyra stumbled over the title like it embarrassed her to use it. "And any direct representatives of Sovereign Prollixer."

"With all these troopers running around, surely you'll be able to find her for him."

It wasn't the news of a contractor suddenly being assigned to the *Bard* that made David's eyes narrow; it was the way Lyra had insinuated that he had left Sara behind. Of course, Lyra assumed he always left people behind. And, at that moment, thinking about all the horrors that could have befallen Sean and Sara, he was beginning to think Lyra was right.

THIRTY-THREE

Rainer stared at the small sparkles in the floor of the *Bard*'s bridge. Even the utilitarian parts of this former pleasure cruiser had beauty. The viewer near him came to life as the passengers returned with their military escort. He knew each of them by sight. Checking their personal histories had registered as high priority even before he assigned himself as Sara's new *bodyguard*.

Prollixer let her walk on here blind, and she never protested. Rainer suspected the drugs Faya had pumped into Sara had impaired her rationality. Or perhaps Sara just had a death wish. Sometimes, when she consumed his thoughts, he feared he could grant that wish for her.

Kenon Brudger was the first of the passengers to wind his way through the forest of crystal trees in the *Bard*'s foyer. His animated face and sharp hand gestures hinted at a disagreement in the ranks. Glancing over the young man's slight build and delicate bone structure Rainer decided the Brudger family circle specialized in looks and nothing else.

The solid stature of the darker man directly behind Brudger spoke of a balanced lineage. Geir Shang had Armadan blood in his veins, but the twinkling eyes and easy smile exuded an overload of Socialite charm, though his file kept any mention of his Socialite ancestors a secret.

Rainer barely looked at Boston Maribu. True Socialite women bored him. And the orange eyes meant she had had a reaction to the Deleinean vaccine when she was a child. A sure sign of faulty genes.

His gaze moved past the Socialites playing at scientists and settled on the navigational leader. David Anlow's large presence probably intimidated the other males aboard, though they would never let him know that. Rainer saw Armadan bulk as a disadvantage. It made them slower, less agile.

Nothing in David's past suggested fragger involvement, and even Prollixer conceded this former captain was no fragger. Yet, the informer Rainer had tortured earlier insisted an Armadan aboard this ship held a high position within the techno-militant ranks. Geir Shang was the only one left. He didn't fit the profile either, but that wouldn't keep Rainer from interrogating him.

Maybe Prollixer's thoughts on fragger resistance to torture were truer than expected, though Rainer couldn't see how anyone would hold back after that many rounds of blade cuffs. It was how he had known Sara was telling the truth to Faya.

Thoughts of Sara pushed through that barrier in his mind where he kept her tucked away. Back on Palomin, when she was vulnerable and had begged for his attention, he had formed an attraction for her and her obvious expression of need. He even entertained thoughts of taking her on as an amour once her contractor training went so well. Then Prollixer shattered Rainer's illusion by hijacking her lineage. Though he never told Sara, there was no doubt in Rainer's mind that once she was of no more use to Prollixer, he would use the hijacking to be rid of her.

No matter how deep the attraction, Rainer would never associate himself with a sterile woman; it could be grounds for estrangement from his family circle. Still, nightly dreams of docking with Sara, her once honey-colored eyes sparkling as brightly as her intra-tat, became false memories, tricks of his psyche. Sometimes he could feel her wrapped around him, but when he opened his eyes, it was Dahlia or one of his other amours under him instead.

Memories of seeing David Anlow so intimate with Sara made Rainer want to draw his cenders as soon as the Armadan burst onto the bridge and started shouting orders.

"Get off my bridge."

"Pilots and their territorial nature." Rainer remained comfortably seated in the nav chair. "Stand down, nav leader. This isn't a battle cruiser. It's a pleasure craft." Then he addressed Captain Simpra. "What's the situation, captain?"

"Contractor Varden." Captain Simpra stepped forward. "One of the passengers, Solimar Robbins, sustained critical injuries. My doctors are doing what they can for her in the *Bard*'s med facility."

"Where is the ambasadora?" Rainer could care less about a Socialite archivist.

No one spoke. Geir Shang lowered his gaze, and Kenon looked at David. The Armadan's visage was stone.

"She and another passenger are still in the Tredificio," Simpra said.

"You left the most important passenger you have—"

"I didn't leave anyone." David whirled on Rainer, but the contractor drew his cender and leveled it at David's head.

"Your aggressor genes not all the way turned off?" Rainer asked.

"That's a myth. Hadn't you heard?" David wasn't backing down.

"I think we need to clarify the new hierarchy on this ship," Rainer said. "I don't know who was the social director before, but I'm the Embassy's voice here now."

The words had their intended effect. David's jaw set. Rainer liked to test the tolerance levels of new adversaries. Little tells while a person was angry or afraid hinted at bigger things to come later. It offered a view into someone's mind. That set jaw told him to keep a close watch on David.

"I was sent from the Embassy to act as Ambasadora Mendoza's bodyguard." It was a half-truth. "She is my only concern. The rest of you simply don't matter." His gaze never left David's. For effect, Rainer lowered his cender. The bigger man would never reach Rainer before he drew again any way. "Captain Simpra, do you still have personnel searching for her?"

"Yes."

"She was in good hands when...we all got separated." David's response reminded Rainer of the typical military drone. No inflection, no emotion, just the facts. Apparently Rainer had really gotten to him. He was drawing on all of his training and every drop of restraint to keep from lunging at Rainer.

"And whose hands would those be?"

"Sean Cryer, another passenger."

"The mech tech?" Rainer's brows narrowed. "What help could he possibly be?"

Cryer's personal history read of extensive academics and Socialite functions, nothing to indicate usefulness in such a situation. "Most Socialites I know, especially techs, would be pissing themselves in this situation."

"Sean's not just some Socialite. He's half Armadan," David said, crossing his arms in front of him.

Rainer's stomach tightened. Nothing about that showed in his personal history. But, the more Rainer thought about it, he realized that history was probably fabricated. Too shiny, too normal—exactly the type of cover an anti-government agitator would use. David's arrogant revelation had just signed Sean Cryer's Writ of Execution.

"Captain." Rainer snapped. "I'll need access to your voyeurs. Transfer a copy of the feed to the *Bard*."

"Contractor Varden, we don't have—"

Rainer walked up to the tall woman. "*What* don't you have, captain? The unsanctioned ability to take control of every voyeur and mind minstrel within the system for the Embassy's purposes or your own? You forget that I'm the Sovereign's Head Contractor."

She took a breath and said, "You'll have your feed. Now, if you'll excuse me, I need to get back to my search and rescue." She didn't wait for a dismissal.

The part of Rainer that liked life simple and neat, controllable and predictable, hoped Sara and the fragger killed one another. But the part of him that saw beauty in complication and chaos, that part needed Sara to live.

THIRTY-FOUR

"Armadans," Sara said.

"Yeah, here to rescue us." Sean's tone said otherwise.

Green energy wells dropped from the immense blue ship. Electric arcs leaped through the cylinder as the Armadans' armor brushed against the well's side on their way to the Tredificio cantilevers that remained standing. Huge thuds peppered the area just above Sean and Sara. The fully armored Armadans were almost as disquieting as lensed fraggers. Almost.

"At least our assassin won't try anything with *them* around." Avoiding the Armadans and finding an alternate way off the island could be her best escape. Simon would assume she perished in the eruption. She could start over, get another identity, get rid of the irradicae. The small hope filled her with vigor. "They won't be able to rescue everyone, though. Probably won't even be able to account for all the bodies."

"Probably not," Sean agreed.

"A person could just disappear among all this chaos and no one would ever know."

"They sure could." Sean stared at her.

She watched the troopers coming closer, her chances of fleeing dying by the second.

"Do you want to disappear with me?" Sean took her hand. She knew he wasn't running just for her, even if he guessed her torture had been Embassy-sanctioned. He had his ghosts, but he was asking her to go with him. To trust him. He had nothing else to lose. Neither did she, and that's what he understood.

"Yes," she said. "How?"

He pointed to a fleet of smaller auxiliary craft. "That's where they're loading the labor force separately. We catch a ride back to the Hub, then I can get us far away from here, somewhere they'll never find us."

"Then, let's disappear."

He smiled from the corner of his mouth and led her inside the glass pyramid and away from their military rescue.

After maneuvering around debris and backtracking to be sure no one, including the contractor with the darts, could follow them, they came to a utility ladder which led down to the next cantilever. Sara grasped the rungs and descended quickly down the narrow ladder, its meager stability welcome after her experience on the damaged walkway.

"We don't exactly look like staff," Sara said as they surveyed the scene from behind a support.

"Other Uppers are boarding." Sean grabbed a guest's discarded wrap and handed it to Sara. "Might be better if they don't know you're an ambasadora." He wrapped the long, silky cloth over Sara's shoulder and around her waist, then tied it at her side.

She tucked her hand in the crook of his arm to hide its faint glow. Linked together, they made their way to the craft farthest from the troopers.

A mishmash of Lower Caste staff and Socialite guests crowded for position at every craft's metal doorway. Uppers were always given preferred consideration, then Lowers with more prominent positions in the labor force.

Sara heard voices raised in dispute as she and Sean waited to board crafts near the middle. She eyed a man dressed in a plain tunic and dirty pants moving toward three hosts. His arms waved madly to keep them away from the craft.

"We're in for trouble. Not everyone's going to fit," Sean said.

A plump man in a filthy maintenance jumper pushed his way between Sara and Sean to the commotion at the far launch. He smelled of grease and fire.

"This is our ship! Get your own," the man roared as he moved through each set of waiting boarders.

"He's drawing too much attention," Sean said.

Sara glanced at the Armadans who watched from the main ship's boarding ramp.

"Wait here." Sean washed through the crowd in the man's wake.

A trooper stepped away from his post. *Or hers.* They may as well have been asexual in that armor.

Sara cut into the next line, aware of penetrating looks from those behind her. She didn't stay among them long before mingling with another group of boarders, slowly making her way to Sean at the far launch. As he talked with the Lowers, they were actually calming down. Then the man in the tunic started screaming again. The maintenance man lunged at him. Sean stepped between them. The maintenance man pulled back an elbow and struck at Sean's face. Sean blocked him, sending him falling into the line of people just in front of him.

Sara stood on the outskirts of the fight, ready to jump in. Sean made a pacifying gesture with his upraised hands to the crowd. A host grabbed Sean around the neck from behind. Before Sara could break through the circle of people, Sean had thrown the man off him, just in time to exchange blows with the maintenance man again.

Three Socialite couples next to Sara took advantage of the commotion to shove to the front of the line. The craft's pilot allowed the group to board even among the uproarious shouts from the agitated crowd. Several men and women from the crowd closed in around Sean; society's hierarchy slid through the fist of panic as it tightened its grip.

A host shoved Sean from behind. The crowd sprung at him. Sean deftly threw the closest man to the concrete with an evasive twist of his body and a well-placed shove to the lower back. Sean used the mob's clumsy aggression against them with well-timed blocks and practiced feints, his moves almost contractor-like, not as polished, but maybe a little more effective.

Sara plowed through the on-lookers. The maintenance man grabbed a bent piece of rebar and charged Sean. Sara shoulder-checked the man, throwing him off-balance. When he tumbled to the ground, she stomped on his wrist to dislodge the weapon. He reached for her foot, but she shoved her heel into his nose.

"Armadans!" A yell from the far end of the dock sent many scurrying from the fray.

Three troopers clomped a path through the Tredificio refugees.

The pilot stuck his head out of the shuttle's grey metal door. "Last call to board."

Sara grabbed Sean's arm and pulled him aboard. Six Lower Caste workers stared at them from the launch. On their faces she read a mixture of hatred, disappointment, and resignation.

"I don't know what they're looking at," a Socialite male next to Sara said. "Like we did something wrong."

"We did," Sean said, his stare remained on their accusing faces until the door hissed shut.

"You're a Socialite. You acted quite within the confines of the law." The man patted Sean on the back.

Sean shoved the man's hand away. "It's an antiquated law."

The few Lowers who made it aboard flicked a look at Sean, but still gave him a wide berth. Sara's heart softened at the shame she saw on his face.

THIRTY-FIVE

Rainer passed through the transparent door of the *Bard*'s medical suite, noting the shelves and cabinets of pastel green glass, the soft blue floors and ceiling. Comfortable and relaxing. The Embassy could take some style notes from this place.

He crossed into a waiting area for the private rooms. Only one of the three doors was shut. He headed for its shimmering metal surface. With the reporter he had lifted from David's chair on the bridge, Rainer keyed the door open.

Solimar Robbins sat up in her temporary bed, light blue braids falling across one mocha shoulder and one wrapped in a silver bandage. Just a curve of her bare breasts peeked out.

She hugged a pillow to her chest.

"Trala, I have to go. Talk with you soon," she said to a viewer on the wall in front of her bed.

The very pregnant woman on the receiving end looked like she wanted to cry. The tight skin around her eyes and mouth suggested she was younger than her amour. "Soon, Soli. I mean you'll come here soon, right?"

"Yes. Now rest. Our daughter needs all your attention," Solimar said in a tight voice.

Before Trala could respond, Solimar ended the transmission.

Her blue eyes, which were much darker than her hair, gave a glimpse into her sensual nature, even as they regarded Rainer with fear.

"Congratulations. Trala looks to be due any day." Rainer enjoyed the way her rounded mouth gaped slightly at the casual mention of her family.

"Sorry. I should have introduced myself." He sat in the dark green chair across from her. Its back attached to the wall by a metal post, much like the matching bed, giving them the appearance of hovering in space.

"I know who you are, Contractor Varden." Solimar's voice sounded small, but didn't quaver.

"Ah, as an archivist you would know all of the Sovereign's closest staff."

"I've also seen numerous clips of you on the Media. A woman doesn't forget a face like yours."

She was playing on his conceit, but he couldn't keep his arousal for females into SG. If they weren't going to respond to him, he couldn't be bothered with them. He thought of Sara's responses—even her anger aroused him. "And, you've been monitoring me ever since you could sit up in that bed, haven't you?"

She answered quickly. "I'm sanctioned through Embassy law—"

"You don't have to quote law to me. I enforce it." *And ignore it when necessary.* "Do the other passengers aboard the *Bard* know you have monitors all over the ship?" he asked.

"Of course."

"Even in their private suites?"

Her blue eyes greyed.

"You see, Solimar, I know more about everyone on the *Bard* than even you do. And, I know you sell private vids of the passengers to pay for your grand lifestyle. I hear the ones of your pilot teaching his young Socialite how to dock fetch the best prices."

Tears flowed freely from the dull lakes of her eyes. "I don't know what you're talking about."

"Yes, you do, and that's why I'm willing to help you. I'll keep your illegal sales to myself if you provide me with all of the raw data from your monitors."

"I didn't keep any of the data."

They both sat very still, quietly regarding one another.

Rainer pushed up from the chair and walked toward the trembling woman. He drew a mini-viewer from his side pants pocket and tossed it onto her lap. It showed Trala back at their estate sitting with a pink-haired contractor. Soli squeezed the pillow closer to her chest and her quiet crying turned to sobs.

"This woman's name is Faya Renault. She's not someone you want around the mother of your child."

"My data cache is at the estate."

"Where?"

"Only I have access to it."

He considered the truth in her revelation. He didn't believe she'd put her family in jeopardy to hide some video footage. "Then I suggest you get dressed. You'll be visiting Trala sooner than either of you expected."

THIRTY-SIX

"They're dropping us at the Hub," Sara said, her voice bouncing as the shuttle lurched in for a landing. Restraints dug into her bared shoulder and tugged at the wrap hiding the other one. Sean held the smothering nylon straps away from his chest with his thumbs.

"We can't stay here long." They were the first words he'd said since they boarded. Several workers looked up at the sound of his voice. He avoided their scrutiny.

"Let's catch a transport out. Any ideas?" she asked.

The bouncing evened out as they descended toward the bustling Hub.

"Latulip," he said.

"That's a high end entertainment district. Not very low profile."

"Its Underground is as low as you can get."

Sara had never visited the Underground and wasn't crazy about the idea now. But it made sense if they were trying to disappear.

A series of bumps signaled their landing.

Sean unfastened his harness and activated the exterior door controls without waiting for the pilot. He and Sara scrambled out ahead of the other passengers. The wrap slid from her shoulder. She thought she caught it in time, but mutters of "Ambasadora" followed them outside.

She and Sean maneuvered through thousands of disembarking passengers. They came from all parts of the system, Upper and Lower Caste alike. Small military transports swarmed from the immense battle cruiser above while dozens of service shuttles joined them in a queue for docking space. They were lucky to have been in the first group.

Sara's apprehension rose as she contemplated danger in each face they passed. A hand snagged her arm. She twisted out of the grip and nearly struck Sean in the face.

"Sorry."

"It's okay. I'm pretty jumpy, too. This way," he said.

She followed him to the transportation schedules nearest them. Magenta text swirled through updates on huge kiosk viewers.

Sean pointed to the one for Latulip. "It's six kilometers to Latulip on the far side of Carrey Bay."

"I think the boats will be faster than the monorail."

Sean looked toward the boat launch. "There's a more direct way."

"Than straight across the bay?"

"Yeah," Sean said. "Under it." Then he asked, "Have you ever ridden a hover bike?"

"A man's headed this way, Sean." Hover bike racers, donning helmets and padded clothing, and fans drinking beer and spirits from bottles roamed around the garage amid the smell of soldered circuits and fuel spills. Up until now no one had paid Sean and her notice, maybe because they looked like poor laborers in their ruined garments. She'd cut off the emerald green train with the bottom part of her gown to be less conspicuous. They had managed to clean off enough ash and blood not to look like evacuees any more. Sean had even *found* Sara a pair of shoes that were only a little too small for her feet.

"Sean."

"Almost there." He tapped a set of controls scrolling across his palm. The heavy bike hummed to life and lifted off the ground.

The man shouted and ran toward them. Sean straddled the bike. Sara climbed on behind him and wrapped her arms around his torso. He engaged the booster and shot past the man and the other racers' berths. When he hit the racing tube, he increased the throttle. Bikes flew through ahead of them, but Sean was gaining fast. Sara hugged his waist tighter and watched the faint royal blue lights that marked the three hundred sixty degree lanes strobe by.

Metal screeched on metal, and sparks filled the dim tube as two bikes clipped each other. A rider flew in the opposite direction as his bike spun out of control on its side. Sean jerked to the left to avoid the collision, sending their bike up one side of the racing tunnel. Sara buried her head in his back to shelter her eyes from the intense wind. She also didn't want to see if they crashed.

Sean kept to the wall lane, but a racer from behind jockeyed for position, trying to force them down. Boosting the throttle again, Sean curved further up the wall. They were almost inverted before he rocketed past the racer and crossed all three ground lanes to reach the wall on the other side. His momentum was so great they almost ran onto the ceiling. She hoped he remembered they weren't actually in this race.

Excitement stirred inside her, bordering on pure delight. The feeling was so foreign after all this time that she wanted to laugh and cry out so loud that she might even be heard above the whir of the engines. Instead, she slid her hand up Sean's chest. She liked the feel of him. His heartbeat was only slightly elevated. Maybe all those restors he took robbed him of any true excitement. It was then she realized her dull heartbeat matched his, even without the aid of drugs.

Much too soon she felt him decelerate. Racers zipped under and around them until they were alone and coming to the end of the tunnel. She peeked around his shoulder to watch their emergence into the Underground.

Sean made a quick right and exited the track up a small grade. He stopped the bike at the top, giving her an incredible view of the cavernous world under Latulip. Above ground, fancy boutiques and expensive restaurants stood in perfect rows along pristine pedestrian streets with manicured fronts. Down here a glowing network of mismatched buildings abutted crooked streets stuffed with bikes, transports, and every type of citizen imaginable. It was a world of perpetual nightlife covered by a ceiling of steel and concrete that was as vast and far away as the sky to her.

Sean reached back and squeezed her leg. "I know a place we can go. Disappear for a while, then decide what to do next."

"I hope it has food and a shower," she said.

"It will, I promise."

They coasted down to street level. Betting salons, bars, v-game parlors, and flesh clubs shouldered around places advertising *INTRA-TATS - just like the ambasadoras* and *Change your genes!* The desperation of Lowers impacted her more and more as she moved among them. To the Upper Caste, manually manipulating your genes was not only illegal, but more shameful than marrying below your status or even being sterile, yet honorable suicide ranked low among these people.

Smells wafted from several unmarked eateries. Sometimes nauseating, sometimes arousing, depending on what notes got stirred about by the passing traffic.

The Underground's decadence was beautiful. Sean had mentioned how no monitoring signals, including those from voyeurs and mind minstrels, could move in or out of the Underground thanks to comm shielding built right into the ceiling. Exactly what they needed in order to get lost.

She wanted to lay her head against his back as fatigue set in, but the possibility that he might be a fragger made images from Palomin trickle through her mind. From the moment she had met Sean, she thought of him as shy and harmless. Now she imagined him with v-mitters, fighting alongside the fraggers at the canyon rim. He showed he had a fighter's skill when he took on the mob back at the Tredificio.

But what bothered her most was wondering if he was the one Simon believed could lift his curse. If so, Sean became the best bargaining chip she had. She hated herself for the thought. To push it away, she hugged him tightly and rested against his back. It was better when she thought he was just shy Sean.

THIRTY-SEVEN

Chen Starrie slumped down in the soft white armchair, glad that the Kelahem Hotel had finally changed out the rigid formal furniture for something a little more inviting. A tall, lanky man stripped parts from a cender on the coffee table. Chen was disgusted by Tennor's too-small nose and lack of muscle tone, but the man's pupils grew within their dull green irises when he caught Chen staring at him.

"How can you be sure the fraggers believe Sean Cryer is responsible for the intel dump?" Chen asked.

"His idents are all over it, just like that e-pulse at the Tredificio." Tennor walked over to a mess of glowing wires on the bed.

"And, how do I know you're not going to get remorseful the next time you see Cryer in the V-side?"

"He's *not* Sean Cryer in the V-side. He's Zak."

"Not interested in the man behind the av?" Chen asked.

"No, just Zak. *Zak* is powerful. Cryer's nothing, just another Socialite living on a pleasure cruiser and pretending to be more important than he is. That's why he doses so much. To keep the real world out and his delusional world intact."

"Maybe he'd prefer you as Ariel, too," Chen said. "I'm sure I would."

Tennor shot Chen an acidy look. "The price just went up for your decrypter. You want more—"

Chen stopped listening to Tennor's rant when one of the vidclips bouncing around on the viewer in front of him caught his attention. All showed some headline about the Tredificio disaster, but Chen enlarged the one which read, *Ambasadora Sara Mendoza Feared Dead in Biome Collapse*.

Finally.

Chen had assumed Sara died at Palomin. When she debuted as a Face of the Embassy Chen couldn't believe her good luck. Or his bad luck. Thoughts of what she may have told them about him, or promised to give them for that kind of status upgrade, made his head throb. At least now she was no longer a threat.

"So you can finally relax," Tennor said. "The amour is dead. I just hope Zak made it out alive. Maybe he killed her for you."

"We were never married," Chen said absently as a message came through on his reporter. The transmission signature was from one of the rogues he sent to the Tredificio. Chen scrolled through the message: *Mendoza at Embassy Hub. With Cryer. Off the grid. Underground.*

"Looks like your lucky day," Chen said.

"Zak's alive?"

"And apparently helping Sara."

The darts were as ineffective as the eruption. They should have gone with force over subtlety. No matter, Chen welcomed the opportunity to kill Sara himself.

THIRTY-EIGHT

Sean pulled the bike into a narrow alleyway which served as a street. They wove their way through spills of luminescent fluid and broken down transports. Several dosed citizens staggered along the side and occasionally out in front of traffic. Sean and Sara had to stop and wait several times while pedestrians crammed into the street after v-games let out.

Too many times Sara was touched by passers-by; the contact with so many people in such a confined, dirty area made her angry and guarded. She pretended it wasn't because most of the citizens here were Lowers. She had never had strong opinions about the caste system before, simply ignored it because she was on the better end of everything. Not anymore. She still had her privilege, more so because of her appointment as an ambasadora, but just like the Lowers, she was a prisoner of her status.

Sean stopped again, but Sara couldn't see any obstacles in front of them, just an illuminated green sign with nude bodies forming letters which spelled out Carnal Escape.

"We need to stash the bike for later." He pulled it up to a stumpy parking attendant. "Can you put this some place safe and out of the way?"

"Safety costs these days," the bearded man said.

Sean pulled a razor disc from his belt and handed it to him. "I got plenty of these."

"You don't have plenty of what's inside."

The attendant inspected the disc further and slid the top off. His eyes lit up at what Sara couldn't see inside.

"You'll get the other half when I come back for the bike." Sean slid off the seat, but kept the bike idling so it still hovered. He helped Sara down.

As they walked away, she asked, "What was in the disc?"

He hesitated. "Half of an electronic siphon that can pull data from any reporter within a ten meter distance."

"Oh, is that all?"

He took her hand. "It's best if we look like a couple, otherwise you'll get some nasty proposals."

"I can handle myself," she said, though she intertwined her fingers with Sean's, not planning to let go any time soon.

"I've seen that first hand. It's just that I don't want to have to pound some poor drunk in the face because he made a crude remark toward you."

Sara was flattered by his protective gesture, but she wouldn't let him know that.

The monstrous bouncer at the door reminded Sara of David. Same jaw line, same physique, no doubt same Armadan bloodline. He waved Sean and Sara through, but stopped an inebriated woman with small hips and a pot belly waiting behind them.

"They know you here?" Sara asked.

Sean didn't respond. He let her step through the open door first.

They entered on the top floor. Below them on varying levels lay dance floors, stim dens, v-game and coiting parlors. Bright green lasers zigzagged from one floor to the next. Bluish vapors wafting up from the lowest level formed a turquoise cloud one level down.

"Ever been to a flesh club before?" Sean asked.

"Not one like this." She and Chen had gone with their rogue companions for post-mission indulgences on many occasions, but those were elite parlors and almost antiseptic compared to the rawness here.

"I'll get us a sky box." Sean gestured her toward a bank of elevators.

When one opened, a mixture of guests poured out along with some of the blue mist. She and Sean pressed in with a large group of men and women, all dressed in black leather with various body parts exposed. They ignored the newcomers, too busy touching each other. Now Sara was the one who felt a little shy. She stared through the glass elevator doors.

The smell of the mist reminded her of blue star lilies. She took a deep breath and the floor of the elevator dissolved into transparency until it disappeared from under her. If she concentrated hard enough, she could see a white capped building at the bottom of a hazy energy well. She stumbled forward with vertigo.

A hand steadied her elbow. "You okay?" The voice sounded muffled.

"She's just having a good slide." This high-pitched voice came from a fragger balancing on a board over Palomin Canyon just in front of her.

"Sara, look at me." She felt a hand nudge her chin.

"Rainer?" She didn't know if she said his name out loud because all exterior sounds died away. All she could hear was the thumping of her heart and the blood rushing through her ears. The world darkened into night, then the blackness became blacker. She thought she felt arms picking her up. Either that or she was floating.

Time passed like a dream. At one point she thought she heard two heartbeats, not quite in sync. Then the blood washed through her ears again and onto her face. She woke gulping air and took in a mouthful of water. Adrenaline shot through her. She struggled against hands holding her and blinked through droplets to see the water's source, a large showerhead raining down on her. Sean held her up from behind. His shirt sleeves were soaked, as were the ruined threads of her gown.

"Thought that might wake you up," he said.

The spattering of the shower on their clothing sounded muffled compared to the drops hitting the tile floor of the huge walk-in shower. Sean released Sara and said, "Take your time. I'll get us some food."

"Do you know why I came to the *Bard?*"

Sean stopped at the glass doorway of the shower. He didn't want to have this conversation. Not after they'd made it this far. It had loomed at the back of his mind since he met her, and he knew it was inevitable. Still, he tried to be coy, hoping he could stop it from playing out, stop either of them from having to say the truth. "The Embassy sent you."

"It wasn't my choice," she said. "Neither was becoming an ambassador." Sara backed against the shower wall and slid to the floor.

Sean didn't say anything, just sat against the wall across from her and waited. The water kept running, as though they spoke from opposite sides of a small, delicate waterfall.

"I never told anyone what happened to me at Palomin," she said. "But I need to tell someone. I need to tell you." She didn't wait for his response.

"I was there celebrating. Chen and I had just become enamoured. He gave me a black bracelet that night, and I should have realized something was wrong, that it was too sudden, that contractors always have ulterior motives. He used me to bit siphon data from the archives."

She was there that night, the night of the uprising. Now Sean knew who siphoned the data. It was probably Chen, or someone working with him, who slipped the data mine into the V-side, framing Bullseye. Separate parts of the same story came together as Sara told her side.

"I got caught in some kind of battle between fraggers and contractors on the rim. Chen saved the bracelet and its data, but left me to die by a fragger's hand."

Sean's muscles tightened at the thought of someone from his organization hurting her. Then again, the same group, *his* group, killed Ephemerata and set him up for mass murder. They wouldn't care about some Socialite who happened to be in the wrong place at the wrong time.

"Rainer saved me, shot the fragger."

Sean recalled watching Rainer kill the Embassy doctor. It seemed the contractor had made himself Sara's protector on more than one occasion.

"Then he shot *me* and delivered me to Simon."

This revelation was shocking. Apparently Sean had misjudged their relationship. Maybe Rainer had been protecting *himself*.

"Simon was panicked because he thought I, or someone with me, had introduced the virus attacking his longevity bots. He had one of his contractors interrogate me."

"Faya?" Sean asked.

"Yes. How did you know?"

"You mentioned her during your slide."

The water splashed rhythmically in Sara's sudden silence.

He knew she needed prompting. "What did she do to you?" He didn't want to know, didn't want to ask her because he was a coward on the inside, but he'd listen to every horrific word because she needed him to.

"Do you know what blade cuffs are?" Sara asked.

"I've heard of them." He'd actually seen them in action on an Embassy surveillance vid of a fragger interrogation. The Embassy had leaked the vid into the V-side to deter anti-government activity. He hoped the footage had been mixed and painted, for Sara's sake.

"There's no way to describe that kind of pain. Feeling your skin slowly sliced open in a dozen different places, seeing it roll up in shreds." Her voice caught in a sob. "You never expect to experience something like that and live through it. It should be impossible, *should be*. In a merciful world. But, in my world, it happened every day for over a month. The only thing impossible in *my* world was escape."

Sean felt physically ill. Acid boiled in his stomach. His chest tightened so he could barely breathe.

"The physical abuse wasn't the worst part, though. The slides multiplied the horror ten-fold. I got lost in my fears some days. The hallucinations were so real. I nearly went insane. That's when Rainer would come to me, clean me up, but he never got me out of there."

"Why?" Sean's voice was harsh, his angry incredulity spilling into his tone. He would have died trying to save her, would give his life for hers right now if he had to.

"He said he couldn't. Maybe he was telling the truth. Or maybe he thought helping me was the easier way to get information from me."

"What information?"

"I don't know. I didn't know anything, Sean. I never did." Sara doubled over sobbing. Sean moved beside her and held her head against his shoulder, hating that he couldn't take this hurt away from her, hating the Embassy and Prollixer, hating Rainer, hating this whole society.

After a long while, she pulled her head away from him so she could look him in the eyes. "That's why I'm here. Because Simon finally believed I didn't know anything, so he made me a deal, gave me a new life with a new title to go along with my new face and body, which I barely recognize in the mirror. To be sure I wouldn't turn on him, he hijacked my lineage."

"That's why you asked me about the irradicae the first time we met," Sean said.

"I thought you would know how I could find out if Simon was bluffing. I thought a lot of things about you during that first meeting."

"Including that I was a fragger?"

"No."

Sean couldn't hide the surprise in his voice. "You really didn't know?"

"Not until the Tredificio," she said. "That's when I was certain you were the one I was supposed to kill."

"Then why did you disappear with me?"

She leaned her head against his. "Because by that time it was already too late. I cared more about you than the deal."

Sean closed his eyes and hugged her close. He'd take this hurt from her somehow, then he'd make sure someone paid dearly for it.

THIRTY-NINE

David ran through the crystal trees in the foyer to catch Soli before she left with Rainer. So much about him didn't make sense, like why such a high-ranking contractor would be assigned to guard one of sixty ambasadoras. Even more absurd was Soli taking him to her estate so that he might meet Trala before recommending their child to Tampa Quad's best nursery. Then there was Rainer's reaction to Sean being part Armadan. It was as if the contractor had just been given the answer to the world's greatest mystery.

David felt as if he had somehow betrayed a confidence by stating the obvious. Granted Sean never mentioned his ancestry, but surely everyone else had noticed the signs too: enhanced skeletal structure, evidenced from the hundreds of times Sean flew into a rage and smashed his hand against some solid object without fracturing anything, and more importantly, the way he could fly into a rage at a moment's notice to begin with. And, his penchant for dosing.

Maybe that final tell wouldn't have been a tip off to the others, but David had witnessed his share of stim abuse at home and aboard the *Protector*. Maybe that's why he was so hard on Sean; they shared a kinship whether either of them would admit it or not.

David reached the gangway as Soli and Rainer disappeared down its glowing throat.

"Soli!"

David didn't miss Rainer's left hand slip to his cender.

"Why don't I go with you? I haven't seen Trala in a few weeks." Her response would tell him if she were in trouble.

"Not right now, David. Trala's not feeling up for too many visitors. I'll tell her how much you miss chatting with her, though."

Rainer tucked an arm around Soli and walked her off the gangway.

Geir sauntered up beside David. "None of us has met Trala."

Exactly.

"I'm going for a walk," David said.

"Mind if I join you?" Geir pulled a cender from behind his back.

"That yours?"

"Yeah." He passed it over to David. "But I could only get one, and you know more about using this than I do."

David heard a pair of footsteps track across the foyer floor. He concealed the cender in his waistband and covered it with his shirt.

Kenon clasped a hand on David's shoulder from behind. "Everyone heading out?"

Mari ran a hand up David's back. "Let's go to Orlando's. I'm starving."

Things just became more complicated. "Actually, Geir and I have an appointment with some potential clients," David said.

"What kind of clients? More passengers? All kidding aside, I don't think we can accommodate any more people on here," Kenon said.

"No, they're clients for me," Geir said.

"Why do you need David at your meeting?" Mari asked.

"It's a group of Armadans." David spoke before he thought. Geir shot him a look.

"But, Geir *is* Armadan." Kenon wasn't helping.

"They're troopers. Geir's never been a military man, so...."

"Troopers like Captain Simpra?" Mari pulled her hand from David's back.

"No," David said. "Retired, like me."

"Which means they don't have a lot of time left, so we better get going." Geir tugged at David's jacket.

David ignored the jab and focused on the disappointment in Mari's eyes. "You and Kenon go ahead. We'll meet up later." He rubbed her shoulder briefly, even in front of the others. "Sorry." Every time he shut her out, she slipped a little further away. One day she wouldn't be around for him to disappoint. Maybe that would be best, at least for her.

The smell of a million gardenias draping the green filigree fence along this part of Carrey Bay masked the water's fresh scent. For as far as Rainer could see, white flowers speckled their verdant trellises. Peeking from a hillside across the roadway were various roofs and towers from this area's mega-estates.

Solimar's private gate stood open, allowing the open-aired transport to continue up the winding drive flanked by blooming plum trees. She must have been selling data for years to afford such luxury.

He followed Solimar to the door. She stopped to enter a pass code on her reporter, but Rainer pushed the double doors open, knowing Faya would have disengaged all the locks and security systems.

Sobbing came from a sun room just off the foyer. Solimar ran toward it.

"Soli!" Trala croaked out between sobs. The blonde pregnant woman pushed up awkwardly from the plush green and lavender sofa. Her large belly impeded her enough without Faya's warning hand pulling her back down.

The passive expression on the contractor as she twisted Trala's wrist made Rainer wonder what she had done to Sara when they were alone in that modification cell.

"Don't touch her," Solimar yelled.

"Faya." Rainer said her name in warning. Then to the women, "This won't end badly if you cooperate."

"The cache is over there on the mantle." Solimar gestured to the room's far corner.

The marble fireplace curved away from the white wall in a half-circle. One artifact adorned its rounded mantle, a tall fish bowl cylinder alive with three small fish, their blue fluorescence splashing the back wall with bits of turquoise.

Rainer led Solimar across the tile floor by the elbow.

"There's a false bottom under the cylinder," she said.

A cheerful melody sang through the sitting room. Rainer glanced toward the entryway. "Where are the servants?"

"Locked in a room upstairs, unconscious," Faya said.

Or perhaps dead.

"Then we'll just wait for your guests to leave," Rainer said.

Everyone remained still. When the door chime remained quiet after an indeterminable time, Rainer used both hands to pull the large cylinder from the mantel.

"Take off the bottom," he told Solimar.

With shaking hands, she gave the thick glass bottom a twist and pulled it free of the vase's real bottom.

Water sloshed onto the toe of Rainer's boot, but his focus trained on the mix of surprise and horror in Solimar's eyes. He spun to look for Faya, but her cender already pressed against his temple. "Hand it over, Rainer."

"Faya, you're an idiot. That's not the data Prollixer wants. It's what *I* need, to prove Sean Cryer is a fragger node." He intended to offer it in exchange for Sara's lineage.

"Still not much of a liar, are you? You couldn't even keep your fallacy for *her* a secret."

Rainer ignored the comment about Sara. "This isn't the Sovereign's data."

Faya took the glass disc from him anyway. Ranier noticed movement out the glass patio doors in his periphery. David quietly pushed open one of the doors with his cender. Faya hadn't bothered to lock it behind her.

The melody of the door chime swept through the room again. Rainer let the vase fall and snapped his head back to the left. With the edge of his right hand he struck the bundle of nerves inside Faya's elbow. Her cender slipped from her numb fingers as the vase smashed on the marble floor. Rainer's hands locked on her wrist and twisted her arm straight over his right shoulder. He pulled down and splintered her ulna.

David fired two shots between Rainer and Faya. Geir followed on his heels, circling around toward Trala.

"Get back!" David yelled, as Kenon Brudger and Boston Maribu ran in from the front entrance. He lunged for the young Socialite as a cender blast zipped past her, destroying the plaster wall behind them.

"Geir!" Kenon yelled a warning that allowed him to dive behind a metal screen.

Faya turned her weapon on Kenon and fired. It caught him in the side and dropped him. His head bounced off the marble floor with a dull thud. Faya fired once more as she leapt through the open patio door.

Trala doubled over, then slumped to the floor. Soli shrieked and rushed to her fallen amour.

David and Rainer squared off, each pointing a cender at the other's face.

Solimar cradled Trala's blood-soaked body in her arms. "No, no, no! Trala."

"Out of the way," Rainer said. "Let me call for help."

"Geir's already sent out a call. Why did your partner doublecross you?"

"You know there's more to it or you would have fired already. Ask Solimar why I'm here." Rainer's words stilled Solimar's hand as it smoothed back Trala's blood-slick hair. "She asked me to help her with Faya," Rainer said.

The archivist would surely see this as a way out for both of them; the others would never know of his coercion, or her deceit. She only needed to agree with him.

"Soli?" David asked.

She cried quietly. "It's true."

"Now, stand down." Rainer kept the relief out of his voice. Solimar placed Trala's bloodied head on the marble floor. "He was trying to save me." Her voice cracked. "To save *us* from that woman."

David lowered the cender and rushed to her side.

Rainer chanced a look around for the glass disc. He saw it shattered with the rest of the cylinder among the flopping fish, gasping with their wide mouths.

Solimar gasped for air, too, and thrashed on the floor, pummeling David as he tried to console her.

Rainer regretted the loss of Solimar's child almost as much as the loss of the incriminating data. The fallout from this violent episode would be far-reaching, especially if Faya gained the Sovereign's ear first. He had allowed his hope of saving Sara and her lineage to dictate his actions. Now he could pay for that decision with his life. He opened his palm to make a call.

How did all this happen?

To David's right the doctors worked on Kenon, to his left they covered Trala's body.

He eyeballed Rainer. The contractor spoke in hushed tones to the Embassy investigators. David knew Soli would never go to Rainer for help. Contractors wielded manipulation better than they did cenders.

David stopped the doctors wheeling Soli out to the transport to ask where they were taking her.

"The Embassy hospital," the one closest to David said.

Rainer stepped in front of David and motioned the doctors out the door. "She'll be treated for her trauma and distress at the psychiatric facility. I'm taking care of the arrangements myself."

David didn't like the sound of that.

Rainer slipped past Mari as she paced in the entryway. She hadn't spoken to David since the Embassy investigators had arrived. He still didn't know what she and Kenon were doing here in the first place. She was either avoiding him because he lied or because she lied.

She strode past David without making eye contact and went to Kenon's side.

"Can you get the bandages *any tighter*?" Kenon asked the doctor. "I already can't breathe very well."

"Are you okay?" Mari asked him.

Kenon pulled in a labored breath as the doctor adjusted his bandage once more. "A little dizzy. Can't really catch my breath."

He held up his white jacket, a bloody hole in its side showed where the cender shot had brushed him. "And a little queasy. You just can't get workmanship like this anymore."

Mari laughed between tears and gave Kenon a kiss on his cheek. "I'm so sorry I convinced you to come with me." She looked at David, shame showing on her face.

"Don't give it a thought. I wanted to see Soli's home anyway." Kenon leaned in close and whispered, "For comparisons, you know?" He pulled a face and rubbed his left arm.

"What is it?" Mari asked.

"My arm keeps going numb."

David squatted beside Kenon and Mari. "Maybe from the electrical discharge of the cender. I've known it to happen."

Rainer reappeared in the room. "We can head back to the ship."

"What about me?" Kenon asked. "Shouldn't I be going to the hospital, too?" His tone sounded panicked. "I was just shot!"

The doctor next to him said, "Your vitals show elevated blood pressure and a slightly irregular heartbeat, but that's consistent with this sort of trauma. I've applied menders under your bandages, so the small second degree burn from the cender flash should heal in a few hours. You're welcome to visit the medical center, though." The doctor looked to Rainer for confirmation on this last suggestion.

Rainer didn't hide his disdain for Kenon's whining. "Do we need to carry you there on a stretcher?"

"I'm not that fragile." Kenon smiled, then his face went pale. "But heading to the hospital seems like the cautious thing to do."

"We'll go with you," David said. He and Geir helped Kenon to his feet.

Kenon's body began to convulse and his eyes rolled back in his head.

David and Geir lowered him to the floor.

Kenon clutched at his chest and squeezed his eyes shut. His breathing became ragged. A foul smell permeated the air. The doctors jostled David and Geir out of the way.

"Cardiac arrest," one of them yelled.

The other tore Kenon's shirt open and attached a defibrillator to his bare chest, then positioned an automatic breather over his nose and mouth. The defibrillator shrieked. Kenon's body convulsed with the pulse of electricity forced through his heart. Then the breather inflated and deflated his lungs, causing his chest to rise and fall, but in an abnormal rhythm. The doctors worked frantically and shouted vitals to each other after each pulse and breath.

Mari buried her face in David's jacket and sobbed. Geir watched in shock.

Minutes rolled by. Instead of hopeful anticipation, the shriek from the defibrillator became horrifying and maddening, like a threnody played over and over.

The doctors called out Kenon's vitals one last time and confirmed what David already knew, Kenon was dead.

"I'm sorry," the doctor closest to David said. "He's gone."

Rainer called for another bag.

Mari pulled away from David in hysterics. "What do you mean *he's gone*? He's dead?" She looked into Kenon's staring eyes, searching for proof the doctors were wrong.

Geir turned away, his shoulders quivering.

"Mari." David reached for her hand. She pulled away. "He was just fine! What happened? What did you do to him?"

"He had a weak heart," the doctor said. "It was a genetic defect."

"How?" Mari looked to David for answers he didn't have.

"The heart defect stays off the report," David said.

"Impossible." The other doctor said, snapping his attention to Rainer.

David snatched the doctor off his feet and pushed him into the wall behind him.

"Don't!" Mari yelled. "Please don't." She pulled at David's arm.

He let the doctor go and stepped away.

"I want him brought up on charges for assault," the doctor said to Rainer.

"Genetic tradition meant everything to Kenon," David said. "He was one of the few citizens I knew who believed in the system enough to make it work for him and his family. Don't let his lineage be tarnished."

Rainer considered for a moment. "Make the report read that Kenon Brudger died of wounds sustained while protecting a fellow citizen."

Then to David, "It will add bravery and altruism to his line. I don't know how well his amours and heirs will appreciate it, though. Some Socialites still think altruism is a defect."

David balked, though Rainer might be right. "They'll know he died a good man. Not all of us will be able to say that."

The doctor looked nervous, but showed Rainer the report before he sent it off from his reporter. "What about the assault charges?"

"No charges. Everyone's just a little tense given the situation." Rainer put a hand to his cender to squelch any arguments.

David almost told him he didn't need any more favors, but realized what did it matter when the first one surely came with a hefty price. In his experience, contractors only helped others for their own substantial gain. He hoped he could afford being in debt to Rainer Varden.

FORTY

"How big is this place?" From Sara's vantage in the sky box she counted at least six levels. Beyond that, the dizzying darkness stole her vision.

She didn't expect a response. Sean was in the shower finally getting to clean up after listening to her babble, then bringing back clothes and something to eat. He'd apologized for the little blue slip dress she now wore, saying it was the most modest piece he could find. She liked it. The skinny straps and little slits up the side made it less binding than the gowns she'd been wearing since becoming an ambasadora.

"I can breathe, for once." Sara often talked to herself, a habit she picked up at Palomin as a way to ground her to reality. Hearing her own voice reminded her that she was still Sara Mendoza, no matter how much of her identity they tried to strip from her. But, thanks to Faya's drugs, Sara took more out of that modification cell than herself.

She glanced at the small black vial sitting on the table by the suite's entryway. Sean had brought the drug back with him, too. She recognized the shimmering liquid as dew drops, a recreational aphrodisiac, but Sean said in this concentration they became powerful neuro-stims, strong enough to help her separate emotion from her terrible memories.

All she had to do was fabricate new memories to layer over the bad ones. The possibilities were endless, any experience she wanted—a cruise on the Kimberly River, walking the gardens at Wright's Landing, dancing under a living, breathing volcano. Sean said he would guide her through it. She picked up the vial, wondering if it were that simple, and worrying that she wouldn't be able to pretend hard enough to make it work.

She needed a real experience to make her forget the horror of Palomin. She picked up Sean's new shirt lying on the table, wanting to smell it, but knowing she'd be disappointed that it didn't have his scent yet. Thinking of how its softness would soon lie against his skin sent little shivers through her fingertips. Just that small sensation felt better than a fake holiday.

She removed the vial's lid. A few drops of the black fluid remained on its flat crystal surface. Touching it against her lip, she tested its taste with a brush of her tongue. Its pleasing sweetness reminded her more of flowers than fruit. She tipped her head back and let the rest slide down her throat.

Sean came around the corner from the bathroom. "Have you seen my shirt?"

His short hair looked darker from being wet, and rumpled, like he'd just taken a towel to it. He stood there in only a pair of pants and looked around the suite. His torso and arms were muscled, but not bulky like David's nor sculpted to detail like Chen's. The natural leanness of Sean's body aroused her.

"You left it here." She walked toward him, his shirt in one hand, the empty vial in her other. "I decided on a new memory," she said.

"Good. I'll talk you through it." He reached for his shirt.

She tossed it on the bed and let the vial drop to the tile floor with a clink. His gaze never left hers. She eased her arms around his neck to whisper in his ear, "I'm tired of talking."

With barely a brush of her lips, she traced a trail along his jaw to his neck. When she found a spot that smelled strongly of him, she ran the tip of her tongue over it. She could feel his pulse quickening under her mouth. Up until now, she had only guessed at his attraction for her.

He slid his hands down the silky slip, then cupped her thighs and lifted her so she could wrap her legs around him. She could feel his arousal, even through the heavy fabric of his pants.

Wanting to relive that feeling from their first kiss, she moved slowly. He followed her lead, but coaxed her lips apart with his. She played the tip of her tongue across his bottom lip, then drew away slightly, teasing him. He pulled her back into the kiss, but she kept up their game. Each time their lips met, heat and pressure pooled between her legs, and her bio-lights pulsed a little brighter. Sean noticed their glow and became more aggressive, pressing her into a deep kiss and swirling his tongue into her mouth. When her tongue met his, he squeezed her thighs in impatience.

By the time he carried her to the bed, her every nerve sizzled in awareness of where he touched her, with his hands, his mouth, his skin, the small swath of stubble coming back to his jaw and chin. The softness of the bed contrasted with his body. She reached for the button on his pants, then unzipped them. When she tried to push them down his hips, he nudged her hands away and pushed her slip up past her belly. Some of the rough spots on his fingertips caught at the silk.

He bent over to kiss the softness above her belly button. She shivered, and not just from the sensation. A nervous excitement rose up inside her, as though it were her first time.

In a way that sentiment was true.

No one had caressed *this* body, this reconstructed shell that she didn't recognize at times. Sean's touch made Sara feel comfortable in her own skin. Whether he knew it or not, he helped her to reclaim ownership of herself because this moment was only for them to share. Not Simon nor Faya nor Rainer could take that from her.

She reached for his pants again, but he pushed the slip up over her breasts and slid it up her arms until it reached her wrists. Instead of pulling it the rest of the way off, he trapped both of her wrists in the tangled silk and held them there with one of his hands, showing he could play his own games.

His free hand stroked one of her breasts with a feather touch as his stare roved over her nude body, then came to rest on the brightening swirl of purple lights on her arm. Drawing his fingers down her arm made the bio-lights pulse into a different pattern. A swipe of his thumb across her nipple sent them flashing brighter. Sean gave a little growl and swept each fingertip slowly against her stiff nipple to make the lights pulse faster. The raw yearning in his eyes excited her. A breathy sigh escaped her lips, drawing his attention back to her mouth. He kissed her, but only briefly before his lips danced down her neck and continued between her breasts. He had turned the tables on her seduction of him. She liked that he challenged her for control, especially the way he commanded a response from her. When he looked up into her eyes as his lips tugged at her nipple, a quick flush warmed her skin. He was winning this round, but, as soon as he let go of her wrists, she let him know it wouldn't be so easy. When he came in for another kiss, she held him back with a hand on his chest while the other tugged at his pants.

Sean gave her his shy smile, and it warmed her like the sun shining down into her heart. He stood up and slid his pants off, but kept his shorts on. She enjoyed this playful side to him. He headed for the bed again, but she placed her foot against his chest to stop him and nodded toward his shorts. He slid those off, too, then kissed the arch of her foot, sending tremors through her limbs. She stared at his naked form, a little timid in anticipation.

His lips continued down the inside of her leg. He kept eye contact with her through each painfully slow kiss, making her body tense and squirm. When he reached her inner thigh, the thought of where his line of kisses would end nearly brought her to climax. It had been a long time since a man had tasted her. The pressure of his tongue on her stole her breath and made her arch her back in response. His lips and tongue moved over her in a circular pattern, working her clitoris until she lifted her hips completely off the bed. She grabbed handfuls of his short hair as the pressure built between her legs. Her bio-lights glowed brighter than she'd ever seen them, the erotic visual putting her over the edge. She whimpered as she came, but Sean was just getting started.

He found her mouth again and kissed her with an urgency spurred on by her quivering body and the brilliance of the dots lighting her arm. She was tight when he first pushed into her and she wasn't used to a man his size. Her fingers pressed into his shoulders, and she squeezed his hips with her thighs. He took the hint and eased himself the rest of the way in. After a few slow strokes, she relaxed and called his name because she liked the sound of it. The encouragement urged him on, as though he had been waiting for her permission to give into his instinct and passion without restraint. This was not at all like the techniques they acquired at school. He excited her with his unpredictability and daring. She was surprised and delighted to find his shyness went only as far as his smile. The feel of him thrusting deep and steady into her was matched only by the words of adoration he whispered against her neck and her lips. He spoke of her beauty, of how much he needed her and wanted her, how much he cared about her.

She felt an intimacy with Sean that she had never known with any other coupling. He helped her to remember what it meant to be Sara. To physically feel Sean's desire and share his pleasure empowered her. Opening herself to him, meeting the rhythm of his hips, she was more alive than she had ever been in her entire life. She was happy that he could see her arousal, exposed and naked, as it burned bright and furious in every dot pulsing up her arm. His intensity increased with the bio-lights' brilliance until Sara panted, trying to catch her breath.

When she couldn't hold back any longer, she gave into rolling waves of ecstasy. The sensation came from deeper inside her than before and was exponentially a greater sensation. Nothing could better erase the horrors she had known than memories of this moment, spread open to Sean's pleasure, the feel of him on top of her, inside her, wanting her and needing her as much as she needed him.

FORTY-ONE

"You may have to wait another year before going rogue," Chen told Faya as she adjusted the bone mender on her arm. "To keep the Sovereign's suspicion down and avoid retaliation."

Chen linked Tennor's decrypter to the hotel's small black viewer unit on the night stand. If it couldn't bypass the Sovereign's codes on his personal transmissions, Chen would break all of Tennor's fingers before shooting him.

"I might not want to go rogue if I can have Rainer's job," Faya said. The bone mender emitted several beeps as she adjusted the cast's pressure again.

A viewscreen pixilated and stuttered to life in the air in front of them, accompanied by Rainer's irritated voice.

"I'll have to fix that glitching for next time," Tennor said.

Never count on a next time.

Although, Chen was loathe to admit that Tennor proved his brilliance time and again. Not that all the brilliance in the system would let him jump castes.

There seemed to be quite a few bright Lowers surfacing recently. If the Uppers allowed exceptions for all of them, then soon the beautiful among the Lower Caste would want exceptions made for them as well. This type of caste jumping became more common with each generation, an affront to the History and a threat to the Uppers' superiority.

Dahlia, Faya's sister by a different father, walked in from the hotel balcony with three of the rogues from Chen's original group, leaving the remnants of their room service dinner on the outside table. A jade-colored bird had already taken the opportunity to swoop in for a bite.

"Are you sure they won't know we're eavesdropping on them?" Chen asked.

"They don't have a clue," Tennor said.

Rainer's face looked strained as he explained what happened at the Robbins' estate, including Faya's role.

"I need a cure, Contractor Varden, not excuses."

"Then blame Faya Renault."

Faya snickered. "Our Head Contractor is scrambling now."

"I've already spoken to Contractor Renault, and the details of her story are quite different from yours. She knew that searching Archivist Robbins' private tapes was a ridiculous idea. You wasted time and gained nothing."

"You would take her word over mine?"

Chen glanced at Faya, who looked a bit nervous to hear the answer.

"Her mind is on the task at hand, not some emotional fallacy. I'm giving Contractor Renault the task of lifting my curse."

Rainer's jaw set and his voice had an angry tone. *"That's a mistake."*

"The mistake was not doing it earlier. Your new assignment is to bring Ambasadora Mendoza back to me. You can stand beside me while she takes her own life in shame. Or put her out of her misery when the irradicae eat away her insides."

So the rumor was true. It surprised Chen that the Sovereign would be so bold and irreverent as to hijack Sara's lineage. The part of him who had foolishly taken her on as an amour after a night of too many neons and too much coupling felt a modicum of compassion for her, but losing her family rights was her problem.

"Sara's dead. Killed at the Tredificio." Rainer's tone betrayed him, but the Sovereign never noticed.

"Then you are useless to me."

The transmission ended.

Chen swiveled his chair around. "Rainer's not quite the liar he believes he is. Must be letting his emotions get the better of him."

"Rainer having an emotional fallacy for anyone is absurd." Dahlia laughed, but her eyes were hard as forged metal.

"You didn't see the footage from the surveillance monitors back on Palomin," Faya said.

Dahlia's breathing deepened, baited by Faya's lie. Chen scrutinized the interplay between the sisters, his cousins on both sides of their family circle. The women's dislike of one another would be useful later.

"They showed it all, how he went to Sara after every modification session, coddling her back to health, docking her every chance he got."

"Data can be manipulated—"

"Not on the Sovereign's personal surveillance monitors," Faya said. "When are you going to wake up, little sister? Rainer is a grand deceiver, one of the reasons Prollixer hired him as Head Contractor, but he's slipping. He just lied to the Sovereign's face to protect Sara again."

"How do you know?" Dahlia asked.

"Our contacts had a visual of Sara and Cryer disembarking here at the Hub some time yesterday."

Dahlia paled slightly. "Why didn't you tell me?"

Chen and Faya shared a look. "You were seen pretty often with Rainer before he ran off to chase his ambasadora around the system," Chen said.

"I don't care what the monitors showed," Dahlia said. "He has no interest in her."

"Why? Because he's married to you and six other women?" Faya circled her sister. "Mother told me about your secret ceremony. She was concerned for the family since rumors have Rainer falling out of favor with the Sovereign." Faya stood in front of Dahlia and stroked her hair. "You can keep secrets from the whole system, but you have to trust your family.

That's why I'm giving you the opportunity to choose your family over your prime amour." The warning in her tone left no doubt she'd make Dahlia pay for any type of betrayal.

"I would always pick family over everything," Dahlia asked.

"Good," Chen said. "Then you'll come with us to find Sara and her fragger. If we can get to Simon's anti-virus before he does, we have the key to the system." Chen hoped to gain a full pardon from the Sovereign as a reward, or a high place among the new governing ranks if he died.

"Tennor, I just hired you for another job. You can be our guide in the Underground."

"I'm better with the tech."

Chen leveled a cender at Tennor's narrow nose. "I think it's time you put all of that V-side combat training to practice, unless you're afraid Zak will kick your ass in the real world."

FORTY-TWO

Like just about every morning since he started dosing, Sean woke to ringing in his ears, but this morning he wasn't alone. Sara lay naked and beautiful, folded in his arms. This was how he wanted to wake up every morning from now on.

Her purple-streaked black hair hung loose around her bare shoulders. The bio-lights twisting down her arm glowed steady and calm. Last night their rhythmic pulses, quickening in time with her heightened arousal, nearly drove him mad. He couldn't remember having to exert so much control in his life. Every time he felt sure he would come, he forced himself to slow down— and not look at those lights. That night was for Sara's pleasure. It was the only way he knew how to help her with her pain. In his mind she transcended being just a pleasant intimacy. He saw her as an irrevocable part of his life. He hoped she felt that way, too. Part of him worried her attraction came as a side effect from the dew drops. It was enough that she had asked him to share last night with her, to use his touch to forget her time at Palomin.

Studying the curve of her body made him want to wake her up with a trail of kisses down her back. He became hard at the thought, but slipped out of bed without waking her, then grabbed his clothes from the floor before heading into the bathroom. He zipped up a pair of comfortable worker's pants and tugged on a light blue shirt.

Life had changed during these past few days. Sean had changed. The emotions Sara stirred within him were the most intense he had felt since losing his brother. Except, these feelings were beautiful and amazing, better than any drug he'd taken, and so much better than the lonely life he lived before. It was the perfect example of an emotional fallacy, according to their society—basing life decisions on what the world considered to be nothing more than fleeting moods and sentiments biased by hormones.

Sean didn't care if all of that were true. He would do anything to keep feeling this way. Of course, that meant making sure he had no more secrets that could ruin things later. Secrets like his family background.

When he returned to the bedroom, he was disappointed to see the bed empty. He heard the clanking of metal and ceramic coming from the kitchen area. Sara sipped on a cup of tea, already dressed in the clothes he *borrowed* for her from one of the shops yesterday. The short white sari looked like something Soli would wear, only Sara had managed to wrap the scarf around her more modestly than Soli would have preferred. Soli had insisted all along that Sean needed someone in his life. It saddened him that he couldn't tell her she was right. Thinking of her grief, made him resolute in this one last confession to Sara.

She offered him a cup of tea. He took the mug and sat it on the counter. "I need to tell you something," he said.

Her smile faltered a little, but she kept a light tone. "I already know you're a fragger. You know I was sent to kill you. And you know what makes my lights flash."

He smiled at that one.

"What other secret could possibly matter?" she asked.

"Your intel was right about the operative being Armadan, except I'm only half, on my father's side."

"Oh." She seemed relieved and not at all surprised. "I guessed you had Armadan blood in you after last night."

"You did? Why?"

She hesitated for a moment, and he thought she blushed a little. "You're a little taller than the average Socialite, your shoulders a little broader, your...*hands* are bigger."

He looked down at his hands, having never really thought about it before.

She seemed a little flustered and quickly added, "You're also much stronger. You hide that strength from people, though, don't you?"

He had for as long as he could remember. "I guess so, but not as much as I hide the fact that my mother came from the Lower Caste." The words came out of his mouth like he'd been waiting to say them his entire life. He sat down on one of the plush dining chairs, wishing he could take it back. He looked at the steam rising from the mug of tea on the counter, avoiding her face, afraid he might see rejection or judgment there.

"That's why your forced handling of the Lowers at the Tredificio caused you so much conflict," she said.

"Probably."

"And, why you feel so comfortable here in the Underground." She said it more to herself.

He didn't say anything.

She ran her hand through his hair, then slid onto his lap, forcing his gaze upon her. "I don't know about you, Sean Cryer, but I'm tired of pretending to be someone I'm not because society dictates it." Sincerity showed on her face. "Does your mother care about you?" she asked.

He was taken aback by the question. "Of course."

"Then be proud of that, no matter who she is." Sara kissed him on the forehead, but he pulled her lips to his. Their kiss was different this time. Instead of just playful or passionate like those hundreds they shared last night, this kiss was a promise of the future they meant to share. He could have stayed in that kiss forever, but they weren't safe yet. He slowly broke away.

"I'm not sure how much longer we can remain here," he said.

"Maybe Simon, the Embassy, the whole system thinks we're dead," she said.

"Everyone might, but it won't stay that way for long. We passed too many voyeurs at the Hub, and I'm sure we didn't hide your bio-lights as well as we should have."

"What do we do?" She looked nervous for the first time.

"We'll bargain for our freedom."

"With what?"

"The cure for Simon's curse," Sean said.

"You have it?"

"I can get it." At least he hoped he could.

Their trip in the elevator this time was uneventful. It stopped at the ground floor and opened onto a sub-street. They exited Carnal Escape and headed across the way to a v-game parlor called Shocker's. All v-game parlors smelled the same, the spicy tang of dosed air drifting above the metallic notes of conductor and cleaner fluids.

Acid pink and rich blue arabesque loops scrolled along silver half-meter portals in the back wall. These were the only lights in the expansive room, aside from the twinkling stars on the walkway.

Ahead of them, at least thirty people waited in a dark line. One woman lay on the floor, singing to herself. A couple near the middle kissed and groped each other, much to the entertainment of those around them. Just in front of Sean and Sara, a group of Lower Caste kids argued with an attendant over the price of admission; they finally left grumbling.

No nurseries or academies for them, Sean thought. They were probably better off.

"They're so healthy," Sara said.

"Who?" Sean asked.

She gestured toward the children hurling back foul-mouthed insults at the attendant. "Their skin is clear, their cheeks rosy, and their muscle tone is better than any of my cousins their age.

Most of my family would have to get little tweaks to attain that kind of look. Where do these kids get that kind of money?"

"They don't. That's just how they are naturally," Sean said.

"Did you ever have any cosmetic alterations?" she asked.

"No." He mused at her naivete, but could forgive Sara for assuming everyone who was attractive owed their looks to selective breeding or cosmetic enhancements. That's how most Uppers viewed the world. She was only now learning to see life from a different perspective. "The diversity of genes among Lowers benefits them in a lot of ways."

"You're a good example of that," she said.

Her last comment made him feel like he'd given her the wrong impression. The Armadan traits he received from his father benefited him just as much as everything his mother passed onto him.

A few meters away three sharp beeps sounded from a portal whose round façade pulsed with an intense white light. The portal and the tube it was attached to slid out from the wall. The v-gamer inside convulsed, vomit splattered over his face and neck.

Attendants pulled the man out, plunged a syringe of stims into his leg, and whisked him onto a gurney and through a back hallway with practiced precision, not even bothering to tear the eye mask from his face. A woman in coveralls raced to the tube and flushed it with a pale green cleaner.

"He dialed up too high. Worked himself into a seizure," Sean said. "Then couldn't unplug."

Sara covered her nose. "Are you getting in one of those?"

"Not a chance."

Another attendant appeared from a hidden door on the wall to their right.

"Cryer?" he asked.

"Yeah."

"This way."

Sean took Sara's hand and led her through the doorway. The pressure of her fingers around his made his arm tingle. He found it hard to focus when she was near him. Once they got out of this mess, he wouldn't have to focus on anything but her.

The room looked like a miniature of their skybox without the windows.

Sean waited for the attendant to exit.

"This shouldn't take more than a few minutes," Sean said. "Don't worry if my arms and legs twitch. It's just reflexes."

"You're not going to come out of this like that last guy, are you?"

Sean took her hand and kissed it; that was a reflex, too. "If you knew how many times I've done this...." *Or knew how many times he'd died in the V-side.*

The thought that this time could bring real death entered his mind. He tried to dismiss it as a left-over bit of paranoia, but knew it wasn't. Ephemerata proved that sides had been chosen, and Sean had ended up on the wrong one. He kissed Sara as though it might be their last.

"Maybe you shouldn't do this," she whispered, her forehead against his.

"I have to. We have to buy our lives back."

He lay on the bed before he changed his mind. "I'll be back before you know it." He closed his eyes, wishing he had his lenses to make the insertion easier. Instead, he had to rely on an old implant behind his ocular nerve. He slowed his breathing and stared at the blackness behind his lids. The seconds ticked by like they were years, but Sean kept his meditation. As the coldness of insertion finally crept into his mind, he was vaguely aware of Sara curling up next to him, her head on his chest.

The watery lobby lapped at Zak's raft. He ignored the blue globes hovering around him and summoned a dark sky through his programs. Stars appeared. The raft launched toward them, forcing a feeling of inertia on his stomach.

Within seconds he was just beneath the sky. This close the stars hung down as shimmering teardrops above his head, each one a portal to a different world. An infinite universe.

"Which of you is hiding the intel dump?"

Zak reached up and combed his fingers through the spongy constellations. They felt wet to the touch, but left no moisture on his skin. Six separate sweeps revealed nothing. The coordinates led to this sector; it had to be there.

Or he was screwed.

A buzzing in his left middle finger alerted him he'd found the one he wanted. He pushed his finger into the membrane. The teardrop stretched down and drew Zak into its protective bubble. Then the sky shed its tear into the purple sea below.

There was no impact with the water's surface; the bubble's velocity remained steady. Smaller aerated bubbles, representing other users, rushed past Zak's clear transport on all sides, yet he heard nothing. A peace settled upon him as increasing pressure squeezed the membrane tighter.

In the illuminated depths of this vast sea, Zak monitored a shadow falling parallel with him. The bubbles obscured its form, but he knew it was moving, *or swimming*, closer. Three hundred meters, perhaps. It picked up speed. Zak calculated the rate of acceleration with dormant programs.

One hundred twenty meters and closing.

Ninety.

Maybe he really was screwed.

Thirty.

The shadow blackened the water in its wake as it closed on Zak. His heart rate and blood pressure sky-rocketed. He forced himself to remember this was just some architect's game, an over-the-top construction meant to inspire awe and fear in the user, but even with his experience, too much of the V-side felt real. A shock rippled through him as the shadow engulfed him.

Complete darkness. Silence. A sucking noise from near his feet. The tickling probe of his idents. He held his breath while waiting to clear fragger security programs. His fate was sealed, as it were; if Ephemerata were wrong about his idents being linked to the dump he'd be dead before he realized she was wrong.

The bubble burst.

Zak landed on his feet in a sunny field of green and blue feathers. The ocean was nowhere to be seen. The landscape stretched on in all directions, no landmarks marred the downy meadow except for one droopy tree thirty meters away. Zak moved in that direction, his booted feet kicking up feathers along the way. Instead of settling back to the ground, they remained suspended in the air just above his knees. There would be no covering his trail, but he aimed to be in and out before another user arrived.

He slowed to a cautious crouch walk when he noticed a circular object nestled in the tree's black roots. If it were a trap, someone went to great lengths to lure him here when they could have disposed of him in the ocean lobby upon insertion. Still, he scanned the horizon to be sure he was alone. He reached the tree and saw a ceramic pot among the roots.

Zak tested the lid with a finger; data streamed through him. He couldn't move. He couldn't think. Just had to let the energy transfer continue. He willed himself to breathe, knowing his body would respond in kind back at the v-game parlor. He believed Sara would pull him out once she saw him in distress…if she could.

A pain stabbed behind his eyes with the final information surge. Zak fell to his knees. Feathers shot into the air around him and hovered there like a cloak. He pushed himself up by his elbows, sorting out the muddling in his head. He recognized the tickle of the intel dump in the back of his mind. He looked for the pot, but it was gone.

He got to his knees and waited while the pain subsided and his disorientation cleared. A large hand reached down to help him up. Cuzco pulled him to his feet and waited for him to speak.

"What are you doing here?" Zak asked. The big guy was the last person Zak would have suspected of stealing the data and letting him take the fall. "Why'd you set me up, Cuzco?"

Cuzco let go of Zak's arm and flexed big fingers around a crafter. "I don't know what you're talking about. I was just monitoring the trap we set. The trap that snared you like a little bird."

We?

"I'm here to find out who's messing with me." Zak tried distracting Cuzco while he called up compression programs. The only way he'd be able to transfer the dump to safe storage in his hidden cache would be to zip the file. He'd decompress it and sift through it when he wasn't at the bad end of a weapon.

"I think you came here to retrieve the data you stole."

"You know that's not right, Cuzco." Zak's transfer was only a third complete. "I don't know who you are in the real world or even in this one, but I believe you're a fragger because the ideology fits."

"From what I hear, you're sporting a new ideology."

Three more portals deposited Topper, Vishnue, and Ariel in a semi-circle around Zak.

Topper leveled a cender at Zak's chest.

"Traitor," Vishnue said.

"Get those out of my face." Zak grabbed Vishnue's wrist and twisted the cender from his grasp.

Eighty percent uploaded.

Topper fired once, but the shot went wild. The tip of Zak's cender pressed into Topper's reptilian neck.

"I'm not here for a brawl," Zak said. "We've got problems in the organization."

"Like nodes who turn traitor?" Vishnue asked.

"Not true." Zak kept an eye on Vishnue's weapon.

A faint buzzing brushed a far corner of Zak's mind. The count stopped at ninety-six percent. Was it feedback? The relentless traffic in v-game parlors often taxed the stream.

"You're not responsible for the intel dump, then?" Topper asked. "And you didn't cause the destruction on Tampa Three?"

"Even though your ident signatures are all over it?" Cuzco added.

"Someone hacked my signature." The buzz in Zak's mind oscillated.

"Impossible." Cuzco was still the most even-tempered of the group, but even his patience appeared to be wearing thin.

"You know it can be done." Zak tried to concentrate, to think of the right thing to say, but the buzzing interfered with his thoughts. A searcher program groped his mind.

Zak released tracing programs to find the source. They were illegal in the V-side, but most everything he did was illegal. Which was the only way he'd ever know about programs like tracers and searchers.

Cuzco was speaking, but Zak couldn't hear him over the program's buzz. The intensity told him the searcher had to be local.

Who—

Zak fired three rounds into Ariel's head. Cuzco knocked the weapon from Zak's hand. The others opened fire. Zak called up his unplug codes, but Ariel had already locked him out. Zak's heart rate increased and his muscles twitched as his contingency threatened to assassinate him. He stumbled to his feet and called upon an emergency weapons program. As cender fire bit into his back, a dozen razor discs materialized over his head and launched at his contingency.

Explosions blossomed around the three assailants, buying Zak precious seconds to scan the data Ephemerata had given him.

There! Just as he had hoped, she provided him with a lockpick.

Zak concentrated on unlocking his codes amidst the onslaught of pain from cender and crafter blasts. He almost had it. An interceptor program latched onto the lockpick, unraveling its code at an alarming rate. Zak struggled to focus, to keep his head clear, working just milliseconds ahead of the interceptor. The tracer reported back. It had Ariel's plug-in location. She was somewhere in Shocker's.

His guard slipped at the revelation. The weapon fire became too much for him. His torn and lifeless body had nothing left.

He thought of Sara, out there watching him die. He thought of her face and how she looked at him like no one else ever had, how she felt in his arms. He'd been prepared to head to the Otherside so many times before, but now felt cheated because he had her. A searing white light burned into his vision and all he could hear was ringing. As the world slipped away, he wondered if this what his brother and his father saw as they died.

FORTY-THREE

"Wake up!"

Sara shook Sean again, calling his name in a panic.

His limbs twitched and sweat poured down his face and chest, like he was in shock. Then his entire body started to convulse. She didn't know what to do, didn't know the first thing about the V-side, or how to get Sean out of it. When they had watched the attendants carry that man out earlier, Sean mentioned something about not unplugging in time. That meant she had to break his connection to the V-side.

She spotted a wireless station in the wall. Ripping the cover away, revealed a mess of wires and an emergency jack coiled up with its plastic-coated cord. If she cut the power, would that work? Probably not, or the attendants would have done that for the man earlier. She abandoned that idea and felt along the inside of Sean's belt for stim patches. Maybe she could pump enough adrenaline and stimulants into him that he'd wake up. She found five patches and three injectors about the same size, then caught the side of her finger on something sharp. At first she thought she had accidentally triggered an injector, but instead, she pulled a thin razor disc from its sheath on the inside of his belt.

She looked at the emergency jack again, an insane idea coming to her. It might work, if it would reach. She uncoiled the cord and made sure it remained attached to the power supply in the wall. It stopped just short of Sean's body. She pulled his twitching arm off the edge of the bed. The cord could reach his hand.

Careful not to cut too deeply, she made a large enough slit in the plastic coating to expose the hot wires inside. They glowed white, warning they were live.

She hoped the sweat on Sean's skin would be a good enough conductor. He was convulsing so badly she feared she'd get zapped along with him, then no one would be around to wake them up. They could disappear to the Otherside permanently. She wanted to see what they could be like together here first.

Ready with the injectors in one hand, Sara brought the exposed wires near Sean's hand. She hesitated. If she couldn't bring him back.... She made contact. A white arc jumped across his hand and a massive convulsion rocked his body. She threw the cord against the wall.

Sean didn't move, not even his chest rising and falling with breath. The absolute stillness of his body terrified her.

She held the ring-sized injector to his neck and felt the needle forced into his flesh by the compressed air triggered inside the tiny plastic case. She used the other two. Nothing happened. She peeled the backing off of a stim, jabbing it into his neck and fumbled to get the next one ready. Then two more. Her hands shook as she pressed the fifth and final patch into place. She felt on the other side of his neck for a pulse. Nothing.

She put her ear to his chest. "Please, please, please." Nothing.

Then his lungs filled, and he sat up with a gasp. His eyes tried to focus, and he looked around in confusion. She held his cheeks in her hands, reassuring him.

"Sara." His voice sounded choked.

"Are you okay?"

He squeezed her hands and calmed his breathing. "How did you get me out of there? I thought I was dead."

"You were." She showed him the frayed wire from the wall. "I stopped your heart."

His expression went from alarm to disbelief. "How did you restart it?"

"I gave you all the dosers you had on you."

His fingers flew to the patches on his neck. "You gave me all five?"

"And, the three injectors, too."

His complexion looked flushed. He stripped the patches away from his skin.

"I thought the more the better, especially for someone who doses pretty frequently," Sara said.

"The injectors were doubles," he said.

Sara felt sick. "Can you handle that much?"

"I hope so." He ripped the last patch out, but the concentrated stimulants from the injectors were already moving through his system. "Right now we have to go. They found us." Sean pushed off the bed and fell against the nearest wall.

Sara steadied him, hoping his disorientation would wear off quickly. "The Embassy found us?"

Sean swayed and pulled a deep breath. "Fraggers."

"If I go, they'll follow me and leave you alone," she said.

"They probably want me more than you at the moment."

"Can you walk?" She let him test his footing. His arms trembled, but his legs seemed to hold his weight.

"Someone from my contingency is here," Sean said. "A woman named Ariel." His breathing evened out and he stood straighter.

"She's in the Underground?"

"She's here in Shocker's."

"Does she know that's where we are?"

"Pretty sure she does." Sean opened the door and scanned the parlor's waiting area. "Never thought I would say this, but we need to contact David for help."

"I thought you two didn't get along."

"We don't. He reminds me too much of my brother, but that's also why I trust him." Sean led the way out into the commotion of the v-parlor lobby. They exited into the traffic-stalled street and picked their way across, back to Carnal Escape.

More people elbowed around the club now than last night.

"What's Ariel look like?" Sara asked, scanning the face of each woman they passed, trying to detect a threat.

"I don't know. My guess is she'll be the one trying to kill us. The dance floor's the best exit. We can use the crowd as cover."

Sara didn't like the sound of this. "She could be any woman here. Does she know what you look like?"

"No. Maybe. Probably." He pushed Sara into an elevator. Blue mist engulfed them. Anticipating a slide, she held her breath. When the dosed air seeped into her lungs, she readied herself, but her mind remained clear. Her strongest memories were flashes of Sean and the phantom feeling of his touch. Only vague hints of Faya and her torture pinched in the back of Sara's mind. Memories, not hallucinations.

Memories were manageable.

The door opened onto a green-tinged dance floor. Half-naked bodies undulated to the oscillating beat of a wooden drum. Strobing purple lights made the movements appear slow, adding to their sensual nature. Couples and groups docked in the cushioned grottoes lining the side walls.

Sean pressed his mouth to Sara's ear to be heard. "There's a service exit at the other end of the dance floor. I've used it before."

They shoved their way through the dancers, Sean guiding Sara from behind. Zealous hands grabbed at the couple in invitation. Several dancers groped Sara as she passed. Her skin flushed from the contact and the drugged mist. She stayed aware of faces in the crowd, but only saw dosed parasites, pleased to be caught up in their own arousals.

Except for one man on her far right. Though the misty interior masked his features, she caught his gaze tracking them across the floor. She felt like she should know him, the way his body moved as he paralleled their progress toward the exit. The blue mist swirled and cleared for only a moment, allowing her to recognize him.

Chen.

"Move." Sara shoved through the last six meters of the dance floor.

Chen ran over dancers to get to them. He drew a cender and fired.

Sean shoved Sara to the floor. With the palm of his hand he absorbed the cender's blast as it burned a glowing wake through the mist. From this close she could see the absorption field came from Sean's reporter. Dancers screamed and stampeded in all directions.

She waited for Sean to orb the energy back at Chen. Instead, he closed his fist around the glowing energy ball until it dissipated. The lights in the club flickered out for a moment.

"This way." Sean pulled her up from the floor and through a shimmering silver doorway. He rushed down the poorly lit grey hallway banging on one closed door after another.

"Why didn't you orb the energy back at him? He'll have the advantage now," Sara said.

"Because he was insane to fire a cender in there in the first place. Didn't you see the mist ignite in its path? Concentrated into orb form, it would have caught all the mist on fire and incinerated everyone inside, including us."

"Where did it go? Did your body absorb it?"

"I grounded out."

"I don't understand."

"I was standing on a port in the floor. Sent the energy through my foot." He picked a lock with his reporter. "Inside."

A blast of cold like the airlock on Nanga Ki rushed at her. Black light played over a long room of freezer cases. Inside were thousands of iridescent blue star lilies, the source of the club's mist. She'd never seen so many in one place.

"Head to the back. There'll be a door in the wall, behind this row of freezer cases." Sean worked on the lock from the inside.

"That won't stop Chen," Sara said.

"Your Chen?"

"*That* Chen." She waited for a reaction or disapproval, but Sean remained on task.

A faint click brought her head around. She saw a triton knife flash in the black light and threw her hand up. The blade sliced a trail down her left cheek. With a side step, she evaded another slash and shoved her knee into the man's groin, then slammed both fists into the back of his neck. His triton clanged to the floor as he fell into a heap. She hit his nose with the butt of her hand until she heard the bone crunch.

Three rogues emerged from the nearest row of freezers. Though she'd met them only on rare occasions, Sara recognized them as Chen's associates.

Sean scooped up the triton and engaged two of the rogues.

The third tried to attack Sara from behind. Sara punched him in the jugular notch, sending him sprawling against a table with syringes and vials marked *BENZOATE FLORAL PRESERVATIVE—TOXIC*. When he slid onto the floor she kicked his spine with her heel. She saw he wasn't getting back up and raced to Sean's aid. He had already dispatched one of the rogues and stripped the downed man of his cender.

The other rogue elbowed Sean in the temple. He repaid him with a slash across the throat. Sean looked around to find Sara.

"Behind you!" Sean lunged toward her.

Something pierced her lower back. Sara fell to her knees. Pain shot into her gut and radiated through her nerves. She fought to see through the tears and stars. The last few centimeters of a metal flower corer stuck out of her abdomen. Her blood dropped from its tip, darkening her shirt. She couldn't quite catch her breath from the searing pain.

Sean had already swept past her, unaware of her injury. He grabbed a large metal syringe from the counter. With a swift move he jabbed the fragger Sara had fought earlier.

The man grabbed his shoulder. Sean freed himself with an elbow jab to the man's throat. He stumbled backward, coughing. He choked out, "You're more like Zak than I thought you'd be." Bloody foam spewed from his mouth.

Brief recognition lit Sean's face. He kicked the man's knee to bring him down and pointed a cender at his head.

"You deserve to suffer, Ariel."

"Piss off." The man spit through the bloody froth.

"Sean..." Sara barely got his name out before pitching over.

Ariel's thrashing and gasping drew no sympathy from Sean. He kneeled at Sara's side and concentrated on her thin breath.

"Pull this thing out of me." Blood seeped around her lips. She lay on her side and wheezed.

"The corer's keeping the bleeding down. It may do more damage if I remove it." He examined where the metal tool had penetrated her back. "You won't be able to ride very far like this. I have to get you to a doctor." He knew where to find one, close, but taking an ambasadora to a covert fragger facility might get them both killed. Still, he had to risk it.

Sara closed her eyes.

"Hey, I need you awake." He stroked her cheek.

Her eyes opened. She tried a weak smile.

Admiration for her grit edged out the panic Sean felt. He eased her to her feet, angry he couldn't take her pain. Figuring Chen was on his way, Sean knew time was short. He scooped Sara into his arms and palmed the door controls open. He took a deep breath, then stepped out into the buzzing street.

The only people who paid any attention to the pair were those who weren't dosed out of their minds or engaged with a partner. The few partiers who did watch didn't find the sight of a man carrying a semi-conscious woman particularly odd. Things like this happened all the time down here.

Sean balanced walking quickly with walking steadily. He felt how the occasional jostles had Sara gasping in pain by the way her breath changed. He had to move faster.

He spotted a transport a few meters ahead. The driver was out of his seat and screaming at a hover bike rider. Under the transport's front left tire were the remnants of the rider's bike. The dispute quickly escalated into a stim-fueled shoving match. Sean slipped Sara into the passenger seat. Before the driver could turn around, Sean had slammed the transport into gear. It shot forward, rolling over the hover bike and clipping the rider.

The driver grabbed onto the passenger door handle. Sara pushed the door's auto-release. The latch clicked and the door swung open, plowing the driver into an industrial trash bin.

Pedestrians scattered. Sean accelerated through the narrow streets like they were part of a memorized v-game map. He waved dosed pedestrians out of the way, shouting and swerving around them before any of them ever even realized they'd been in serious danger of being run down.

Sara's breathing slowed.

"Stay awake, okay? Almost there." She couldn't die, not after he finally found a reason to live in this world. He grabbed her hand.

Hitting the decelerator, he made a sharp right and stopped less than a meter from a heavy metal gate. He held his hand under a small white box with multiple sensors and scanners attached to it. The box contracted around Sean's fist like a clamp and shot tracer pulses through his body, searching for idents.

Three seconds later a chime sounded and the clamp released Sean's hand. The gate squealed open.

Sean palmed his pilfered cender, never knowing for certain the difference between good will and a trap. He ran to the other side of the transport. Sara's head lulled back and forth on the seat. Her blood, lots of it, added to the stains on the grimy seat. Sean suppressed his alarm and slid his arms beneath her. He glanced at the sleeve covering the bio-lights on her arm, rested his cheek against it and tried to assure her she was safe now. The glowing on her hand would be harder to hide, and it was better if the fraggers at this medical outpost didn't know she was an ambasadora. The doctor would find out soon enough. Fortunately, this particular doctor trusted Sean, even if no one else did right now.

A woman with bobbed lavender hair waited for them at the end of the passageway. It smelled antiseptic compared to the street outside.

Sean called out, "I need a stretcher now."

The woman crossed her arms over her chest.

"Did you hear me? She needs help."

"Who's *she*?"

"My prime." The moment he brought Sara through the grate, the scanners had alerted those inside that she didn't have idents.

"She's not authorized. You can't bring her here even with your node status." The fragger's gaze took in the blood trailing Sean down the passageway, but it didn't change her mind.

Sean pushed forward. She blocked the way and let her fingers slip to a cender strapped on her thigh.

"She needs help." Sean's voice amplified his desperation. "Yul knows me. He took care of my initiation, and I've been in his service before."

The woman's delicate features were offset by her aggressive stance. She looked from Sean to Sara.

"Just ask him!" Sean forced himself to remain calm. He knew his attitude wouldn't help here.

A man said, *"Let him in."*

For a moment Sean thought the voice had come from behind him, and half-turned before realizing it was the cocom Ephemerata had forced on him at the Tredificio. It took another moment to realize he was actually eavesdropping on this fragger's subvocal conversation.

The woman stepped aside and motioned Sean through a sliding metal door.

Three men rushed at him with a stretcher and equipment. He didn't want to let Sara go. He believed as long as he could hang onto her he could protect her. Relinquishing her to the others left him shivering and cold.

One of the men snagged her sleeve, exposing her right hand. Sean's muscles tightened as he prepared for an argument, or a fight. When the men failed to respond, his stomach fell. Sara's bio-lights had faded so badly he had to concentrate on her skin to find their patterns.

Another sliding door opened to a blinding white light. Sean pushed after the stretcher bearers, but a large man stopped him with a hand to his chest. "You have to wait."

Sean's frustration level ratcheted up by a factor of ten. Uncontrollable anger made his face hot, pushed away his ability to see reason. He gave the fragger an upper cut to the jaw. The bigger man staggered backward, due to surprise more than the pain. Sean tried to push past, but got tackled from behind. The big fragger threw Sean to the ground, knocking the wind from him. Sean struggled and landed a damaging kick to the man's shin, but couldn't break free.

"Zak!"

Sean twisted his head up to see Yul hovering over Sara. "You're not helping. I'll let you in if you promise to behave." Sean nodded.

Yul motioned to the man perched on Sean, who let him stand after bouncing his shoulder off the floor to make a point.

Sean flew to Sara's side. Once it was just he and Yul, he asked, "Will she be okay?"

"She's an ambasadora." Yul ran a sterilizing irradiator over Sean. "What were you thinking bringing her here?"

"I was thinking she needs help. You're still a doctor, aren't you? Now, is she going to be okay? She lost a lot of blood." Sean felt panic welling inside of him, an emotion he hadn't felt full-blown in years.

"If that lot out there finds out who she is, they'll tear you both to bits. Maybe me, too."

"She's worth the risk," Sean said.

"What is she to you? Not your prime. You were never the type to take an amour."

"She's more than that to me." Speaking the sentiment out loud made Sean face the idea that at some point since first meeting Sara Mendoza he decided he wanted to spend the rest of his life with her. And just her. It must have been his Lower Caste monogamy genes kicking in. Maybe he had just bypassed the emotional fallacy stage and was full-blown delusional, but so far the delusion of Sara outshined his dark reality.

Yul cut her clothing away from the wound. "I'll do what I can for her."

"I need you to do more than that. Please." Sean wondered if he should mention the irradicae. Yul would notice them before he tripped them anyway, and he might be reluctant to help her at all if he knew there was greater medical risk involved.

"I can trust you to keep her safe and locked away until I get back?" Sean studied Yul's face.

"You're leaving?"

"I need to find us a ride out of here. Can I trust you?" Sean asked.

"You wouldn't have brought her here if you didn't already know the answer to that question," Yul said. "Besides, I owe you."

The sincerity of Yul's words alleviated some of Sean's guilt.

"I'll keep this room locked down. My codes for entrance only," Yul said. "But secure a way out of here fast. Not everyone here can be trusted."

"Thanks. I'll be back soon. If I don't, make sure she gets in touch with David Anlow, the pilot from my ship. And, tell her...." He couldn't imagine saying good-bye to her.

"I'll tell her you saved her. That she was worth the risk," Yul said.

Sean stroked the skin on her arm one last time. He wanted to kiss her, but feared it would be too much like a good-bye, so he left, promising himself he'd kiss her again, soon, or die trying.

FORTY-FOUR

Chen stood over Tennor's writhing body. The freezers' black light highlighted the white thread of his clothing and the foam spattered on the floor around him.

"What happened?"

Tennor clasped his stomach and continued to roll back and forth. "Kill me."

"Looks like someone stuck you with a preserving agent. That's some tough stuff. You'll writhe for an hour maybe. If the pain doesn't kill you, the convulsions will. Snap your neck right off your spine."

Tennor whimpered and shook.

"Where's Sara?"

"Fragger doctor."

"Where?" Chen asked.

"Please kill me." Tennor's blued lips spat out the plea.

"Tell me where."

"Lindenn Street. First gate." Tennor's head snapped back and his body spasmed so violently he almost came off the floor. He reached for Chen's cender, but Chen held it just out of his reach. Tennor's knees jerked. He kicked the concrete floor so hard the bones in his feet and ankles splintered. He pounded the floor with his fists, breaking the bones in his wrists and hands with muffled little pops. His body straightened with a series of escalating cracks, then just as suddenly was still.

Chen tapped his reporter and spoke into the empty air, hoping the signal Tennor had boosted for him earlier would reach Faya a few streets down. "Ariel's dead. Sara and the fragger are still here in the Underground. They went to see a fragger doctor. I'm heading there now."

"Are you insane?" Faya's gravelly voice mocked him.

"What's the problem?"

"A contractor walking into fragger territory by himself. They'll slice you then fry you."

"We can't let them disappear again." Chen noticed a strip of light on the floor behind a freezer case and walked toward it.

"Stay where you are. I'm coming to you," Faya said. "There may be a way to flush out Sara and Cryer."

"Fine. I'm on Lindenn Street. Near the first gate." Or he would be soon. Chen ended the communication and stepped into the bright lights of the street.

FORTY-FIVE

Ear-shattering wails and electronic screeches blasted from a raucous group of street musicians further down Lindenn.

Sean made a left and slipped into an alley. He glanced around for spying eyes before pulling himself up onto a low-hanging roof. The rusting metal groaned under his weight in places, but held him. When he reached a circular exhaust chimney, he stooped down and removed the pale green plastic cap that kept pests out.

His hand slid down the narrow tube. The inside was smooth ceramic. Once he pushed in up to his elbow, he rubbed his fingers along the side in all directions until he found his prize. He pinched a small bit of metal like a builder's nail between his thumb and forefinger and carefully lifted it to the surface.

The jack's sharp point glinted in the streetlights. Jacking was standard practice a decade ago, until fraggers invented jackless reporters. The Embassy killed a few operatives and stole the design for their contractors. So, the fraggers released the tech into the general population as revenge. The Embassy still took credit, however, citing it as an example of how the Sovereign's scientists had found a way to improve personal communication.

But, there was only one way to communicate with the outside world here in the Latulip Underground, with an old-fashioned jack.

Taking a deep breath, then releasing it slowly, Sean pushed the jack into the soft skin on the inside of his wrist. With a little effort he threaded it into the nerve cluster which held the brain of his reporter. His mouth twitched at the insertion. He clenched his teeth. The sting brought tears to his eyes, even with the extra stims in his system. He'd forgotten how much it hurt.

Sean searched his mind for the transmission signature he needed.

An androgynous voice filled his head. *"This is a scientific vessel owned by the Embassy. Your communication is illegal."*

"City girls." Sean spoke the password he'd programmed a while ago. He held his breath until it cleared him.

"Please specify which passenger you would like to communicate with." The androgynous voice was the same, but this time it was interactive.

"Navigational Leader David Anlow."

"Connecting to Bard *secure line."*

While Sean waited, he scanned the area from his rooftop vantage point. Even the scant light up here seemed harsh compared to the darkness below. His heart felt just as dark thinking about Sara.

"Who is this?"

Though Sean couldn't see David's face, he could hear tension in the man's voice.

"David, it's Sean."

"Sean? What th—? Where are you?" The tone changed slightly, but not necessarily for the better.

"I'm..." He hesitated, second-guessing his decision to trust David.

There were few alternatives at this point. Deep down Sean knew the Armadan was honorable. Besides, anyone who walked out on the military couldn't be all bad. "I'm in the Underground with Sara. She's been hurt."

"*Injuries from the Tredificio?*"

"No."

There was a pause on both ends.

"We need a discrete pick up, David."

"*No good.*"

"What do you mean 'no good'? I know we've had some problems, but Sara doesn't have time—"

"*Sovereign Prollixer's Head Contractor is on board, guy by the name of Rainer Varden.*"

Sean's heart stuttered. "What's he doing there?"

"*He says he's Sara's bodyguard, but there's an awful lot going on behind the scenes. You know all about that, though, don't you? It's why you two left.*"

"Sara never mentioned a bodyguard." If that euphemism was the contractor's idea of a joke, Sean would cut the smile right off his face when he finally met him.

Then again, what if Sara hadn't told Sean the truth. He snapped a piece of metal from the rusted roof and rolled it back and forth between his fingers. He shook the thought off. That was his stim-induced paranoia talking. After all they shared, he would trust her with his life.

"*Kenon's dead, Sean.*"

The news stunned him.

"What happened? Did he make it out of the Tredificio?" He had known Kenon for six years; though not the best of friends, they had some good times.

"*It wasn't the eruption. He died protecting Geir from a female contractor at Soli's estate.*"

"What were they doing there? Is Soli okay?"

"*She's alive, at least in body. Trala was killed, too.*"

"Trala?" Sean squeezed his eyes shut. He had been closer to Soli than anyone else on the ship, mainly because of her refusal to leave him to his own misery. He couldn't imagine the pain she must be feeling. "What happened?"

"*My guess is the contractors were after Sara and her fragger operative.*"

Sean couldn't say anything, and David's sudden silence made his point clearer than his accusatory tone.

"Why involve Soli?" Sean asked.

"We may never know the truth. Rainer had her committed to the psych ward at Embassy Hospital."

"You just let all this happen?" He didn't mean for it to come out that way, but frustration and guilt got the better of him.

"I didn't just let this happen, Sean. You did. You and Sara and whatever games you're playing."

Silence.

"I'll come for you and Sara somehow, but I can't promise the others will welcome you back," David said.

"All of this is wrong. A misunderstanding." He wanted to explain what had happened to Sara, to him, but there wasn't time.

"I don't care what your excuses are. Two of our crew are dead, people who meant something to me, and who knows what will happen to Soli. I'll come for you, not because you mean anything to me. I'm coming because I don't leave people behind, even if they deserve it."

Sean drew in a breath. "Understood. As soon as Sara stabilizes I'll transmit again."

He cut the transmission and sat very still. Things were completely out of control. The cacophony of sound floating up from the street mirrored the chaos in his life right now. If it weren't for saving Sara, he might do exactly what Ephemerata had warned him about—stare into the abyss and jump. And, if Sara didn't make it, that jump would be far too easy for him.

He climbed down the side of the building and headed back toward Lindenn.

A small boy waited for him at a blind corner. "Don't go back there."

Sean looked around while he questioned the boy. "What are you talking about?"

"Back to the gate with the claw box."

Sean grabbed the kid's wrist.

The boy's eyes opened wide and he talked fast. "A contractor gave me six blocks to tell him where you took the bleeding girl from that transport."

"Why are you telling me now?"

"So you'll give me more to tell him you left the Underground."

Sean hesitated putting his trust in someone who could be bought so easily by so little, but he needed to get Sara out of there while Yul still held sway with the other fraggers. He couldn't do that with Chen trailing him.

He let the kid go. "I don't have any blocks."

"They said you wouldn't." The kid ran.

Something hard hit Sean in the back of the head. Pain streaked through his mind and blurred his vision. He heard his assailant step onto the street behind him. Even as his consciousness spiraled away, Sean's training took over. His right leg kicked backward like a piston. The move rewarded him with the satisfying crack of a knee joint splintering in the wrong direction followed by a suppressed scream.

He turned around and stepped forward in a basic fighting stance. His eyes wouldn't focus. A dark figure lay on the ground, grasping its damaged leg. Sean went for his stolen cender when he caught movement to his right.

Smooth, hard muscles propelled him into the battle. A blur of black topped in pink flashed past him on the left. The hair on the back of his neck rose.

Cender.

The shot sizzled into his brain. Burning pain spread through him, but the level wasn't high enough to kill him. He collapsed to his knees.

A female voice buzzed in his ears. "Where's Sara?"

"I got rid of her," he said and threw his forehead into the woman's.

Another set of hands secured his arms behind him. The pink-haired contractor pushed herself up with one arm, the other secured in a bone mender. With her free hand she stuffed a rag in Sean's mouth. It smelled of strawberries. Or maybe the scent was hers. With a raised boot, she kicked him onto his side. His shoulder took the brunt, but his head still hit the ground with a crack.

"We need you alive, not necessarily in one piece. I've been wanting to get my hands on you for a while."

Sean knew they were after the data. If he didn't make it, Sara would need it to make a deal for her life. He opened his subvocal link to Yul. Since others would be eavesdropping like Sean had earlier, he said what they would consider jibberish, but what Yul would figure out later.

"Compromised. Take Sara to my initiation. Check the lights—"

The female contractor kicked Sean in the jaw, breaking his subvocal link and nearly stealing his consciousness. She slid Ariel's plundered triton from a sheath under Sean's pant leg. The cold steel burned as she worked it into the skin of his wrist. Warm blood leaked down his arm. Feeling the point of the knife probing under the skin and slicing through nerves kept Sean from passing out. With a final, violent rip and a blast of searing pain, the woman tore the reporter and jack from his arm.

FORTY-SIX

Rainer stared at the white walls of Sara's suite. The mirrors at the far corner only reflected more of the alabaster nothingness. His fingers kneaded the Deleinean silk gown on the bed where he sat. Her soft scent hung on the turquoise fabric.

No more roses. Instead, there lingered a light smell he didn't recognize. The mech tech fragger had taken that scent memory from him.

He tossed the dress aside. His relief that she lived through the Tredificio destruction twisted into suspicion. He now accepted that she wasn't with Sean Cryer against her will, that maybe she had run off with him. Perhaps she was playing an angle to get at Prollixer. The theory rested on shaky ground. He despised the fact that he even cared what happened to her at this point. At one time he imagined her as his amour. Her elevated status as an ambasadora would make her more acceptable to his family circle. Then the good Sovereign ruined her.

The disappointment he felt troubled him. That's why he'd rebounded with Dahlia when she'd asked, and why he'd agreed to a child with her immediately. Yet, here he was, chasing Sara for the Sovereign, at least that was his official story.

Her resilience fascinated him. Though Simon would never admit it, Sara had a certain power. When the Embassy thought they could use her for their own purposes, she surprised them, turned on them, even Rainer.

His shoulders rolled back as he tried to dismiss thoughts of her, not the images of her from after her modification sessions, times when she needed him most. He wanted to be rid of those thoughts, instead focusing on Sara after Prollixer had *changed* her, when she became defiant. He remembered pressing against her in the communications kiosk, of the harsh words they had spoken to one another. When he called her a liar, it was because he recognized an attraction she still held for him, one she'd fiercely deny by the time they could finally act upon it.

She blamed him for not helping her sooner. He figured if anybody could've gotten her out it would've been him. But it would've cost him his position, his family. No reasonable man would take those kinds of risk, no matter the intensity of the attraction, yet guilt stirred inside him. And desire. All he wanted to do was feel her, taste her, have her. Like the way she once wanted him.

Rainer picked up a chair by the bed and threw it into the corner mirror. He looked at his reddened visage, mimicked over a thousand small shards, and hated her for introducing this weakness, this emotional fallacy, to a life he'd built on strength and careful analysis.

He needed to talk to Dahlia. She allowed him to remain focused because he would never burn for her like he did for Sara. Dahlia needed him for a breeding relationship, nothing so personal and complicated as what he had with Sara.

He opened an air screen and punched in Dahlia's code.

Her surprised face appeared in the space in front of him. She was prettier than Sara, but the observation didn't make him feel any different. Sometimes she reminded him too much of her sister, Faya.

"*Rainer?*" Dahlia's voice betrayed a nervous pitch.

"Were you expecting someone else?"

"*You shouldn't be contacting me.*"

His brow knitted. "What's happening, Dahlia? Is it something with Sara?"

The mention of Sara's name turned the nervousness into irritation. *"She'd be smart to hide. The Sovereign wants her brought in, and Faya's pushing for a Writ of Execution."*

So she could collect on Sara's death.

"What is Faya using as her argument?" Rainer imagined it stemmed from her own miserable failings during the modification. Maybe it was just to get to him.

"Under the auspices of treason. Because of the Palomin data cache. Faya has help. From Chen Starrie. He was the rogue who used Sara to siphon that data in the first place," Dahlia said.

"What does he get out of it?"

"Faya promised Chen a full pardon and re-instatement as a guild contractor once all this is over."

"She's making some big promises for a mid-level contractor."

"A mid-level contractor who has the Sovereign's ear."

Apparently the confidence did not go both ways, otherwise Faya would have known that Prollixer hijacked Sara's lineage. Rainer was certain that seeing Sara disgraced, in pain, and forced to take her own life would have been more appealing to Faya, even if she wouldn't receive any remuneration for it. Still, Rainer worried because Faya's power play couldn't have come at a worse time.

"Rainer, she's pushing for collusion with a known fragger operative and a rogue contractor."

The mention of Sara with Cryer made Rainer's jaw clench and his chest tighten. "If Prollixer's pardoning Starrie, can he really make a case for Sara's collusion?"

"Chen's not the rogue he's talking about."

Rainer's mind ran through lists of names and faces of contractors who could be involved. Nobody else was in any kind of position to do the kinds of things Simon.... The hairs on the back of Rainer's neck stiffened. There were no other players except the original ones.

"Prollixer put the writ out on me, didn't he?"

"*Yes.*" Dahlia's bottom lip twitched, but otherwise she showed no emotion.

Reality slammed into him like a runaway monorail. The Sovereign knew how Rainer had helped Sara during Faya's modification sessions, why he'd taken on the responsibility of being Sara's bodyguard. Maybe he even knew about Rainer's fallacy for the woman.

"Tell me everything, Dahlia."

Her gaze met his through the viewer. *"We have Cryer, but Sara's still somewhere on Tampa Quad."*

Dahlia blinked one too many times when she spoke about Sara. Rainer balled his hand into a fist. Even his amours were lying to him now.

"Is she hurt?" Rainer's voice remained steady, his gaze fixed. He never gave up tells.

"Probably. But it will be worse when Faya finds her." Dahlia's half-smile dared Rainer to reveal something.

"If your sister's smart, she'll control her homicidal tendencies. Sara's too valuable. She may be the only one who can get us out of this mess."

"What do you mean?" Dahlia's eyes widened a bit too much, pretending innocence.

"Stop it, Dahlia. You don't have it in you to bluff. I need exact locations."

"Do you plan to save Cryer, too?"

"He can rot. But knowing where he's being held could be good leverage." Rainer wasn't sure if Sara cared, but David Anlow wasn't about to let another person under his watch disappear.

"Sara's in the Latulip Underground."

That's why he couldn't find her through the minstrels and voyeurs. He would never have thought Cryer would risk taking Sara into fragger territory and a dead zone. "Where's Cryer?"

"I don't know." Dahlia swallowed after she spoke.

"Stop lying to me, Dahlia. Writ or not, I am still your amour and the father of your child. I can make life very difficult for you once this is all cleared up."

The cock of her head showed defiance, so he added, "Don't underestimate me or you'll end up on the losing side."

Rainer's heart raced with news of how badly the odds had become stacked against him, and his mind flooded with options, including running. But, none of that showed on his icy exterior, he made sure of it. A Writ of Execution was just paperwork—showing weakness was the real death sentence.

Dahlia's tanned face became pale and splotchy. He was slightly relieved that she still feared his power.

"They took the fragger to Palomin. Don't contact me again until this is over. I have a child to think about." Dahlia's image dissipated.

Rainer ignored her last jab. He was already planning his next move. If he played all his options well, there wouldn't be a need to go back to Palomin. Once Sara was safe, Sean Cryer's bones could crumble to dust in the desert sun.

FORTY-SEVEN

This had better work.

David watched the night side of Tampa Quad come into view. He'd already been concocting a reason to land at Shiraz Dock and find a way to get to Sean and Sara without anyone knowing.

His response to the question, as it surfaced every few minutes in his head, was always, *because I have to*. It wasn't duty. It was emancipation from guilt.

Most citizens only saw the military in action during major rescue operations, like the recent destruction of the Tredificio; yet, they were in combat situations often enough: quelling uprisings when specialized contractors would be wasted on the effort, closing off borders near the unstable Giovani Territory, even breaking up siphoning stations along the Kimberly River.

The Embassy had always kept them away from fragger activity, however. David never knew why until his last official mission, when Lyra and some of the others began *to turn*, when he had to leave some of the mutineers behind.

Because of David's relationship with Lyra, he had kept her secret safe. So what did the military do? They promoted her. That's when David left both Lyra and his commission. If the Sovereign knew how the Armadans were working more for themselves than the Embassy, he'd have the whole military disbanded. He preferred his mercenary contractors anyway.

A tell-tale clump of rubber soles preceded Rainer's appearance in front of David's holo-controls. The contractor's black boots nearly blended into the dark floor. "Land at the Hub. I need to pick up Ambasadora Mendoza at Latulip."

"You heard from her?" David feared Rainer had been listening to his conversation with Sean.

"Sara was seen there, and she may be injured."

David didn't miss the fact Rainer had called her by her given name. "You know this for certain?" David tapped his reporter and stood over Rainer in the fading control icons.

"Yes. We're wasting time. My only objective is to bring her back. Shouldn't that be your objective as well?"

"What about Sean? Is he with her?"

"No mention of the mech tech. He's not my concern. Now get me there."

"I can go with you and help you bring them back."

David expected a sarcastic remark or an argument, but Rainer looked to be considering the idea. Maybe he was getting desperate. David sweetened the deal. "I'm weapons trained and discreet." David knew the only way Sean might get back alive was with his help. He waited for Rainer's reaction.

The contractor didn't twitch.

David changed tactics, hoping he had correctly read the signs of Rainer's attraction to Sara. "You need someone who wants to get her back as badly as you do."

"This all finally makes sense," Rainer said. "I saw the vid of you with her from Nanga Ki. Is that why you want her back?"

The edge in Rainer's voice put David on guard.

"You can't believe everything you see. I would help anyone in her situation." He left Sean out of it this time, wondering if Rainer would be more likely to accept assistance if it were only for Sara. David had no intention of leaving Sean behind, but Rainer didn't need to know that right now.

"Get me there first." Rainer said. "Then we'll discuss it."

"We agree to it now or we go nowhere."

"For all your talk of helping others, you seem anxious to risk Sara's life for principle. I suppose all those rumors Captain Simpra's been spreading have an edge of truth to them."

Rainer played this game better than David because Rainer Varden would risk many lives just to prove his authority.

Every kilo of David wanted to tackle the man to the bridge floor and smash in his smug, perfect face. Instead, he dropped back into the holo-controls. "We arrive in thirty minutes."

And that was exactly how much time he had to think of something.

FORTY-EIGHT

"Who are you? Where's Sean?" Sara's speech was mostly sputtering.

She heard pounding, and not just in her head. Her eye lids drooped as she struggled to wake herself, but she kept forcing them open. The rhythmic insistence of fists on metal sounded from the white door behind her.

The man in the room took a silver flask from the counter and popped its cap under her nose. The metallic smell invaded her nostrils and her brain. Its familiar tang brought brief panic when she thought she'd found herself back in a modification cell. She believed she could feel Faya's hair tickling her cheek while she administered Sara's drugs. She pulled her arm up in defense, but a restraint dug into her wrist.

"Sorry. Occupational precaution. Seems silly to use on an ambasadora," the man muttered, unlocking the padded metal bands. "I'm Yul, by the way."

Sara took a breath and the strawberry brush of Faya's hair became a scratch from Sean's stubbly cheek. Remembering their night together calmed her.

The pounding halted.

Yul's head snapped up. "They'll hack my door soon." He grabbed a fresh blue sheet from a cupboard and placed it beside her.

"Where's Sean?" she asked again.

The frantic alarm from the door hinted that they didn't have much time. Yul tapped a finger to his palm. The alarm died.

"He went to get help, but he'll be too late. I'm getting you out of here because I promised him no harm would come to you."

"How will Sean know where to find us?"

"I'm hoping to contact him on the outside." Yul's gaze drifted away from hers as he said this. The alarm shrilled again. He tapped his reporter, but the alarm wouldn't respond this time. "I'm sorry we have to go now. I'll explain once we're safe."

Sara slid from the table and nearly toppled to the floor. Yul ran to her side and steadied her. "Careful. You'll tear all that newly-mended tissue."

She wrapped the sheet around her like a sari, while Yul worked at a wall box beside the door. The alarm bleated out of existence. "Lucky for us, they underestimate me. I wasn't always a doctor, but that was my last trick."

"Let's go before they get savvy."

"Right." Yul palmed open a panel in the wall and ushered Sara into the awaiting darkness. The panel snapped shut behind them.

"You're glowing again." Yul motioned to Sara's bio-lights. They were bright enough to make out their swirly pattern. "That's a good sign."

The illuminated floor outshone her body art, revealing the room's giant occupants. At least a dozen metal spheres, measuring half her height and just as wide, rested at the bottom of matching launch tubes. Sara's gaze followed the tubes angling high into the wall.

"Parcel launches?" She touched her back where the corer had penetrated. "I'm not crazy about bouncing around in a high-speed metal ball being sucked through a vacuum tube in my current condition."

"Let me see how your mending is holding up." Yul unfolded the sheet to expose her lower back. "The synthskin patch doesn't show signs of corruption, and my reporter verifies the mender beneath it is healing the tissue already. Even with some jostling in there, you won't have scarring. Most fraggers don't care, but a woman in your position relies on her image." He lowered his eyes as though she were the Sovereign herself.

His response unnerved her, embarrassed her. There was nothing special about her, except for some purple bugs living in her arm.

"I'm just a Socialite who got captured and tortured and modified and forced to do Simon Prollixer's bidding."

The shock in his face made her regret having said anything.

"Then you are more remarkable than I could have known. I understand why Sean's taken with you."

"He's more remarkable than I am," she said, worry creeping into her voice.

Yul popped the seal on one of the grey spheres. "I'm not the only one who knows about these abandoned launches, so they'll figure it out eventually." Taking her by the elbow, he helped her inside.

Sara stopped him from closing the lid. "Where am I going to end up?"

"Shiraz Dock by Carrey Bay. See you there in ninety seconds. And if anything should happen before then, it was nice to have met you, ambasadora."

That was encouraging.

Yul pulled his arm away and slammed the lid closed. The sudden darkness startled her. Sara braced herself, hoping the thin foam padding would be enough to keep from being knocked out. She held her breath.

The tube launched.

Sara's stomach fell from the force of acceleration. She had the slight sensation of spinning, but was unable to tell up from down at this speed. It was like blasting off in a starship without the reassurance of restraints.

The coffin-like claustrophobia of the parcel sphere squeezed her mind. Images of Sean rushed with her through the vacuum. His crooked smile. The stare of his brown eyes. His kiss.

A sudden jig to the left shoved her shoulder into the concave wall. She felt a tear at the tender synthetic skin over her wound. Her mind grabbed for calming images again: His kiss, not Sean's. Chen's. At Palomin. Before he left her. Had he kissed her good-bye? Rainer never did.

A spin to the right knocked her head.

Rainer. His dark hair. Hands that barely touched her. Stopping the pain. Not quite pleasure. Pleasure was Sean. Not an emotional fallacy. But, Sean was gone.

Sara's body became heavier. The sphere decelerated. When it rolled to a gentle stop, she suddenly felt very alone.

FORTY-NINE

The sunset spread onto Carrey Bay from the West, leaving the brightly lit shops of Latulip to their purples and blues.

Rainer tossed a few blocks to a street vendor, then left the kiosk's hot pink glow to offer David a bottle of water. He needed an excuse to stay topside in Latulip until he grabbed another read from Lyra's network of voyeurs and mind minstrels. Once they hit the Underground, there would be no outside communications.

He'd like a better read on David, too. He brought the Armadan along to watch his back, especially with the Sovereign passing out Writs at Faya's every whim. Rainer only hoped he wouldn't regret arming David with a pair of cenders.

The big man may have suspected his role as shield for now, but his nonchalant posture masked all but the most subtle cues. David's apprehension only showed in his wide stance and crossed arms. And though he'd flipped the cap off the water bottle several minutes ago, he hadn't taken a drink.

"What are we waiting for?" David asked.

Rainer took a draw from his bottle. A melody carried on the slight breeze as the synth spiders began spinning their electric webs on Carrey Bay. "I want an update before we storm in there." Rainer could manipulate the situation with half-truths and outright deception, but wanted to observe David's reaction to the truth. "About Cryer."

"I thought you said there was no mention of Sean. Something change?"

"Nothing that concerns you."

David's body language remained neutral and gave no hints to his intentions. Rainer stayed alert.

"He's part of my crew. It concerns me," David said.

"You have no crew. Just passengers."

David uncrossed his arms.

Rainer put a hand to his cender. His other wrist vibrated, indicating an incoming message on his reporter. It scrolled across his palm. David stepped closer.

Rainer tapped his palm. Music played in his head, a snippet from a mind minstrel stationed along the parcel launch docks on this side of Carrey Bay, filtered to him via Captain Simpra's network. The cadence was choppy and fast with breaks into a liquid refrain.

His smile. His eyes. His kiss. Sean.
His kiss. Chen's kiss. Before he left.
Before Rainer.
His touch.
After Rainer.
His pleasure. His kiss.
Not a fallacy.
Sean.
Alone.
Not a fallacy.
So alone.
His smile. His—

The song looped, but Rainer caught what he needed the first time.

"Sara's at the docks."

They caught a water transport. Rainer crushed his empty bottle and threw it into a disposal unit as Sara's song replayed over and over in his head. He wondered what it meant.

FIFTY

"Let me out." Sara screamed, panic invading her already too small space.

For several minutes she felt along the sides of the sphere, looking for the release. She found it near the bottom, just when she thought for sure her oxygen had run out. With a racing heart and shallow, labored breaths, she rocked the parcel launch back and forth until the release was on her left. Jamming a thumb into the depression, she released the seal with a hiss.

She spilled out into the Tampa Quad night and onto a heap of spheres; their grey coatings reflected repeating images of blinking purples and blues. A breeze cooled the perspiration on her face. She rolled over onto her hands and knees, her head hanging low to control her deep breathing before she hyperventilated. Her fingers probed the area where the corer had penetrated. No seepage, but still some pain.

Under and around her were thousands of parcel spheres. Crawling over the shifting mass, Sara reached the edge of a large cargo container. The purple and blue reflections took shape as strands of lights strung between nearby buildings. Just a few meters beneath those, hundreds of citizens sat at café tables and danced in the cobbled alleyway. Smells of fried fish and spilled alcohol wafted up from the carnival atmosphere.

Though she hadn't eaten in a while, the aroma of food turned her stomach.

Melodies from a pair of synth spiders and Media commentary from multiple air screens competed with the raucous crowd.

Sara ducked when a voyeur drifted up out of the partiers. Once a beacon of safety, the floating transmitters had now become deadly tattles, promising her capture if they looked her way.

She scanned the crowd, looking for Sean, but knew she wouldn't see him. Abandonment never crossed her mind. Her instincts said he was in more trouble than she was right now.

A metallic clunk nearly sent Sara out of her skin. Yul emerged from his own sphere and crawled the unstable gauntlet to her. She waved him down as a voyeur crested the cargo container from behind. He dropped and lay still. The voyeur kept moving over the spheres and settled over the front of the container and into the festivities below.

The dock parties, infamous for their cheap booze and fights, were more interesting than two people crawling out of a parcel launch.

Yul dragged his body up to hers. "Hello again."

Sara eyed his olive shirt, then peered over the container's far side, away from the carnival. "Take off your shirt."

"Why?"

"Because we need my sheet, and I'm not walking around that dock in just a pair of panties."

Yul pulled the shirt over his head and handed it to Sara. "The sheet will only give us about three meters."

"Not if we tear it into sections."

"Still a nasty drop."

"Do you have another way to get down?" Sara untied the sheet and slipped on Yul's shirt. It smelled like talc with a tinge of chemicals from the medical suite.

"I've been trying to think of one ever since I climbed into that parcel sphere." He grabbed one side of the sheet and thrust his triton into its center.

Seeing the doctor rip through the powdery blue fabric with the knife gave her chills. Until that point she had considered him harmless, but he was still a fragger. She held onto the thought that he had risked his own life to save her.

"Sean's in trouble, isn't he?" she asked.

"Yes, he sent me a subvocal transmission just before I woke you. The others in the fragger compound heard it. That's why they came running."

"Where is he?" Sara felt sick.

"I don't know, only that he's been compromised."

"What does that mean?" Panic rose inside her.

"Most likely he's been captured. He asked me to get you to a fragger initiate center in Rushow. It's a safe house with people we trust, and he told me how to access the data. We can use that to get him released."

Another voyeur peeked from the far corner of the cargo container. Sara and Yul lay as flat as they could among the parcel spheres. As soon as it wandered away, she tied one end of the sheet to an opening in the lip of the container where the automated cranes grabbed the monstrous spheres for removal.

Yul tugged at the knots where he joined the sheets and helped her over the side. "Remember, I'll be at Rushow, at the end of the dragon's tail."

"You're not coming with me?"

He was already gone. "Yul?"

Sara was on her own again. Her bare feet stuck to the metal sides in the humidity of Carrey Bay. Hoping not to draw any attention from the revelers on the other side, she half-walked, half-rappelled down the cargo container. When she reached the end of the sheet, she didn't even look down. Dropping feet first onto the cobbled stone surface jarred her body. Her lower back throbbed in response.

She looked up, hoping Yul had decided to follow.

The side of the cargo container was bare. No Yul, no sheet.

A hand wrapped around her mouth and pulled her to the shadows behind the container. She pummeled and kicked at her captor, but her weakened condition hindered her ability to defend herself.

The assailant pushed her to her knees. The sudden contact with the cool cobbles forced pain up through her legs and into her back and abdomen, where it pooled and reverberated within her wound. At one time she would have welcomed pain like this to quell her panic. Not anymore.

She looked up into the end of a cender held by a tall woman. A couple of males as large as David flanked her. Maybe Simon sent the military for her.

"We need the data you got from Sean Cryer," the woman said.

"I don't know who or what you're talking about."

The woman smashed the cender against the side of Sara's head. She crumpled sideways. Her shoulder bounced off the rounded stones.

"Did that help your memory?" the Armadan asked.

Pain blurred Sara's vision, but she still caught movement at the top of the cargo container. A barrage of parcel spheres rolled off the side, the rumbling drawing the Armadans' attention.

Sara rolled out of the way.

One of the male Armadans leaped in the wrong direction and caught a sphere to the chin. The female noticed Sara's escape and fired a cender at her, but an incoming sphere bounced in the way. The static blast blew a hole in the side of the sphere. It rained down large pieces of hot metal shrapnel.

Sara pushed to her feet and sprinted around the side of the cargo container, targeting the green lights of the docks. She could hide among the hundreds of ships berthed there.

A hand on her left arm jolted her reflexes into fighting mode. She thrust her index and middle fingers from her free hand at her assailant's eyes.

Icy blue eyes.

Rainer caught her by the wrist.

Her relief at seeing him gave way to a tired embrace. His woody scent masked the smells of the dock. Out of the corner of her eye, she saw Yul at the top of the cargo container. He waited for a sign from Sara that she was safe, then disappeared over the other side. David appeared from the other direction. "Are you okay?" he asked Sara. Then, he drew his cenders and pointed them past her.

The Armadans, bloodied and bruised, faced them, weapons drawn.

"What are you doing here, Lyra?" David asked.

"She watched the feeds like we did," Rainer said.

Sara felt lost. Apparently every one knew each other except for her.

"You got here faster than I expected," Lyra said.

"Did you think you'd be in and out with her before anyone knew?" Rainer asked.

"Something like that," Lyra said.

"What do you want with me?" Sara asked. If they were working against Rainer, then Simon had stepped up his game, and she was losing fast.

"Answering a Writ of Abduction for the Sovereign's errant ambasadora."

"A writ?" The warmth drained from Sara's cheeks.

A voyeur slid around the side of the cargo container. Rainer blasted it with his cender, sending it plummeting to the ground beside them. The action put the Armadans on high alert, alternately scanning the skies for more voyeurs and keeping track of Rainer's itchy trigger finger.

David put his hands out in a peaceable gesture. "Are we going to be able to walk out of here without someone getting killed?"

"You should know I don't negotiate." Rainer's finger moved to the trigger.

"I don't care about you, Rainer. I want Cryer's data." Lyra stared at Sara.

"So Simon asked you to recover what I couldn't? No wonder he wants me dead," Sara said. "Too bad Sean's gone."

"You know where he is," Lyra said.

"Would I be running around like this if I did?" Sara never blinked, and her tone was strong. "I guess you can't trust many people these days."

"You're lying." Lyra's voice trembled slightly. "Where is he? People will die without that information!"

"Simon's the only one dying, and I don't see where that's a bad thing," Sara said.

"It's not just him," Lyra bit out.

"Ah, Lyra. Please tell me you didn't let them inject you with those bots. Is that what happened to the others before the mutiny?" David lowered his weapon. His tone hinted at an intimacy they may have shared at one time.

"She has Simon's curse." Sara looked at the male Armadans and realized they, too, had been affected.

Lyra didn't bother to make eye contact.

"I told you not to do it, Lyra." David's voice came as a sad whisper. "I practically begged you."

"You cursed yourself," Sara said without pity. "Just like Simon."

Rainer's face screwed up in disgust. "You've polluted your line. A true Upper never resorts to gene manipulation, not even for procreation."

"Save your lecture. It was my duty to the Embassy." Lyra stood a bit straighter.

"Duty never usurps family," Rainer said. "And, there are horrors worse than death, like having your family circle disgraced and marked in shame forever."

Lyra stepped toward Rainer. "You say things like that because, no matter hard you try and how many generations go by, contractors will never be what they pretend to be—Armadans. There's nothing special about you, Rainer. You're pretty and you're devious, but in the end, you're still as much a Socialite as the woman standing beside you, only with a weaker gene—"

"Stop it, Lyra." David stepped between them.

Rainer dialed up his cenders. Sara put a pacifying hand against his chest and pleaded with him. "We need her."

"For what?" Rainer asked.

Sara focused on Lyra. "I'll make sure you get the data if you secure amnesty for all of us, including the other passengers on the *Bard*."

"Agreed," Lyra said.

"I'm not done," Sara said. "I want you to help me find Sean and bring him back."

"She can't keep that promise," Rainer said.

"She's in a better position than you are right now," David said.

Sara walked over to Lyra and looked up into her eyes. "If you help me get Sean back, I'll turn myself in with the data," Sara said.

"Don't be foolish, Sara," Rainer said.

"If I have the cure, I won't need you," Lyra said. "You can go and live your life with your fragger or your contractor or both, if you want."

"Then gather whatever force you can. I'll be in touch soon."

Sara took a risk trusting Lyra, but then desperate people were sometimes the most reliable…until they got what they wanted.

FIFTY-ONE

A final clang of metal on concrete marked the end of Sean's struggle with his steel bindings; he managed only to work them deeper into the flesh on his wrists and ankles. The muscles in his back bunched up in spasms. After leaving the cargo hold of the light cruiser, the contractors shackled him again in this dank cell. He tried keeping track of time by counting his heartbeats, but lost count too many times already. For all he knew, he could have been here for an entire day.

Heaps of garbage ship parts and outdated tech fragments littered every corner. In some places the junk spilled out into the center of the room. He had the impression they used this space more for storage than modification. With the eye that wasn't swollen shut, Sean scanned the scraps for something he could use as a weapon.

Chen Starrie hobbled back into the room. Even in these circumstances, Sean sized up the man Sara would have taken as an amour. She could have done better.

"You broke my knee." Chen stood in front of Sean. "And, I hate wearing bone menders."

"You must have hollow bones. All that inbreeding catching up with you?"

Chen punched Sean in the nose. The bergamot smell of the contractor's knuckles lingered before the irony tang of Sean's blood permeated his taste and smell.

"Sara never told me you liked it rough," Sean said.

Chen snickered. "You can't goad me with Sara. She was fun in the beginning, then a means to an end. And she should have *ended* back here."

"Here? Where are we?"

"Palomin." Chen adjusted a setting on the mender wrapped around his knee.

"Sara liked it here." The female with the pink-streaked hair strolled up beside of Chen. "Did she tell you about me?"

Sean's right wrist suddenly ached in its makeshift tourniquet; it dangled from the binder, a broken monument to her earlier slicing and paring. "Who are you?"

"I'm Faya. Surely Sara told you what kind of fun we had, or maybe she was sobbing too hard to be coherent. She babbled a lot during our sessions. And screamed. It was sad and pathetic."

"Don't ever remember her mentioning you," Sean lied. If he could get just one hand free, he'd snap the bitch's neck, even if Chen killed him for it.

"I think you're lying." Faya handed Chen an arm's length of a broken auxiliary engine rod. "But I like your attitude. Let's see if you last longer than she did. I'm sure you will the first time. She begged right away." Faya chuckled. "But, she got good at taking the pain. I bet you don't have that in you."

Metal glinted under the harsh white ceiling lights as Chen held the rod over his shoulder like a club. Sean tensed. Chen brought the rod down on top of Sean's knee cap. His left knee gave way with the impact. Bones crunched and the engine rod resonated in a high-pitched ring as it bounced onto the concrete floor.

Sean clenched his teeth to keep from screaming or vomiting. He lost his breath and shook as waves of pain radiated from his busted knee. His eyes watered, and bloody drool dribbled out of the side of his mouth.

The stims were wearing off. Now, he wished he would have kept the patches on, but his heart probably would have exploded before they even got him here. Maybe that wouldn't be such a bad idea, considering his nervous system was so raw to the pain.

"That's not how you handle a fragger." Faya glided over. "They like the pain. Hadn't you heard?"

"I always wondered where that rumor started." Sean's words came out in a pant. Most likely fragger operatives were so dosed upon capture that they didn't really feel much. Sean was feeling everything.

"You plan to kill him with kindness?" Chen asked.

"We're not going to kill him—yet. There's some very important information locked in here." Faya leaned close and rapped a fist on Sean's head. She produced a long-needled syringe and jammed it into the soft flesh of his inner thigh. The thick green liquid split his muscle and pushed into his veins.

He was about to make a desperate move when he saw the third contractor, the other female, leveling a cender at him from the room's doorway.

Not now. The time would be right. He could handle what they threw at him to know Sara was safe.

"Help me, Sean."

The voice echoed inside his skull like Ephemerata's through his subvocal link.

"Please. Help me."

The whisper floated to him from somewhere in the room, everywhere. It sounded like Sara. He twisted his head around.

"They're going to hurt me, Sean."

"Sara?"

"Yes, she's right here." Faya's voice modulated from normal to tinny, stuttering at times. "We have her and we'll cut her unless you cooperate."

Sean searched for Sara, but couldn't find her through the blue mist filling the room. In the beginning stages of a full-on panic, Sean fought for breath. He was sliding. And, it was some heavy stuff. Nothing like he'd ever had before. If this was what Faya had forced on Sara time and time again....

"Sean, we'll be okay, right?" Sara's voice tickled his left ear. She clung to his neck and buried her face in his chest. His heart pumped faster, but his mind slowed. "Yes," he said. "I promise." He wanted so much to hold her, stroke her hair, but—He took a deep draw of her scent, the scent he made for her, but choked on a heavy perfume of sweet berries and musk.

She raised her head. The dark locks were streaked magenta instead of purple, her eyes a frozen blue, not rich and dark. He pulled back from her. Sara's oval face bounced with a giggle. Her lips pulled back into a shrill laugh, cracking her beautiful face. Higher cheekbones and a pointed nose erupted from the split, desiccated flesh. Bright pink roots pushed out the shiny black hair.

"Get away from me." Sean's words dripped from his tongue with blood.

"Should I play with *her* instead?" The voice was Sara's but the head belonged to Faya. She grabbed his face and forced his focus to a pile of discarded view screens and voyeurs in the corner.

An arm peeked from the bottom of the junk heap, its olive skin dirty with bruises.

It's not her. It's not her. Not her.

The arm twitched, then the fingers moved. The discarded viewscreens burst to life, throwing images from every angle. Rapid flashes of code, a flickering of prismatic light, bursts of static, chatter in unknown languages. Then they all tuned to the same channel. A blurred picture and silence.

A muffled rhythm played, but not from the speakers. It came from Sean's head. The fingers twitched again. The screen shot widened. As the picture focused, the volume boomed, filling his head. It was sobbing—Sara's sobbing.

The screen's image cleared.

A woman's naked torso filled his view, repeated on every viewer from every angle. The body quivered, its skin split in a thousand places and oozing black fluid. The shot flashed to the head, bald and bruised, a hand hiding the face.

No. He told his mind not to believe his eyes, but his logic slipped away into some dark crevice of his consciousness as he watched the fingers claw at the concrete floor, splitting the nails, scraping the skin from the knuckles. The arm bent backward at the elbow to reach the closest viewscreen, its shoulder still lost under the pile of metal and plastic. The hand pushed into the viewscreen, pulling at the hand hiding her face. The hand slipped away to show Sara's face.

"Sara." Sean's tears slowly blurred the image once again.

"Tell me where the data is, and I'll help her, let you keep your promise to her." Faya's whisper was a scream in his ear, making him flinch. "And I'll stop hurting you. Trust me, you want to make that deal now because I learned a lot about how to break the tough ones from your little ambasadora."

Faya pulled the triton out of her waist band with one hand and grabbed his bound wrist with the other. "If I see her, I'll give her the few pieces of you that are left…before I start cutting on her, too." One quick slice severed the smallest finger from his left hand.

With no more help from the stims, Sean screamed. Faya started on his next finger.

FIFTY-TWO

"Thanks for the clothes." Sara tugged a long-sleeved black dress over her head; the swirling white vortex crawling down its front was like a graphic reminder of her life since Palomin. Except for that night with Sean. Their coupling was the only time she hadn't been blinded by hurt and suffering. She missed his touch. He made her feel safe.

"I would prefer you in one of the Embassy gowns," Rainer said.

"Yeah, well, I'd prefer not to be here at all, so I guess we're even."

Even though Rainer had managed to secure her proper attire and passage aboard this ferry, she wished he had gone back to the *Bard* with David. The ferry's small quarters suffocated her. Too many accidental touches in the tight corridors. Too many unguarded looks. From both of them.

But maybe David wasn't coming back. His attitude upon leaving was non-committal. Diffusing a fight with the Armadans seemed to be the end of his involvement in this mess. She couldn't blame him for that.

Sara's choice would have been to run and hide, but not without Sean. The stress of not knowing where Sean was, or if he were safe, made it impossible for her to control her breathing.

He was a fragger. He would be fine.

"Isn't the point of this so no one recognizes me as an ambasadora?" She continued stuffing her dark hair into a bobbed green and silver wig. They had both changed their appearance enough to throw off the voyeurs. Though she scolded herself every time she looked at him, she admitted Rainer's clean-shaven face and flattened hair gave him a softer look and enhanced his features.

"You should talk about fashion choices," she said.

He looked down at his new clothes, a pair of light grey tailored pants and a button up white shirt with navy blue pin stripes that any Embassy worker would have been proud of. "I take your point."

"Do you think David will show?" Sara asked.

"He seemed hesitant. We'll be fine without him."

"You don't like him, do you? Or anyone who's different from you."

Rainer fingered a few green strands of her wig in appraisal. "It's not about *liking* people. It's about their value. David's an Armadan, and most Armadans, are of value to our society."

"Lyra lost her value in your eyes."

"She chose her shame."

"Lyra's not the only one cursed. Shouldn't Simon bear just as much shame in your eyes, or more?" she asked.

Rainer plucked a decanter from the bedside table and poured three fingers of brandy into Sara's glass. "Prollixer corrupted himself for power. He's not whole, no matter how long he's Sovereign. He hasn't had an amour in decades. No children left, not that most citizens believed those were his original children to begin with."

"Then how does he stay on top?" Sara sniffed at the brandy before taking a sip. Sweet, verging on the edge of sour.

"The Sovereign gets by with the help of key individuals. He probably cursed some of them, too."

"*You're* working for him. What if he cursed you?" she asked.

"*Used* to work for him. I'm rogue now, remember? Becoming your bodyguard has done wonders for my career." Rainer filled his glass. "And I would know if anyone tampered with my genes."

Sara was surprised by his earlier comment. "He didn't order you to watch over me?"

"No."

The admission hung in the air. She didn't know what to say. Now was not the time for her to begin believing Rainer could actually care. Still, she had to ask, "Did my reconstruction devalue me?"

He brought the glass down without taking another drink.

The fantasies that kept her alive during her modification were all about Rainer. Now his attraction to her was obvious, but aside from fulfilling her physical needs, what more could he offer her?

"They just reconstructed your shell," he said. "What's in your line remains more or less unaltered."

Typical Rainer response. "What does that mean?" she asked.

"So long as those irradicae are still on your ovaries, you'll be little more than a tumble to any Upper who has a true pride in his heritage." He emptied his glass without looking at her.

Part of her didn't believe him, knew he was trying to convince himself that he didn't want her. It didn't matter. She no longer wanted him. *Rainer* had now become the empty shell, at least to her, because he'd never be the man Sean was.

The glass domes in the city of Rushow glowed from the inside with soft blue light, spreading their warmth through the gloomy afternoon. Above, a green-grey sky threatened rain. Sara breathed the loamy scent of the approaching storm with anticipation. A rising wind pulled at the fine hairs of her wig.

She and Rainer mixed into the crowd of passengers bustling down the gangway. They hadn't spoken in hours. What else was there to say?

It was only her third time to this part of Tampa Quad, yet Sara marveled at Rushow's stately architecture. The buildings in the main square intersected at a series of glass elevator towers, giving the impression of one huge complex of alternating walls of slate and windows.

"Hard to believe this city was designed as a virtual world first, then built here in the real world," Sara said. They had been watching vids about Rushow on the cruise over, partly for research, partly to fill the uncomfortable silence. She had been painfully aware of his every movement, and forced herself not to stare at him and wonder at how things could have been different.

"Ridiculous." Rainer moved past her into the street.

Their previous conversation had gotten to him, which surprised her because he wasn't the brooding type. She told herself it was being cast out of Simon's powerful circle which had brought about the change in Rainer. But, she recognized a lie, especially when she was the one telling it.

The steps were the same ash grey slate as the exterior of the buildings. Coils of fossilized sea creatures, metamorphed by the planet and buffed to a shine by human hands, twirled up and down the façade, complementing the round domes and windows and glass elevator towers. She recognized the great silica dragon skeleton winding around the side of the third building on the left. This had to be the dragon Yul had hinted at.

"This way." Sara tugged at Rainer's arm.

The elevator doors opened from opposite sides, one leading to the second building, the other letting off passengers to the third. A few other Socialites entered. Sara sneezed from the mix of floral and musky fragrances spewing from their scentbots. They all stared out different sides of the glass elevator box. She concentrated behind them where the dragon's skull rested just outside the elevator tower.

"What floor?" A platinum-haired man asked.

"Three."

Sara watched the vertebrae in the dragon's tail get smaller and smaller as the elevator crept toward the higher floors.

The doors chimed and opened at the third floor of each building, but the dragon's tail continued to curl upward. Everyone stepped off except for the platinum-haired man, Sara, and Rainer.

"Sorry. Next floor, please."

The man smiled and pressed the button with a shiny fingernail.

Another floor and the dragon tail slithered still upward. She tried to crane her head to see further up the wall, but couldn't see past the current floor.

"My mistake," she said. "The next one, if you would? Thank you."

The man nodded, no smile this time.

Rainer shot Sara a look and gestured to the number nine button the man had lit upon entering. He might be in for a long ride.

Even before the lift settled again, Sara knew it was the wrong floor.

"Six, please."

The man cleared his throat, about to protest, when three Socialite women swept into the elevator. One with clover pink hair piled high on her head asked for floor six, as well, and he readily complied.

Socialite men. Sara shook her head. They had never held her interest, no adventure; they never got dirty.

The sixth floor slipped into view. On the stone wall outside, framed perfectly by the glass lift's window, was the silica dragon's perfectly coiled tail.

The females glided out in a chatter. Sara stepped to follow.

"Are you sure this is your floor?" The man sniffed.

Rainer dropped a shoulder into him on his way out.

"How do you plan to find this fragger doctor now?" Rainer asked.

"I'm hoping he'll find me."

They stopped in the middle of the hallway, the circular stained-glass window refracting every wavelength of blue light over Rainer's white shirt.

"You said you knew where to find him."

"Approximately...." Sara ripped off the wig and walked around in a circle, staring at the walls and ceiling.

"What are you doing?"

"Trying to get noticed."

Click.

A door to her right popped open a few centimeters.

Rainer reached for cenders that weren't there. Sara had insisted that if he were going to walk around with weapons strapped to his thighs, there was no need to alter their appearances in the first place. He had back up weapons secreted somewhere, she was certain, otherwise he would have never agreed to give up his guns.

She edged toward the door, but Rainer stopped her with a raised hand.

Standing to the side, she spoke. "Yul. I need your help."

Seconds ticked by. Sara stared at the thin line of white light that slipped through the portal. The crack widened. Rainer held a razor disc in the hand at his side. Sara shot him a look of alarm.

A redheaded woman dressed in a light pink mini-dress stepped through the doorway. "How may I help you?" she asked.

"I need to see your doctor, Yul."

"We have no doctor in this suite. Perhaps you could try three floors up."

"Tell Yul that Zak's life is in danger." Sara stepped closer. Anger and impatience threatened to break through her dam of resolve as her panic rose. "I need him. Please."

The woman cocked her head, listening to a subvocal feed. "This way." She put a hand on Rainer's chest. "But the contractor has to leave his toys behind."

Rainer shook his head no.

"Then stay out here," Sara said. She wouldn't lose a chance to save Sean because of Rainer's stubbornness.

Rainer handed over the disc.

"And, the others?" the redhead asked.

"That's it," Rainer said.

"Then you wouldn't mind if I searched you, would you?" Her tone was mild, but conveyed a warning.

"You're not going to search me." Rainer made it sound like an order.

"Then you'll wait for her here," the woman said.

Sara headed for the door, but Rainer grabbed her hand to stop her.

"Fine." Rainer allowed the woman to search him and take three razor discs and a retractable whip. When he didn't show any real indignation about the confiscated items, Sara knew there were a few weapons the redhead had missed.

Inside, Yul waited for them behind an empty medical table in the center of the spacious room. It was a silvery island amidst a sea of blue tile. Sara rushed to greet him.

"I can't believe I found you." Tears puddled in the corners of her eyes. "We've heard the Embassy has Sean," she whispered.

Yul looked nervously at Rainer, but his words were tender. "I know. Word came through the ranks that they took him to Palomin."

Sara's heart sank. Until that moment there was still the possibility that all this was misdirection on Simon's part, but hearing that Sean was imprisoned at Palomin almost undid her.

Yul reached a hand toward her arm, but stopped short of touching her when Rainer stepped forward.

"We have to contact Simon to make a trade—his cure for Sean. I'm surprised you haven't done that already." Sara's chest tightened as she thought of what Simon's contractors were doing to Sean right now. If he hadn't helped her, he could have escaped, dropped out of society, been safe, but saving himself wasn't in Sean's make up.

"I don't have the data," Yul said.

"Why not?" Sara's voice rose in anger. "You said he told you where to find it."

"Yes, I know where to find it, but I can't access it inside the V-side. I was locked out on my first attempt. Too many fraggers in that Underground compound heard Sean's transmission."

"Why didn't you send in another operative?" Rainer asked.

"Because I traced my lockout back to *this* location. Aside from my assistant," he motioned toward the redheaded woman. "I can't trust anyone else here."

"Then send her in," Rainer said.

"She's not a fragger." An unexpected fierceness came into Yul's voice. "She's my prime, and I'm sorry, Sara, but I can't risk the mother of my children, even for Sean."

Sara regarded the redhead, who looked away as if in guilt. "It's okay. I could never ask you to sacrifice your family after all that you've done for me. Send me in instead."

"Absolutely not." Rainer's tone made Sara and Yul jump. Stepping between them, Rainer spoke to Sara. "He can get someone else to go in. There's no reason for you to do this."

"Didn't you just hear him? There's no one else. It has to be done. Now."

"I would have to agree with him," Yul said from behind Rainer. "To get you into the V-side would involve implanting idents, and in your condition...that's not advisable."

"You mean the irradicae," Sara said.

"I found them during a scan before I removed the flower corer from your abdomen. That's why I didn't give you any immune boosters."

"Would that have set them off, so to speak?" she asked. It was the first time she had gotten any real answers about what was happening inside her. She hadn't felt pain or discomfort, not so much as a cramp, but maybe she wouldn't, maybe her eggs would just shrivel inside her. Or, maybe it would kill her immediately with an onset of severe hemorrhaging, sparing her the Passing Ritual. Either way, she believed she'd know when it happened.

"Yes," Yul said. "Irradicae *are* immune boosters, on stims. They don't just go after diseased cells, they look at everything as a threat and devour whatever's in their path. That's why they were banned by the Embassy."

"Except for purposes of genetic blackmail," Sara said.

"I can't give you idents without giving you immune boosters, not after your recent injury. It may seem almost healed, but I scanned your vitals upon entering, and there is a small spike in your white blood cell count. Probably an infection."

"Then that's the end of it," Rainer said. "We'll find another way—"

"It's not your decision."

"You'd give up your lineage for *him*? Shame your family and take your own life, if you eventually survive this?"

"Yes." Her response held more weight than she felt. "He'd do all he could to help me, and has."

"He wouldn't do this."

"How do you know, Rainer? Because *you* wouldn't? Not every man in this system is like you and Chen. Get everything ready, Yul."

Rainer's expression went from anger to alarm. He took her hands in his, the most touching gesture he had ever made toward her. "Sara, I'm begging you not to do this. There's still a chance they can be removed without any damage to you. Still a chance that we could...."

She waited for him to continue, knowing he'd never speak the words. "Could what? Fly back to your place and play at the perfect society couple? The only reason you want me is because I'm taboo in your world."

"You don't understand what you're risking."

"Sean's already risked more for me than anyone else ever has. He has an ideology, a sense of honor in this place so corrupted and decadent that most people don't even remember what commitment means." She had been afraid she might not be able to do what was necessary, but now she was certain she could do anything.

"You wouldn't understand, Rainer. Life's about more than passing on your genes." Her tone was gentle, free of judgment. "You have six amours and a dozen children. Sean only has me, and I only have him."

He released her. The disappointment in his gaze tore at her, but she lay down on the table, resolved, but frightened. "I'm ready."

Yul pressed a sedative patch into the crook of her arm. His talc smell comforted her. She held her hand out to Rainer. He reached out, but pulled back. Then he left. The sight of him walking away was all too familiar.

FIFTY-THREE

Chen ducked as the Sovereign lobbed a razor cuff at the room's blood-splattered wall. Thanks to his atrophying muscles and fading motor skills, the cuff clinked harmlessly to the concrete without leaving so much as a dent in the stucco.

There were few options left to Chen—either Prollixer would grant him his pardon for his continuing efforts in the data recovery or he would order Chen's immediate execution. Chen knew Faya was the better shot, but Dahlia was much closer.

He edged his nervous fingers toward his cenders.

Sean Cryer let loose then with a roar of rage at some vision only he could see. Prollixer shrank away from the noise.

Chen gripped his weapons.

Prollixer shook visibly. "Stop that," he yelled at Cryer. "Make him stop!"

Faya kicked Cryer in the stomach. He doubled over, but continued to snap out terrifying screams and growls. Chen hoped the bindings held against Cryer's vicious thrashing. Faya had really pissed him off when she mentioned cutting on Sara this last time.

Sweat poured down the Sovereign's face, and Chen realized he was looking at him. "Who are you?" Prollixer asked. The facial twitch which accompanied the question showed the old man was slipping away fast, and not just physically.

He didn't recognize Chen, even after their ongoing negotiations. The Sovereign lost interest in Chen when Cryer took another fit and pulled his undamaged leg free of the manacle. He kicked Faya in her chest as she tried to secure him again and knocked her backward onto the floor. Chen pulled his cender, his heart slamming against his rib cage. Before he could fire, Faya sprang to her feet, sucking in air and ready to punish Cryer. She pulled his head back and pointed the triton knife at his good eye.

"Stop." The Sovereign grabbed Faya's wrist. Chen knew she could have easily twisted out of his feeble grasp, but she wasn't ready to defy Prollixer yet—that was a path of no return. She sheathed the knife.

"How can you expect to get anything coherent from him in this state? These facilities weren't built to fulfill your personal masochistic desires."

"He's already given us some information," Faya insisted. "We just need to play up his emotional fallacy with the ambasadora."

"Emotional fallacy? He's a fragger. They have even less emotion than contractors." Prollixer muttered something about the groups being one and the same, but Chen couldn't catch it all.

Faya set her jaw. "And less emotion than Simon Prollixer."

Chen held his breath. Part of him enjoyed this showdown and wanted to see how it would end, but the preservationist inside him backed toward the door.

"You don't speak to me that way." Prollixer suddenly seemed lucid. The coldness in his voice was terrifying. "I am still your Sovereign." He walked toward Faya. "I am still your Sovereign!"

Prollixer grabbed a fistful of Faya's shirt, a surge of strength, fueled by rage, rose from his gaunt frame.

Faya pulled back from him in shock, but he held tight.

"What do you know so far?" The nervousness in his voice from a few moments ago turned into fierce accusation.

Chen believed Prollixer was almost as messed up as Cryer. Faya cleared her throat. "He didn't take the cache—"

"What?" He shook Faya in a panic.

Faya looked as though she wanted to tear his eyes out, but her tone was matter of fact. "But he did receive possession of it, then hid it somewhere within the V-side."

"Where?" The Sovereign's eyes lit up and he actually smiled. Chen noticed dark spots discoloring Prollixer's teeth in places. It was as haunting as it was disgusting. If Chen looked close enough, he could also see those same spots erupting on the man's neck and hands.

"I was just about to find out," Faya said.

Prollixer released his hold on her. "I think we've come as far as we can with your tactics."

Cryer's broken body, which had been so loathsome to the Sovereign only minutes before, now seemed to stir him. He touched Cryer's shoulder and asked, "Do you miss Sara?" Cryer's head lulled on his chest at the mention of her name. Dried streams of blood zigzagged down his bared back and his temples, while bright drops still puddled around him from deeper wounds. The Sovereign avoided the mess and squatted next to Cryer.

"She misses you, too." The Sovereign's voice was soft.

Cryer's head lifted slightly, but his gaze couldn't focus.

"She's here. Sara asked for you. I told her you were helping me lift my curse. That made her very happy."

"Sara." Cryer's voice barely got the word out.

"Yes, Sara. As soon as you tell me where to find that cache, we'll let you see her. She's waiting for you. You don't want to disappoint her, do you?"

"The lights," Cryer said. "The lights."

"What was that?" The Sovereign leaned closer. Faya had a cender trained on Cryer, not taking any chances after the kick he gave her moments ago.

Chen didn't think this was a ploy, though. Somehow Prollixer had managed to convince Cryer what Faya couldn't—that Sara was here waiting for him.

"Tell me what you said again," the Sovereign said.

But Cryer had slipped into unconsciousness. Faya had gone too far with the drugs in an attempt to pluck a fast and easy confession from the fragger.

Expecting the Sovereign's earlier rage, the three contractors backed toward the exit. Chen stopped dead when he saw the Sovereign lean over and cradle Cryer's head against his shoulder. He cooed to him as if to an infant. "Everything will be fine. Just fine."

Chen looked to Faya and Dahlia for validation. Their startled expressions mirrored his thoughts. Dealing with a sane Sovereign was delicate at best; dealing with whatever he was turning into might mean the end of all their lines.

FIFTY-FOUR

"Yul?" Sara awoke to a sweetness on her tongue and a fuzziness on her teeth. She tried to swallow, but the dehydrating sedative made her tongue feel like chalk. The medical table chilled her skin, even through the soft blankets.

Yul rushed over. Tilting her head, he held a glass to her cracked lips. "Sip."

The same sugary taste dribbled into her mouth. Coughing and clearing her throat a few times she managed to say, "Am I okay?"

"It appears so, though it may be too early to tell." He squeezed her arm.

She didn't feel any ill effects, but that didn't mean she was fine and her feelings offered her little in the way of real relief.

Rainer appeared in her periphery and occasionally touched the table's rounded edges, but never her. She smiled faintly; he looked away.

Yul passed a hand-held scanner over her body. She scratched at her wrist as the scanner's fingers of light played over her.

A stinging pain forced her to clench her fist. A small streak of blood dripped from the inside of her wrist down to her fingertips.

"Sorry. I should have bandaged that." Yul held a sterile pad over the incision and applied steady pressure.

"What is it?" Sara tried to lift her hand to see exactly what he'd done to her.

"An internal reporter. No more bracelets for you. I'll explain how to use it later. Now you need to rest."

A sense of urgency gripped Sara. She fought to push her grogginess away. "No, Sean doesn't have time."

"Normally an initiate would wait thirty hours before attempting her first post-op insertion—"

"Out of the question."

"I figured you'd say that." Yul handed her a case.

Sara flipped the lid open and saw a pair of silver lenses.

"I sent you an invite to the area where Sean hid the cache. It took me a while to figure out what he meant by check the lights. You will, too, once you're inside the right world."

"How do I get there?" she asked.

"You'll arrive in the lobby, a sort of waiting room that looks and feels like an endless ocean. A sphere will rise out of the water. Just touch its surface. It will take you where you need to go. I've set up an automatic streaming program for you, which allows me to siphon the data and pull you out as soon as the capture is complete."

So much information. Sara's head swam, trying to shake off the sedative and process Yul's instructions. "So, I'm stealing back the same data that got me here to begin with."

"I've always felt life is circular," Yul said, then seemed embarrassed by his wistfulness. "Anyway, the lenses will adapt themselves to the pattern of blood vessels on your retina."

"Can I go in without them?" The stigma of the v-mitters stayed with her after Palomin. She was glad Sean hadn't used them back at Shocker's.

"Not at your level," Yul said. "It's painful enough the first time. Let the lenses make insertion easier."

Sara held her breath against the faint chemical smell. The lens didn't slide on as easily as she'd hoped. The longer it took, the more she wondered if this was really the path she wanted to take. When it finally slid into place over her iris she immediately wanted to rip it right back out. "Is it supposed to burn like this?"

"Stings a bit."

She kept her eye still. The drying burn became a series of minor irritations tingling randomly beneath her lid. She held her breath and tried the other before she changed her mind altogether. Thankfully, it adjusted quicker.

Now she only saw blackness with an occasional spark of light to accompany the tingle. She imagined looking down on herself from above and seeing the silver v-mitters in place of eyes. She closed her lids, wondering if wearing the lenses in the real world really made a difference. Only areas which had already been mapped virtually like Palomin would even show up. She suspected some fraggers hid behind the lenses' anonymity or wore them for intimidation.

In a way, these v-mitters, which had once haunted her dreams and visions, were now the final piece of her transformation. Stripped of the shell she'd been born into, she finally knew who she was, and the thought gave her courage for whatever lay ahead. So did the promise of seeing Sean again.

Her ears popped, then a brilliant new landscape flashed into being all around Sara. A purple sea shimmered in every direction. It was so real. She trembled from the shock and curled her toes.

Her toes. She could feel her toes. Sara looked down to glimpse her bare feet, her av's bare feet. They were the same, felt the same, reacted the same. Everything was the same, except no bio-lights. A black sarong brushed her ankles, its Deleinean silk sliding along her legs. Matching black scarves, their ends wrapped snugly around her wrists, blew freely in the slight ocean breeze. Long waves of dark hair fluttered against her shoulders. Her hand went to her abdomen, and for the first time in weeks, she let herself entertain a feeling of hope. She was one step closer to freedom, hers and Sean's.

A blue sphere rose from the purple water just as Yul had said. She cautiously touched its shimmering surface. Electricity swept through her. Her instinct was to pull away, but she remained still, balancing on the little floating raft which bobbed slightly on the ocean lobby. The sphere expanded. Her heart pounded as she stepped inside.

It was like a door into another world, but a world all too familiar to her. Sara placed her foot down on the onyx floor of the Embassy Hub. Disorientation flooded her mind, a remembered fear simmered in its wake. A darkening sky barely filtered through the chalcedony wall. This Hub was exactly like the original. Just no people. The magnoramps were lifeless. The seating areas empty. The silence was almost complete, except for a distant buzzing. For all she knew, that could have been inside her head or a result of her popping ears during insertion. As the light of the Tampa Quad sky continued to fade, the interior lights of the Hub came up.

A green shaded floor lamp flickered from a far corner, the only animate feature of this doppelganger Hub. She walked toward the lamp. The light brightened and the buzz intensified with each step. Her eyes darted from corner to corner. She expected someone or something to jump at her from the shadows. She stopped a meter from the lamp. It shined with a steady intensity.

The buzz evened out into a high-pitched whine. She covered her ears, but forced herself to inch closer and closer until she was within touching distance of the lamp. Tentatively, she reached out a hand.

The lamp exploded.

A blue arc jumped from the conduit into Sara's chest. The intense heat washed over her face, but her chest burned with cold. Her breaths came in ragged gasps. Her heart pounded out of control. Her vision blurred. All she could think about was how Sean's body had convulsed when he was last in the V-side, how he could have died in here, how she might die in here.

Then all sensations stopped, and she stood in front of the same lamp, now in pristine order and glowing steadily once again. No more buzzing. She controlled her breathing, confident she had the data and that Yul would pull her out at any moment.

"Looking good, Zak."

Sara spun around.

A large, barrel-chested man walked toward her from the bottom of the inert magno-ramp. "Or are you just a little friend he sent to retrieve his cache?"

A hand grasped her shoulder from behind. She shook it off and backed up enough to put each of the intruders in her sight. This second man was smaller, but the fierce, dead stare of his green eyes was almost reptilian. Darkness bloomed as a portal opened beside him. A third man in a blue shirt stepped through the portal, brandishing an odd-looking cender. The same weapons materialized in the other men's hands.

"Yul, get me out of here." Sara had no idea if he could hear her. She worked around one of the white plush couches, never taking her eyes from the threats in front of her.

"It's not Zak, Cuzco," the man with green eyes said.

"So the idents affirm," Cuzco said. "Can you get a read on her real identity, Vishnue?"

"Doing it now, but I need a location from Topper first."

"Working on it," the green-eyed man said.

Sara didn't understand what they were talking about, but knew it couldn't be good for her.

"Whose side are you on?" Cuzco asked.

"I'm on Sean's side," she said. "Zak's side. He's innocent. The contractors are trying to split the fraggers, can't you see that?"

"So, he's not the one who hid the data you just recovered?" Vishnue asked. "Remember, lies will get you killed here." He shot, but aimed high so the massive blast of energy would miss Sara by fractions of a meter.

"He had no choice." Sara scanned the Hub, hoping Yul would open a portal for her any minute, or maybe just rip her out of this world like she had Sean. She'd even be happy if Yul had to stop her heart to do it.

"That doesn't sound like Zak. Always struck me as the kind of guy who made sure he had plenty of choices to fall back on," Cuzco said.

"Got an insertion location for her," Topper said. "Rushow."

If they contacted operatives at Rushow, Yul, his wife, and Rainer might not have a chance, and if Sara couldn't get out of here, Sean's chances died with her.

"You ready to give us some answers?" Cuzco asked.

Her patience wore thin. "You know the truth." She walked toward the trio, ignoring the raised weapons aimed at her. "Otherwise, I'd already be dead."

"It's not too late for that," Vishnue said.

Sara never blinked. "Stop hiding behind your avatars and fight for your ideology. Sean's *dying* for his at Palomin right now. If you had half the courage and passion that he has, you'd gather as many fraggers as it took to bring him back. But for all of the blustering and rhetoric that comes out of this organization about marriage rights and destroying an antiquated caste system, all of you just stand in the background, waiting for the right time. This is it."

A portal opened to Sara's right.

"Simon is dying and the Embassy will be up for grabs," she said. "All you have to do is put your training into practice. You can start by helping Sean. He would have done it for any of you. And, if you're afraid to come out of this…." She looked around. "This antiseptic, shell of a world, and fight in a real battle, then stay here. Sean's probably better off without you." She backed into darkness to the rejoin the real world because she wasn't afraid to fight for him.

FIFTY-FIVE

David squeezed Mari's hand and followed the funeral procession into the memorial hall. She probably hadn't been to many funerals in her short life; David had attended too many.

Leading the mourners, a synth spider played the lively tune of Kenon's family circle on his mother's side and spun a bright blue web of light between its sinewy legs. Its sound politely covered the soft crying of Kenon's family and friends.

"I always thought these places were too beautiful to cry in," Geir whispered. "I don't want—" His voice broke and he had to clear his throat to continue. "I don't want my family crying for me in a place like this. Don't want them crying at all. Have a party for me when I die."

They glided past endless rows of sparkling silver monoliths that stretched into the dimly lit depths of the cavernous room.

Mari's gaze stayed on the white marble beneath their feet.

David envied her hyper-emotions—the extreme sadness and clingy vulnerability she showed now complemented her usual bouncy cheer and mouth-pursing determination. She was never embarrassed by her feelings, the complete opposite of David's Armadan upbringing.

His children, *their* children, would be raised to value emotions, not hide them.

He put his arm around Mari and followed the mourners, forcing himself not to count the monoliths as they walked by. Not superstitious in nature, David wasn't taking any chances that cosmic luck, bad or otherwise, actually existed.

The six-sided monoliths had narrow bases that widened like inverted pyramids to a flat base at top, rising like the decorative bird baths in his mother's gardens in the Koley Mountains. But unlike the many-storied baths, the monoliths of the passed barely reached a meter. Their granite tops, set with gemstones in every hue of the spectrum, gleamed within a halo of blue from lights shining down from the ceiling.

David passed a man and three children on his right who watched a holovid play just above one of the pedestal's surfaces. The young woman in the vid chased the same three children around a manicured lawn. They were all laughing in the captured scene, but here in the memorial hall, the children wept and clung to their father's side.

A somber glow beckoned the processional from an archway.

"What do we do now?" Mari whispered, looking up without moving her head.

"We just follow the people into the Sculptorium."

"We won't actually be in there when they burn him—the body, will we?"

"Yes, but we'll leave before they begin the sculpting." David was thankful for that. It was one thing to see a finished pedestal of ash and gems, another to witness The Passed molded into their own memorial.

David and Mari followed the men in front of them in ever-larger circles. Each sweep strategically placed members of Kenon's extended family around an oblong impression in the floor. Within the impression lay Kenon's body, dressed in formal attire. David, Mari, and Geir's view near the end showed three hundred odd mourners radiating outward.

Giselle held the spot of honor at the front with Kenon's mothers and fathers. She kept tight hold of Hailey. Mikail stood next to her, holding Sasha. A dark-skinned Armadan rounded out Giselle's inner circle. Kenon's remaining amours and their amours were positioned according to the hierarchy.

The synth spider played its last strand, signaling Kenon's mother to begin. She looked like she could be David's age. Socialites always started their families young, why they had so many more children than the average Armadan.

With a steady voice and a rigid stance, she said, "Today we gather to *remember*."

The assembled recited, "We remember."

"Though Kenon Jean-Luc Brudger has passed to the Otherside, today he becomes part of the History and will live there with us forever. We remember you, my son."

"We remember," Mari spoke the words quietly with those around them, but David remained silent.

"*I* remember. I remember the beautiful smile I gave to you. I remember the darkness of your hair that came from your father."

Mari choked back a sob against David's chest as Kenon's mother continued her eulogy. Geir bowed his head.

Lost another one, Anlow. Another dead kid. What kind of captain are you?

He knew this wasn't his fault any more than it was Sean or Sara's fault, but he needed someone to blame, otherwise he'd have to accept that bad things could happen to any of them at any time. That was more difficult than accepting he was no longer a captain in the fleet. He hugged Mari a little closer. Civilian life was growing on him.

Mari looked at him and just cried, harder than he'd ever seen her cry. He kissed the top of her head. "At least it wasn't you," he whispered against her hair. "I couldn't have handled that." The thought of losing her paralyzed him. "I will never let anything happen to you."

Several more of Kenon's mothers spoke and his birth father. Then Giselle stepped forward, her formal strapless gown hugging her tiny figure and making her the most radiant woman in the hall. Kenon would have been in awe of his prime. Of course, they all knew he had been in awe of her every day of their marriage.

"We remember you, Kenon." Giselle's voice was thin and wispy, even though she tried to project for all the mourners to hear.

"We remember," came the refrain.

"*I* remember you. I remember the brush of your hand, the looks from across a crowded room. I remember the words we spoke and those we didn't, the vows we took and those we broke. I remember naming our child. I remember making our child. I will *always* remember you."

To David's surprise, tears poured from Giselle's closed eyes. He always assumed Kenon's emotional fallacy for his prime was one-sided. She held her arm out over Kenon's body. A silver chain and black pendant swung in her hand. She let it fall back to Kenon in the funerary niche.

Hailey followed her mother's lead. "Good-bye, Daddy." Her sapphire ring fell short of the pit. She ran forward to pick it up. This time it fell from her little fingers onto her father's chest.

Mikail held the younger Sasha near the niche. Together they offered a small green stone. "You live on through your children, Kenon. And through your family," he said. "We are strong because of you. You live on because of us."

As Kenon's other amours and children stepped forward to say their final words, David understood why Kenon followed tradition so closely, why having his own circle was so important to him. He *lived* the History. And, like his mother said, he would live forever through that History, through generations of an extended family and their genes.

When the last of the offerings were made, Kenon's birth father proudly held a flickering torch over the niche.

Mari buried her head in David's shoulder. He held her for a long time before taking her hand and leading her away from the ceremony. He touched her cheek with the back of his hand. "There could have been a better time for this, but...." He slipped a ring from his pocket and slid it onto her middle finger. The shine of three obsidian spheres set atop the silver band made up for its loose fit. "I want you to be my prime, Mari, so we can laugh, and dock, and fight every day for the rest of our lives."

A small smile shone through her tear-streaked face. "You're leaving, aren't you?" she whispered.

She was intuitive, another quality David admired, and he felt guilty for his answer. "Just to help bring them back." David wasn't sure if he meant Sean and Sara or the crew he walked out on so many months ago. Maybe in a way it was for all of them. "Then I'm yours for good."

"You better know I'm holding you to all three of these." Mari wiggled the ring on her finger.

"That's why I chose that one." He kissed her like it was their first kiss.

FIFTY-SIX

"I can't believe I'm going back there." Sara studied the purpled contours of the slot canyon below. The wavy edges of eroded rock snaked away for kilometers, eventually emptying into Palomin Canyon Reserve in the southeast. Lyra and a group of nineteen Armadans she had managed to gather stood watching with Sara and Rainer.

"It would have been easier if Simon hadn't installed rim scanners after that first fragger attack," Rainer said. "Approaching from this far out leaves us exposed too many times along the way."

It amused Sara that Rainer now freely referred to Simon by his given name. He was either picking up her habits or had decided there was no point in keeping formality with a man who had ordered his death.

"It doesn't bother you to come back to Palomin?" she asked.

"I'm not proud of what happened, Sara."

The near-apology caught her off-guard, and she didn't like how her feelings toward him softened.

"Is that why you're doing this, some type of redemption?" she asked.

Lightning speared the desert sky behind them. Thunder clubbed the black clouds in the distance. Sara's skin tingled, a mix of anxiety and inevitability. A sudden pinch in her side heightened her apprehension. She pressed a hand to the pain.

"What's wrong?" Rainer asked.

His alarmed look mirrored her thoughts—that the irradicae had begun their assault.

Whether in denial or because she didn't want Rainer to know, she lied. "I'm fine. Just need to adjust this grappler belt." She loosened the nylon, hoping that would bring some relief. It didn't.

"It's more awkward than the thigh holsters, but you should be able to get rid of it once we deploy the grapplers." He pulled out one of the cenders holstered around her legs and checked the energy level, even though he'd seen her do it a few minutes before.

"You never answered my question," Sara said.

Rainer replaced the cender and inspected her harness. "These leg straps are too loose." He grabbed the strap on the inside of Sara's right thigh and pulled it snug.

She reached for the other strap and grabbed Rainer's hand by mistake. He caught her fingers with his. "I'm here because our situation could have been different." He tested her other cender.

His words sounded tragic to her. "You could have made it different."

He handed the gun back to her this time, instead of replacing it himself. "It's too late now, huh?"

She wondered if he wanted a response from her. She didn't have one.

"The truth is," he said. "We probably both would have ended up dead."

That last statement put her on guard. As much as she wanted to, she couldn't believe Rainer would have changed that much. If he wasn't willing to risk his life for her so many months ago, he certainly wouldn't be putting himself in peril now simply to save Sean. Rainer had his own agenda. It just so happened that his and Sara's goals overlapped presently. At least that's what he thought since she lied to him about not finding the data.

Yul had played along when she came out of the V-side and said the data was still in Sean's head. It was the only way to insure his safety. If Rainer were playing both sides, he still would have to get Sean out alive in order to obtain his prize. Yul had the cure now, and even Sara didn't know where he went after fleeing Rushow. She was a quick study of contractor ways after being around so many for so long, and the first lesson she learned was deceit. The second was manipulation. A part of her felt guilty for it, but the larger part of her just wanted Sean back.

A swirl of sand appeared over Rainer's shoulder.

"What's that?" Sara asked.

Lyra squinted through one eye in the dust cloud's direction. "Incoming rover."

"Nice optical implants. They're illegal, you know," Rainer said.

"You can turn me in when we break into the Sovereign's estate."

"They've found us." Anger and fear flooded Sara's system at giving up the advantage of their surprise entrance.

The Armadans readied static rifles simultaneously. Sara aimed a paired of cenders. Rainer stood there with his arms folded. "We're out of range for weapons that small."

"I know," she said. "It just feels better to have a weapon between me and whoever's headed our way."

Lyra squinted again. "Calm down." She lowered her rifle. "It's the rest of our team."

"I didn't know there were others joining us," Sara said.

"I wasn't sure they would until just now," Lyra said.

An open-air desert rover rambled into view ahead of the whirling cloud from the west. Sara counted a full load of six Armadans, three of whom were women, sitting on bench seats under the roll bars in the transport's bed, plus a male driver and passenger.

A force of thirty against a hundred or more. And that was if they did it the easy way.

When the rover lumbered to a stop, David was the first to hop over the side. Sara wondered how a former fleet captain felt about sitting in the back. Not sure if he were still angry with her, she greeted him formally by placing her palm against his chest.

"Thank you," she said.

"Duty calls. Can't let one of my crew down, even if he is a cocky, dosed up mech tech who's too smart for his own good." He gave her a small kiss on the forehead.

Sara knew David cared about Sean, otherwise he would never risk his life to bring him back. She handed him a harness.

"You've been hanging around Socialites too long. Picking up their posturing," Lyra said.

"It's a sign of affection, Lyra. Something you wouldn't understand," David said.

A light breeze blew among them, making Sara shiver. Thunder banged off the rock walls. The storm to the north had begun.

"It won't be long now," Rainer said.

Sara snapped into the boot restraints on her swivel board the way Rainer had showed her. She shouldn't have been surprised that board training was now mandatory for contractors after they were introduced by the fraggers at the last battle here. Any seven year old could master the gyroscopic maneuvers of the hovering plank, but the unsteadiness still made Sara's insides churn. The pinching in her abdomen didn't help. It was constant now, intensifying a little with each breath.

The wind picked up, stirring from the slot canyon below. It smelled of fresh clay and reminded her of the first notes of Sean's scent. A rumbling shook the ground. Lightning filled the air with the smell of ozone. The temperature dropped suddenly.

"Ready?" Rainer moved the small force into position at the canyon's lip. He turned a slow semi-circle on his board, watching for signs of confirmation from every man and woman.

A deafening roar belched up from the slot canyon. Purple brown water raged below them, shaking the ground with its passing.

Rainer dropped his board into the churning waves, followed by Lyra. One after the other Armadans disappeared over the rim.

David motioned Sara in front of him. With a twist of her body, she moved her board to the edge. She didn't hesitate, afraid her legs would lock up out of fear, just dropped into the flash flood. The sound was deafening, and the narrow canyon eclipsed the sun except in patches. Out of instinct, she braced for impact. But the board's absorption field ate her momentum and left her bouncing just above the gnashing water. Splashes drenched her boots and pants, and the spray soaked the rest of her. While the muddy water painted the canyon walls a dark charcoal, it splatted her black shirt and pants with a greyish purple scum.

She shifted the weight to her back foot slightly to make the board climb a little higher. The front end angled too high. She threw her weight forward, but overcorrected. She swung her arm to the opposite side to regain her balance. A startled cry echoed below her. One of the Armadans had dropped into the flash flood. Sara saw his head, then only an arm and a foot pass under her before the body disappeared completely. Her heart thundered nearly as loud as the rushing river. She looked up in time to see the canyon wall jutting in front of her. Taking the brunt of the hit with her shoulder, her center of gravity shifted. The board spun ninety degrees.

She adjusted right before smashing into a ledge on the opposite side. David nearly missed her and surfed past just over her head. She held her breath and found her balance. One lean too far to the right or left and she'd end up grated against the sandstone. Adrenaline masked the pain in her shoulder and belly.

The side entrance to Palomin approached rapidly. All the force in the universe wouldn't stop her now. Sara tried to guess how far she was from the ever-widening sliver of light that floated just above the flood. She hoped the water contained enough force to blind the entry sensors, otherwise the harrowing trip through the slot canyon would have been as ineffective as driving right up to Palomin's rim and jumping into direct contractor fire.

Three troopers and David surfed and bounced out of the slot canyon in front of her and into the main expanse of Palomin. Sara followed their route, though the waves were unpredictable as they jostled for release at the mouth of the slot canyon. One rose high. Sara had nowhere to go. She burst through the wall of water and surfed into Palomin. The cluster of white buildings appeared ahead. Their white towers rose three hundred meters high, capped by the rounded remnants of a worldship hull.

As the canyon widened, the water level dropped significantly. The boarders fell into formation, five abreast. David dropped in beside her. "That was close back there. You look pretty shaken."

Actually, the adrenaline was wearing off, leaving a roiling pain in her abdomen in its wake. David didn't need to know this, though. "I'm worried about what we'll find inside. Whether Sean's...."

"Sean's going to hang on just to keep pissing them all off." Despite the joke, David's tone indicated that he worried, too.

Sara's board jerked. The bottom skipped off a rock, exposed by the dwindling flood waters. She compensated and climbed a bit higher with the board. David gracefully swerved and maneuvered on the board like he'd done it all his life. His agility surprised her, and made her feel a little clumsy. Apparently, her few weeks training as a contractor wasn't enough to erase eighteen years as a coddled Socialite.

They pulled up to the others at the nearest tower. Sara dismounted from her board into the shin-deep water. Her legs wobbled as she settled into a thin layer of mud on the canyon floor. No alarms, no sign of contractors.

She walked up to where Rainer and Lyra looked to be in a heated discussion.

"You'd better be right," Lyra said. "Because we only have one shot at this."

"I've scoured every inch of this compound on security detail," Rainer said.

"I don't believe the Sovereign's Head Contractor performed his own security detail," Lyra said.

"Rainer doesn't leave anything to chance," Sara said. "He's Head Contractor because he does the job the best."

"*Was* Head Contractor," Lyra corrected.

"You either trust me or turn back now," Rainer said.

Sara held her breath at the bluff. Rainer was gambling with Sean's life by making the ultimatum. He knew as well as she did that they needed the Armadans' skills and numbers if this plan were to work.

"We'll follow you," Lyra said. "But, if this goes wrong, I'll kill you myself, Rainer, and collect on your execution writ."

Rainer's look said she'd *try* to kill him, but that he wasn't envisioning the same ending she was. Sara knew Rainer would win. Because he always stacked the odds in his favor.

Sara unholstered the grappler gun, then unbuckled the nylon belt and let it fall to the thick mud at her feet. The receding water had also left a strong organic smell behind, not as pleasant as when the torrent first rushed through the canyon.

The reinforced aluminum stock of the grappler had little heft and fit neatly in the palm of her hand. She flipped on the laser sight and painted a dot on the bottom of the balcony railing suspended three hundred meters above her. She pulled the trigger. A click preceded the whooshing of the aluminum grappling hook carrying the silk rope up to the balcony. It pierced the concrete just under the railing and locked in place. Sara secured her right hand to the grappler with the strap on its side and held tight with the other hand. She pressed the retract button by her thumb and shot into the air.

Sara and the rest of her group zipped toward the balcony. The wet skin on her hands and face tingled with the rush of wind. Her clothes clung to her, sucking away her warmth. She watched the concrete supports of the balcony loom closer. Her ascent slowed automatically as the grappler reeled in its last twenty meters. She reached for the railing with her free hand, ignoring the throb in her arms.

Rainer and Lyra were the first two to climb the railing and hop onto the balcony. Sara and David took their turns with the remaining Armadans. Rainer stood in front of the double doors leading inside.

"How long do we have until the contractors inside react to your access code?" Lyra asked.

"Hopefully they'll think it's a glitch and not check at all, or send one guard," Rainer said. "If they're anticipating a move like this, then about six minutes. If so, that fragger camera loop program will be worthless."

"It's better to have it just in case," Sara said. Yul had been busy loading them down with tech before she and Rainer left him at Rushow. Though she had full faith in Yul, she still held some trepidation that one of the cameras along the way wouldn't pick up the signal from her reporter in time, therefore not prompting it to show the same loop of video of the few seconds before their arrival.

"Then, let's get this over with," Lyra said.

Rainer tapped his reporter. A small green circle lit on the door's lock. He shouldered the door open and followed the muzzles of his weapons inside. Lyra stayed close on his heels. One by one the troopers filed through the door, each one covering a different direction. Sara swept with David. No one spoke.

Inside the sounds reduced to the buzzing of lights in the grey hallway. With sudden alarm, she remembered being here. Her mind went back to that night after the fragger attack, after Rainer had shot her. She had traveled this same route to her torture. Doors marked with signs for the hippodrome confirmed her surroundings. The elevators would be coming up in the hallway on their left.

Sara felt nauseous, whether from reliving her last moments before imprisonment or from the increasing spasms in her abdomen. When they reached the elevators, she clenched her cenders tighter to keep her world from spinning.

Cameras rotated within their white sphere casings, but didn't zoom into any one spot. She hoped that meant Yul's trick was working. Rainer inclined his head toward the stairwell door by the elevator bank. Lyra entered first as he covered her.

They all spiraled down a staircase, cenders and rifles drawn, boots tapping the concrete stairs in a soft cadence. They descended floor after floor. The overhead white lights burned into Sara's retinas with an unrelenting intensity. When they reached the bottom landing, Rainer pushed open the door just enough to peek through. Satisfied, he slipped onto the awaiting metal catwalk. Single file, their rifles against their shoulders, the Armadans traversed the catwalk. Sara didn't remember this accessway, nor the cavernous room thirty meters below it. The low level lighting allowed her to see large shipping crates stacked like buildings underneath them. Aisles crisscrossed among the crates like a street grid. She froze when she thought she saw a figure dash behind a stack. David bumped into her and immediately trained his rifle where she pointed her cenders.

Then, she felt it. The hair on her arms stood straight up, charged with static. Cender fire splashed off the railing to her right, sizzling through the trooper standing there. She dove for the catwalk floor.

"Covering!" David aimed the rifle through the exposed rails of the catwalk. He sent alternating bursts flying into the aisles below. Sara aimed her centers at the oncoming static trails. Their flash dissipated just before reaching the ceiling lights above the catwalk. She crawled toward the other end of the accessway where part of their group laid down more cover. As she approached the end, Lyra yelled. "Incoming grenades."

A shrill series of beeps cut the air. Rainer grabbed Sara and pulled her to her feet, then shoved her through the door. A silvery light from the exploding catwalk blinded her. The force threw a body into the stairwell on top of her legs. The world cut out from her for just a moment. She fought off a wave of oncoming blackness.

Pain wrapped around into her lower back, and her ribs ached, but she held her hands to her ears against an unbearable ringing. She shouted for Rainer, for David, until a coughing fit took her breath. She coughed and spit grit from her mouth, then stood and shook off the dust. Her vision returned in a spotty mess. The dust swirling through the concrete stairwell didn't help her visibility. It was if time played in slow motion. She looked for familiar faces, spotting David among the other Armadans. His face was bloody, and shrapnel peppered his right cheek and neck.

She shouted for someone to close the door to the stairwell, but realized it had been blown off its hinges. The closest trooper nudged her up and shoved her forward. She looked around frantically for Rainer. There were only twelve of their group left here in the stairwell. She ducked around the trooper to look for Rainer.

David caught her arm as she went for the doorway. She skidded to a stop. It was gone. The contractor force below had taken down the entire accessway. Bodies littered the floor below. She could hear muffled bursts of gunfire as her hearing tried to come back. David pulled at her arm. She punched at it, not going anywhere until she knew for certain. He grabbed her chin and pointed her face toward one of the stacks.

Rainer lay face down among the shredded steel. A dark stain oozed beneath him. She stared at his lifeless body in disbelief as David dragged her away.

FIFTY-SEVEN

Chen held his cender to Sean Cryer's head. It felt a little cowardly considering the fragger was so dosed out of his mind that he couldn't tell reality from hallucination any more, but Chen wasn't feeling overly brave after the Armadans took out forty contractors during the skirmish in the warehouse. The troopers had taken heavy losses, as well, but not in comparison to the defense they mounted on the contractors' surprise attack.

"I say we get rid of Cryer now and cut our losses," Chen said. "The Sovereign is as good as dead any way. You saw him. He's lost his mind. His body will follow soon enough. It's better for us all if he dies, especially with Rainer dead. All we have to do is bide our time to see how the new government shakes out and force our way to the top of it."

"I'm not leaving without the cure." Faya leveled her cender at Chen. "So step away from him."

She was obsessed. Chen lowered his weapon, not really caring if Cryer lived or died. "Weren't you listening to me? We don't need the cure anymore."

"I need it."

For the first time Chen noticed the little shake in Faya's hands. He understood how Cryer had gotten the drop on her, even in his condition. "Prollixer gave you his curse?"

"It wasn't a curse when he gave it to me. It was a gift."

"Prollixer doesn't give gifts," Chen said.

"I was special."

The way she said it left no doubt what she meant. And, here they all thought the Sovereign wasn't interested in pleasures of the flesh. Chen wasn't sure what disgusted him more—the thought of Faya docking Prollixer or the fact that she would alter her genes in such a drastic way.

"Did Rainer know that his days as Head Contractor were numbered because he wasn't providing the same type of services that you were?" he asked.

She ignored the taunt and picked up the knife she had been using on Cryer for the past hour.

"I think you're already losing your mind." Chen made for the door.

"Dahlia and the Sovereign are halfway to the docking pad by now. You'd never reach the ship before they take off," Faya said. "Besides, I need someone to watch my back. I almost have him broken."

Cryer wasn't giving her anything more, but her desperation outweighed the obvious. "The few remaining contractors we have left out there won't be able to hold off those troopers before our reinforcements arrive. I'm getting out while I can. You're on your own."

"I'll remember this when I'm controlling the Embassy," Faya shouted after him.

Chen wasn't worried. If she did make it out of here alive and managed to cure her curse, he knew her dirty secrets. That kind of blackmail would be worth a power position. He had nothing to lose, unless he couldn't get to that ship before it left. He dialed Dahlia on his reporter.

FIFTY-EIGHT

"That's it," Sara said. Their small team stood outside her former modification cell. Of the remaining Armadans, only two troopers, a male, Markus, and a female, Tamasine, stayed with Sara, David, and Lyra. The others split off in the stairwell to assist their comrades on the warehouse floor who managed to survive the fall and were still battling contractors.

A distant sound of footfalls echoed from around the corner. With quick hand gestures, Lyra and David signed to one another, then to the troopers. Each of them took a position along the concrete walls. David motioned Sara toward him, then cupped his hand over her ear. "Could be an ambush. You and I will watch the rear."

Sara aimed her cenders at a small imperfection about two meters high on the wall down the hallway behind them. It was unnerving to be facing away from the action, but if this were an ambush, she and David would have plenty to deal with on their end. The footsteps were louder, but also more hesitant as they approached the hallway. Sara wanted to see what Lyra and the troopers were doing, but kept her discipline and never deviated from her spot on the wall.

The footsteps stopped just before turning the corner. Sara controlled her breathing, though the soft exhalations still sounded deafening to her.

The smack of a weapon into bone and flesh made Sara flinch. From behind her, she heard a thump, like a body hitting the floor.

"Clear," Tamasine said.

David held up a hand for Sara to stay and cover. Sticking to the wall, his compact rifle butted against his shoulder, David hurried to the end of the hallway. Sara maintained her concentration, even with the scuffle erupting behind her. David peered around the corner, keeping most of his body in cover. "Clear," he said, though his stare remained on the adjoining hallway.

Sara finally looked at the contractor held to the floor by Lyra and Markus. Though Chen's features were distorted by the gag stuffed in his mouth, Sara recognized his eyes. Not quite Rainer's icy blue, but piercing enough. She had never seen Chen's eyes so rounded in fear. Maybe she should have felt a twinge of pity or nostalgia for him, but it was as if that life, the one where they were together, wasn't hers anymore.

"Where's Sean, Chen?" she asked.

"You know this man?" Lyra and Markus hoisted Chen to his feet and slammed him against the hard concrete wall. His one knee couldn't hold his weight and a bone mender beeped in alarm. The trooper kicked it off, sending Chen into a fit of muffled shrieks.

"He's working with the group who has Sean," Sara said. When Rainer initially mentioned this to her, she thought it was a bluff, but meeting Chen here at Palomin was no coincidence.

Lyra grabbed Chen's head and slammed it into the wall again. She flipped open her knife in front of his face. "I'm going to remove this gag, and if you make any noise except to answer her, I'll jam this knife between your ribs and deflate your lung so you'll barely be able to whisper. Do you understand me?"

Chen's gaze darted from the knife to Lyra to Sara and back.

"Do you understand me?"

He nodded his affirmative. She plucked the rolled up piece of shirt from Chen's mouth.

"Will you let me go if I tell you?" he asked.

Lyra stuffed the gag back in and jabbed the knife under his ribcage. Chen jerked in pain, his screams muffled by the gag. "You don't listen very well," Lyra said. "I didn't nick your lung this time, but if you don't answer her question, next time I'll plunge the blade in up to its hilt."

Chen quit squirming. Lyra ungagged him, pressing the knife to his side.

"Cryer's in the storage room at the end of the next hallway."

Sara's mouth went dry. "Is he alive?"

"For now," Chen said. "But Faya's still working on him."

Sara bolted around the corner and ran down the hallway. The pain of twisted muscles gathered in her abdomen. Her heart banged against her rib cage, terrified at what she might find inside that room. She heard David shout, "Targets this side." Weapons fire sounded behind her, but Sara's mind had one purpose, get Sean away from Faya.

She was within a meter of the storage room door when a hand snatched her by the shoulder and flipped her to the floor backward. Sara rolled to her feet and kicked the cender out of Faya's hand. A bone mender chimed from her other arm as Faya used it to smash one of Sara's cenders into the wall. Sara fired the other one. The shot grazed Faya's shoulder, but she wrestled the weapon out of Sara's hand before she could do more damage.

Sara plowed her head into Faya's solar plexus and knocked her down. Faya kicked Sara in the chest with the heel of her boot. Pain surged through newly bruised ribs, the sharpness in sickening contrast to the dull, constant pain in her abdomen. Faya regained her feet and locked her arms around Sara's head and shoulders from behind. Sara jabbed her thumb back into Faya's left eye. She cried out and loosened her grip. Sara twisted out of her hold and tackled Faya to the ground. Jamming her elbow into Faya's throat, Sara pushed away, but not before grabbing a fistful of pink-streaked hair. She slammed Faya's face into the floor and ripped out the pink streak by its roots. Sara went right back for another section of Faya's hair and dragged her to the storage room door.

When Faya bit Sara's leg, she kicked her in the teeth. She trapped Faya's arm between her legs and accessed Faya's reporter. The lock mechanism lit green. Sara pulled Faya to her feet and shoved her into the room first, in case another surprise might be waiting inside.

There were no sounds, no words, when Sara saw Sean's body. She was paralyzed. The bile in her stomach rose from the stench of chemicals and blood and torture. Sean was slumped over on the floor, his hands bound behind him, blood streaking his head and bare chest, soaking the waistband of his pants and pooling on the floor around him. Ugly bruises covered his fair skin in deep purple blooms.

David stormed inside with the troopers. She threw Faya at him and ran to Sean.

Seeing him broken like that made her sick. She noticed how his leg from the knee down rested at an unnatural angle. Then, she saw his missing fingers and how his wrist dangled from his arm. She couldn't imagine she'd ever looked this bad. Her hands shook as she reached for his arm. She had to know for certain. His skin felt chilled under her touch.

"Sean."

She leaned closer, afraid to look at his face, afraid to see how Faya might have butchered his handsome features. A small movement from his chest, as though he were taking a shallow breath, sent a shiver of hope up her spine. "Sean? Can you hear me?"

He groaned, a small, wheezy, pathetic sound that sent her into a sob because it meant he was alive, but that he had suffered horribly at Faya's hand. Discarded at his side lay her weapons of choice—syringes of hallucinatory drugs and the triton knife he had taken from Ariel at the Underground.

Sara picked up the knife. Bright red dripped over blackened flakes of dried blood, Sean's blood. She flew to where David still held Faya back. She screamed and kicked at Sara and struggled against David like a deranged animal. Sara pulled Faya's head back to expose her throat.

"Sara—"

Her look silenced David. "Just hold her."

It was her fight, her past.

"I want you to know this isn't because of what you did to me," Sara said, staring into Faya's eyes. "It's because of what you did to him." She slid the knife across Faya's throat. It split as easily as Sara's skin had so many times from the blade cuffs. Sara watched Faya's head flop with each gush of blood until the contractor's blue eyes stared into the Otherside.

David let her body drop to the ground.

A moan from Sean drew Sara's attention. Lyra and Markus had Sean sitting up against the wall. Sara shoved Lyra away from him and kneeled in front of him.

His right eye had swollen shut, and the surrounding skin shined black and purple, all the way down to his broken nose. Crusting rivulets of blood matted his hair and painted his cheeks, and his lips were split and cracked. She cradled his head and begged him to come back to her, even just a small part of him.

An explosion from the floor above dimmed the lights and shook the room. They choked on dust that fell from the ancient structure.

"What was that?" David asked.

"Not from us," Lyra said. "Unless some of our troopers found a supply of rocket launchers hidden in that warehouse."

"Not likely," David said. "If the contractors had rocket launchers, they would have used them when we were most vulnerable, on the catwalk."

"Then, someone else has joined the party. We need to go now," Lyra said. "The fragger's sliding pretty badly. We don't have time for him to pull out of it...if he even can."

"Sean, we're getting you out of here," Sara said as Lyra picked the lock on his restraints with her knife.

No response. Dizziness slammed into her, maybe because the pain in her belly was almost unbearable, maybe because she might have come all this way and still not get Sean back.

David lifted Sean onto his shoulders, pinning Sean's arm and his bad leg against his chest with one hand. In the other he brandished a cender.

"We're on the bottom floor, right?" Lyra asked Sara. "All we have to do is get back into the canyon and onto our boards—"

"This level is actually below ground," Sara said. "We need to go up four floors to exit out onto the canyon floor."

Lyra shot David a concerned look. "Can you do the stairs carrying him?"

"It'd be better for both of us if we could take the elevator."

Sara refused to think about the difficulties they faced trying to transport Sean by swivel board back to the slot canyon. She would drag Sean out of Palomin if she had to. First, they had to make it out of here.

A second blast shook loose tiles from the ceiling. With an electrical hiss the lights began to oscillate and strobe. Ozone wafted through the room. Explosions and voices came from upper levels through new holes in the structure.

"If there's an elevator left," Sara said.

The strobing lights showed their exit in slow motion. Lyra led them down the hallway; Sara followed David, helping Tamasine sweep. She leveled her cenders, ready to take out anyone who might be following them.

The muscles in her abdomen contracted so hard, she doubled over, riding through wave after wave of nauseating blackness.

"What's wrong with you?" Tamasine asked, her personality less hard-edged than Lyra's, more like David's and Geir's.

Sara forced herself upright. "Nothing."

They waited for Lyra's "all clear" before rounding the corner. As they waited in front of the silver elevator doors, Sara was mesmerized by their reflections flickering in and out with the strobing lights. They looked like battle-worn ghosts returning from the Otherside.

When the lit display showed the elevator descending to their floor, the group took up posts to either side of the doors. At the chime announcing the elevator's arrival, Lyra and Markus readied themselves.

The doors opened.

Swinging around, cenders first, Lyra yelled, "Clear."

They boarded. Sara rubbed a hand over Sean's back. There was a whirring sound and a feeling of inertia as the number display counted up from sublevel four.

Another distant explosion rippled above them. The elevator jerked and the lights went out. Dim emergency lighting popped on in one corner.

"How far did we make it?" Sara asked.

"The display is out," Lyra said.

The main lights popped on again and the elevator dropped. This time Sara's stomach floated.

The number display flashed, all the floors lit.

Sara jammed a fist against the emergency halt button. The elevator lurched and stopped.

"Looks like we're at sublevel three," David said. "Not much progress."

Lyra and the female trooper pried the doors apart. "We're between floors."

A narrow opening greeted them at eye level. The larger opening went to the floor below. Sara stuck her head out and looked up at the wall of the elevator shaft. "There's a big two painted on the wall above us."

"We'll take the stairs up the last couple of levels," Lyra said.

"I hope we can squeeze through that." David eyed the bottom space.

Lyra slipped through first, followed by Tamasine. Markus had a harder time squeezing his chest and shoulders through. Sara dropped down next and waited for David to maneuver Sean through the opening with Markus' help. David managed to slide through with only minimal scrapes and scratches.

Lyra and Tamasine checked the stairwell. "Clear."

Sara brushed sweat-soaked hair from her forehead and swallowed back her rising nausea. She was losing the battle against her pain. It took concentration just to remain upright. Pushing off the wall, she ascended the steps on Lyra's heels. Sara once again relied on her pain for focus, like she had during her imprisonment here.

If nothing else, the pain meant she was still alive.

FIFTY-NINE

Finally.

David's neck and shoulders burned under Sean's weight. He was heavier than he looked. Once Sean was well enough, David wouldn't let him forget how big a pain in the ass he was for making them come all the way to Palomin for him. But, the joke landed flat, even in David's head because he wasn't sure Sean was going to survive. It made him sad because, despite Sean's moodiness and arrogance, David appreciated his spirit, his drive to be self-sufficient, and his unguided passion. Sean would have made a good fleet officer. David smiled, knowing Sean probably would have punched him in the mouth for such blasphemy.

The massive white doors that opened to Palomin's canyon floor loomed twenty meters away. A fresh coat of silt deposited by the flash flood covered the floor. The smell of mud reminded David of the slot canyon and just how far away that escape route was now. He slipped, but managed to catch his balance, even with Sean's weight making him top-heavy. Sara didn't fair as well. She hit hard on her shoulder and didn't get up right away. Tamasine helped her to her feet, and after a few words between them that David couldn't hear, Sara continued toward the door with cautious steps and a hand wrapped around her belly.

He had never seen combat take such a toll on a person so quickly, then again Sara was no warrior. She looked like she'd aged twenty years since this morning. Her ashen complexion and bleary eyes reminded him of a private on his first commission who'd taken a low level cender blast to the gut. The severe internal injuries weren't enough to kill him right away, so he suffered greatly until finally succumbing to the pain. Maybe Sara had been injured during her fight with Faya.

He liked how Tamasine had taken to watching over Sara. Lyra could take a lesson in leadership from the younger woman.

Standing at the door controls, Lyra said, "Ready?"

Tamasine and Markus took up position on either side of the doorway. On Lyra's command, they each kicked a door open.

Windblown grit washed into the room on a sound wave of dissonant music. The lyrics screamed death to the Embassy, and called for Sovereign Simon to be castrated. Refrains of *Kill the castes* echoed from a hodge-podge of ships—space transports, cruisers, sanitation vessels, an old medical frigate. They all vented fragger boarders out of their bellies, thousands of them that surfed through the air around a few huge Embassy transports.

David's whole team stood dumbfounded in the cap-shadowed doorway. The thick scent of ozone mixed with the smell of canyon mud.

"What the...?" Lyra stepped back.

Heavy weapons fire pelted Palomin. Soft metal surfaces melted in the inferno. Cascading booms caused rock columns to fall from canyon walls. Light strobed through smoke just before bone-softening thunder wracked David's body. The cleansing light of revolution had descended into this part of the world. The contractors countered with grenade launchers and heavy static guns mounted in the back of rim transports, but they were outnumbered three to one.

Plasma bombs ate through the old buildings and glassed the canyon walls. Energy waves rippled through the sand. Prop wash blew dust and ash into their faces. It was impossible to shield their eyes from the energy that erupted all around.

Combatants on both sides yelled orders through speakers, trying to be heard over the blaring music. Waves of mismatched fragger surfers shot through the air dodging contractor fire. Every so often one would fall straight to the ground as a lucky contractor hit his mark.

"We won't make it through that," Lyra said.

"There's another slot canyon behind us," David said.

"With no transport waiting at the top," Lyra said.

"Once we make it topside, we can do a rim skim and circumnavigate all this." David had doubts about how well he'd be able to maneuver along the inside of the canyon rim with Sean on his back, but would deal with that when the time came.

"Agreed," Sara said. "Sean won't last much longer."

David wasn't sure she would either.

The team worked its way around the base of the building they'd just fought their way through. Sara could tell David grew weary from carrying Sean. She couldn't imagine that strain, considering she could barely place one foot in front of the other in her current condition.

"Everybody down!" Lyra jumped back against the wall. Sara pulled her cenders.

A transport filled with contractors rolled toward their small group. Though they didn't have one of the large mounted static guns, the half dozen contractors in the open air bed fired their cenders.

Markus took fire to his shoulder. David had dropped Sean and grabbed his rifle.

Sara threw her cenders to the ground. She ran to the front of the fray, rage and pain controlling her mind and body. Blasts sizzled around her. Standing in the middle of the heated onslaught and staring down the oncoming transport, she held up her palms, not certain the convertors in her wrist implant would absorb the incoming cender energy and not really caring anymore. Her body shook. Her heart raced. The energy compounded until she labored for breath. She staggered backward.

From the corner of her eye she saw David rush at her, then stop and simply watch. She was watching, too, from somewhere outside of her body, watching and crying.

Blinding light emanated from an orb at the center of Sara's palm. She screamed with the effort to control the energy. The pitch of her voice melded with the squeal of overcooked cenders and the ringing in her ears. She smashed her palms together, forcing the light into one large, quivering orb and launched it at the contractors.

Glowing hot light blasted through the men and women. Sara dropped to her knees and covered her eyes. She expected silence like when she had first witnessed the orb weapon used on Palomin's rim, but the sounds of battle never relented. She opened her eyes to watch the last dying flash reveal the contractors' charred bodies.

As she pushed to her feet, fragger boarders dropped in around them, surrounding the group. The low whir of their boards was nearly lost in the noise of battle. Each fragger wielded dual cenders, the modded kind like she had seen in the V-side.

"Don't fire." A female fragger, her long blonde hair whipping around her face, jumped from her board, her eyes hidden by dark shades. She held her palm screen up to read from it. "Fragger idents."

Her attention snapped to Sara, honing in on the bio-lights peeking around rips in the dark sleeve. "Nice to finally meet you in the Realside, Ambasadora Mendoza."

Sara stumbled forward. Her eyes crinkled at the corners and her nose scrunched up from the pain, but she stood tall when she reached the fragger. When she asked, "Who are you?" her wispy breath barely carried the distance between them.

"Yadira, but you know me as Cuzco," the small woman said. "Yul is waiting for you. And Zak."

"What about the rest?" A boarder in back pointed a cender at the Armadans.

"They're with us," Sara said.

Several fraggers dismounted and attended to Sean. Sara wondered if any of them were in the V-side with Cuzco that day, not that she would recognize them without their avs. Cuzco/Yadira said, "We'll go two per board and make the run for our ship."

"I don't like this." Lyra's grip remained tight on her weapon.

"Mount up, Lyra," David interrupted. "You know better than to refuse aid from allies."

"You trust a bunch of fraggers?" Lyra asked.

David looked at Sara. "Do you trust them?"

"Yes. They came here for Sean. They didn't have to."

"There's your answer, Lyra," David said. Tamasine stepped forward to stand with him. Sara didn't miss the scathing look Lyra gave David, nor the way he ignored her.

SIXTY

A rumbling explosion woke Rainer. He tasted blood in his mouth. Unable to pull a full breath, he realized he was lying on his chest. Before he moved his head, he tried moving his fingers in case he'd suffered neck or spinal trauma from the fall. He remembered the fall, the explosion on the catwalk, shoving Sara out of the way.

Confident he had full use of his limbs, he pushed himself up onto his knees and took inventory of his injuries. Some broken ribs, to be sure, and a cut to his forehead—that explained the large amount of blood since head wounds tended to bleed more—but aside from the bruising and general all-over pain and stiffness he could expect from falling a hundred meters into a cargo crate, he was fine.

And he was alone. He wouldn't let himself read too much into that thought. Looking down the side of the crate stack showed nothing but darkness. Even the scant light from the ceiling and at ground level had been extinguished. He grabbed for his cenders. His holsters were empty. They would be; he'd had his weapons drawn when the catwalk collapsed. He searched for them among the crate debris, but they were gone.

He had no choice but to take his chances on the ground. Each movement on his climb down sent electric jolts of pain up into his groin, through his back and neck, and settled in his damaged ribcage. Muffled sounds of heavy weapons fire bounced along the exterior walls. Maybe Prollixer had gotten wise to their plan and called in the military. Maybe Dahlia had told him everything.

At the bottom, he flicked on his palm screen to light his path through the carnage of a battle. It looked like the contractors had gotten the worst end of it. He noted a prompt on his palm announcing a message waiting for him from Dahlia. *Stalling take off.* It was sent twenty minutes ago. No follow up. He sent back, *On my way. No cure.* According to their prior arrangement, she would know to bluff Prollixer. If Dahlia decided to turn on Rainer, he would lose completely. Not just the cure. And not just Sara. But his life, his family honor.

He considered searching for Sara's body among the burnt and cracked contents of upended crates, but he knew in his gut she wasn't dead. She had made it inside the stairwell before the blast. When his mind wandered to darker possibilities, Rainer repeated to himself that she had made it. She was alive.

He picked his way through crumpled bodies and still burning table linens and broken dishes meant for the ballroom upstairs, then had to detour around large engine parts and crushed ceiling lights. His focus returned again and again to a pink emergency exit light hanging above a doorway where the door itself had been blown from its hinges.

His head throbbed with each exertive step.

He felt the air rush at him, carrying the scent of the recent flood. The sounds of a full-scale battle boomed louder. When he rounded the corner, he saw the right side of the building had a ten meter gouge which opened it to Palomin Canyon. Rainer stood at the edge and witnessed war raging outside.

Perhaps because he was still dazed from the fall or because he held tight to his stoicism for focus, he watched the brutal battle between fraggers and contractors as though it were a Media vid. In the back of his mind he contained the small fear that one of his brothers or sisters could be fighting for their lives or already lying in the mud at the bottom of Palomin. Or worse, one of his amours. The idea that his line, his family, could be destroyed, if not in this particular battle, then one like it that was sure to come after today, cemented itself in a primal spot within his brain. He had lost sight of his priorities, given into emotion, and he would pay for that indiscretion.

His reporter buzzed with an incoming message. Dahlia responded, *Hurry*. That one word, coming from his seventh amour, the woman carrying his thirteenth child, a woman he had all but ignored except to conceive and to plot with her, gave him hope like he had never felt before.

He sent back, *Soon*.

The easiest way to the transport pad was the obliterated catwalk or the internal elevator. Both ways were cut off now. He'd head for the stairwell.

At the end of the featureless hallway, Rainer signaled a door control with his reporter. It ignored him. He pounded it with his fist. The decorative cover split open, spilling a busted responder and fingers of twisted cable, but the main door remained shut.

He carefully played two wires against one another, short-circuiting the electronic lock, but the door jammed after opening only a crack. He used his leg as leverage and pried the door open. Centimeter by centimeter the gap widened. Sweat mixed with the dust that coated his face and hands. He pried the door a little further and wriggled his body through, catching his side against the door frame. The pain shot through him. He closed his eyes to it, trying to breathe.

He pushed open the door to the stairwell and started his climb up forty flights. Each time his boot slapped off the concrete, he heard its echo and felt its jarring in his body. Each step ate through his stoicism. He fought the onslaught of emotion at first until he stumbled on tired and bruised legs, falling against the grey wall like a child just learning to walk. His anger boiled to the surface, and he welcomed its hot flush like an amour's touch. Someone would pay for all of this.

When he pushed open the door onto the launch pad, his stride was purposeful, concealing his pain and extent of his injuries.

Dahlia and the Sovereign waited for him by an Embassy ship.

The access iris above the transport pad remained closed. The sounds of the fragger bombardment outside would necessitate waiting until a moment or two just before lift-off to open it to the sky above.

Prollixer's face split into a crazed smile. "Contractor Varden, I knew I could count on you. Please, give me my cure."

Rainer walked past him and straight up to Dahlia. He stroked her cheek and pulled her into a tender kiss, then whispered, "Thank you." While he nuzzled her neck, he slid his hand down her thigh to her holster. He pulled out her cender, drawing in shallow breaths of her rosy scent. It smelled better on her than Sara.

"Where's my cure?" Prollixer clasped a hand on Rainer's shoulder. Rainer elbowed him in the jaw, knocking him to the ground.

Then he fired his cender into Prollixer's face. The Sovereign's head jerked back and settled against the concrete floor.

The pilot rushed down the gangway, cenders drawn. Dahlia drew and fired, dropping him as he stared at the Sovereign's dead body.

Rainer saw her with new eyes. She had stood by him when abandoning him would have been easier.

She trained the cender on Rainer. "I need to know if you did this for her."

Rainer looked into Dahlia's cender barrel. Mourning filled him, mourning for a life he was afraid to ever want in the first place.

"I did it all for her. But now it's time to move on." He walked past her and into the ship.

As he started the lift-off sequence, he figured Dahlia would either shoot him or slide into the seat next to him.

She followed him into the ship, then stood over him, almost like she still didn't know which she'd choose. After a tense moment she settled into the seat and buckled her restraint.

Rainer opened the ceiling and held his breath. The transport pad began to rise.

"Where will we go?" Dahlia asked.

"Somewhere safe. Somewhere together."

The transport cleared the pad. Turbulence rattled the hull as shells from the fragger conflict exploded and echoed throughout the canyon. Rainer deftly maneuvered the Sovereign's ship in the opposite direction, leaving the fighting behind him, only to seek comfort in the darkness ahead.

SIXTY-ONE

"He's so cold," Sara said. Her body shook as she tried to rub life back into Sean's arm. "Will this work?" She looked at the three swivel boards lashed together into a makeshift stretcher.

"We're only going a few hundred meters. It's risky, but our only choice," Yadira said.

David hoisted Sean into a sitting position on the boards, lashing his back to the middle boarder's legs. Sean was completely unresponsive. The rest of Sara's group doubled up on boards.

"Ready?" Yadira reached a hand out to pull Sara onto her board.

Sara forced herself to move toward the board. A wave of pain forced her to her knees. She collapsed into the mud and vomited. Her vision blurred; she pounded her fists into the ground to keep from screaming. She felt the blood trickling down her thighs. A crazy vanity inside of her was thankful no one could see the proof of her suffering, of her loss.

David kneeled beside her and pulled her into a hug. He pushed the sweat-soaked hair from her neck and produced a stim patch from his pocket. "You should have told me earlier how bad you were hurting." He pressed the patch into her neck.

"This is faster acting." Yadira handed David an injector. He held it against Sara's neck. Its air-forced needle jabbed into her skin, delivering the entire dose at once. David helped her onto Yadira's board. Sara wrapped her arms around the tiny woman's waist. The boards moved out, and though the pace was excruciatingly slow due to their overload of cargo, Sara still had to close her eyes from time to time to quell her sickness.

Blasts of music alternated with the gunfire until they became part of the same composition. Exploding rockets echoed off the canyon walls and the hulls of burning ships. It was a cacophony of death, but also the birth scream of a new system, conceived in discontent and born naturally into the raw, naked glory of war.

Overheated cenders popped and smoked, making breathing difficult. Each cough wracked Sara's body with pain. The system could eventually return from this violence, but she wasn't sure she could ever return from sterility.

The boards carrying David and the healthy troopers arrived at the ship first. Yadira held back, sweeping the area while the boarders carrying the injured crawled into the ship. A sudden lurch forced Sara to the ground. A rocket exploded in front of them and rained down dirt and stone.

Sara crawled through the swirling dust and smoke. A hand on her arm helped her stand.

"My propulsion's shot," Yadira said. "Run for the ship. I'll help the others."

Sara scrambled after Yadira through the clearing dust. She could only run doubled over, her arms holding her mid-section. Coming up on her left, she saw a trio of crumpled boards still lashed together with bodies sprawled around it.

"Sean!" She ran for the downed men. The direct hit from the rocket left them bloody and lifeless.

She turned over body after body. None of them were Sean. She looked for Yadira amidst the mayhem.

She helped another fragger from a wreck further ahead. Fire from grenade launchers had sent them crashing to the ground. Return cannon fire sounded from the ship. David and a combined force of Armadans and fraggers laid down cover while Sara's group struggled toward safety.

Through the smoke, she spotted a group unloading Sean.

Relief and a sense of accomplishment swept over her. Her efforts to save him had been worth every kilo of pain. Now she needed what was left of her strength to save herself, vowing not to be abandoned in Palomin again. She stumbled and fell. Pain seared through her belly and ribs, a fiery kick that felt like her insides had grown a hundred times too large.

She didn't have the strength to stand up again, so she crawled on her elbows. A million little explosions pounded through her abdomen, the pain pulsing through her was worse than if it'd come from the rockets that ripped through the sky all around her.

"Sara?" David called to her from behind a curtain of smoke.

She tried to respond, but at first only raspy croaks issued from her dry throat.

"Here," she managed.

David appeared on her left.

"I'm here," she said.

Lifting her up into his arms, David cradled her against his chest and rushed for the waiting load ramp. She wanted to tell him about the pain, to slow down. Each of his wide steps brought the taste of blood onto her tongue. She wiped her mouth, streaking blood across her cheek.

He placed her on the cargo bay floor. Medics ascended on her as the ship lifted off. Sara pitched forward and vomited again. Rolling onto her side, she cradled her belly and rocked back and forth on the metal floor.

"She's bleeding out." Yul's familiar voice rushed into her ear.

Several pairs of hands lifted her onto a hovering stretcher.

Sara screamed as her insides twisted, trying to discharge the mess that the irradicae had left behind.

Yadira held one of her hands and Tamasine held the other. Sara squeezed them for strength. A steady ache pushed against the walls of her belly. Yul pumped stim after stim into her system.

Her vision went dark. Frantic voices tried to comfort her, to bring her back into the world. Pricking needles on her skin gave way to numb coldness. She'd look for Sean on the Otherside, but hoped he would live many long, happy years before he made his way back to her there.

SIXTY-TWO

ONE MONTH LATER

Sara changed Sean's bandages on his knee the way Yul had showed her. She'd move onto his wrist and fingers next, a routine she had developed since last week when she had finally felt well enough to stay on her feet for a few hours at a time.

Sean would finally be able to wear a bone mender on his leg after this last surgery. The wrist would have to wait. He'd had so many surgeries, so many scares. He remained sedated most of the time, but occasionally he'd wake up and ask for her. She would hold his hand and talk to him, usually about her family and her childhood, until he drifted off again. The reconstruction took its toll on his body almost as much as Faya's torture.

She missed him, but he was alive and healing, and they were together. Actually, they were all together, David, Lyra, Tamasine and Markus, Yul and his pretty wife, hiding from the Embassy on the fragger ship with Yadira and a dozen other fraggers, most from Sean's contingency. Sara's contingency now. She took his place as node and worked tirelessly in the campaign against Simon and his corruption. The fraggers had won at Palomin, but their resources were limited, their leadership still fractured. Falling back to reorganize in the V-side would allow them to prepare for the next stage.

Yadira walked in and put a hand on Sara's shoulder. Since Palomin, the two women had become good friends, as had Tamasine, who resigned from the fleet in order to join the fragger organization, much to Lyra's disgust. "How's he doing?" Yadira asked. "His color looks better, no ugly black and blue patches anywhere."

"He's strong," Sara said, pride and adoration creeping into her voice. "He'll be up and trying to take his job back from me in no time."

"Speaking of...We have to send the message to the Embassy now," Yadira said. "Sorry to pull you away, but once we reach Archenzon, broadcasts will be impossible due to the communications net and the embargo. Are you ready?"

Sara was ready. She volunteered to be the face for their revolution. There was more danger to her than any real power, but the cause needed a shell to embody their ideology.

The right shell, an empty one, like hers.

She kissed Sean, realizing she really wasn't that empty anymore.

THE PLANET MOONS

TAMPA ONE
The first to be terraformed, Tampa One was only halfway settled before its larger neighbor, Tampa Deux, was ready for habitation. Home to large swaths of unspoiled wilderness, like Archenzon, much of the moon remains a preserve for millions of species of animal and plant life.

TAMPA DEUX
Heavily populated, even after Tampa Three was terraformed, Tampa Deux's popularity still grows because of its infrastructure and planning.

TAMPA THREE
The smallest of all the moons, it was originally meant to be an exclusive world for Socialite families with the most money; however, bad terraforming and rushed planning made this the least desirable planet in the system.

YURAI
This world was terraformed to compete with Tampa Three as the optimal planet. Socialites left it to the Armadans because they believed its potential wasn't as high as Tampa Three, but now Yurai's size and wealth is rivaled only by Tampa Quad.

TAMPA QUAD
The most populated planet in the system, Tampa Quad is the center of government and commerce. As the largest moon, Tampa Quad boasts more inhabitants per square foot than any other, while still maintaining as much wild space as Tampa One.

DELEINE
Deleine was the newest planet to be terraformed, mainly so that workers could be close to the plethora of uranium, iridium, and boxite mines there. The extensive mining has caused health issues, especially among the less genetically diverse Socialites.

Heidi Ruby Miller writes stories where the relationship is as important as the adventure. She teaches creative writing at Seton Hill University where she graduated from their Writing Popular Fiction program. She is a member of The Authors Guild, Pennwriters, Broad Universe, and Science Fiction Poetry Association. *Ambasadora* was her thesis novel. Visit her online at *heidirubymiller.blogspot.com*.

Made in the USA
Charleston, SC
27 August 2011